CRITICAL ACCLAIM FOR WENDY PERRIAM

Wendy Perriam is one of the most interesting unsung novelists of her generation. Intelligent and accessible, she is fighting for the same bit of turf as Joanna Trollope, but she is probably the more accomplished and varied writer of the two. She writes beautifully about relationships and hilariously about sex. Her work can be recommended without reservation for its honesty, its acuteness and its wide-ranging humanity. *Sunday Telegraph*

Nobody does deep feelings better. *Sunday Times*

Each book is a magnificently orchestrated orgy in which her potent blend of sex, religion and humour takes the reader on a spiritual odyssey from the solid rocks of safety to the wilder shores of fantasy. *Time Out*

Perriam writes brilliantly about fear and grief, but she is also hilariously funny. *The Times*

Perriam has the knack of being explicit about sex without being crude or embarrassing. She teases us to the end with twists and turns in the plot, but just as accomplished is the novel's moral debate. *The Literary Review*

Perriam writes passionately and movingly about the sad and the bad, but is brilliant on the funny side, too. Bravo! *Daily Mail*

Perriam must be a strong contender for Britain's most underrated novelist. *Daily Telegraph*

Perriam is sometimes very funny, sometimes very sexual, sometimes very painful, and always difficult to pin down. *Standard*

Perriam is both clever and funny, as well as being a skilled artist with something to say about life. This is an author who has learned how to face the world and tame the horrors of life: we should be grateful for her optimism – it is infectious. *The Tablet*

Perriam addresses serious issues, but she writes with such verve and such delight in the language that the touch is light even when the themes are weighty. *New Books Magazine*

Perriam makes waves with her novels because each of them is an unusually honest projection of her personality and each of them is sustained by a fine command of her craft. *Glasgow Herald*

Perriam is rare among contemporary writers in the breadth of her canvas and the boldness of her colours: a sort of literary blend of Benjamin Haydon and Stanley Spencer. *Books and Bookmen*

Perriam is one of the funniest writers around. *Daily Telegraph*

Wendy Perriam is a real find. For she has that magical combination of a brisk, lively style and a literate intelligence. Her characters are vibrantly realistic; her understanding of human hopes, selfishness and absurdity sympathetic, but sharp and funny; the dialogue twists absolutely right. Perriam is a very welcome discovery. *Sunday Express*

Perriam's shrewd, sharp prose style is complemented by a marvellous talent for satirical observation. *The Scotsman*

Never predictable, never sentimental, she is a terrific champion of the powers of the imagination to transform individual lives. *The Tablet*

It is impossible to categorize this prolific novelist, whose work is a bizarre mixture of intellectual gravitas and sex scenes more steamy than any you'd find in a bonkbuster. Perriam has a pacy Polaroid pen. *Daily Mail*

Wendy Perriam puts the soul back into sex. *Irish Independent*

Perriam is a skilled and sympathetic observer of contemporary life, so there is a lot of truth about contemporary morals, manners and fantasies. *Sunday Telegraph*

Wendy Perriam is bursting with ideas about sex, death, grief, celibacy, the problems of old age, of guilt, of mother-daughter relationships ... The problems of women of all ages are described in a flexible lucid style, with humour and exuberance. *Irish Times*

It is Wendy Perriam's gift to set out a chessboard of conventional characters with whom the reader can identiy, and move them, perfectly plausible, into the most extraordinary situations. You settle down for a nice, undemanding read, then you are hooked and finally you cannot put the book down. *Daily Telegraph*

Her books will surely live on as great literature long after she and the rest of us have gone. *Surrey Comet*

Wendy Perriam was born to write. She looks at the world with a different eye from the rest of us. Her work refreshes and exhilarates. She gets to the heart of the matter, and there, lurking beneath the seriously mundane, we discover the spiritual underpinnings of the universe. I am her greatest fan. **Fay Weldon**

An Enormous Yes

An Enormous Yes

Wendy Perriam

ROBERT HALE · LONDON

© Wendy Perriam 2013
First published in Great Britain 2013

ISBN 978-0-7090-9385-5

Robert Hale Limited
Clerkenwell House
Clerkenwell Green
London EC1R 0HT

www.halebooks.com

2 4 6 8 10 9 7 5 3 1

Typeset in 10/13.5pt Sabon
Printed by MPG Printgroup, UK

For my brother Robert Brech –
quite simply, the brilliant best.

On me your voice falls, as they say love should,
Like an enormous yes.

Philip Larkin, 'For Sidney Bechet'

Begin

Begin again to the summoning birds
to the sight of light at the window,
begin to the roar of morning traffic
all along Pembroke Road.
Every beginning is a promise
born in light and dying in dark
determination and exaltation of springtime
flowering the way to work.
Begin to the pageant of queuing girls
the arrogant loneliness of swans in the canal
bridges linking the past and the future
old friends passing through with us still.
Begin to the loneliness that cannot end
since it perhaps is what makes us begin,
begin to wonder at unknown faces
at crying birds in the sudden rain
at branches stark in the willing sunlight
at seagulls foraging for bread
at couples sharing a sunny secret
alone together while making good.
Though we live in a world that dreams of ending
that always seems about to give in
something that will not acknowledge conclusion
insists that we forever begin.

Brendan Kennelly

Reproduced with kind permission from *The Essential Brendan Kennelly:
Selected Poems with Live CD* (Bloodaxe Books, 2011)

Chapter 1

'BLOODY PRIESTS!' SHE muttered, slamming two cups and saucers on the tray. The best china, naturally. Priests were superior beings – or so she had always been taught. In fact, the way some Catholic females fussed and flurried round them, one might imagine they were gods themselves, rather than God's servants. Certainly, they couldn't be fobbed off with a chipped and uncouth mug.

Having spread a hand-crocheted doily onto a floral-patterned plate, she arranged chocolate fingers and custard creams on top. If this young, gangly Father Andrew expected home baking, then he had failed to understand her current situation.

While waiting for the kettle to boil, she glanced out at the sodden fields; grey beneath a greyer sky. A few dirty-white sheep, bedraggled in the rain, were the only signs of life. November. Useless month.

The priest's cheery voice echoed from the sitting-room – the only voice, of course. For the last fifteen days, her mother hadn't spoken a single word; not uttered so much as a grunt or sigh.

'Well, Hanna, it's a wonderful age!' she heard him continue, maddeningly, as she carried in the tea things. Nothing very wonderful about being ninety-five – at least not in her mother's case. For all Hanna knew, this tow-haired youth could have been Mickey Mouse or Peter Pan. Admittedly, he was a stranger – standing in for Father Charles, while the latter was in hospital – but it was achingly long since her mother had recognized even Father Charles.

'Only five more years till your hundredth, Hanna! I expect you're looking forward to that telegram from the Queen.'

Clearly, Father Charles had been unable to find a substitute who might have had the savvy to avoid fatuous remarks. Priests were in short supply. Still, at least Father Andrew's clumsy gait and booming voice hadn't frightened Hanna; indeed, had failed to arouse the slightest reaction.

'Do sit down,' Maria urged. So long as the lanky fellow stood, he was blocking out the only available light. 'And please forgive the clutter. I've had to turn this into Mama's bedroom, now she can no longer manage the stairs, and there's barely room for the sofa, let alone a bed.'

The bed in question was jammed against one wall; the sofa positioned at a strange diagonal angle, to accommodate the tiny table, as well as the two armchairs. At least she had made an effort: dusted and deodorized the room; changed Hanna's blouse after the mishap with the breakfast porridge; hidden the incontinence pads tactfully away.

'How do you like your tea, Father?' At last, he had settled back against the sofa cushions, his black-trousered legs sticking out at full skinny length, revealing incongruous pea-green socks.

'Nice and strong, please, with two sugars.' He rummaged in his briefcase and withdrew a small, slim book. 'This is published by an organization called *Dementia Positive*! I hope you'll find it useful.'

Unlikely, she thought, judging by the cover, which showed a happy, smiling couple, arms entwined. To be part of a couple at any age was something of a luxury, but for the over-nineties with Alzheimer's, extremely, tragically rare. The Creator, she felt, had missed a trick in fashioning people as individual units, rather than as indissoluble pairs, the one cemented to the other, so that death, abandonment or widowhood became de facto impossible. Often, she had tried to picture her literal other half: part Byron; part William Wilberforce; part Leonardo da Vinci.

'Thank you, Father,' she murmured, leafing through the book. Positive it undoubtedly was. *Encourage the patient to take up new pursuits – swimming, painting, tai chi classes, amateur dramatics.*

The chance of finding a tai chi class in a remote Northumbrian village was pretty close to zero, and there were enough amateur dramatics in her own struggle to keep sane, whilst helping Hanna survive. Swimming might be possible, though – in the swollen river, or flooded lane.

'Shocking weather, isn't it?' the priest remarked, as if tuning in to her thoughts. He appeared to have given up trying to engage with her mother, who sat mute, remote and trapped in her own silent world. The pink cheeks and snowy hair made her look healthy, even pretty. Only the eyes betrayed her: haunted, frightened eyes, surveying some unspeakable void.

After a few superfluous remarks about the rain, the floods and the huge puddles on the road, Father Andrew returned to the object of his visit. 'She's not responding too well, I see.'

Maria bristled at that 'she'. Her mother was *there*, and she hadn't lost her hearing, whatever other faculties had vanished. Even if the words made no sense, his downbeat tone would register.

Having poured some milky tea into a beaker, she rose from her chair and went to stand beside her. 'Mama, it's Maria,' she said, never quite sure if Hanna required these constant reminders, or whether she recognized, at some deep level, the person who had shared her life for so long. 'And here's some nice sweet tea.' She held the spout against her mother's lips, inserting it as carefully as possible. 'It's not too hot, so try to take a sip or two.'

Hanna pushed away the beaker and, when offered a custard cream, stared at it in suspicion, even fear. If a mere biscuit was an unknown, dangerous object, how perilous her entire universe must be.

Father Andrew, for his part, was making serious inroads into the plate of chocolate fingers. 'That book has a Resources section,' he mumbled through a mouthful, 'with a lot of useful websites.'

'Yes, I'm sure I'll find it a help, Father.' Dutifully, she opened it again, only to light on another couple – ballroom dancing, this time. 'Positive' could verge on plain improbable.

'More tea for you?' she asked, having removed the untouched biscuit from her mother and returned to her own chair.

'No, I'm afraid I'll have to make a move soon. I promised to look in on Mrs Chalmers, and it's quite a tricky drive with the roads the way they are.'

Stay, she almost begged. Stay and hold the fort for me. She yearned for a brief escape; a walk outside in the downpour; the chance to hear another voice; the bleat of a sheep, the roar of the wind, the sly chuckle of the stream. 'Well, thank you so much for coming,' she said, instead, politely.

'Don't mention it. I wish I could do more to help, but with Father Charles off sick, I'm covering for several different parishes.' He lumbered to his feet and, pausing by Hanna's chair, gingerly patted her shoulder, before intoning a prayer. 'May the Lord of all mercy help and comfort our sister, Hanna.'

The Lord of all mercy, Maria reflected, had been stingy with his mercy, when it came to Hanna's life. 'Amen,' she muttered nonetheless; respecting Hanna's own deep religious faith.

Once she had bade the priest goodbye, she stood a moment at the door, breathing in the cold, enticing air and envying the Bradleys' collie, Bess, who was romping joyously past, intent on some doggy pursuit. If she, like Bess, were free of responsibilities, there was so much she yearned to do. Just a simple trip to Hexham and a wander round the shops was now an impossible luxury, and joining her friends in the pub for the odd Sunday morning drink seemed equally out of the question. She was tempted to embark on some drawing and painting – activities once central to her life, yet abandoned decades ago – but feared it might distract her from her more crucial role as carer.

Returning to the sitting-room, she sat, as usual, beside her mother, clasping her frail and scrawny hand; a hand mottled with brown age-spots, traceried with swollen veins. The ponderous ticking of the clock seemed to be deliberately spinning out each torpid hour. If only she had sisters, brothers, uncles, aunts – someone else to help – but the only relatives she and Hanna could claim were a few unknown ones in Kostenberg and Villach.

'It's all falling apart,' the old lady said, suddenly, abruptly, raising her head and staring directly ahead.

Maria jumped. After so long a silence, the words were startling – no less in the fact that they actually made sense. It *was* all falling apart, and at a terrifying rate. Uncurling Hanna's fingers from her own, she went to fetch the Treasure Box. Her mother needed comfort – that was clear. Besides, *any* words were a good sign, so further speech must be encouraged. But barely had she unpacked the photos and untied the bundle of faded letters, when the phone shrilled, with its loud peremptory ring. Dr Lloyd, most probably, or perhaps the mobile library, with news about the books on order.

'Hi, Mum, it's me!'

'Amy, how lovely! It seems ages since you've rung. It's Amy,' she mouthed at Hanna; always careful to include her mother, however slim the chance she would understand.

'Sorry – life's been hectic. But how are things up there?'

'OK-ish. Grandma's much the same.'

'Poor Grandma. Poor *you*. But, listen, Mum, Hugo and I want you to come for Christmas. You simply have to see the new house! We're thrilled with it and, anyway, you need a break.'

'It's out of the question, darling. You know I just can't—'

'Mum, you always say no, but, honestly, it *is* feasible. You could arrange respite care for Grandma – No, don't interrupt. I'm only asking just this once and only for a week, that's all. I'd adore to have you visit and, besides, if Grandma's as confused as you say, she won't even realize she's somewhere else.'

'Oh, she will, Amy. She's very sensitive to atmospheres.' Maria had already moved into the kitchen, not wanting her mother to hear. 'Even that time when Deidre took over, Mama hated every minute, yet she was still in her own home, then. And, when I got back, she'd definitely deteriorated.'

'But that was almost a year ago. From what you say, she's hardly aware of anything now. And, d'you realize, Mum, apart from that one weekend, we haven't seen each other for nearly four years?'

'But how could we, darling, with you and Hugo in Dubai?'

'There *are* things called planes, Mum, and we did invite you to visit dozens of times. You'd have loved it in Dubai – the sunshine and the beaches and the souks and everything, and those amazingly tall skyscrapers and ...'

Maria gave an inaudible sigh. Even four years ago, her mother had been severely confused – and an agitated, panicky confusion, almost worse than her present slumped passivity. She could no more have jetted off to Dubai than boarded a rocket to the moon. That one weekend in London last October had taxed *her* as much as Deidre: the continual guilt and worry; the fear that something would happen the minute she wasn't on hand to help.

'I love Grandma to bits – you know that, Mum – but I still think it's time you put yourself first, for a change. Or, if you won't do that, put *me* first. I'm dying for you to see the house. And we've invited some super people for Christmas Day lunch. I'd really like you to meet them.'

Amy's 'super' people were bound to be stylish and sophisticated. Maria glanced at her shapeless slacks, her stained and baggy top. Coping with a messy eater, who also happened to be incontinent, didn't exactly encourage dapper dressing. And even a trip to the local hair salon required careful advance planning and the kind cooperation of a neighbour. Besides, she would hardly be a scintillating guest, with her mind constantly on Hanna.

'Mum, if it's a question of expense, I'll gladly pay for Grandma to have a week in the snazziest care home you can find.'

Care homes by their very nature were unlikely to be snazzy. Old folk made smells and mess, and all the money in the world couldn't overcome that fact. 'It's sweet of you, darling, but—'

'No buts, Mum! I want you to promise, this time, that you'll really, truly investigate what's available. I mean, if there's nothing local, go further afield.'

'She can't travel, Amy. I told you.'

'Well, maybe not in your midget of a car, but she could in a nice big limousine. I'll hire one for her, there and back – make it her Christmas present, if she wants.'

Hanna wouldn't want *any* car, however grand, to whisk her away from her only place of security and the one person in the world she trusted. Maybe the only thing she wanted, in the jumbled, scrambled chaos of her mind, was an end to her undignified state – a truly horrifying thought.

'Mum, are you still there?'

'Yes, 'course.'

'Well, I haven't heard you promise.'

'OK. I promise,' she said, weakly. Amy had always been persuasive, even as a child. 'But, look, tell me more about the house.'

'Sorry – can't! Must fly. I'm due at a meeting – overdue, in fact. But you'll see it for yourself in less than six weeks' time. Oh, Mum, I just can't wait! I miss you terribly.'

'Miss you, too.' She had grown used to missing Amy, whose visits had become less frequent since she'd moved to London and started building her career. Even long ago, when Hanna was still her efficient, coping, cheerful self, it had been difficult for Amy to make the long, time-consuming journey. And her marriage to a husband equally clever and high-powered had only compounded the problem.

Returning to Hanna, she explained patiently (for at least the fifth time this month) that Amy and Hugo had moved from their rented London flat and bought their own house near Victoria. Did her mother even remember who Amy and Hugo were, or have any idea where Victoria might be? Nonetheless, it was important to communicate – just in case, just in case.

Besides, the fact that Hanna had spoken a coherent sentence was a definite advance, however pessimistic its content. Her mother needed distraction from the horror of things 'falling apart', so she picked out a letter from the bundle in the Treasure Box and, sitting companionably close, read it aloud, slowly, phrase by phrase.

She scanned her mother's face for any sign of recognition of a letter she knew off by heart – in fact, her favourite of the entire 207. But Hanna's eyes were still turned inwards; focused on some unspeakable loss. Was she recalling her husband's death, the horror of the telegram, the mass grave in France she had never seen?

She tried another tack. 'Remember Papa's gallantry medal?' she prompted, having fetched it from the Treasure Box and placed it in her mother's hands. As recently as last December, Hanna had recognized that six-pointed star, but now it might as well have been a piece of junk for all the reaction it induced.

Nonetheless, she refused to lose heart. In the past, her mother had seemed to rally when she heard various well-known songs and hymns, especially the Lourdes hymn, 'Immaculate Mary'. Despite its dirge-like tune, it had sometimes raised a smile of recognition. Perhaps its endlessly repeated 'Aves' were soothing, like a mantra.

'*Ave, Ave, Ave, Maria,*' Maria sang, with all the conviction she could muster.

No response.

Undaunted, she continued. *'In Heaven, the blessed thy glory proclaim ...'*

Unlikely, she thought, that her father would be proclaiming Mary's glory, although, as a child, she had always felt distinctly muddled when reciting the Our Father. *Our Father Who art in Heaven* was obviously her dad. His photograph had confused her even more. The Almighty, as she knew from His pictures, wore a flowing white robe and had long hair and a beard, so why was her father wearing army uniform, with a crew-cut and no facial hair at all?

'Ave, Ave, Ave, Maria ...'

At least twenty *Aves*, by now, yet not only had her mother failed to respond, she had actually nodded off. Which didn't reflect too favourably on her own talent as a vocalist, or as a carer, come to that. She seemed to be failing in all departments – unless it was simply the new drug that had lulled Hanna into an almost vegetative state. Perhaps Amy was right and she wouldn't actually notice if she was sent away for a week.

Still unhappy at the thought, she removed the medal from her mother's lap, tucked the rug more securely round her legs and tiptoed out of the room, leaving the door ajar, of course. Then, wearily, she trudged upstairs, glad of the chance to snatch a rest herself. As her mother's nights became increasingly disturbed, she'd had to train herself to doze with one ear open, so she could instantly go down to help, at the slightest sound of movement or distress.

Only as she stretched out on the bed did she realize how hungry she was. Her mother ate little now, and preferred slushy foods like soup or Complan, and it seemed pointless, if not self-indulgent, to cook solely for herself.

Closing her eyes, she remembered Hanna's weekly baking sessions: apple dumplings, fairy cakes, sultana scones, jam tarts; delicious smells of cinnamon and hot pastry wafting through the cottage. Taking a scone from the cooling rack, she crammed it into her mouth, still warm, followed by another and another. She continued eating piggishly, voraciously – although a thousand scones or cakes or buns couldn't satisfy her greed. Good Catholic girls weren't greedy, not for food or love or sex – all the things she craved. Good Catholic girls denied themselves and shouldn't even think of sex.

Long ago, in the absence of a man, she had taken to sleeping with her heroes – John Donne, Caravaggio, Dante Gabriel Rossetti – romantic, sensual geniuses who would never abandon her, or tire of her. Unbuttoning her blouse, she let her fingers stray across her breast: John Donne's fingers, knowing exactly how and where to touch. His beard was on her belly now;

exquisite roughness and softness mixed; his full sensuous lips travelling lower; his roving hands doing everything he promised in his poem: going before, behind, between, above, below ...

She lay back, recovering, aware of her heart thumping through her chest. No one ever warned you that you could still feel lust at the age of sixty-five; still long for a thousand men. Men, scones ... Why did she always crave excess?

Hanna, in marked contrast, had invariably given the impression that she regarded sex as sinful, dangerous and definitely distasteful. Sometimes, Maria wondered how she herself had come to be conceived, unless it was another Virgin Birth. Yet even her friends in the village – earthy types like Carole, June and Jacqueline, each with a big brood of kids – seemed to lose all sexual appetite once they passed the menopause. 'Eddie leaves me alone now, thank God!' Carole had remarked, just the other week.

She summoned Eddie to bed: a burly, weather-beaten man, with a head of strong white hair and powerful, muscly hands. She made him use those hands; enjoyed the sense of his solid bulk astride her; inhaled his masculine smell of gun-oil and tobacco. Eddie was a thruster, and not a man to tire. He might be seventy-odd but, frustrated by Carole's tepidity, he was ardently determined to make up for lost time.

A wild cry escaped her lips, followed by a sense of deep embarrassment, not to mention shame. She was far too old for these ersatz thrills and, anyway, it was adultery by stealth, and adultery was not only a sin but signally disloyal to Carole.

However, even now, she wasn't satisfied; yearning for some more substantial pleasure. Was something seriously wrong with her – stuck in perpetual adolescence, despite her pension and her bus pass? Or was she simply reinhabiting her rebellious, twenty-something self?

That memory set off another fantasy: her imperious and talented first lover kissing away her scruples and her nerves; simply overruling her, through the force of his own passion. His urgent, seeking mouth was clamped against her own; shockwaves shuddering through her body as—

She sprang off the bed at the sound of something being overturned in the sitting-room below; charged downstairs, full pelt.

Rebellious youth was over; it was time to return to her present, burdened self.

Chapter 2

'AND THIS IS our lounge,' the worryingly young nurse announced, opening the door to a large, institutional room, its walls painted a depressing sludge-green. 'Just look at that fantastic view!'

Maria glanced out at the bleakly empty flowerbeds and naked, shivering trees. Admittedly, the prospect would be much improved once spring brought leaves and blooms but, judging by the inmates here, it would take more than a view to rally them. Twenty aged females and two still more ancient men were sitting in a circle of identical green-padded chairs, facing a large television that was tuned to a children's programme featuring quacking ducks and mooing cows, all giving tongue at full volume.

'We have to turn it up loud,' the nurse explained, apologetically, 'with so many of our residents being hard of hearing.'

Maria did a quick appraisal. The furnishings couldn't be faulted: the carpet decent quality, the curtains properly lined, the residents themselves all respectably dressed. It was just the general atmosphere that seemed so sadly wrong. For one thing, no one was talking – no interaction, no friendly exchanges – but then conversation would have been well nigh impossible, with so much competition from the screen.

'Do they watch television all day?' she dared to ask. Hanna had lost the distinction between flesh-and-blood people and their on-screen counterparts, so she kept their own set firmly switched to 'off'.

'Oh, *no!*' The nurse sounded genuinely shocked. We employ a dedicated activities co-ordinator – Danielle – she's lovely! She arranges things like carpet bowls and handicrafts. And, although we don't have a specialized dementia programme, there are reminiscence sessions, which, from what you say, might be very helpful for your mother.'

Maria nodded abstractedly, taking in the Christmas decorations: tinsel, streamers, tall tree festooned with fairy lights; the glitter and adornment an ironic contrast to the marked lack of celebration in any other aspect of the place. Except for the brochure, of course, where, once again, smiling couples took precedence; one ecstatic pair even toasting each other in champagne. And the photo of the dining-room showed beaming gourmets tucking in with gusto; no one wearing a bib, or requiring to be fed, mouthful by laborious mouthful, or, worse, spitting clotted morsels of half-masticated food onto the table and themselves.

'Could I see the dining-room?' she asked.

'Of course. We pride ourselves on our home-cooked food and, if your mother's vegetarian, or on some special diet, that's no problem for our catering staff.'

Slops three times a day might strain their staff's resources, Maria refrained from saying, as she followed her cheery guide back into the corridor and the now-familiar smell of urine, overlaid with sickly floral air-freshener. Nonetheless, this was decidedly better than the first home she'd inspected.

The dining-room was empty, save for two girls laying the tables, banging down the knives and forks with unnecessary force. One of the knives went flying, but the taller girl retrieved it from the floor, spat on it, to clean it, then wiped it dry with her sleeve. Maria's frown went unnoticed. Would her mother's already compromised immune system be able to withstand the germs? She just hoped this teenaged duo didn't double as care assistants, or, indeed, help out in the kitchen, since their long, loose hair would dangle in the food.

'And we provide a really top-notch Christmas dinner,' the nurse continued, with a smile. 'Turkey and all the trimmings, and wine for those who want it.'

All wasted on Hanna, Maria reflected, sadly.

'Well, shall we go upstairs now? Then I can show you one of our bedrooms. They're all en-suite and quite spacious, so there'll be room for your mother's things, if she decides she'd like to stay on after Christmas and make this her permanent home.'

Emerging from the lift, Maria and the nurse proceeded down the corridor to the last room on the left. 'Spacious' seemed hardly the word, but then 'home' itself was somewhat inappropriate for such an unhomely place. On the other hand, Hanna was used to cramped conditions and, certainly, an en-suite bathroom would be an advantage, as would the sturdy rails around the bed.

'And all our rooms are connected to a central Nurse-Call system. Your mother only needs to press this bell and a nurse will come immediately.'

Maria didn't bother pointing out that Hanna wouldn't have the faintest notion as to how to press a bell. If only, she thought, for the millionth time, she had overruled her mother's life-long reluctance to admit illness or defeat, and insisted she see a doctor earlier, rather than waiting till the stage when she had started putting pepper in her tea, or scissors in the fridge, or hiding her nightgown behind the bathroom basin, for no explicable reason.

As they left the bedroom, they stood back to let two wheelchairs pass, each pushed by a care assistant, who looked neat and well turned out, and was well above playschool age. A definite improvement. The occupants of the wheelchairs, however, gave little cause for hope. One, shaking uncontrollably, was uttering pitiful cries, whilst the other was so crippled by osteoporosis, her pathetically balding head was almost level with her knees. In some ways, Hanna was lucky. At least she hadn't succumbed to bone-thinning, or Parkinson's Disease, not to mention the various cancers that had felled so many of her contemporaries.

'Well, I think that's all,' the nurse said, as they descended in the lift. 'But do come back to the office and have another chat with our manager.'

Maria checked her watch. 'Actually, I really ought to be off now, I'm afraid. One of my friends is kindly looking after my mother and I don't want to impose on her too long.'

'No problem. Just give us a ring. You already have all the necessary forms and a copy of our terms and conditions. Although I do advise you to book as soon as possible. We're already getting quite full up for Christmas.'

'Yes, of course. I'll phone tomorrow.'

Maria noted with approval the profusion of green plants, ranged along the window ledges, and the large sign informing residents: TODAY IS TUESDAY, DECEMBER 7, 2010. It would mean nothing to Hanna in her present state, of course, but might be very helpful to those less hopelessly confused.

'And be assured, Miss Brown,' the nurse concluded, warmly shaking her hand, 'that if you entrust your mother to us, we'll do everything we can to make her stay enjoyable.'

Enjoyment had never featured prominently in Hanna's ninety-five years – not that she ever complained. Suffering, in her view, was to be positively embraced as a chance of gaining grace and releasing her long-dead relatives from Purgatory. Besides, her mother firmly believed that God sent only so much trauma as each individual soul could bear. She herself disputed such opinions, but she had learned, long ago, to conceal her scepticism.

Dusk was falling as she drove away, along the sweeping drive, yet it was barely four o'clock. Only a fortnight now until the shortest day of the year, yet every day seemed longer, longer, longer.

The countryside stretched bleak and vast beneath a lowering sky, its uncompromising ruggedness making her feel almost daunted, despite its familiarity. Apart from her few years in London, she had never ventured far from this isolated region of her birth.

The roads were near deserted; her mind, too, strangely empty, as she drove, perilously fast, in an effort to reach home in record time.

'She was no trouble at all,' Carole reported, once the two of them had excused themselves from Hanna and were safely out of earshot in the kitchen. 'Except feeding her's no picnic, is it?' Her neighbour gave a bellow of a laugh. 'She seems to regurgitate more than she swallows!'

'I'm sorry,' Maria murmured. 'I should have warned you.'

'Don't worry. My grandsons are worse! But tell me, what did you think of Forest Court?'

'Well, the hygiene left a lot to be desired, but in some respects, it was better than I dared hope.'

'So have you booked Hanna in for Christmas?'

'Not yet. It's quite a lengthy process and I didn't want to hold you up.'

'Well, do it first thing tomorrow. I'm fond of your mother, but elderly folk can be tyrants and there comes a point when you have to say enough's enough. And, anyway, Maria, you owe it to Amy to put her first, for once. The very old have *had* their lives, so the young ones should take precedence. But,' she added, moving to the door, 'I'd better be on my way. You know what Eddie's like if his tea's not on the table on the dot of six o'clock!'

'I just can't thank you enough, Carole.'

'The only thanks I want is knowing you're going to get away for Christmas. And honestly, Maria, your mother hasn't a clue what's going on. If you moved her to Timbuktu, she wouldn't know the difference.'

'Yes, Amy said much the same. Although, actually, it's so hard to tell. I sometimes feel she's aware of things, even if she shows no sign.'

As Carole's ancient Land Rover bumped along the rutted lane, Maria closed the door and remained standing where she was, struggling with her dilemma. Was there any way that Hanna's needs and Amy's could be somehow reconciled? Perhaps it *would* help her mother to move permanently to Forest Court, since there was just a chance that the expertise of a care home might resurrect the old, familiar Hanna; the independent, energetic woman who had sewed and knitted, cooked and gardened, always been in charge and on the ball, and was more concerned with helping others than accepting help herself. That version of her mother had died a good ten years ago, but an activities co-ordinator might know how to rouse a patient from a seemingly comatose state. A trained professional would undoubtedly have more resources than a few songs and hymns, and letters from a long-dead spouse. Besides, the *Dementia Positive* book had made the point that apathy and lassitude could be due not to medication but to lack of stimulation, and there was certainly a dearth of stimulation with just her and Hanna stuck in one small room at home.

In any case, if her mother lived to be a hundred, as Father Andrew anticipated, how would she herself survive five more gruelling years? She already felt close to cracking up, especially when her mother cried – a hopeless, silent weeping that seemed almost worse than the fretful agitation of three years ago. Yet, it seemed unutterably selfish to be thinking of her own needs when there was no guarantee that Hanna would improve at Forest Court. Indeed, the move itself might be so disorientating, it could actually make her worse. And what about the risk of abuse: untrained, low-paid carers victimizing patients when no one was around to check?

Suddenly, all vacillation vanished from her mind. Returning to the sitting-room, she knelt in front of her mother so she could look right into her eyes. 'You're *not* a tyrant, Mama,' she said. 'You couldn't be. It's just not in your nature. And,' she added, speaking loudly and distinctly – to herself as well as to Hanna; to Amy, Carole, Jacqueline and June, and to all her other friends and neighbours, 'I promise faithfully I shan't leave you – ever – not this Christmas or any Christmas, let alone for longer. You can stay here, safe at home with me – yes, however long you live.'

Her decision was right – she knew that. Hanna had looked after her when she was at her lowest and her worst – ill, despairing, reckless and rebellious – and then looked after Amy, too; a devoted mother and grandma, not sparing a thought for her own needs, or life, or job.

The least she owed her in return was to be equally devoted.

Chapter 3

'ETERNAL REST GRANT unto her, O Lord, and let perpetual light shine upon her ...'

Maria was unable to shift her gaze from that loathsome, hateful coffin. Despite its gleaming mahogany and the shower of white chrysanthemums extravagant on top, it seemed cruel in the extreme that her beloved mother should be cramped up, claustrophobic, in a box, when, apart from the last tragic decade, she had been always busy, active, upright.

'Mum, *darling*,' Amy whispered, seeing her distress.

Maria clutched her hand – a life-raft. She had been on tenterhooks all week, acutely worried that Amy and Hugo might not make it for the funeral, with such heavy snow blocking roads and disrupting all the trains. Her overwhelming relief at their last-minute arrival had made her realize just how hugely she had missed them during her long, lonely years of daughter-deprivation. Indeed, since Hanna's death, they had become even more important, as her only remaining family.

'Lord have mercy ... Christ have mercy,' Father Charles intoned, resplendent in a black-and-silver chasuble. 'Absolve, we beseech thee ...'

Words were flashing past, but it was impossible to grasp them. She was reliving the shock of Boxing Day, when she had dragged herself downstairs, pre-dawn, to take Hanna her usual tea and milky porridge, and found not a living, breathing mother but an already stiffening corpse.

'O God, Your nature is ever-merciful ...'

Mercy, mercy – the word was near unbearable. If God were truly merciful, He would have given her a chance to say goodbye; ensured she was there when Hanna actually died; allowed her time to hold her mother close, comfort her and pray with her, as she had always planned and promised.

'... bid Your holy angels lead her home to Paradise ...'

Could Hanna really be in Paradise, joyfully reunited with her husband after sixty-six years of widowhood? Or was she simply decomposing, soon to be food for worms? The thought induced a wave of nausea, not helped by the overpowering scent of the lilies on the altar, or the choking fumes of incense that seemed to have lodged deep in her throat

She jumped as Hugo squeezed past her in the pew, having totally forgotten that he had agreed to give the first reading. The last ten days had passed in a sort of churning fog of desolation, disbelief and endless busy-ness – a whole tidal wave of arrangements and decisions, at a time when she could barely decide whether to offer people tea or coffee when they called to pay their respects.

She tried her best to concentrate by focusing on Hugo's tall, athletic figure, standing by the altar; his blue-grey eyes and neatly cut blond hair. How extraordinary it always seemed that Amy should marry someone so *English*; someone from a good professional family, his father a retired head-master, his mother a magistrate. If only she could run time back to Amy and Hugo's wedding, held in this same church; be singing celebratory hymns rather than mournful dirges.

Hugo was now returning to the pew and she hadn't taken in a single word he had read. And when the congregation stood for the Gospel, she was still lost in her own thoughts and had to be nudged to her feet. Her distraction was due partly to the fierce internal battle she was fighting: one part of her determined to remain courageous and controlled, as her mother would expect, while another, reprehensible part wanted simply to give way to her grief; startle these worthy villagers with wild shrieks of lamentation. And didn't she have reason? Since the moment of her birth, she had been the centre of her mother's life, the main point of Hanna's existence, her overriding concern; and now mother and daughter were cut callously adrift. Yet, whatever the pain of losing such a bond, she knew she must restrain herself. Grief could be excessive; even a sort of greed – and greed was sinful and selfish, as Hanna had taught her early on.

'Amen,' she said, as much to her mother as to the Gospel, before settling wearily back in the pew for Father Charles's homily.

He smiled around at the congregation, extending both hands in his usual declamatory manner. 'Welcome to you all, dear people. We are gathered here to mourn the passing of our sister, Hanna, and I like that phrase, "the passing of Hanna", rather than Hanna dying, because, as Catholics, we know that death is not the end. Our faith tells us that Hanna lives still …'

If only, Maria thought. If her mother could be granted just one more hour of life, with all her faculties intact, then she could apologize for her grouchiness on what had proved to be their final day together. How appallingly remiss it now seemed to have spent Christmas Day resenting her captivity and longing to be with Amy in London, surrounded by cheerful people, instead of being cooped up with her silent, brooding mother, who had refused to swallow anything beyond a dab of mashed potato and a scant spoonful of custard.

'It seems a paradox,' Father Charles continued, against a background of muffled coughs, 'that at baptism we celebrate dying to this world, whereas at funerals we celebrate rising to new life.'

Her shame mounted as she remembered Amy's baptism – again, in this same church; Hanna her usual valiant self, but she a mutinous rebel, thinking less of her new baby than of her shattered hopes and dreams.

'Hanna's faith never wavered throughout her long, unselfish life, despite the crosses she had to bear, chief of which was the loss of her husband, Kenneth, a heroic sergeant, slaughtered in France, after the D-Day landings. And, only three years earlier, she'd had to endure the equally tragic death of her mother.'

Father Charles paused to clear his throat, then raised his voice above a wailing infant. 'When she came up here as an evacuee, she was pregnant and alone, yet she didn't waste time feeling sorry for herself. She thought only of the welfare of her baby, who was born here in the village, of course. So, when the other evacuees were sent back home, she decided to stay up here and make a new life for herself and her child. And we're very glad she did stay, because she's proved an extremely valuable member of our community. Right from the start, when she had very little to live on, she proved her independence and resilience. She took in sewing, found a job at Wood End Farm, helping with the paperwork and typing and, later, worked at Mrs Plowden's, the draper's, where many of us older folk remember her.'

Maria's cheeks were burning at the contrast with her own behaviour, when she, too, had a baby, and no man around to help. She had cursed the Pope for banning contraception; cursed even her saintly mother for bringing her up a Catholic.

'So today, dear people, we celebrate the life of Hanna and her many sterling qualities. But we mustn't forget that there's another, even greater celebration, taking place in Heaven, because not only has Hanna been reunited with her husband, at last, but one of God's most faithful servants has come home to her eternal rest.'

Maria had to clench her fists and clamp her lips together to stop herself from breaking into sobs. And she could no longer cling to Amy, because she had arranged with Father Charles that, at the end of his sermon, her daughter should say a few concluding words about her beloved grandmother.

She watched as Amy went up to the lectern, amazed, as always, that she had produced a child who was all the things *she* wasn't: slim, stylish, elegant, successful, clever, confident. In all those aspects, she resembled Hugo, yet in appearance they were strikingly different: Amy sultry-dark and exotic-looking; Hugo tamer in his colouring and dress.

'I owe so much to Grandma,' Amy began, in the refined accent she'd adopted at Cambridge; a marked contrast to her former Northumbrian burr. 'She more or less brought me up, because Mum had to work, of course.'

Maria shifted in her seat. Did Amy even *know* that, far from working, she'd been plunged into depression, unable to change so much as a nappy, let alone earn the money to buy them? Hanna, always loyal, had never divulged to a single soul the sad truth of those first years.

'We were three women in the house,' Amy went on, showing no trace of nerves or hesitation, 'but we all pulled together to make it work and I can honestly say that there's no one I love more than Mum and Grandma – well, except for my husband, of course,' she added, flashing Hugo an apologetic smile, which produced a ripple of laughter from her listeners. 'Father Charles has already praised my grandmother, and all of us here know how special she was. But I want to praise my *mother*, because she deserves a tribute, too, for her unswervable devotion to Grandma during the last extremely difficult years. I know, because I've barely seen her. However tired she was, or desperate for a break, she refused to come and chill out with me in Dubai, or even London, because she knew how much her absence would upset Grandma.'

Maria's flush had now changed to one of embarrassment. It seemed wrong to hear herself lauded, when, in point of fact, she had often been in tears of frustration at her mother's increasing dependency, or racked with fear about how much longer she could cope with her at home. No one, not even Amy, realized quite what huge reserves of patience it required. And, even now, she felt burdened by the amount she had to do – not just the whole business of probate, but the total renovation of the cottage. Whilst devoting her time to Hanna, she had neglected the house and garden, and now the latter was overgrown and choked with brambles, and the former sorely in need of a face-lift.

She glanced up at Amy, svelte in her smart black suit; her dark hair swept up on top; a single strand of pearls – a gift from Hugo's mother – gleaming in the light. 'Stop!' she wanted to shout, as her daughter continued singing her praises. 'I don't deserve this tribute.'

'So I'd like to conclude by saying, "Well done, Mum!" I know everyone here agrees with me that you're every bit as unselfish and remarkable as Grandma was herself and, to me, you're simply the best mother in the world.'

'Hear, hear!' Hugo whispered, edging a little closer in the pew and laying his arm across Maria's back and shoulders. And, only then, did she sob, letting her tears fall unchecked. She was crying not for her mother, nor in response to Amy's truly touching words, but because she had never had a husband to put his warm, supportive, loving arms around her.

Chapter 4

'I DON'T KNOW about you two, my loves, but *I'm* completely knackered.' Maria collapsed into a chair, kicking off her tight black shoes. 'Mind you, the wake went well, don't you think? I mean, all those people turning up, even in this lousy weather. Thing is, it's so hard to keep chatting and smiling when ...' Her voice tailed off.

'Yes, *I* felt choked, too,' Amy said, 'especially when I got talking to that weird old Mrs Melrose. I hadn't realized she's the same age as Grandma. She said they've been friends for over sixty years, and she was telling me how hard it was when Grandma first came up here, not knowing a soul and being billeted on strangers. And even on VE Day, when everyone was dancing in the streets, Grandma must have felt more like howling, especially with her mother dead as well. I never even knew how that happened, but according to Mrs Melrose the house suffered a direct hit in the Blitz. '

'Yes,' Maria reflected, 'in 1941. And Mama only escaped because she was working in a munitions factory and so not allowed home except at week-ends. The bomb fell on a Tuesday and your great-grandma was killed outright. In fact, her life was pretty wretched altogether, as far as I can gather. Mama never said a lot about it but apparently Theresia was orphaned very early on and brought up by nuns in a convent in Ossiach. Eventually, she became a maid to Lady Stanley, who was a benefactress of the convent and living locally. And when her ladyship returned to London, she took Theresia with her, which is how she came to be in England.'

'So how did she meet Great-Grandpa?' Amy asked.

'Oh, that's quite a romantic saga. He fell head over heels in love with her when she was only sixteen, but, of course, the nuns weren't having any of that! They brought her up incredibly strictly and refused to let her even *look* at boys. But, once she was in London, Franz-Josef simply followed her over and kept on pestering and pestering until, at last, she agreed to marry him.'

'I know the feeling,' Hugo laughed. 'Amy took a fair bit of persuasion before she married *me*.'

Amy gave him a friendly punch. 'Only because life was so hectic. There just wasn't time to plan a wedding.'

'Well, you didn't do too badly,' Maria said, smiling as she took a sip of her wine. 'The whole village still talks about it – your fantastic dress and the amazing cake and everything.'

'But what about Theresia?' Hugo enquired. 'Did things go well once she'd tied the knot?'

'Not really. Lady Stanley dismissed her, for a start, and money was terribly short. So she had to take in sewing, and Franz-Josef was only a waiter, so he can't have been earning much. But, despite the lack of cash, he remained a romantic at heart and had plans for a great big family – five boys and five girls was the general idea, I think. But those other nine were never to be, because, of course, he was interned and, after that, he became a broken man.'

Amy shuddered. 'You know, when I first told Hugo that my own great-grandpa was sent to break stones in a prison camp, like a common criminal, he was gobsmacked, weren't you, darling?'

Maria flushed, aware of the contrast between her own beleaguered ancestors and Hugo's well-to-do family, rooted securely in Shropshire from generations back. 'Well, you see, he was classed as an "enemy-alien" and so a danger to national security, because no one really understood that Austro-Hungarians were different from Germans. Which is why, all the time she lived here, Mama never breathed a word about her foreign origins. She didn't even confide in the parish priest, which I suppose is understandable. I mean, she was miles from home, and pregnant, and recently bereaved, so better to play safe. The last thing she'd want was to be shunned as a "bloody German".'

'But, going back to Franz-Josef,' Hugo said, draining the last of his wine, 'what happened to him after his release?'

'Well, for one thing, Mama was distinctly put out, when this haggard stranger showed up! She was only four at the time, you see, and had no idea who he was, because he'd been interned in 1915, just months after her birth. And, anyway, she tended to be excluded, as he became increasingly dependent on his wife and perhaps resented having to share her with a child. And he couldn't get work, since people still suspected him of being on the enemy side. And, saddest of all, he died of pneumonia, when Mama was only sixteen, so she and Theresia were on their own in London, again, and had to get by as best they could. And being Austro-Hungarian must have been even more of an issue then, what with Theresia's foreign accent and her unpronounceable surname.'

'Oh, Mum, it's all so tragic!'

'Well, I can't speak for Theresia, but as far as Mama's concerned, she *wasn't* a tragic person, as you very well know. And life was easier for her than it ever was for her parents. I mean, she didn't have an accent and no one knew her maiden name, Radványi. Hanna Brown sounded reassuringly English. She was actually christened Johanna – shortened to Hanna in the convent – and most people assumed it was the *English* Hannah, with an "H" at the end.' Maria gave a sudden laugh. 'It was the Brown that saved her bacon, though! In fact, I sometimes wonder if she married Papa just on account of his surname.'

'Yes, and then her darling Mr Brown goes and gets blown to bits,' Amy said, bitterly.

'But, even when she was widowed, which was devastating, obviously, she always made the best of things. She told me once, much later on, that the night she heard the news, she happened to be knitting Papa a sweater, and she insisted on finishing it during the next few weeks, because she couldn't believe he'd never actually wear it. And, apparently, he'd given her this bar of chocolate – part of his army rations, I suppose – which she said she kept for years and years, as a sort of precious memento, even when it had gone all grey with mould.'

'*Don't*, Mum – I'll be in tears again.'

'Yes, but in one way she was fortunate, because Papa was allowed one last leave before he was sent to Normandy, so they had some time together, a few months before he died. And, without that final visit, I'd never have been conceived. And, of course, she saw me as *part* of Papa, so, in a sense, she hadn't lost him entirely. And you mustn't forget that her faith was a tremendous support. I suspect it got her through more than anything.'

'I wish mine did,' Amy muttered, ruefully. 'But, to tell the truth, it doesn't mean much any more. And Hugo's even worse, aren't you, darling?'

Maria envied the pair their casual stance on religion. The one time she had left the Church, she had paid extremely dearly for it.

'Well,' said Hugo, with a yawn, 'this poor degenerate Catholic is not only lapsed, he's pretty dead beat, too! Isn't it time we went to bed? I didn't sleep much last night.'

'No wonder – in that bed.' Maria felt a twinge of embarrassment every time she thought of Hugo – a six-foot-one ex-rugby player – trying to cram himself and Amy into a small and saggy divan. His parents owned a substantial house, with a tastefully furnished guest bedroom, complete with king-size bed. 'You should have let me book a hotel. But I can get you in for tomorrow, if you like. At least the roads aren't quite so bad now.' She went to the window and lifted the curtain aside. The landscape was still blanketed in white, but the whirling, frantic flakes had stopped falling late last night, as if respecting Hanna's funeral.

'We wouldn't dream of it, Mum. You need us here and here we'll stay. I feel bad enough, in any case, turfing you out of your room.'

'Don't worry, Mama's bed did me proud.' Although Eddie had moved the bed back upstairs, she wouldn't dream of allowing Amy and Hugo to sleep on a mattress stained with urine – and worse. In fact, she hadn't actually slept on it herself, unable to face lying in the very spot where her mother's corpse had lain. Instead, she had crept downstairs and curled up on the sofa, beneath a heap of rugs; spent the night counting the endless minutes until a grey and grudging dawn broke, reluctantly, half-heartedly.

'Hugo, you go on up,' Amy said, giving him a kiss. 'But I'll stay with you a bit longer, Mum. Hugo likes to read before he settles down, so he won't mind, will you, honey?'

'Not at all. See you later, darling.'

Having bid goodnight to her son-in-law, Maria listened to his heavy footsteps tramping up the stairs. He was really just too tall and broad for this squat, low-ceilinged cottage, although it was something of a luxury to have any man sleeping here at all. On all their previous visits, Amy and Hugo had stayed at the Rose and Crown, but it had closed down just last year.

'More wine?' she offered, once she had moved across to join Amy on the sofa. 'Or how about a hot drink?'

'Nothing, Mum – relax! And, listen, now it's just the two of us, if you want to go ahead and have a good old cry, I'll completely understand. In fact, I feel close to tears myself every time I think of Grandma all on her own in that grave, instead of being buried with Grandpa.'

'Well, I'll be joining her eventually.' Maria forced a smile. 'We bought two plots, ages ago, side by side, of course.'

'Mum, you're not even to *think* of dying. I need you to be around for years and years and years yet.' She broke off, awkwardly. 'Actually, I wasn't going to tell you this until tomorrow, at the earliest. Hugo said you were shattered and best leave it for a while. But maybe it will cheer you up.'

'What will? What d'you mean?'

'Well, I hope you're sitting tight, Mum, because this may come as a bit of a shock. Fact is – I'm pregnant. Eight weeks exactly. The doctor confirmed it just before we left.'

Maria stared at her, incredulous. Long ago, she had come to accept that

Amy and Hugo would never start a family. After the first five years of their marriage, she had begun to drop broad hints, or issue not-so-veiled warnings about biological clocks, but since Amy resented what she saw as interference, she now deliberately avoided the subject. Invariably, their careers came first. One or other of them was always working flat out for promotion, or Hugo was abroad on some construction project and, after that, they were both in Dubai and then—

'Mum, what's the matter? You haven't said a word. I thought you'd be over the moon.'

'I am, I am!' Maria felt a colossal smile spreading from her face to the whole triumphant room. 'I just couldn't take it in, that's all.'

'No wonder. We've kept you waiting long enough.'

'But the timing's sort of … perfect.' Maria enfolded her daughter in a jubilant hug. 'It's almost like it's *meant* – you know, one life ending as another starts.'

'Well, actually, if it's a girl, we've decided to call her Hannah.'

'Oh, Mama would be really chuffed.' Maria had always seen her daughter as having broken the chain of suffering, which seemed to have dogged their family from generations back. And now, she dared to hope, this new trend of success and happiness might continue down the ages.

'I'm afraid Hugo's so conventional, he insists on an "H" at the end, but I'm sure Grandma won't object to that.'

''Course not. Oh, darling I'm just so excited! When's your actual due date?'

'August 16th.'

'Good – a summer baby. *I* was born in a snowstorm, remember.'

'Yes, I was telling Hugo,' Amy laughed, 'how Grandma couldn't get to the hospital, because all the roads were blocked, and a midwife couldn't get out to her, so a kind but clueless neighbour did her best to deliver you at home. The poor darling looked quite terrified and said not to count on *him* as midwife!'

'But he's pleased about the news, I hope?'

'Delighted. This wasn't a mistake, Mum, in case you're wondering. We planned it very carefully, to fit in with the house move and Hugo's new job and everything.'

Maria hid a smile. Her ultra-efficient daughter would, of course, plan every last detail of a conception, and her confidence was such it would never even occur to her that she might encounter fertility problems and not conceive exactly when she chose. 'And how about his parents? Are they excited, too?'

'We haven't told them yet. We wanted you to be the first to know.'

'Oh, that's lovely, Amy – I'm flattered. But shouldn't you be resting, darling, taking things more slowly altogether?'

'No way. I'm as fit as a fiddle! OK, thirty-eight is old for a first pregnancy, but three of my friends had their first children in their forties, so it's all relative, you could say.'

'But you'll stop working once the baby's born?'

'Not for long – you know me! Anyway, we need two salaries to pay our whopping mortgage. It was totally my fault, of course, for choosing a house in SW1, rather than further out. But it's wonderfully convenient being so close to the office, instead of having a long trek every day.'

'So do you intend to get a nanny?' Maria tried to keep any hint of disapproval from her voice. Who was *she* to disapprove?

'No, you have to pay them a fortune, and buying the house has more or less cleaned us out. I read, the other day, that the cost of rearing a child till the age of twenty-one is somewhere in the region of a hundred thousand pounds – and that certainly doesn't include a nanny or private education.'

Again, Maria had to hide a sense of wry amusement. How could anyone spend so prodigious a sum on raising one small child? Both she and Hanna had done it on a shoestring.

'We might just about manage an au pair. Otherwise, we'll use a local childminder.'

Maria said nothing. From what she knew of au pairs, they were usually more interested in learning English or finding a boyfriend than in looking after their charges. And a childminder might be worse. They tended to take in far too many children, which made it most unlikely that any individual would receive personal attention.

'Actually, we did think about asking *you*, now that Grandma's passed away. Hugo and I discussed it on the way up here, and I told him I was worried about you living on your own, especially when you get older. But we didn't want you to feel we were simply using you, you know, as a way to solve our own problem: we can't afford a nanny, so let's call on Granny instead.'

Maria could barely digest this new proposal which, anyway, was surely premature. The pregnancy was very new and fragile. However tragic the thought, there was a chance that Amy could lose the baby, considering her age and hectic lifestyle. Once she had passed the twelve-week stage, things would be more stable, of course. But even then, the idea of moving to London seemed too radical to contemplate when her mind was still besieged by the churning mix of grief, remorse, relief and regret that had dogged her since her mother's death. Besides, the thought of leaving behind not just her friends but the only home she had ever known was daunting in the extreme. And suppose Amy *was* just 'using' her?

On the other hand, she craved the same close bond as had existed between Hanna and Amy; a bond certain to develop if she was in charge of the baby. And it would save her precious grandchild from some bungling, inept minder. In any case, didn't she owe it to her daughter to make some recompense for her own inadequacies during the first two shaming years?

'Maybe I've sprung this on you too soon, Mum. But, d'you know, the more I think about it, the more I feel it might benefit us all. I mean, do you really want to vegetate up here until you're as old as Grandma, but with no one to look after you?'

Maria bristled at that 'vegetate'. She had never vegetated in her life and didn't intend to now. In fact, considering she was free of ties for the first time in a decade, wasn't this the perfect chance to do some serious painting and start building up a substantial body of work? Anyway, she couldn't imagine her daughter looking after her. Amy would always be busy, even twenty or thirty years hence.

She sat in silence, torn two ways: her selfish side wanted time for herself, after her long stint as a carer, while another, equally compelling side longed to be totally involved with the baby, from the moment of its birth.

'And, if you did decide to come and live with us, don't worry about us being in each other's hair. The top floor of our house is more or less self-contained. It used to be the attic, which makes it sound all small and poky, but actually it's very light and bright, and there's a fantastic view across the rooftops.'

'But what about *this* place?' Maria felt she was being moved, lock, stock and barrel, before she'd had time to catch her breath.

'Best sell it, Mum. It's so remote.'

'But I have to get probate first, which could take five or six months. Anyway, no buyer would consider it in its present shabby state. And even if I spruced it up, I can't be showing people round if I'm three hundred miles away in London.'

'Mum, you need to use professionals, which is far less hassle, anyway. Just get a good solicitor and a decent local estate agent and they'll handle the whole thing.'

Maria gave a noncommittal shrug. Amy was so persuasive, she could talk a tortoise into surrendering its shell. Indeed, her daughter's voice had taken on an authoritative tone, as if she were exhorting one of her clients to follow some recommended course.

'Listen, Mum, I've got a good idea – why not give it a trial run? Come for just three months and regard it as more a visit than a total long-term commitment – and see how it works out. And if the arrangement doesn't suit you, then I'll investigate the situation with au pairs and local child-minders.'

Maria tried to get to grips with what this might entail. 'But if it was just a trial, I'd need to come to London really soon. Otherwise, if I did decide against it, it would mean letting you down pretty late on in your pregnancy, when it might be much more difficult to make alternative arrangements, and when you'll be feeling tireder anyway.'

'Great! The sooner the better.'

Maria shook her head with a certain irritation. 'Amy,' she said, more sternly than she'd intended, 'I'm not free to just drop everything – and it's far too late to discuss all this, in any case. We need to go to bed.'

'Yes, but—'

'No "yes buts". Hugo's been waiting ages and, if you don't need rest, your baby certainly does.' She laid a gentle hand on her daughter's still-flat stomach. 'I'm absolutely thrilled to bits that I'm going to be a grandma. It's the best news in the world – don't doubt that for a second – and, of course, I'll help you any way I can. But let's leave the actual decisions of exactly when and how I help for just a little bit longer.'

'But, Mum, don't you think—'

Maria rose from the sofa and, having coaxed Amy to her feet, steered her gently towards the door. 'Not another word, OK?'

Once alone, she made no move to go to bed herself, knowing that, with all the ramifications of the pregnancy seething in her mind, she was unlikely to get to sleep. How could she sell the cottage, as if it were nothing but bricks and mortar, rather than her mother's lifelong home? Or move to London, when she was so firmly rooted here?

Yet, whatever she decided, the dizzyingly exciting prospect of being a grandmother was still worth celebrating, so she poured herself another half-glass of wine and drank a toast to that fragile, precious foetus.

Chapter 5

MARIA GAZED OUT at the rooftops, surprised to see a faint glow in the sky, despite it being only 5 a.m. At home, it would be inky-dark but, here in London, presumably, the sheer volume of street-lamps would always mitigate so intense and deep-dyed a black. And the array of roofs and chimneypots provided a jolting contrast to her usual view of rolling fields and undulating hills.

She jumped at the sound of a siren, followed by the vroom of a police car speeding past the house. How did Amy and Hugo *sleep*, especially with the intrusive noise of the planes that had started droning over as early as half-past four? And an hour before, she had been woken by a crowd of drunken revellers staggering home after a Saturday night on the town. She had groped her way to the window again and watched their unsteady progress as they lurched along the street, spilling shouts and laughter in their wake.

She let the curtain fall and ventured into her tiny mini-kitchen; filled the squat red kettle; fetched milk from the bijou fridge. Ironic that she should miss her morning ritual of making tea for Hanna, changing her incontinence pad, and struggling to wash and dress her. But, in truth, she felt a little purposeless, with the long day stretching ahead and no role for her to play as yet. Perhaps she could cook Sunday lunch and insist her daughter rested, after the sudden scare last week that had brought her rushing down to help.

Except Amy didn't *need* help. 'I'm fine now, Mum. It was only the weeniest bit of bleeding – a false alarm, the hospital said, and I was discharged within a few hours. Still, I'm so relieved you've come, then if there's any further problem you're right here on the spot. Oh, I know it's a lot earlier than we planned, but that's all to the good, because it'll give you more time to adjust.'

So, there was no going back, apparently. She was now the full-time, live-in granny, but four months before the date agreed and with no baby to look after.

With a shrug, she took her tea to the window and scanned the vista beyond the road, in an attempt to get her bearings. Having arrived only late last night, she hadn't much idea, yet, of where Victoria might be, or even which was north and which was south. She winced as another plane roared over, seemingly all but skimming the roof, but however great the noise outside, there wasn't a sound from within the house. Amy loved her Sunday lie-ins, so she wouldn't be up for another five hours – a long time to wait for breakfast. As yet, her little food-cupboard was unstocked with provisions, apart from tea and milk, but Amy had told her to help herself from the oversized fridge downstairs.

Throwing on her dressing gown, she tiptoed down the narrow attic staircase, pausing a moment outside the master bedroom and imagining Amy and Hugo curled companionably together. She had never shared a bed, apart from that one brief period with Silas, which, even at the time, had seemed miraculous. To be that *close* to someone; share their smells, their fidgets, listen to their breathing; to wake, frightened, from a nightmare and find a reassuring presence to dissipate the fear and, if they were wakeful, too, to chat with them in the middle of the night; to reach out for them, embrace them.

She walked softly on, down the grander staircase and into the sitting-room. What had struck her last night was its stylishness – combined with its complete unsuitability for children. The two pristine-white sofas would be marked by grubby fingers; the expensive white silk cushions used as Frisbees; the precious ornaments and fragile lamps in constant danger from curious little hands. And was that highly polished dark-oak floor the most comfortable of surfaces for a baby learning to crawl?

She shifted her gaze to the two pictures on the wall, which appeared to have been chosen to blend with the colour scheme rather than for any intrinsic merit. Considering Silas's talents and her own artistic bent, she had expected Amy to grow up to be some kind of artist – a poet, painter or rock guitarist, not an executive-search consultant – but then Amy differed from her and Silas in almost every way.

Sweltering in the over-heated house, she loosened the belt of her dressing gown. The cottage would be perishing cold this early in the morning, the first week of February, and she would be bundled up in several woolly sweaters.

Creeping on to the kitchen – almost twice the size of her sitting-room at home – she again marvelled at its almost clinical neatness. No clutter on the worktops, or dirty dishes in the sink; the gadgets spanking new; the oven never used, by the looks of it. Well, she would put that right today; fill the room with homely smells of roast beef and apple pie. For now, though, she must content herself with a bowl of cereal.

Except there didn't appear to be any, or anything in the way of bread. Having searched the cupboards, she tried the fridge instead, but none of its contents seemed remotely suitable for breakfast: Camembert, smoked salmon, a bag of ready-washed rocket salad, a selection of stuffed olives and two bottles of Chardonnay. She pounced on a single yogurt, half-hidden at the back. She would replace it as soon as Sainsbury's opened – in fact, do a full-scale shop. She had come down here to help, so, even if she couldn't persuade her daughter to rest, at least she could take on the major chores.

'Hi, Mum! Sleep well?'

'Yes,' she lied, admiring Amy's slinky black-lace peignoir. Thank God she was now dressed herself, rather than wandering round in a hefty, hairy dressing gown. 'Can I get you some breakfast, darling?'

'No, thanks. We don't eat breakfast.'

'But surely now you're pregnant...?'

'Mum, don't fuss, OK?'

Deflated, she said nothing. When *she* was pregnant, she'd had to eat a couple of biscuits the minute she woke up, just to prevent her vomiting, and even then she had suffered extremes of nausea the whole of the first trimester. And at fourteen weeks, two bouts of glandular fever had left her so low in mind and body, her initial resolve to return to a Whitechapel bedsit and make it as a single mum had been swallowed up in a tide of despair. But Amy, thank God, was never ill; hadn't experienced even a twinge of morning sickness and, apart from that slight show of blood, claimed to barely notice she was pregnant.

'Well, how about a nice pot of tea?'

'Mum, there's no need to wait on us. Hugo and I are so used to doing our own thing, we don't expect room service!'

Maria decided to make herself scarce. 'I thought I'd have a little recce, to get to know the area. So, if there's any shopping you want ....'

'Don't worry, we're eating out today.'

Well, so much for her cosy Sunday lunch. 'In that case, I might go further afield – take myself to Tate Modern, perhaps.'

'No, we're going to a lunch party and you're invited as well. Sorry – I forgot to tell you last night. Nicholas and Chloe said they wanted you to come.'

'But won't I be in the way?'

'Far from it. Chloe said she can't wait to meet you. She's pregnant too, you see, and madly jealous because she's going bananas trying to find a nanny – or at least one who won't break the bank or run off with Nicholas! But if she tries to poach you, beware, Mum! *She's* expecting twins. And, by the way—'

She broke off as her mobile rang. 'Stephen? … it's OK, I can talk…. Oh, I see. I'm extremely sorry to hear that.'

Having seen Amy's look of despondency, Maria prayed that nothing dire had happened. She wasn't to know, however, since her daughter told the caller that she was moving to another room, to ensure total privacy. And, as she made her way towards her mini-office, Hugo drifted in, looking equally snazzy in a striped silk dressing gown.

'Morning,' he yawned, pouring himself some orange juice, before filling the coffee percolator.

Maria itched to do it for him, but that, too, might be classed as 'fussing'. Besides, she always felt slightly daunted by her son-in-law. When Amy first announced she was in love with an engineer, Maria had imagined a down-to-earth mechanic and was thus unprepared for the suave, well-spoken Cambridge graduate, already working as project manager on a huge, upmarket shopping mall. Even now, she hardly knew him, apart from his outward shell. His confidence and competence were so different from her own self-doubt; his unqualified success a reproach to her hapless early life.

Apart from his one-word greeting, he hadn't spoken another syllable and she feared he might resent her presence in the house, especially on his precious Sunday off. Yet it was he, in fact, who had phoned her after Amy's mini-crisis and begged her to come immediately. Like Amy, he was busy, though, and, indeed his mobile was now shrilling, too, so she tactfully retreated to what Amy called 'the granny-flat'. If she had nothing else to do, at least she could pass the time trying to find a suitable outfit for a stylish London lunch party.

'Delicious chicken,' Maria enthused. 'You must let me have the recipe.'

'Ask Waitrose,' Chloe laughed. 'I never cook – can't see the point, with their "Gourmet Entertaining" range. All you have to do is heat it up – which even I can manage!'

'So that paté wasn't yours?'

'God, no! I wouldn't have a clue as to how to make a paté. All three courses are courtesy of Waitrose. Though I sometimes ring the changes by buying M&S. They're pretty good as well.'

Good, maybe, Maria thought, but much more economical to buy a whole chicken, make the casserole from scratch – and several other meals as well – and have the liver, giblets and carcass to use for a nourishing soup.

'So how does it feel,' asked Julian, the tall, distinguished-looking barrister, sitting on her right, 'to be here in the capital, rather than in a village in the wilds?'

'Well, I haven't seen much of it yet – although we came here today on the underground and I was amazed by how crowded it was. When I lived in London in the sixties, the tube was almost empty on a Sunday. I was also struck by all the different nationalities and hearing every language under the sun. That's another big change from forty years ago.'

'Still, I envy you being around then,' Deborah chipped in – an elegant and ultra-skinny female, who looked as if she might snap in half. 'Or weren't the Swinging Sixties quite as swinging as they say?'

'I think it depended on who and where you were. I happened to be at art school, so my friends were pretty bohemian.' She wouldn't admit what an outsider she had felt – a devout Catholic and a country cousin, with only mediocre talent and none of her fellow students' vaunting ambition and self-belief. In truth, she had been out of tune with almost every aspect of the sixties. Drug-taking, mini-skirts, sexual licence, student protests and the hippy quest for freedom – all went against her Church's stress on chastity, obedience, modest dress and self-abnegation.

'And do you work as an artist now?' Nicholas enquired. 'Actually, we're looking for a painting for our sitting-room, so if you have anything we could see ...'

If only, Maria thought. She had sold nothing since two tiny watercolours, way back in 1968, and had painted depressingly little during most of her adult life. For many of those years, she had, in fact, worked in galleries, but more as a glorified sales assistant than as a dealer in fine art. And such jobs had been hard to find in rural Northumberland. Even those galleries that did exist only managed to survive by making frames and selling art materials.

'I'm sorry, no,' she said, embarrassed at being the centre of attention and even by her voice. The others' Oxbridge accents made her own Northumbrian burr seem somehow more pronounced.

Fortunately, Chloe changed the subject and began extolling some fantastic day-spa she'd discovered near Sloane Square. 'Amy, if you feel in need of a boost, book yourself in for a "pamper-day". I had one last week and it was total and utter bliss! It started with a mud treatment. Mud draws out all the impurities in the skin, you see ...'

A pity she hadn't known, Maria reflected, then she could have utilized the facilities of the deplorably muddy lane beyond the cottage. Judging by the pre-lunch conversation, these modish thirty-and-forty-somethings all tended to favour a hedonistic lifestyle – although it had struck her as peculiar that, while they had no time to cook, 'me-time' was apparently no problem. Fiona met her personal trainer for daily sessions in the gym, Caroline 'couldn't survive' without her weekly facials, and even Alexander had actually admitted to having Botox treatments. And, as for manicures and nail extensions, they were clearly *de rigueur*.

'I've been using our local nail-bar,' Deborah observed, returning to the subject. 'But I'm not exactly thrilled with it, so maybe I'll change to your place.'

Maria studied Deborah's nails: super-scarlet, super-long. Wasn't it just a tad absurd to waste an hour or more varnishing or extending ten outgrowths of dead keratin?

'Yes, I highly recommend it. In fact, I intend to be a regular now, and in just a few years' time, we'll be going *en famille*. You see, they already do men's grooming days and they're about to introduce these special pamper-packages tailored to the under-fives.'

Maria found it hard to countenance that tiny tots at playschool were in desperate need of body-wraps or pedicures. She knew her mother would be horrified by these lives of high consumption and high debt. Economy had always been Hanna's watchword, since, if you did have money to spare, your duty as a Christian was to give it away to those in greater need. She would scrape out the last morsel from every can and carton; fry left-over Christmas pudding in slices, long after Christmas Day; iron the Christmas wrapping-paper so it could be reused the following year; save scraps of soap, to be melted down into a serviceable new bar. And, because she and Hanna shared a home, she herself had adopted similar practices. Now, she worried that perhaps Amy had resented such a frugal way of existence and that her present pursuit of wealth and power was simply an overreaction. Although, in all other ways, of course, she and Hanna had showered 'their' child with love. Indeed, ironical as it might seem, it was *she* who had made her daughter confident, ambitious and with a deep sense of inner worth, so determined had she been to compensate for those first two years of neglect.

'What do you do as your job?' she asked Fiona, the blonde and bosomy woman on her left, once the conversation had moved away from beauty salons.

'I'm a headhunter, like Amy, only I specialize in financial services rather than in marketing and retail. I see my role as a matchmaker – trying to pair the client with his ideal, perfect candidate.'

Maria disliked the word 'headhunter', with its overtones of cannibals, but her daughter used it all the time. She glanced anxiously at Amy, knowing how dejected she was about this morning's phone call. Apparently, the man who'd rung had been her lead candidate for the post of marketing director of some prestigious firm but, just this weekend, he had decided against the job and so was pulling out of tomorrow's meeting with the CEO. Which meant that Amy's months of hard, painstaking work and delicate negotiations had been a total waste of time and, the minute this lunch was over, she would have to sort out the mess.

Aware her mind was wandering, Maria resumed her small talk with Fiona. 'So I suppose you're as busy as Amy?'

'Absolutely. High pressure goes with the job.'

'And have you also worked in Dubai?'

'Sadly, no. They say it's the shopping capital of the world and I'm an incurable shopaholic!'

Was she a prig or, worse, a killjoy, Maria wondered, in that she regarded shopping in the same light as manicures? Hanna's influence again, of course. Her mother considered it wasteful to buy more clothes or household wares when the old ones were still serviceable. Luckily for Hanna, though, she had never had to mix in so fashionable a milieu. Compared with these sophisticates, she herself felt overweight, under-dressed, homespun and decidedly ancient. The irony was that, when caring for her mother, *she* had been the 'young' and trendy one.

As if for comfort, she forked in more potatoes – Waitrose again, presumably, since they had been lavishly cooked with onions and cream – then took a swig of her Sauvignon Blanc, savouring its bouquet. It was an unaccustomed treat for her to eat and drink so well and, indeed, to eat and drink in company, and as for the voguish dining-room, it was like something from the Design Museum, with its extensive black-glass table and high-backed, grey-steel chairs. Even the vase of roses – exotic beauties in the subtlest shade of pink – looked as if they'd been hothoused in Kew Gardens.

'No, we thought we'd try the Maldives this year. We did consider Peru, but ...'

The talk was now of holidays, although, distracted by her surroundings, she had missed the details of who was going where.

'No holiday for us, alas.' Chloe gave a sigh. 'I'm already as big as a house, so I wouldn't be seen dead in a swimsuit. You're lucky, Amy. You hardly show at all.'

'You're meant to flaunt your bulge these days,' Caroline observed, pausing with a forkful of chicken halfway to her mouth. 'Even wear a bikini at nine months!'

'Oh, that's just gross.' Chloe shuddered.

'So when are your babies due?' Maria enquired, feeling guilty for not having asked before.

'Well, officially, it's May 5th, though they'll probably be delivered early. But, however gruesome the labour is, I honestly can't wait.' She patted her protuberant stomach with a grimace. 'What I'll be like in another three months doesn't bear thinking about.'

'Don't they usually do a Caesarean for twins?' Maria asked.

'Yes, that's the norm, but you can opt for vaginal delivery if the babies are in the right position and there aren't any complications and, frankly, I'd prefer that to having an ugly scar.'

'Is a scar any worse,' Caroline demanded, 'than being left saggy and incontinent, which you risk with a normal birth?'

Alexander screwed up his face in revulsion. 'Look, we're meant to be eating, if you *don't* mind! And, anyway, all this pregnancy-talk is really pissing me off. I hope you lot realize that, as little as a year ago, none of us was even thinking about procreation. Yet now three of our number have fallen for the myth that life's not complete without an adorable little sprog – or three.'

'It's not a myth. Speak for yourself!'

'I am – *and* for Deborah, too. Neither of us have the slightest desire to clutter up our lives with dirty nappies, screaming infants and – least of all – sky-high university fees just as we're hoping to retire.'

'Infants don't have to scream,' Chloe retorted, tartly. 'Nicholas and I are studying Gabriella Bruno's book and—'

'Who's she?' asked Deborah.

'The latest parenting guru. If you follow her methods, you can train a baby to sleep through the night when it's only a few weeks old.'

Maria tried to keep a straight face. Gabriella Bruno had clearly never met a baby as restless and super-alert as Amy. In any case, 'training' made babies sound like dogs.

'She's called the Queen of Routine,' Nicholas chipped in. 'And she insists on a super-strict timetable. It pays off, though, she claims, because you don't hear a squeak from your baby, once it's been broken in, so to speak.'

Maria winced as the terminology changed from dogs to horses. Poor Nicholas and Chloe, she thought, picturing their hungry, self-willed twins blithely ignoring any guru's strict routine. Thank God *she* would be in charge when it came to Amy's baby and could feed it on demand and give it nice, old-fashioned cuddles in the middle of the night, if it so desired. None of those present actually had children yet, so the reality might come as something of a shock. Chloe and Nicholas's place was as unscathed as Amy and Hugo's – in fact, it put her in mind of a show-house – and she feared its serene perfection was unlikely to withstand the chaos of the new arrivals.

'Another thing,' Chloe added, 'is that, according to Gabriella, once your children are older, you need only spend fifteen minutes a day with them, so long as it's quality time and you switch off your mobile and don't do emails and stuff.'

Maria all but expostulated. A mere dog or cat required more than fifteen minutes' 'quality time'. And even if the children went *en famille* to a day-spa, presumably they and their parents would all be in separate cubicles, each with a different beautician.

'Spare me the details,' Alexander yawned. 'I still stick by my belief that Deborah and I have chosen the better path.'

'Absolutely,' Deborah echoed, giving her husband a maddeningly complicit smile. 'I mean, if you're supposed to learn from your mistakes, why do some parents have more than one child? Take our friends, Nigel and Fay. Fay gave birth to this horrific little creature who shrieked the place down and more or less destroyed the house. And, would you believe, far from learning their lesson, they went ahead and had a second son, equally delinquent.'

'Never mind Nigel and Fay.' Alexander made a sweeping gesture, all but overturning his wine glass. 'It's *you* poor sods I'm worried about. When you're haggard and near bankrupt – and about to be landed with grand-kids, even more expensive and unruly than your own – Debs and I will be going on world cruises, or relaxing by the pool of our luxury villa in Mustique.'

And, thought Maria, taking an instant dislike to this smugly arrogant banker and his unsympathetic wife, you won't have the faintest notion of just how much you've missed.

Chapter 6

'MEET MARIA,' THE tutor said, steering her towards the group of men and women, all standing by the window, chattering and laughing. 'She's new – and new to London, so be sure you make her welcome.'

Everyone began telling her their names, half of which she missed, as they melded in a jumbled blur. At least the class seemed friendly, though – people clustering around her and asking her about herself. And the studio was the perfect setting: a bright, high-ceilinged room; all the available wall-space hung with paintings in a brilliant edgy style.

'Is this all *your* work?' she asked the tutor, once the general conversation had died down.

'No, none of it,' he laughed. 'This isn't even my studio. Mine's a bit on the small side, so a fellow artist lends me his, just for these Friday classes.'

She was still surprised by how different he was from the persona his name suggested. Felix Frances Fullerton had led her to imagine someone distinctive, or maybe eccentric; not this average sort of chap, of middling build and height, conventionally dressed in grey trousers and blue shirt. The only things that marked him out as an artist were the length of his hair – grey, untidy hair, falling onto the collar of his shirt – and the paint-stains on his battered leather boots.

'Right, we ought to make a start,' he said, raising his voice above the chatter, 'so could you all settle down, please. Maria, I suggest you sit in this armchair, then if you need any instruction, I can perch on the arm and talk to you, without disturbing the others.'

'If you need any instruction … ' She needed almost fifty years' worth! Perhaps it was bumptious to have come at all, when she had done practically no life drawing since way back in the sixties. But she had acted on a whim; grabbed the phone, two days ago, and rung her old art school, to enlist their help in finding a class, driven simply by a sense of being aimless and expendable. She had no wish to fill her days attending further lunches

or functions with Amy and Hugo's stylish circle – she would only feel
distinctly spare, not to mention ancient. Despite the restrictions of her
previous role as carer, it had given her a definitive function and made her
central to her mother's life, whereas at Amy's she was simply marking time.
She couldn't even do the housework, because they already had a cleaner –
one she'd met this morning: an elderly Indonesian, spindle-thin and barely
five feet tall. In fact, a Friday class was perfect, because it allowed her to
escape Sumiah, who came on Fridays and whose fragile build and air of
cowed submission were bound to be a source of guilt.

'Janina, are you ready?' Felix called.

'Yes, 'course.' The model removed her silky robe, to reveal a full, curvaceous figure.

'I'd like you to begin with a few short three-minute poses, OK?'

'OK.' Janina took up a position in the centre of the room, one small,
blunt-fingered hand supporting her pendulous breasts, the other resting on
her neck.

Maria's chair was so placed that she could see the woman full-on.
Nervously, she picked up a pencil, wondering if she would remember how
to draw at all. Yet, to her great surprise, the lines began to flow with such
freedom and fluidity, it was as if a dam had burst and all her pent-up
longing to express herself was now pouring onto the paper. Instead of the
former buzz of conversation, there was now reverential silence in the room;
the only sounds the whisper of pencils on paper, the purr of an occasional
rubber, and a sudden rasping noise as the man beside her sharpened his
pencil with a Stanley knife.

Felix was also drawing, standing in front of the model and so absorbed
in the task he seemed to have forgotten about her instruction, or that of
anyone else. Not that she minded in the least. She was making up for those
deeply regretted 'lost' decades, and all that mattered was to continue at her
present white-hot pace.

'One minute left,' Felix announced, and her pencil moved still faster,
eager to make the most of that one remaining minute.

'Thirty seconds left.'

Hardly had the last second elapsed when Janina took up a new pose.
Maria was now presented with her back view: the shoulders squarish,
solid; the back itself broad and well upholstered, with an interesting roll of
flesh above the waist. Right from the start, she had felt an instant response
to this woman's ample body, its generous proportions and air of relaxed
abandon. Her pencil swept down the page as she sketched the mane of
near-black hair tumbling over the shoulders, the exaggerated arch of the

back and voluminous curve of the buttocks, the chunky thighs and heavily muscled legs.

'Thirty seconds left.'

She almost voiced an objection when, once the thirty seconds was up, the model relaxed a moment before adopting the next pose. She had been trying to capture the exact way the left leg was crooked, and now Janina had straightened it.

'Can we have a longer pose next?' a tall, willowy woman asked – a plea Maria echoed silently.

Felix nodded. 'Certainly, if that's OK with everyone. How about you, Janina? Are you happy with, say, twenty minutes?'

'Fine.' The model went to sit on the edge of a straight-backed chair, her legs splayed wide, her fingers caressing her squat, brown nipples, as if inviting all eyes to study them.

Maria envied the way she flaunted her body with such a lack of inhibition. This brazen pose displayed her tangled mass of pubic hair and even the lips of her vagina. *She* had been taught, as a convent girl, never to sit with her legs apart, and also warned that bodies were perilous, so the less known about them the better. Even in her twenties, she had been unaware that she possessed such things as labia, until Silas discovered them for her.

Well, if nothing else, her pencil-strokes were becoming increasingly daring, as she endeavoured to catch the nature of that unbiddable pubic hair, which grew even down the tops of Janina's thighs, as if refusing to be confined. Her concentration was so absolute, she didn't notice Felix glide across the room and, when he stopped beside her chair, she started in surprise.

'That's really expressive drawing,' he whispered, seating himself on the chair-arm and peering over her shoulder at her work. 'Honestly, I'm impressed. All it lacks is a certain degree of technical skill. You need to work out how the legs relate to the thighs, the thighs to the stomach and the stomach to the chest.'

His soft, intimate tone reminded her of the confessional. Despite the proximity of the others, the two of them seemed to be in their own private space; his hip nudging against her upper arm; his voice murmuring in her ear; his eyes meeting hers a moment.

'A grasp of anatomy is essential for an artist,' he added, in the same hushed tone. 'Stubbs had whole dead horses hung up in his studio, so he could study their basic structure, and Leonardo da Vinci was always dissecting cadavers.' He broke off with a smile. 'I don't expect you to go as far as that! And, anyway, don't worry too much at this stage. You'll find, with more practice, it will just come naturally.'

She was distracted by his hand, gesturing to her work: the strong but stubby fingers, the tiny scar on the wrist, the hairs on the back of the thumb.

'What you also need to consider,' he continued, seemingly oblivious of her scrutiny, 'is the model's relationship to the chair. The chair has an angle, and *she* has an angle, so try to get a sense of exactly how she's sitting. But, technicalities apart, what I really like is the freedom of your drawing. It has this huge exuberance, almost an anarchic quality. But I reckon your sketch-book's too small to do justice to the boldness of your style. Wait a sec – I'll fetch you a board and larger paper.'

He returned in less than a minute; several sheets of paper clipped firmly to a board. 'No, keep it upright,' he advised, 'not balanced on your lap. And I suggest you draw standing up. You may find that still more freeing.'

Although embarrassed to be singled out in this fashion, she was so elated by his praises, she wouldn't have minded if he had asked her to stand on her head. Besides, the others were so lost in the process of drawing they were blind to everything except the model and their sketchbooks, their gaze continually flicking from one to the other and back again.

She, too, must resume her former focus – not difficult, in fact, since her long years of prayer had taught her a basic discipline, as well as the ability to fix her mind on one all-important figure. Indeed, the fervour and the sense of rapt attention, so apparent in the room, did have certain similarities to intense religious devotion. She made a silent vow: to be as observant in this new artistic practice as in her old religious one.

'So where were you at art school?' Elizabeth enquired.

Maria took her time in answering. Elizabeth herself had been to the Royal College, so she'd been informed, and Helen to the Slade – both highly distinguished establishments. The Cass was hardly in the same league, despite its full, aristocratic name: the *Sir* John Cass School of Art. And, during her time there, it had been in a state of some upheaval, evolving from a charitable foundation to becoming part of the City of London Polytechnic – not that she would mention the word polytechnic in this exalted company.

'Well, I was a bit clueless, to be honest,' she mumbled, finally. 'You see, I'd lived my whole life in the depths of the country and never met any artists, so I didn't really know where to go, or even what courses to study.'

She was glad when Elizabeth changed the subject, being reluctant to dwell on that period of her life, when she had felt daunted by her tutors (who were sometimes brusque and frightening), and by those students with exotic names – Aida, Scarlet, Roderigues, Ché – and confidence to match. And, apart from the other frustrations, she seemed always to be broke, despite having worked for four years in Northumberland, straight after leaving school, and saved all she could for the course. But, when she'd eventually made it to the capital, everything cost far more than she'd imagined, including the rent on a small, squalid bedsit in Whitechapel. As for Silas, he hadn't appeared on the scene until she'd almost completed her foundation year and was about to move to another – even less prestigious – school, since the Cass offered no further courses in Fine Art. But at least he had solved one problem by inviting her to share his flat, despite the fact it wasn't strictly 'his'. The rest was history – or perhaps the *end* of her history would be nearer to the mark.

'More wine?' Felix asked, doing the rounds with the bottle.

Elizabeth shook her head. 'No, I'd better not. One glass is enough at lunchtime.'

'Who says?' he laughed. 'One glass is *never* enough! How about you, Maria?'

'Yes, please.' She intended to get her fill of this blissful Friday lunchtime. However inexperienced she might be, compared with all the rest, she did, in fact, feel surprisingly at home, surrounded as she was by laid-back, congenial people, rather than high-powered business types. There wasn't a suit to be seen. Helen was wearing mustard-coloured leggings and a blue embroidered waistcoat; Barry sported purple corduroy trousers, while Robert's tawny hair clashed deliciously with his crimson shirt. No one was ultra-stylish, ultra-gorgeous, or even particularly young, so she could hold her own, she felt. Even Felix must be sixtyish, although the lively way he moved and spoke made him seem much younger.

Robert passed her a plate of oatcakes; some spread with hummus, others with cream cheese. 'So will you be coming back next week?' he asked.

She reflected for a moment. This class would give her a much-needed sense of purpose until the baby was born and, if she practised regularly, would fill the long and lonely days. 'Yes,' she said, with a sudden surge of contentment, 'most definitely I will.'

On the way back to the tube, she began thinking about her grandchild, whom she intended to teach to draw, as soon as it was old enough to hold a crayon, and also take to the London galleries, in its pushchair. In fact, she could start going to them herself, to study the great masters' nudes and try to pick up some basic techniques.

All at once, she recalled Hanna's utter horror when she'd first mentioned her weekly life class, back in 1965. Her mother shared the Church's view of nakedness, as shameful, if not sinful. In fact, she sometimes wondered if even her father had ever seen his wife in the nude. After all, many women in those days wore their nightgowns during sex, and often regarded their marital duty as indeed a duty, if not an actual burden. As for oral sex, Hanna had no idea such a thing existed until, very late in life, she had read a magazine article and expostulated in obvious shock, 'But that's like putting a cesspit into your mouth!'

Maria gave a rueful grin as she descended to the underground. Despite the crowds, she was still amazed by how quick and easy London journeys were. Maida Vale to Sutherland Street might seem a longish trek, yet a mere thirty minutes later, she was back in Pimlico and striding down the road to Amy's house. As she turned the corner, she jumped aside to avoid a small girl on a scooter, hurtling towards her on the pavement – but jumped a fraction too late. The front wheel caught her shin, resulting in a sharp pain in her leg. The child was unhurt, thank God, but its mother came rushing up to investigate the damage, followed by a second, older girl.

'Oh, Lord, you're bleeding!' the woman cried. 'And there's a big hole in your tights. I'm so terribly sorry. Polly's such a clumsy child. Look, I'd feel a lot less bad if you came home with me and let me patch you up. I only live in the next street.'

'And I live in *this* one,' Maria replied, with a smile. 'So please don't worry – it's nothing.'

The woman returned her smile. 'That means we're almost neighbours, which seems a pretty good reason to get to know each other. This area's not exactly friendly.'

'Mummy, I'm *cold*,' the small child wailed.

'You should be saying sorry to the lady, not complaining.' The mother shook her head in exasperation. 'I'm afraid she never looks where she's going.'

'Sorry,' the recreant muttered, clinging on to her scooter as if she feared it might be confiscated.

'*I'm* cold, too,' the older girl interjected, giving a histrionic shiver.

'OK, hot chocolate for all of us, once we've dealt with this poor lady's cut. I'm Kate, by the way. And this is Clara.' She indicated the coltish older child. 'Polly you've already met – although hardly in ideal circumstances! I can't tell you how sorry I am.'

'Don't give it another thought. These things happen, don't they? I'm Maria and, thanks, I will pop in.' Having enjoyed the class so much, she had no desire to return to an empty, silent house and wait an age till Amy got back – *if* she got back at all, rather than going straight from work to some networking engagement. She could hardly believe what punishing hours her daughter and her son-in-law both worked. Hugo's present role as project manager of a major Olympic structure meant he was required to be on-site by 7.30 each morning, and the drive to Stratford East was invariably long and stressful. As for Amy, she rarely finished work before seven in the evening and, if she was negotiating an offer, or involved in a client presentation, it could easily be nine or ten when she finally left the office.

'Right,' Kate was saying, 'we just cross this road, turn left and our house is a few yards along.'

It proved to be very similar to Amy's – the same four floors, elegant sash windows, white exterior and black iron railings. Inside, however, the place looked both more cluttered and more comfortable, with evidence of children on all sides. Kate took her coat, ushered her through to the kitchen and sat her on a chair.

'Does it hurt?' asked Polly, the prettier of the sisters, with blonde curls and peachy skin. The darker, more sallow Clara had disappeared upstairs. 'I always cry when I'm hurt. Mummy says I'm a cry-baby.'

'We're all cry-babies sometimes,' Maria told her, remembering how she had cried for Hanna, yet again, last night. She still missed not just her mother but the cottage and her friends, although now, it seemed, there was a good chance of making new ones.

'I'm six and a half,' Polly declared, abruptly changing the subject. 'How old are you?'

'Well, I had a birthday on 26 January, so I'm sixty-six-and-three-weeks.'

'That's *old*.'

'Polly, I hope you're not being a pain?' Kate said, returning with the first-aid box.

'No. I'm looking after Maria.'

'Well, that's very kind of you, but I'd prefer it if you changed out of your school uniform and left us grown-ups in peace. Right, Maria, I'll just boil up some water and, if you wouldn't mind slipping off your tights, I can give the wound a proper wash.'

'What's a wound?'

'Polly, what did I just say?'

'Change out of my uniform. Can we have cream on our hot chocolate and those little sprinkly things?'

'Yes, but only if you do as you're told.'

Once Polly had gone stomping off, Maria removed her tights and let

Kate bathe her leg. Although embarrassed by this fuss over a mere superficial cut, she also felt a curious pleasure at being looked after for a change. She sat back in her chair, gradually thawing in the cosy heat of the kitchen: a cheery room, with yellow walls, pine cupboards and an old-fashioned rustic dresser.

'Good – that looks better.' Having applied ointment, gauze and plaster to the cut, Kate went to fetch some replacement tights.

'Take your pick – thick or thin, dark or pale. They're all new, by the way. The damn things ladder so easily, I always keep some spares.'

Maria chose thick, dark ones – suitable for the frosty weather – and eased them up and on, while Kate washed her hands at the sink.

'Do you have children?' she enquired, pulling up a chair and joining Maria at the table.

'Yes, one daughter. But she's hardly a child. She's thirty-eight and expecting her first baby.'

'Oh, she left it late, like me,' Kate laughed. 'I had Clara at forty-one and Polly at forty-five – which is really truly ancient! No doubt you were more sensible and got down to things at an earlier stage.'

'Well, actually, I was twenty-seven, which was considered very old in those days.' As a Catholic – and pious Hanna's daughter – the concept of keeping her virginity until her wedding night had seemed crucially important. Sex and children were both impossible in the absence of a husband, and she had remained steadfast to that view even through her years at art school. Only Silas had finally worn her down, replacing her once-firm Catholic faith with a faith in *him*, as demi-god.

'But, reverting to this age thing, I don't think it matters a toss, do you? I mean, I'm getting on for fifty-two, and if sixty is the new forty, as everybody says, then I'm looking forward to it! Frankly, I don't intend to get old. If it takes a few nips and tucks, that's fine by me, and I hope that when the girls are in their twenties, I'll be wearing the same type of clothes as them.'

Maria glanced at Kate's present attire: skin-tight denim jeans, leopard-print top and skittishly high-heeled boots, which made her own outfit look distinctly matronly. Yet the idea of refusing to age struck her as a futile form of denial. Surely it was better to embrace one's increasing maturity and feel comfortable in one's (admittedly) slackening skin. Of course, for Clara and Polly time stretched ahead – endlessly and infinitely – whereas in thirty years or less, she herself would no longer be here at all. As for Amy and Hugo, they were so busy juggling work and social life, and multi-tasking generally, they rarely spared a thought for time in the abstract.

'Well, I'd better get our tea,' Kate said, fetching a loaf from the breadbin. 'It's only sandwiches, at this stage, because later we're having dinner as a family. The girls barely see their father just at present. He's a management consultant and involved in a project in Frankfurt at the moment. He's here tonight, but off again tomorrow, which means he'll miss their Valentine's party. They're having it this Sunday, the 13th rather than the14th, because weekends are so much easier if you're planning a big bash. Hey, why don't you come, Maria? I'd love to see you again.'

'Won't the girls mind, if it's their thing?'

''Course not. Polly's taken a shine to you and it's her we have to blame for the idea. She said it wasn't fair that only grown-ups got to celebrate St Valentine's, so she's invited all her school friends and wants a red-heart cake, and red balloons all over the place!'

'Well, it'll be a first for me. I've never been to a Valentine's party.'

'And I've never given one.'

'Look, if you'd like me to make the cake, I have lots of free time at the moment.'

'Oh, no, it's already ordered. I use this marvellous firm of caterers and they're laying on the food, all themed to red and pink.'

Did anyone in London cook, Maria wondered, as she watched Kate make the sandwiches with a carton of Sainsbury's egg mayonnaise. *She* would have boiled a couple of eggs, but then she was clearly something of a dinosaur in this modern convenience world.

'Actually, I plan to send both Clara and Polly a gorgeous Valentine's card – anonymously, of course. I don't want them feeling left out or rejected if their friends receive cards and they don't.'

Maria was lost for words. Valentine's cards for the under-twelves seemed a step too far.

'There's so much competition at their school, even over things like cards. And parties themselves have become a definite form of one-upmanship. All the parents try to outdo each other – you know, a Harry Potter theme trumped by Pirates of the Caribbean, or whatever the latest craze is. And the party-bags are a nightmare! The last party Clara went to, each child's bag contained a piece of really ostentatious jewellery, hand-made by some local artist. How the hell do I rival that?'

'I wouldn't bother,' Maria dared to say. 'Give them a penny-chew and let them be grateful!'

'You don't know modern kids. Their parents would probably sue.'

They both laughed conspiratorially.

'Right – sandwiches done. Now all we need is—'

'Mummy,' Polly interrupted, reappearing in a pair of tartan trews, teamed, oddly, with a sequinned lilac top. 'Can I show Maria my dolls' house?'

'Maria might prefer to rest her leg.'

'No, I'd love to see it, Polly.' She followed the child downstairs to the basement, which had been turned into a gigantic playroom, complete with two computer stations, one for each girl, and every type of game and toy. Amy and Hugo had deliberately chosen a house without a basement, because even one storey fewer reduced the price considerably. (It had been sold off, years ago, to a French businessman, who used it as a pied-à-terre, although, in fact, was seldom there.) But Kate and her husband, presumably, had no such financial concerns.

'This is Mrs Brown,' Polly explained, indicating a superbly dressed lady-doll, primping in front of her dressing-table mirror. 'And that's Mr Brown downstairs.'

'*My* name's Brown,' Maria informed her.

Polly gave a delighted giggle. 'That means it's your house, then.'

Unlikely, Maria thought, noting the sheer luxury of this mansion-in-miniature.

'Girls are better than boys,' Polly announced, changing the subject in her usual sudden fashion.

'Better in what way?'

'Every way, of course.'

Maria only realized at that moment that she desperately wanted her grandchild to be a girl. Not because girls were 'better', but because the women in her family were invariably the ones who survived.

Clara swivelled round from her computer. 'Do you have a dog?'

'Not now. I used to have one called Heidi.'

'What happened to her?'

'She died, I'm afraid, but she was very old and she'd had a lovely life.'

'The most wonderful thing in the world,' Polly declared, hands on hips, 'is to have a dog.'

'No,' countered Clara, 'the most wonderful thing in the world is to be so rich you can buy whole countries like Greece and Malta and America and Italy. I've been to all those four and I really, really loved them.'

Maria declined to admit that her own travels had been confined to London and the Lake District – Hanna's influence, again. Having been a 'foreigner' in England, her mother had no desire to repeat the experience in any other country, nor any wish to visit her native land. It wasn't just Theresia who had endured a wretched childhood there, but many of her ancestors had also lived unhappy lives in Austria.

'I'd like to be so rich,' Polly trumped her sister, 'that I could buy the whole world and all the planets, too.'

Was it any wonder, Maria thought, that these girls' aspirations should reach so far, when, judging by the contents of this playroom, they already owned such a wealth of consumer goods? She resolved to bring up her own grandchild with a different set of values. In fact, she had decided not to sell the cottage, but keep it as her refuge in older age and a holiday retreat for any grandchildren she might have. She would probably have to let it in the meantime, but she wanted Amy's children to get to know their ancestral home, however modest it might be.

Polly had already lost interest in the dolls' house and was now raiding the dressing-up box. 'Here, wear this!' she ordered, plonking a glittery gold crown on Maria's head.

Maria eyed the contents of the box, most of which were spread out on the floor. The Queen herself would surely have been impressed by these sumptuous gowns, magicians' robes, pirate costumes, fairy wings and dresses, and by the versatile range of wands, masks, hats, veils and flower-wreaths. When *she* had dressed up as a child, it would have been in some old tablecloth or tea towel, or she'd have clumped around in her mother's gingham overall and oversized brown lace-ups. But then she had probably been every bit as happy as Polly would in a jewelled tiara and beribboned princess-frock.

'Tea's ready!' Kate called from the top of the basement stairs.

Maria was soon seated between the two girls and, whilst munching sandwiches and scooping the froth off hot chocolate, they chatted to her about their likes and dislikes, hobbies, homework and future ambitions – Polly's to be an angel, so she could fly without an engine. Maria let her mind take flight, as well, imagining two very similar granddaughters, but sitting in her cottage, enjoying simple country pleasures: baking scones, grooming dogs, washing the feathers off newly laid brown eggs – and doing lots of drawing, of course. And, by *that* time, she resolved, her own pictures would be so accomplished they would surpass those of every member of the life class.

Chapter 7

'Hi! I don't think we've met. I'm Tim.'

'And I'm Maria. Great to meet you, Tim.'

The wiry, tow-haired man was sitting cross-legged on the floor, a baby in the crook of his arm, whom he was feeding with its bottle. She edged her chair towards him, glad to make conversation, since she was feeling rather out of things, being the oldest person present. Grandmas seemed an unknown quantity, at least in this milieu. She had offered to help a dozen times, but Kate required no help. As well as professional caterers, she had professional entertainers: a magician and a clown, who'd been holding the children in a state of enthralled attention since the party first began.

'And which of the little girls is yours?' Tim asked.

'Oh, I'm just a neighbour, not a parent,' Maria answered, embarrassed by the question. Unless she had gone in for surrogacy, she could hardly be the mother of a six-year-old – or even of an eleven-year-old. 'How old's your baby?' she asked, keen to shift attention from herself.

'Six months.' Hoisting the infant over his shoulder, he brought up its wind with surprising expertise. 'And our other child's in the same class as Polly. My wife's gone back to work, so now it's my turn to look after them. I actually work in PR, but they've given me paternity leave and I'm learning how to cook and iron, as well as basic baby-care.'

The contrast with Silas was searing. The very thought of babies had been totally abhorrent to him: their messiness and insatiable demands; their galling lack of reason. Although even Hugo, she imagined, was unlikely to rival Tim's domestic skills. As the only child of doting parents, he had probably never cooked or ironed in his life. But at least he was *there*, to provide the child with a father – something she and Hanna had been forced to do without.

'And, of course, I accompanied my wife to all the antenatal courses, including a special class to prepare us for the psychological pressures of being parents.'

Maria forbore to mention that the psychological pressures of bringing up an illegitimate child in a gossipy, finger-pointing village were probably somewhat greater than any Tim might encounter.

'Daddy, I'm hungry.' Tim's daughter had come looking for her father.

'Tea won't be long, I'm sure. This is Clementine,' he said, introducing Maria to the child, who was dressed in floor-length frills and a sparkly gold-and-silver crown.

'Hi, Clementine.' These parents certainly favoured fancy names. So far, she'd met an Amber, a Viola, an Orlando and a Zebedee.

'Tea's ready, everyone!' Kate announced, as the clown and the magician made their final bows. 'So if you'd like to move into the dining-room ...'

That room proved as spacious as the sitting-room and was equally awash in hearts: red-heart balloons, red-heart bunting, red-heart bows on the table-legs, and the red-heart cake in pride of place on the red-heart-printed tablecloth.

Once everyone was seated, Kate explained which of the food was gluten-, nut- or dairy-free. Half the children had allergies, apparently – or so their parents claimed (although Kate had told her earlier that it was another form of one-upmanship to have produced a child so sensitive it could eat no normal food). Maria eyed the table with interest. The sandwiches were heart-shaped, with additional heart-shaped slices of ham, beef and smoked salmon placed on top, to show off the reds and pinks. Nor had vegetarians – or even vegans – been forgotten. As well as bowls of radishes and cherry tomatoes, there were roasted-red-pepper wraps, bagels topped with pink-tinged cream cheese, and dishes of every conceivable fruit in the red/pink spectrum: straw-berries, cherries, raspberries, redcurrants, cranberries, watermelon. Elaborate red jellies were studded with yet more scarlet fruits; a profusion of cupcakes had been iced in red and pink and decorated with pink sugar hearts, and the Valentine's Day cake itself was a triumph of the confectioner's art.

Although more than ready to eat, Maria deliberately held back, since no one else appeared to be showing much interest. Some of the mothers looked semi-anorexic and were toying with a single prawn or radish, but none was doing justice to the spread. And Kate herself was busy filling glasses with a strawberry-coloured smoothie, and thus had no chance to eat.

'I want pizza,' Clementine wailed, pushing away the sandwich Tim had given her.

Another child was clamouring for crisps, while two small boys were fighting over the same cheese bagel, despite the fact there were dozens more. Clara, ignoring the savouries, was making serious inroads into a dish of foil-wrapped chocolate hearts.

'They all have a message, printed on the inside of the wrapper,' she explained to her friend, Fenella, smoothing out the foil, to read it. 'Yuk! Listen to this: "With you by my side, every second of every day is deeply precious." Doesn't that make you want to puke?'

Intrigued, Maria took a heart herself and, having unwrapped the foil, read the message on its underside: 'Love is never impossible.'

That she doubted. Silas had been the one great love of her life – or so she'd thought at the time. She had often wondered, since, if he had ever really loved her, or was merely attracted by her innocence, naiveté and subservience. And what about her own love for him – a love so over-whelming and immoderate, it had marked her ever since – had that also been a delusion, the substitution of one unobtainable God for another, human one? All she really knew was that love brought punishment – a deeply depressing thought. She reached out for a couple more hearts, hoping for a message that might strike a chord.

The words on the first declared: 'The only truth is love beyond reason.' Again, she strongly disagreed, but maybe third time lucky.

'Love is the sweetest poison,' she read. Yes, dead right, this time.

'It sounds to me, Maria, as if your needs have never been met.'

Maria flushed. Although the concept of 'needs' was foreign to her (apart from the aberration in her twenties), she had certainly been indulging herself in the last few days, what with the life class and the Valentine's party and now this post-party tête-a-tête.

'You're entitled to some pleasure, you know, especially after martyring yourself, tending to your mother all that time.'

Maria's flush intensified. She barely knew Kate as yet, so should never have confided the details of her private life. 'Please don't use that word.' Martyrdom involved being burnt at the stake, or tortured on a rack, not a few years of paltry service to a much-loved parent. 'I *wanted* to do it, Kate.'

'That's not the point …'

'Let's change the subject, OK?'

'OK, but at least let me give you a top-up.' Kate leaned across to grab the half-empty wine bottle.

'No, actually, I ought to go.' Firmly, she stood up, ignoring Kate's pleas to stay. She already regretted the third glass of wine, since it had made her relax her guard.

'Well, huge thanks for all you've done. I'd never have got the house to rights without your help.'

'Don't worry – I enjoyed it.' If nothing else, the party had been an eye-opener. After tea, the children had played pass-the-parcel – a rather different version from that current in her childhood. Instead of one small, inexpensive present, wrapped in layer upon layer of old newspaper, each and every layer had contained a lavish gift. (Apparently, it was wrong for any child to have to suffer disappointment.) Luxurious metallic gift-wrap – red-heart-emblazoned, of course – had replaced unhygienic newspaper, and the scratchy borrowed gramophone been superseded by a state-of-the-art sound system.

'Well, I suppose we didn't do too badly,' Kate commented, getting up to fetch Maria's coat. 'A few tears and squabbles, maybe, but no out-and-out fisticuffs, or hissy fits from the parents. The only thing I really misjudged was the food. I ordered loads too much and, in fact, you'd be doing me a favour, Maria, if you could take the bulk of it home. My fridge is overflowing as it is.'

'But surely Clara and Polly will eat it?'

'Oh, no! They'll turn up their noses at having the same thing twice. And Paul's away till next Friday and *I'm* on a diet.'

If slender Kate was on a diet, then *she* should embark on a total fast. But she was seriously tempted to accept this banquet-to-go, if only to save it being disposed of in the waste-bin.

While Kate stacked the food into Tupperware boxes, Maria went downstairs to the playroom to say goodbye to the girls. Clara was on her mobile and Polly playing some game on her laptop, while simultaneously listening to her i-Pod. The scene reminded her of Amy and Hugo, at weekends and in the evenings: shut off in their private worlds, texting, tweeting, Googling, FaceBooking. Even when physically present, they remained emotionally absent. Was it right to assume that every technological advance was an undisputed advantage; one of the so-called blessings of contemporary life? When it came to her own grandchild, she would aim to wean it off all its digital dummies, at least during their spells in the country. Or was that a mere pastoral idyll?

''Bye,' she mouthed to Clara, while Polly removed her earphones and came to see her off.

'Is your cut still bleeding?' she asked, eyeing the Elastoplast on Maria's leg.

'No, it's healing nicely, thanks.'

Next, the child observed the Tupperware cartons Kate was stowing in Maria's bag.

'Is all that food for *your* children?'

Maria laughed. 'Well, yes, my daughter, Amy, might like some.' Except Amy and Hugo were out till late tonight, and she couldn't see them scoffing jelly on a busy Monday morning.

Nonetheless, once she got home, she put the fruits and jellies in the fridge and the cupcakes in a tin, hoping they might be eaten by someone besides herself. The sandwiches wouldn't keep, though, so she laid them on the kitchen table and, safe from disapproval, started tucking in to cream-cheese bagels, roasted-pepper wraps, salmon sandwiches and roast-beef hearts, in glorious succession.

After all, hadn't Kate just told her she was entitled to some pleasure?

Chapter 8

'MUM, WE'RE LEAVING now,' Amy called from the foot of the attic stairs.

'Oh, right – just a sec.' Maria glanced at herself in the mirror, suddenly regretting the tight blue-denim jeans and brilliant swirly top. She was about to be a grandma, for God's sake! Too late to change, though, since she wanted to go down and see Amy and Hugo off.

'Wow, Mum, you look amazing!'

She flushed. 'You don't think it's – you know, mutton dressed as lamb?'

'Well, to be perfectly frank, you look nothing like the mother I've grown used to, but I'd say that's all to the good. Why the change, though?'

She hesitated. 'I ... I've been feeling a bit frumpy in the life class.' That was true, at least. 'The others aren't particularly young, but they *dress* young, certainly. And they've invited me to supper this evening, so I thought I'd make a bit of an effort.' 'They' was safely vague.

'Oh, I'm glad you have something planned. I hate leaving you alone on a Sunday. It's bad enough in the week, with me and Hugo both so busy. You should have mentioned it before, though – saved me all that guilt!'

'It came up sort of ... suddenly.'

'So are you all going out as a group?'

'No. One of them's asked us all back to her flat.' 'All' and 'her' weren't true. She hated lying to Amy, but she just couldn't admit the truth. Indeed, she could hardly believe how ridiculously apprehensive she had felt since Friday's class, when Felix had suggested she go round to his place this Sunday evening, to see his recent paintings. Never would it have occurred to her that he had anything more in mind than an appraisal of his work, were it not for the signs he had given during the last few classes. These had escalated from a hand on her arm as he leaned over to assess her drawing, to the brushing of his body against hers, to direct, almost provocative eye-contact, to compliments on her hair and even figure. And, just last week, when all the others had left, he had actually taken her hand and slowly traced each finger with his own. The soft, mesmeric pressure had been so sensual, so surprising, she had felt its shockwaves throbbing further down. But then he'd laughed and made a joke of it; said he was simply checking to see if she had artistic hands.

'Mum, I've the perfect scarf to go with that top – a red and purply one. I haven't time to find it now, but just rummage through my drawers and help yourself to anything you want. And I think a paler lipstick would work better than that vivid red, so feel free to borrow mine.'

Having thanked her daughter, Maria added, with a sudden guilt, 'Darling, you mustn't think I've been throwing money around. I bought this entire outfit at Tachbrook Market for less than twenty quid, and that includes the boots.'

'Mum, for heaven's sake, you've *never* thrown money around! You should see my friend, Beth. She spent over a thousand pounds on some Balmain jeans last week.'

Appalled, Maria did a speedy calculation: a thousand pounds would probably buy a sandwich for almost every homeless Londoner.

'OK, that's over the top. But you don't have to keep economizing. Why not spoil yourself for once and buy some decent clothes?'

'Why, do these look cheap and nasty?'

'No, they look surprisingly good. In fact, I doubt if I could tell the jeans from Beth's, apart from examining the label. Hell! Is that the time? I told Hugo I'd only be a sec. And he's pretty pissed off as it is.'

'Why, what's wrong?'

'Oh, it's connected with his old firm in Dubai. Apparently, a major problem's developed in that huge hotel complex he built.'

'But you left Dubai a good nine months ago, so surely it's not his responsibility?'

'Well, actually it is. You see, there's a clause in the contract that says if any defects are discovered in the materials or workmanship within one year of completion, the contractors are liable and have to—' She broke off, impatiently, with another glance at her watch. 'I'm sorry, Mum, I can't go into all the details now – it's just too complicated. Basically, Hugo blames the contractors, but *they* say he approved it, so it's actually his fault. It's a major hassle for him – poor darling! He has enough on his plate with his current job, without all this exploding in his face.'

As if confirming his tense state, there was a tetchy shout from downstairs. 'Get a move on, Amy! We're going to be frightfully late.'

Together, they hurried down the two flights and found him pacing up and down the hall. However, his expression changed as he gave Maria an appraising glance. 'Hey, you look great!' he exclaimed.

Well, at least *one* male approved, but Felix and Hugo were entirely different types and, if the artist was less impressed than the civil engineer, then it was Kate she had to blame. Now that they were seeing each other more often, the younger woman's influence was beginning to rub off on her. At first, she had strongly resisted Kate's suggestion, saying she was far too old and fat even to consider wearing jeans.

'Don't put yourself down, Maria. You're not fat, you're voluptuous. And as for being old, I have a couple of friends in their *eighties* who still look fantastic in jeans.'

Far from being an octogenarian, she was only forty-six – if sixty was the new forty, as Kate had again insisted. Although, to tell the truth, she felt more like seventeen inside: excited and terrified by turns. Would Felix be disappointed, once she was alone with him; feel her conversation lacked sparkle or authority? And did she possess the right vocabulary to comment on his work in any depth? Or suppose she disliked the paintings and was lost for any words at all? When it came to art, she was a mere novice in comparison: unconfident, unskilled and rusty. Yet, at every class so far, he had singled out her work as 'exceptional', 'original' and 'erotic'.

Erotic .... Had he used that word with regard only to her drawings or—

''Bye, Mum. Have fun!'

'You, too.'

She just hoped the Dubai problem wouldn't spoil their day. Despite her fervent wish to make their lives easier and reduce the pressures on them, there was so little she could do in point of fact. Her frequent offers of help were usually declined and, as for Hugo's construction contracts, they were so bafflingly arcane she simply couldn't grasp the technicalities.

Once Amy and Hugo had left, she nipped up to their bedroom to find a suitable lipstick and the scarf. The large, all-white room made her troublingly conscious of the two small, shabby bedrooms in the cottage. However, now that the baby had quickened – a truly special moment, as much for her as for her daughter – she was all the more determined to keep on the place for her grandchild, as well as for herself. And although it would need total renovation, inside as well as out, Amy had generously offered to foot the bill, since she, too, liked the notion of a holiday retreat.

Returning to the attic with her booty, she paused a moment to study the new drawing on her easel. Although a definite improvement on her earlier attempts, it required a lot more work. But she couldn't settle to anything in her present state of mind, and the easel only engendered further questions.

Why had Felix given her an easel – an old one, admittedly – which he claimed he no longer used? Nonetheless, it marked her out as special. She simply couldn't believe that all other eleven members of the class had been presented with free easels.

Weary from her constant introspection, she stretched out on the bed and deliberately switched her mind to something else – something mundane and practical: namely probate and the cottage, and the various minor matters still outstanding after Hanna's death. In fact, she ought to make a trip back home, to check on the cottage, give the car a run, and put flowers on her mother's grave. And she could take the chance to visit the solicitor, and also catch up with her friends, Carole in particular.

Suddenly, Carole's husband Eddie was lying naked astride her, as so often in the past: thwacking, thrusting, whipping her on, as if she had become his sweaty, lathered horse, and they were careering over hedge and ditch in a mad gallop to the finish, the room vibrating with the thunder of hoofs.

Breathless, she slumped back, feeling her usual disquiet. Did other women of her age carry on in this feverish way, or was something seriously wrong with her? And it seemed all the worse considering it was Lent – a time of penitence and self-denial, not of steamy gratification. Yet, however hard she tried to resist, thoughts of Felix began creeping back again and, all at once, he was there beside her, his stubby, paint-stained fingers brushing lightly against her lips, coaxing them to open, then kissing her so wildly, she ...

'*Stop,*' she muttered furiously. It was ludicrous, if not conceited, to imagine he had designs on her. Men preferred younger women – that was a fact of life – and only her long-thwarted desire had made her misinterpret a few merely friendly gestures.

Restlessly, she shifted on the bed. Truth to tell, she had been in a peculiar state since her recent extraordinary massage at the day-spa. Amy had given her a voucher for several treatments there – a present she was reluctant to accept until Kate offered to come with her. Hedonistic Kate had no qualms about 'indulgence'.

Closing her eyes, she felt the masseuse's hands again, stroking her naked body; that amazing physical contact of one person with another; the touch of skin against skin; the sense of being accepted, safe, protected. It had struck her at the time that this was what a baby must feel when cradled by its mother, and – suddenly, upsettingly – she had realized at some deep, instinctive level that *she* had never felt it as an infant.

She sat up on the bed, speculating, as in the spa, on the circumstances of her birth – in a severely cold and snowy winter, with the war still dragging on, and her mother an evacuee, billeted on strangers. Perhaps poor Hanna – widowed, grieving and miles from home – had simply been incapable of nurturing a child, and was possibly much more vulnerable than anyone suspected. The mother she had known – strong, religious, dutiful – might have temporarily cracked at such a traumatic time. And perhaps her devotion to the infant Amy had arisen partly on account of guilt: what she had failed to give her own daughter she must give to her daughter's daughter. The implications for *her*, as a grandmother-to-be, were overwhelmingly clear: if, for any reason, Amy couldn't provide her baby with that essential early sense of safety and security, then she herself must impart it to the child – repeating history in the process, perhaps.

She walked slowly to the window, reflecting on all the mysteries embedded in her family; the things she would never know; the father she had never seen, the grandparents and other distant relatives who were only faded photographs.

But brooding over her family was no advance on fretting over Felix. However, it had at least brought her down to earth and put a halt to the erotic extravaganzas. She suspected, though, that if she didn't have a change of scene and a breath of bracing fresh air, she would probably wheedle Felix back to bed. So, since it was a bright spring day, she decided to take a walk to Victoria Street and buy a gift for the baby. It was only 2.45 and Felix wasn't expecting her till six, so she could wander round the shops, pick out something suitable and give it to Amy on Mother's Day – when she would be getting on for twenty-one weeks pregnant.

At least a shopping expedition would help to pass the time.

Proceeding along Carlisle Place, she stopped to listen, puzzled by the sound of drums, which appeared to be coming from the cathedral piazza. Intrigued, she wandered over to investigate and found an event in progress. Crowds of people were milling about, some with banners and placards; stalls had been set up all along one side and, yes, a group of drummers were filling the square with urgent, rhythmic noise.

'What's going on?' she asked the young lad manning one of the stalls.

'It's a protest,' he informed her, 'against a proposed new Westminster bye-law that'll make it a crime to give out food to the homeless.'

'That sounds a bit extreme.'

'It's barbaric!' he replied. 'It means all those charities that organize soup-runs and the like will now be heavily fined. And even sandwich shops won't be allowed to give away their unsold stock. They'll have to chuck it out in future, which is a shocking waste of food.'

'But why?' Maria asked.

'Oh, the council have their reasons, but they don't hold water, actually. I mean, they complain that local residents get hassled by rough-sleepers drinking in the street, but it's just as easy to be hassled by groups of toffs spilling out of ritzy clubs, all disgustingly pissed.'

She nodded, having experienced something similar last week. Besides, living in Amy and Hugo's decidedly upmarket house had made her shamingly aware of the contrast between her own cushy lifestyle and that of the rough-sleepers.

'Do sign our petition,' the fellow urged, handing her a clipboard that held several sheets of paper, all already scrawled with signatures.

Once she had added her own, the young man went on to tell her that, at four o'clock precisely, a group of core supporters planned to lie down in the piazza, as a gesture of solidarity and to mark the end of the protest. 'Why not join in?' he suggested.

'Maybe,' she said, slightly uneasy at the prospect and hastily moving on to another stall. There, she was given a handful of leaflets and soon engaged in conversation once more and, only minutes later, she was served a free dish of rice and got talking to a woman who had helped organize the protest.

'I'm prepared to go to gaol,' the fiery redhead declared, 'if this bye-law comes into force. And anyone who calls themselves a Christian should jolly well feel the same. Christ commanded us to feed the poor, so what the hell would He think if He knew that His command was now a criminal offence?'

'Yes, I must say I agree.' Maria was all too conscious of the soaring façade of the cathedral; the whole impressive building and its contents were so richly ostentatious that, if they were sold for ready cash, the proceeds could have fed every homeless person in the land.

'And He told us to love our neighbour – meaning *all* our neighbours, not just those with a foot on the housing ladder.'

As the woman continued to express her indignation, Maria suddenly realized that she felt part of a community for the first time since she had moved to London. All the people here were exchanging views and mingling, instead of the usual London habit of simply looking through their fellow human beings, as if they didn't exist.

So, on the stroke of four, she abandoned her misgivings and stretched out on the pavement, along with everyone else – young and old, well-heeled and homeless, all lying down in unison. At first, she did feel a certain embarrassment, in case one of Amy's wealthy local friends happened to pass by, saw her lying on the ground and recoiled in horrified dismay. She was also worried about dirtying her jeans before this all-important evening. Yet, as she glanced around at all the prostrate bodies, she experienced a sense of solidarity, just as the man had said. Her feet were all but touching another woman's head; her hand brushing some old fellow's arm. These people might be strangers, but she was joined with them in body and in purpose.

She gazed up at the sky. However hard the ground might be, above her were soft fluffy clouds, and she spotted one lone gull, flying high, high, high, and began following its progress, until white was swallowed up in white.

Her spirits seemed to rise with the bird. She knew Felix was a radical type who might well approve her action and, if nothing else, it would provide her with a talking point this evening. And, she realized, with a sense of mingled surprise and relief, for the first time since his invitation, she actually felt confident.

Once the protesters had disbanded, she couldn't resist slipping into the cathedral. Since her return to the faith in 1974, she'd been as assiduous in her religious practice as she had before her fall from grace, and the ensuing decades of fervent devotion had left an indelible mark. Even now, when her religion constituted little more than a bedrock of indoctrination, suffused with incense-clouds of nostalgia, churches still attracted her; seemed to answer some deep-seated need.

She walked slowly up the aisle, thrilling, as always, to the sheer splendour of this place. However uneasy she might feel about ecclesiastical wealth, when it came to aesthetics, she couldn't help but respond to the gleaming marble and glittering mosaics, the theatrical sense of space.

She stopped to peer up at the huge painted crucifix suspended over the sanctuary, recalling, with wry amusement, that the only naked male body she had seen until her twenties was that of the crucified Christ – a body racked with pain. But it had seemed normal, as a child, that religion should be so deeply infused with suffering, what with the Agony in the Garden, the Passion and the Crucifixion, and the emphasis on this earthly existence as being, essentially, a Vale of Tears. Yet only now did she recognize that there had also been a strongly sexual element: the way she had burned with rapture when kneeling for hours in front of the Blessed Sacrament, and her all-consuming passion for God, not just as Father, but as soul-mate and spiritual lover. Even Confession possessed an erotic charge: whispering her secret sins to a *man* – and not just any man, but God's representative on earth.

As she passed a stand ablaze with votive candles, she remembered, as a girl, spending all her pocket money on lighting candles for her school friends, or for anyone in need. And she still felt, quite irrationally, that those flickering flames could somehow reach to Heaven and influence the Almighty – however childish such a notion. Indeed, she intended to light a candle for herself, and light it just outside the Lady Chapel, since her name-sake, Mary, had been as familiar a figure in her childhood as her other mother, Hanna. Forty years ago, she had begged the Blessed Virgin for the strength to resist Silas's strong sexual drive and thus retain her own virginity; now she was doing something much more reprehensible.

Having made her way to the far end of the cathedral, she put her money in the slot and lit her candle from one already burning in the stand. Then she walked towards the image of Our Lady, shimmering blue and gold above the Lady-Chapel altar.

'Holy Mary,' she mouthed, 'what I'm asking – all I'm asking – is for this evening to go well, in every way.'

Chapter 9

MARIA PAUSED OUTSIDE the tall, terraced house, almost tempted to bolt for home. Inhaling deeply to try to calm her nerves, she made herself descend the basement steps – a basement very different from the one in Amy and Hugo's house which, neglected by its (mostly absent) owner, looked drab and uninviting. Here the paint was bright and the brickwork spruce and on the edge of every steep stone step stood a flourishing green plant. Pots of cheery daffodils blew their yellow trumpets on the window ledges, and the front door had been painted in a geometric pattern, almost like a canvas itself.

She raised her hand to the knocker – a curious bird-shaped one, in bronze – then changed her mind and rang the bell instead. Awful if Felix didn't hear and left her standing on the doorstep.

'Maria, you look sensational!'

If only she didn't blush – additional proof that she was still stuck in adolescence. He looked different from the Felix of the life class, dressed in a smart grey jacket and an open-necked red shirt.

He ushered her into the hall which, although dark and narrow, he had totally transformed. Literally hundreds of picture frames, all different styles and shapes, had been arranged side by side, one above the other – and even one inside another – floor to ceiling, on both walls, yet none of the frames held a painting.

'It's a sort of joke,' he explained, as he watched her absorbing the display. 'I mean, why bother painting anything at all, when an empty frame looks good in its own right?'

'And they *do* look good – amazingly so. Are some of them quite old?'

'Yes, a few date back to God knows when! Sometimes, I just pick one off the wall because it happens to be the perfect size or shape for a painting I've completed. But, look, come upstairs and let's have a glass of wine.'

A twinge of panic rippled through her stomach. If she drank too much, she might lose control. 'No, let me see this room first,' she said, boldly venturing through the open door on the left. 'Oh – it's like an Aladdin's cave! Where did you find all these fantastic things?'

'Mostly on my travels. The textiles come from Egypt and this wrought-iron lamp from Turkey, and that maquette over there I bought from a Dutch sculptor when I was teaching in Maastricht. It's actually his mother, but it's so expressionistic, the figure and the chair are fused into one shape. And those wooden masks are African, of course.'

Maria nodded, hoping he wouldn't quiz her about her own travels – remarkable only for their absence.

'I love searching bazaars and markets and hunting down something really special. Although I must admit I often have to sort through loads of tat before I find a treasure. See this,' he said, gesturing to a glass case on the shelf, which held a desiccated brown object she couldn't quite make out in the dim light of the basement. 'It's one of my best finds – a shrunken human head from Papua New Guinea, which I picked up in a Parisian flea market a good thirty years ago.'

'It looks far too small to be human,' Maria exclaimed, half-fascinated, half-repelled.

'Well, most so-called human heads turn out to be fakes, but this one's probably genuine.' He removed the glass cover and ushered Maria closer to the shelf. 'You see, I know a bit about the shrinking process and it appears that all the different steps have been taken with this chap. What they do is remove the skull and brain, sew the eyelids shut, and keep boiling and re-boiling the remaining skin and flesh, until it gets smaller and smaller. Then they dry it and reshape it and coat the skin with ash.'

Maria suppressed a shudder as she stared at the shrivelled head; still recognizably human, despite its diminutive size and distorted features.

Felix caressed its fringe of coarse black hair. 'It's odd to think I share my flat with a fellow human being who lived aeons ago, in a completely different culture. Sometimes, I even sense his presence, however strange that sounds.'

The pained and almost pleading expression on the unfortunate man's face made Maria feel uneasy, so she turned away and began looking at the paintings on the opposite side of the room. 'Is this your work?' she asked.

'Well, yes, but very ancient stuff. My more recent work is upstairs in the studio.'

Despite his dismissive tone, she studied one of the canvases with close and careful attention, admiring the swirls of black and scarlet, overlaying a deep ochre ground. 'It has such energy,' she enthused, 'as if all the colours are flying out of the frame!'

'I did it years and years ago,' he gave a casual shrug, 'when I was more into abstraction.'

She scrutinized another painting, in which a female figure's lips and brows seemed to have been rendered in 3D. 'Is that some sort of textile?' she asked, indicating the mouth.

'They're actually those miniature trees that architects use in their plans. I cut them even smaller, then painted them brown for the eyebrows and red for the lips, to give a sort of textured effect. But, look, don't waste your time on these. I'd prefer you to see what I hope is my better work – although, I have to say, I'm dying for a drink. I've had a pretty hairy day, to be honest, so I'd really like to sit down and relax. I can show you my studio later, if that's all right with you?'

He led her up to the ground-floor sitting-room – unlike any room she had ever seen, with its wooden shutters and panels of rough brick, set between plain whitewashed walls and, again, a wealth of objects arrayed on every side. The room was small, in fact, and the remaining three floors of the house belonged to another tenant, so he had told her at the class, yet the impression was one of expansiveness, largesse. Amy and Hugo's house might be markedly grander, but considerations of fashion and 'good taste' dictated its general style, rather than springing from an original mind, as here.

'Do sit down.' He gestured to the sofa, itself draped with some exotic fabric, presumably from another of his trips. 'And I'll open a bottle of wine.'

'Lovely,' she said, vowing to restrict herself to just one glass.

He returned with two pewter goblets and set hers down on a small table beside the sofa, then seated himself, rather too close, she felt. All at once, the images of his naked body, conjured up earlier today, began returning in a fevered rush, increasing her apprehension.

'Well, here's to your work.' He smiled, touching his goblet to hers.

'It's hardly "work", as yet,' she said, struggling to censor the images and adopt a detached and distant tone. 'I'm shamefully out of practice.'

'So you keep telling me, Maria, but that makes me all the more impressed by what you've done so far. No, don't contradict me – I've been teaching for donkey's years and I know talent when I see it. Some of my other students have been slaving away for decades, but they lack that vital spark that marks them out as special. They also lack your total commitment. I noticed that at the very first class. You seemed to be drinking in everything I said, as if you just couldn't get enough of it. In fact, you reminded me of a starving woman suddenly offered food.'

She gave a nervous laugh. 'I'm afraid I'm a hungry sort of person altogether. Even as a child, I was greedy for all sorts of things. At my convent school, they came down really hard on that and insisted I learn strict self-control. They kept stressing that greed is one of the worst of sins, because it meant I was selfish and acquisitive.'

'Greed is *wonderful*,' he contradicted. 'It goes along with exuberance and enthusiasm. Blasé, cynical people are very rarely greedy, because nothing seems worth their while. And, anyway, it's built into our DNA, to help us humans find the best food and shelter – not to mention the best mates! And, as artists, it's one of our duties to be greedy for success – which you *are*, Maria. I can see that very clearly.'

He flung his arm along the sofa-back; his hand a provocative hairs-breadth from her neck. 'If you really want to know, what first attracted me about you was your total engagement with every aspect of the class – Leo's studio, the model, the other students, the view from the window, even that board I gave you, for heaven's sake! I found myself intrigued by your famished desire to cram in even....'

The rest of the sentence was blurring. She was still focused on his earlier words: 'What first attracted me about you....' So she *hadn't* imagined his interest, but how on earth would she handle it? She might be out of prac-tice as an artist, but when it came to real relationships with men – as against mere fantasy and longing – she was almost a non-starter. Silas had been life-changing, but only a one-off – a single, shameful lapse – and, since her return to the Church, she had maintained a strictly celibate life. However incredible that might seem to her less devout and more promiscuous friends, she had seen it as her basic religious duty, and also a private atone-ment for the pain she had caused her mother and the stigma laid on Amy. And although nowadays, with her faith so weak and wobbly, there was less need for sexual abstinence, she'd had no chance to change her habits, since at her age lovers were conspicuous by their absence.

The arm along the sofa-back was moving down to encircle her shoulders and began pressing insistently close. 'In fact, I've been asking myself contin-ually what it would be like to kiss you. Would you show the same enthusiasm, I wonder?'

Warning voices in her head, long entrenched since childhood, were giving her advice: 'Leave immediately! Don't consider such a thing. Show him you have standards.' And Hanna's voice was admonishing, 'He's simply taking advantage of you. Don't risk your eternal soul.' And, added to those, her own diffident self was reminding her that encouragement at this stage might well mean that, at some point in the future, she would have to reveal her body and, since it was a mature and far from slender body, risk rejection in the process.

Yet, above all the cacophony, another voice – a voice she didn't recognize, brazen, wild and, yes, ravenously hungry – was already giving him his answer.

'Well, why don't you try and see?'

Chapter 10

MARIA GAZED, ENTHRALLED, at the fuzzy black-and-white shapes on the monitor.

'Those are the heart valves,' Sue, the ultrasonographer, explained, 'and you can see they're opening and closing exactly as they should. In fact, the heart looks fine altogether.'

Maria exchanged a smile with Amy, who was lying on her back on the couch, her naked belly exposed. As she glanced at its gently swelling curve, then back to the amazing images on-screen, Maria felt secretly glad that Hugo had left, late last night, for a lightning trip to Dubai, so that it was *she* who was here with her daughter, bonded in so intimate a way. He had, of course, accompanied Amy to her first scan, but this second, twenty-week one was actually more important, since all the structures of the developing foetus were now clearly visible, making it easier to detect any abnormalities.

So far, there had been none, thank God: head, brain, eyes, lips, spine, heart all given the OK. But although Amy seemed supremely confident about every aspect of the pregnancy, she herself was worryingly aware of the high incidence of stillbirths and intrauterine deaths, especially in older mothers. So, as Sue continued checking, first, the foetal lungs and diaphragm, then the stomach and abdominal wall, Maria realized she was holding her breath. One anomaly and the baby's whole life and future could be threatened.

'All fine,' Sue declared, moving the transducer slightly lower. 'And the kidneys look perfectly normal,' she added. 'The urine's flowing freely into the bladder – again exactly as it should. You may not realize, Amy, that for the last few months your baby's been doing a secret little pee every half an hour.'

Amy laughed. 'Good for him – or her!'

'Well, if you *want* to know the gender, we can probably tell you at this stage.'

'No,' Amy put in, quickly. 'We'd prefer it to be a surprise.'

Maria knew that Hugo was hoping for a boy, whereas her daughter hadn't stated any preference. She herself had maintained a tactful silence about her fervent wish for a girl. That wish was even stronger since Amy had told her, earlier this morning, that if the baby *were* a girl, she would be christened not just Hannah but Hannah Maria. The news had touched her deeply; even made her feel that, in some mysterious fashion, both she and her mother would live again, in and through this child – and live richer lives, in every sense. Amy had also confided that she and Hugo planned on having a second child, which had delighted her still more. Neither she nor Hanna had managed more than one – nor Theresia, either – so Amy and Hugo's eventual family would break the unhappy pattern of only children and absent fathers.

'The placenta's in a good position,' Sue confirmed, as she continued with the scan, 'well away from the cervix. And there's sufficient amniotic fluid for the baby to move freely. Everything looks fine, in short – no anomalies at all, not at this stage, anyway. I'll just take a few more measurements and then you're done and dusted, Amy.'

While her daughter was getting dressed, Maria returned to the waiting-room, where she was surrounded by women in various stages of pregnancy. Despite the inappropriate environment, she took the chance to luxuriate in the Kiss again, as she'd been doing almost every minute during the last nine heady days. Not only did it merit a capital letter, it deserved a place in the *Guinness Book of Records* as the most electrifying Kiss in history – and that despite her initial fear that she would be unable to respond. Yet, for all the aching length of time since anyone had kissed her, her lips and mouth and tongue had instantly quickened into life. And the effect had lasted hours. Too fired up even to think of going home, she had walked for miles – walked rapturously and blindly – reliving every tiniest sensation; his tongue still probing hers; his hands still on her breasts ....

'Right, Mum, all done.'

As Amy breezed back in, she rocketed from Felix's embrace, experiencing an undertow of guilt. No way could she tell her daughter that she was entangled with a man – a man she hardly knew, a man she was seeing again tonight, when things might go still further. It would seem totally inappropriate for someone of her age; someone about to be a grandmother.

'I suggest we take a taxi,' Amy said, buttoning up her jacket, 'and scoot along to Sloane Square. There's this new baby shop just opened, so I thought we'd have a look at it and maybe buy a few things.'

'But shouldn't you be resting after the scan?'

'Whatever for? It's just a routine check-up. Damn! I've broken a nail. Hold on a sec while I file it smooth.'

'Sit down to do it.' Maria patted the adjoining chair. 'You need to take the weight off your feet. But it's fantastic, isn't it, that the scan was so reassuring?'

'I'd say! And Hugo's delighted, too. I gave him a quick ring just now.'

'Lord, how are things going? It must be pretty tense.'

'Well, of course, he'd no idea when all this first cropped up it would ever involve a court case. He just assumed they'd sort things out in an informal sort of way. But the client's breathing fire and has now issued writs against the main contractor, the sub-contractor *and* the consultancy firm that originally appointed Hugo to take charge. Apparently, this particular client is a notoriously bad payer, so I suspect it's just a ruse on his part, to avoid handing over the final whack of the total cost. Also, Hugo says the wretched guy tends to issue court proceedings on the flimsiest of grounds, so it seems they're up against a rather tricky character.'

'I'm sorry to be thick, darling, but I still don't understand quite what's going on. I know about the basic problem, but how is Hugo implicated?'

'Well, as project manager, the client blames him for any fault that develops. And it appears they used an inferior coating to protect all that fancy steel cladding on the hotel's exterior. In Dubai, steel corrodes very rapidly, because most of the buildings face the sea and there's masses of salt in the air, so it needs a high-grade protective coating. It's actually called pvfd – poly vinyl fluoride – but forget the technicalities. The crux of the matter is that the paint's beginning to peel and the steel's already rusting. It's meant to last a good twenty years but, from the looks of things, it won't last more than a couple. The client's claiming they deliberately used an inferior coating to save on costs and ratchet up their profits.'

'But surely Hugo wouldn't do a thing like that?'

'No, 'course not. But corruption's rife over there, so a suspicious Arab client might smell a whiff of it, even when there's not the slightest cause. Or he may just be indulging in brinkmanship – doing everything he can to get his outstanding payments reduced. And, as far as I can gather, the contractors *were* rather rushed to complete the project on schedule and may have failed to check the detailed spec. I seem to remember Hugo saying he passed it over to an assistant, and – who knows? – perhaps the fellow just didn't have the necessary experience.'

'Gosh, what a ghastly mess!'

'Yes, and I suspect it'll drag on quite a while yet. I mean, this is only the initial meeting, when all the experts get together and exchange opinions and facts. But there's still a chance they'll manage to settle out of court, so let's not spoil our day, Mum.'

Maria concurred entirely. However worrying the whole imbroglio might be, the all-important fact at the moment was that the baby had been given the all clear, at least until the next scan.

'Right, let's go.' Amy jumped to her feet, having finished the nail repair.

Proudly, Maria took her arm as they emerged from the antenatal department and sauntered down the corridor. Once they had negotiated the hospital's huge revolving doors and were outside in the street, Amy darted forward and flagged down an empty cab. An unnecessary extravagance, Maria couldn't help but think, when three buses were approaching on the opposite side of the road. And, considering the heavy traffic all along the Fulham Road, a taxi would be no quicker than a bus.

'*Enjoy* it, for heaven's sake!' she heard Kate whisper – a voice often in her head these days, now that she and Kate were closer. So she settled back contentedly while Amy rang the office. A taxi ride for her daughter was invariably a chance to catch up on her calls and she was already deep in discussion with Rebecca, her PA.

So, creeping back to Felix again, she relived last Friday's class, when he'd had a private word with her and begged her to come home with him, once the class was over and the others had all left.

'Yes!' her avid body whooped, but her spoilsport mind took a rather different view, urging caution, circumspection; for fear of seeming too eager or – worse – an easy lay. Only after protracted argument had she agreed to postpone the visit till this evening, and her nervousness had been building ever since, wondering what might happen between them. And, if it came to undressing, he was bound to regard her body as too fat. He might even lose all desire and –

'Great, Mum!' Amy said, snapping her mobile shut. 'The client's not expected until three, which means we can have lunch out, once we've been to Babybliss.'

Maria made an effort to banish Felix from the cab. 'Perfect, darling. It's a real treat to have some together.'

'You're not lonely in London, are you? I'd hate to think you wished you hadn't come.'

'No, I'm absolutely fine. I did feel a bit spare at the outset, but now I have my weekly classes and Kate just round the corner, I've plenty to do till the baby arrives. Oh, by the way, talking of babies arriving, how are Chloe's getting on?'

'Really well, apparently, although she complains she's as big as three elephants and too uncomfortable to sleep at night. But the twins are moni-tored every second minute by some frightfully eminent obstetrician. Nicholas works as a hedge-fund manager, so they can afford to go private, you see – and private schools, as well, of course. He's already planned for the twins to follow him to his old prep school and then to Marlborough. Which reminds me, Mum, we've decided to put the baby's name down for St Peter's Primary School.'

'What, now?' Maria exclaimed. 'Before it's even born?'

'The earlier the better, if you want to be sure of a place. We can't do a Chloe-and-Nicholas – not with our hefty mortgage. But, according to reports, St Peter's is the next best thing. And we *are* in the catchment area.'

'Is that the school behind the cathedral? I've passed it several times.'

'No, that one's Catholic. St Peter's is C of E, which poses a bit of a problem, because the vicar's incredibly strict about prospective parents being paid-up Anglicans. Hugo and I are agnostic, if we're anything, but we've decided it might be worth our while to start showing up at church each week.'

Maria could barely conceal her sense of shock. For all her scepticism towards aspects of the Church, religion for her was so serious a matter it seemed profoundly wrong to adopt a set of beliefs, or change denomina-tions, simply to further one's own advantage. 'But isn't there a good state *Catholic* school?' she asked, partly out of loyalty to Hanna. 'I went to a pretty decent one myself and that was in the wilds – and so did you, for that matter.'

The car behind started hooting so obstreperously they could barely hear themselves speak. Amy raised her voice above the din. 'No, nothing in the same class as St Peter's – or not locally, in any case.'

'But maybe in the next five years there will be,' Maria persisted, wondering why she was championing Catholic education when her own faith was so half-hearted. 'Do you have to decide things quite so early?'

Amy nodded vehemently. 'The competition's really fierce, so the sooner we establish an interest, the greater our chances.'

Best let the matter go, she decided, and simply be glad that her grand-child would receive a decent education. Besides, the taxi had now pulled up at Babybliss.

'Oh, what a darling little shop!' Amy enthused, once they were inside and surrounded by racks of babygros, diminutive sailor-suits and frilly party frocks.

Maria felt it was tempting fate to be buying baby clothes at so early a stage – although Hugo's mother, Beatrice, clearly didn't share her concern, since she had already sent a parcel containing four exquisite matinee jackets and an ostentatious christening gown. Maria gave silent thanks that Hugo's parents lived in deepest Shropshire and apparently had no desire to pitch in with hands-on baby care, but simply planned occasional visits and a financial contribution. She couldn't compete when it came to such largesse, but at least there would be no rival grandma vying for the day-to-day role. Beatrice had even remarked that she found the title 'Grandma' ageing and downbeat and would prefer to be known as 'Glam-ma'. But how long would glamour last, Maria reflected wryly, when one was intimately involved with a puking, pooing infant?

'Don't you just love this shawl?' Amy held the fine lace against her cheek. 'It's so soft it's like a cobweb.'

'Yes, it's beautiful – and I'm going to buy it for you.'

'Don't be silly, Mum. It's not exactly cheap.'

'No arguments. I want to give you something special for once. It can be your Mother's Day present – the first time you've qualified!'

Amy's mobile shrilled through her words of thanks. 'Shit! I hope that's not Rebecca.'

It *was* Rebecca, so while Amy moved to a quiet corner of the shop to continue with the call, Maria grabbed the shawl and took it to the cash register. Once it had been double-wrapped in layers of tissue and embossed white paper printed with gold storks, she hid it at the bottom of her bag – a surprise for Sunday next. Her money was dwindling fast, since she had splashed out only yesterday on a black lace bra and pants. Tachbrook market had been no help this time: it sold only passion-killing styles in puce-pink nylon or prim white interlock. Not quite the thing for—

'I'm sorry, Mum,' Amy said, re-joining her. 'I'm afraid there's a bit of a problem. They need me back at two, not three. But don't worry, we can still have lunch – we'll just have to cut the shopping. I know – let's take a cab to Victoria, then I'll be right on top of the office if anything else crops up. We can have a bite in the Grosvenor Lounge. It's mainly sandwiches and suchlike but at least it'll be quick.'

'We can always skip lunch, darling, if you'd prefer to go straight to the office?'

'No, Mum, this is *our* day, even if it's shorter than I'd like. Anyway, I want to hear about you – how the classes are going and everything.'

Well, Maria thought, suppressing a guilty smile, it'll have to be the censored version.

*

'Anything to drink, *mesdames?*'

'I'd better stick to orange juice,' Amy said, patting her little bulge. 'But you have wine, Mum. They do a rather special Pinot Grigio here.'

Maria deliberately quashed her instinctive twinge of guilt – her former Catholic self would never have been indulging during Lent. 'Sounds lovely. Thank you, darling.'

Once the waiter had departed, Maria gazed around at the spacious room, with its high, decorated ceiling, its gleaming chandeliers and the floor-length curtains, looped back with golden tassels. Chopin was playing softly in the background and on the centre table stood an enormous vase of exotic Madonna lilies. Indeed, if everyone in this crowded lounge were given a lily to take home, there would still be a creditable display left over in the vase. No wonder a sandwich here cost £14.95, rather than two quid at Sam's Sandwich Bar.

'Stop fretting about prices,' Kate advised. 'Amy can afford it, so relax and make the most of being with her.'

So, leaning back against the padded seat, she allowed herself to enjoy the stylish ambience. 'What's great about London,' she said, 'is—

'I'd love to chat, Mum,' Amy interrupted, 'but we're pushed for time, and there's something really important I need to discuss with you – and discuss on my own, without Hugo. So would you mind if we got down to it right now?'

Maria felt a flurry of unease. Had her daughter found out about Felix? Impossible. In any case, there was nothing to find out – or not as yet. It was hardly a crime to kiss one's tutor.

'I'm afraid it's something you're not going to like….' Amy shook out her napkin; seemed to take an age arranging and rearranging it on her lap. 'It's about my father,' she blurted out, at last. 'I *must* know more about him. Apart from anything else, they keep asking me at the hospital about inheritable diseases, but how the hell can I tell them when he's always been a total mystery?'

Maria stared at her, aghast. Extraordinary as it might seem, she had managed to avoid this conversation for all of Amy's thirty-eight years. Amy had asked about her father, of course, especially as a child, but a string of pretty, not-quite lies had sufficed to fob her off and – thank Christ – she had never persisted in the enquiries.

'Oh, I know you promised Silas you'd never get in touch with him, but frankly he had no right to make you give that promise. It wasn't fair to me, for one thing. And anyway—' Amy broke off as their waiter reappeared with a cheery smile and the drinks.

Never, Maria thought, had a smile seemed so inappropriate. She willed the man to stay, to engage them in some idle chatter about the menu or the wine list – anything to stop her daughter continuing with a subject she had no desire to discuss, either now or ever.

But Amy had already returned to the offensive. 'Up till now, I've tried to spare your feelings. I mean, I understood how fraught the whole thing was for you. But don't imagine it was easy to be left in the dark on such a crucial matter. Hundreds of times, I've wanted to ask you loads more details, but I knew, from past experience, that even a mention of Silas made you terribly upset. But now I'm pregnant, it changes the whole situation. Surely you realize it affects the baby, as well?'

Yes, she did realize and, yes, Amy did have a right to the truth, just as the baby had a right to know about its grandfather. Yet that truth was so harsh, so wounding, how, in all conscience, could she reveal it? Besides, Silas didn't even know that any child of his existed.

'Mum, you haven't said a word.'

There were no words. It would be appallingly destructive to admit that Silas had blamed her for the pregnancy and insisted she had a termination. How could she tell her beloved daughter that her own father had wanted her destroyed? Not that she had ever considered such a thing. The very notion was unthinkable for a cradle-Catholic and for pious Hanna's daughter. Pre-marital sex was crime enough, but abortion was a heinous sin that would damn her for all eternity. Hanna regarded any developing foetus as a new and precious soul for God, to be nurtured, cherished, honoured, not chucked out with the trash. So, when Silas issued his ultimatum – she either 'got rid of the thing' or he would never see her again – there had actually been no choice. Frightened in the face of his anger, she had pretended to agree to an abortion, but that, of course, meant she *couldn't* see him again, or he would notice her swelling stomach.

The loss had been colossal. Silas, her first and only lover, was a poet and a lyricist, and the most intoxicating person she had ever met or dreamed of. None of the men back home had shoulder-length black hair, so fiercely, emphatically dark it made jet and coal seem pallid, or eyes that could blaze a hole through steel. None wore Edwardian jackets or purple velvet trousers, or had such extreme opinions on art, religion, poetry, politics and sex: the Catholic Church was a self-serving patriarchy that oppressed women, forbade freedom of thought, and had long since over-turned all Christ's basic precepts; art school was a waste of time and suppressed most students' talent rather than encouraging it; poetry didn't exist before the Beat Generation; and all governments were corrupt – only anarchy should rule. As for sex, it was a primeval force that must be subject to no limits or restrictions.

Everything she had ever believed had melted in the white heat of his certainties. Whether she agreed or not was immaterial. All that mattered was the stupendous fact that he had chosen *her* – a country mouse, with few opinions of her own – rather than the sophisticated women in his circle; the fellow poets, fellow revolutionaries. She had gained lustre from his status, from his greater age and experience, his—

'Mum, are you ever going to speak, or am I wasting my breath? I actually have a *right* to know my father and that's the end of it.'

Maria glanced around in panic, as if someone, in this room of strangers, could help her find some words – correct, consoling words she wouldn't later regret. But the people at the next table were giving raucous bursts of laughter as they drank toasts to each other, while the lone man on the other side was engaged in a long confab on his mobile. Nobody could help and, as for her, she had no idea where even to begin. Silas was completely unaware that she had given birth to the infant he had condemned to early extinction. And the whole ghastly muddle was totally her fault. She had let him believe she was on the Pill; allowed her own impassioned desire to possess a permanent part of him overrule his own distaste for procreation. Greed again on her part – demanding more than he could give, and profoundly wrong, she had realized only later in her life.

Amy, however, was waiting for an answer, so she had to break her silence yet still endeavour to hide the hurtful truth. 'Darling,' she began, her voice constrained and hesitant, 'you say you have a right to know him, but he … he didn't want to know *you*.' She took a gulp of wine, to try to dilute the sting in the words. 'Oh, I realize how appalling that must sound, but it was nothing to do with you as a person. How could it be when you were only a tiny blob? It's just that he made it clear from the start that he didn't want commitment – not of any kind. He opposed marriage on principle and, in any case, he was planning to go abroad, so it wouldn't have been easy to drag a wife and baby along.' In point of fact, she was pretty sure that Silas's travel plans were more a dream than a reality. Nonetheless, she had relayed them as genuine to Hanna, if only to excuse her lover from seeming just too callous.

'He sounds frightfully dominant. Didn't you challenge him or argue your case?'

How could she explain that no one ever argued with Silas? He was like a force of nature, sweeping everything aside that might hinder his ambition or his will. She had always submitted, in return for the thrill of being in his bed; being both his mistress and his muse. 'I did try, honestly, but he said I'd broken the terms of our relationship. You see, right from the beginning, he'd made it clear that he had to be free to pursue his art, which meant no ties or obligations whatsoever.'

'If you ask me, he's just a selfish shit. I'm not sure I *want* to know him.'

'Well,' Maria said, clutching at any straw, 'it might save a lot of heartache if you just let the matter rest.'

'I can't. I promised Hugo I'd find out. And, remember, Mum, it wasn't exactly easy for my poor husband, marrying someone illegitimate, and even more awkward for his highly conventional parents.'

Maria winced at the word 'illegitimate' – one she had always detested, yet she couldn't avoid the fact that for Beatrice and Tom, their only son's marriage to a girl from a humble family, born out of wedlock to a Bohemian mess of a mother, must have been a bitter blow.

'And it wasn't easy for me. Even at school I was bullied – called a bastard and worse.'

'But that's *awful.*' Maria pushed her glass away. Impossible to eat or drink when she felt such extremes of guilt. 'Why did you never tell me?'

'I had to protect you, didn't I?'

'I'm so terribly, terribly sorry. I just don't know what to say.' The music had changed to a jaunty tune, every note of which seemed to mock her desolation.

'Even at Cambridge, I felt inferior. Most of the others had wealthy, doting dads, who'd turn up in their swanky BMWs and take their little darlings out to five-star restaurants and the like.'

Maria put her head in her hands. Everything was crumbling: her daughter's carefree years at school and euphoric time at university; her own now clearly premature belief that Amy had reversed the family's misfortunes. 'But Hanna and I thought you were so happy at Cambridge.'

'I know. It was *because* of you and Grandma that I just put up with it. I mean, I realized what a lot you'd both given up, for my sake, and you were so proud of me and everything, so....' She shrugged ' ... it seemed wrong to make a fuss. Anyway, I *was* happy after the first ghastly year. I decided to show the snobs that I was every bit as good as them, with or without a father. So I deliberately went all out for success – changed my accent, read the right books, was seen in the right places. But this is all beside the point, Mum. I'm not interested in years ago; I'm interested in *now*. And what I want *now* is for you to track down Silas and arrange a meeting for the three of us.'

Track him down? Impossible when they had parted on such bitter terms.

And that was her fault, too. She'd felt so utterly rejected and so terrified of giving birth alone, she had lost her cool and shouted abuse: the first and only time in their relationship. And, in the heat of that moment, the hateful things she'd said made any sort of rapprochement completely out of the question. The whole affair with Silas had been one of wild extremes: frantic love, voracious need, then unrelenting fury at the break-up.

'It's really simple nowadays. You can trace more or less anyone online and with a name like Silas Keegan it'll be a good deal easier than hunting down a John Smith or David Jones. And easier still if he's a published poet.'

'He's not.' Maria picked up her knife and jabbed it into her palm. She deserved punishment for what she had done.

'But you told me he was famous – on a par with Keats, or some such.'

Maria cursed the lies. Her sole intention had been to make Amy feel good about herself, so she had deliberately stressed the superior genes passed on to her daughter; those of an exceptional man with outstanding talent. Yet, even when she had known him, Silas hadn't actually written much. Poetry for him had been less a daily practice than an ambition and a calling; something that imbued him with an aura, a mystique.

'Well, we know his age, which helps. And he must have done some sort of job, so we can search professional organizations and company records and all that sort of thing.'

Maria refrained from comment, unwilling to admit that Silas had never had anything resembling a career and had somehow managed to get by without even a basic job, crazy as that sounded.

'And how about his school or university? They'll have old-boy networks and alumni associations, which are often a good source to try.'

'I'm sorry, Amy, I'm not trying to be difficult, but he didn't go to university and, as for his school, I'm not sure he ever mentioned it – well, except to slam education in general. That was one of his great bugbears. He hated rigid syllabuses and saw schools as sort of … prisons that force children to conform to some tamely bourgeois model and stifle all their natural talents in the process.'

Amy banged down her glass impatiently. 'Mum, unless we refine the search, it's going to take forever. We need more detail and, preferably, a few solid facts. A definite town or region always helps, so let's start there, OK? Presumably he'll still be living in London.'

'We can't assume that, no. As I said, he had plans to live abroad – maybe America or …' Why was she perpetuating the myth of Silas's globetrotting, when it had been obvious at the time that, for all his grandiose ideas of relocating, he couldn't actually survive without the life-support system provided by his London friends? Admittedly, he had often complained that the English literati didn't rate him and thus reckoned he would have more chance somewhere like New York. But he would be forced to live on air if he moved away from that cosy little circle who were invariably on hand to bail him out. Besides, however would he raise the cost of a Transatlantic fare? She was beginning to see, as she reflected on the past, that while her lover could talk the talk, following it up with action was a different matter entirely. And, even if he had totally changed in the forty years since she'd seen him, she still had a strong gut feeling that, with his high-flown love of culture, he would never have left the capital. So why not share that feeling with Amy, who, like a tenacious terrier determined to track its quarry down, was continuing to question her?

'Is there anyone you could contact who knew him in the past and might have kept in touch right up till now?'

'No, not a soul.' Maria was increasingly aware how woefully negative all her replies must sound. But Silas's associates had been eager moths circling the flame of his brilliance and had barely even noticed her own dim and wavering light. And once she had fled back to Northumberland, she had never seen or spoken to a single one of them again.

'What about his relatives?'

'I feel awful keep saying no, but to start with he's an only child, and his parents would almost certainly be dead by now, and actually I never heard him mention a single member of his family.' Again, she forbore to say that Silas regarded families as pressure-cookers of seething, bubbling resentments.

'Well, however little we have to go on,' Amy said, decisively, 'I'm sure we'll find him in the end. We need to start with the obvious sites – Google, Facebook, MySpace, Twitter – and, of course, try the online phone books and the mail-address directories. And if we draw a blank with those, we'll use one of the specialist people-finding services. There's a whole load out there, covering almost every country in the world. OK, they charge, but their fees are fairly reasonable and I'll pay, in any case.'

'It's not a question of money. I—

Amy cut her off. 'Remember my college friend, Henrietta? I'm still in touch with her and, last time we spoke, she told me she'd used a site called Tracesmart to find a long-lost uncle and, within seconds – literally seconds – she had his details, including his address and phone number.'

'What, they give out people's private addresses?' Maria asked, in horror.

'Absolutely. All those companies have access to vast databases: electoral rolls, public records, census records and God knows what else besides. A few clicks of the mouse and by this time next week I could be sitting oppo-site my father.'

'No!' she said, appalled.

'What do you mean, "no"? If *you* won't do it, I most certainly will. In fact, I've been an absolute saint not doing so before. I promised you I wouldn't and I've kept that promise all this time, despite the fact you don't seem to have the slightest notion how difficult that was. Again and again, I was tempted simply to type in Silas's name and conduct a private search, without telling you a word about it. But you've always played fair with me, so I felt honour-bound to do the same. Now, though, things are different, and I feel obliged to act, for the baby's sake, as much as mine.'

'No, no! Please don't. Leave it to me, I beg you. Except,' she added, wrestling with her conscience, 'that means breaking *my* promise – the one I made to Silas.' It had been more like a solemn vow – he had made her swear on the Bible, on her very life, never to contact him again. She had insulted him so deeply, he averred, he wanted to eradicate not just the baby but all memory of their affair.

'I've told you, Mum, he had no right to—'

'Your sandwiches, *mesdames*.' The waiter set down two large platters, garnished with tomato flowers and fronds of curly lettuce. 'Enjoy!'

Enjoy? No word could be less apt. 'Look, he may well be dead by now. He was ten years older than me.'

'Well, better for us to know. At least I'll have something to tell Hugo. He's involved as well, Mum, which you seem to keep forgetting.'

'I don't forget. I'm well aware how much this means to both of you. It's just that if we track your father down, that may open up a can of worms and I'm frightened you'll get hurt. Suppose he doesn't want to see you even now?'

'I can handle that.'

'Or he may think you want revenge, or money.'

'I'll make it clear I don't – that I'd simply like to get to know him.'

More gales of laughter rose from the adjoining table. How could *anybody* laugh, Maria wondered, as she tried a different tack. 'There might be other people involved and you'll get entangled in a whole web of messy relationships. Surely you don't want that?'

'I'm not a child, Mum. I can deal with any complications that may or may not arise. Anyway—' She glanced at her watch '—we haven't time to argue the toss. I want you to find Silas and, if the free sites get you nowhere, then I suggest you use Tracesmart, OK? Henrietta's no fool and if she thinks highly of them, that's good enough for me. But will you make a start this week, please?'

'Amy, I … I *can't.*'

'You owe it to me, Mum. To be brutally honest, I've never understood how you could take the risk of bringing up a child without a father, when you knew from your own experience what a huge loss that is. It's almost like you said, "*I* had no dad, so I'll make sure my child doesn't have one either."'

'That's totally unfounded!' Maria cradled the knife – sharp, cold, unkind. '*And* cruel.'

'Well, *you're* being cruel, refusing even to let me meet my father.'

'Look here, Amy, you seem to think you're the only one who suffered. Have you ever stopped to wonder what it was like for *me*, bringing back a fatherless child to that narrow-minded village and having somehow to explain it to Hanna's ultra-pious Catholic circle? Things were very different then – far less liberal than nowadays. People used to talk behind my back – you know, about how I'd gone to the bad and what a shock it must be for my poor, long-suffering mother. And there was endless speculation about who the father was and why he'd left me in the lurch. One neighbour even said she hoped I felt thoroughly ashamed, because my own father was a war hero and I'd let him down in the most appalling way. And, if that wasn't enough, I had to give up all my dreams of being an artist.'

'So you're blaming me for that?'

'I'm not blaming anyone. It was just hard, that's all. I was like a fish out of water, up there in the sticks, after my years at art school. And I never met another man – not with Hanna breathing down my neck. She seemed to think that if I got the slightest bit involved with any other male, the same thing would happen again and, since I was living in her house, it wasn't exactly easy to invite a bloke back, or even stay out late.'

'So that's my fault, too, I suppose?'

'No, of course it isn't. I'm just trying to make you realize that *I* paid a high price, too. It's not easy being a single parent and seeing everyone else in couples. You take all that for granted, Amy – Hugo and your marriage, and being loved and cherished, not to mention having money to do anything you like. I'd have given my eye-teeth to be in that position. OK, I was totally in the wrong. I've never tried to dodge the fact that it was *my* fault, a hundred per cent, but I did my bloody best trying to make it up to you. All through your childhood, and afterwards, I showered you with devotion.'

'And now you regret it, I suppose – wish you'd buggered off and left me alone with Grandma?'

'Amy, that's unforgivable! How *could* you say such a thing?'

Amy sprang to her feet, rummaged in her purse and flung a handful of notes on the table. 'Well, since you're obviously so resentful, maybe it would have been better if you *had*.' Then, bursting into tears, she swept towards the door.

Chapter 11

'MARIA, YOU *must* stop crying. Of course you're upset – any mother would be – but it's not the end of the world.'

'It feels like it,' Maria sobbed, sitting hunched over the kitchen table, the pale pinewood branded with dark stains from her tears. 'I've never said those things to Amy before, so now she thinks I didn't *want* her.'

'Of course she doesn't.' Kate sat, helpless, beside her, the table strewn with soggy balls of Kleenex. She had offered lunch, and coffee; both had been refused. 'I've seen you two together and it's obvious how close you are. In any case, why would she have invited you to live with her if she didn't love you to bits?'

'Well, she won't any more – not after today.' Was there such a thing as love?, Maria wondered, desolately. Silas, she was increasingly sure, had loved only her submissiveness and the rare prize of her virginity. And when Amy trotted out her frequent 'Love you, Mum!'s, was she hiding huge resentment?

'Look, let's try to work out a rescue plan. Why don't you write her a note and leave it in her office, later on today? You can say you're really sorry for the row and that you'll agree to search for Silas.'

'But I *can't* – I've told you, Kate.'

'I'm sure it won't be anything like as bad as you imagine. Either he'll be dead, which will be sad for Amy, of course, but at least that will let you off the hook. And if he's still alive – let's face it, an old man of nearly eighty is hardly going to be breathing fire. He'll have mellowed hugely by now – maybe married with kids and grandkids of his own and only too glad to welcome a few new relatives.'

Maria tried, in vain, to picture such a scenario. The Silas she had known was egotistic, self-absorbed and wary of true intimacy. On the other hand, she had to concede, if only from her own experience, that people could change, and change profoundly. The besotted, reckless, love-enslaved mistress-of-a-would-be-poet of 1969 had morphed into the manic, hate-filled termagant of 1971, then changed again, radically, to the devoted mother and dutiful daughter of 1974, even her former steadfast religious faith restored.

'And *I'll* help, if you want. It'll be far less nerve-wracking, if we do the thing together. And better for us to do it, anyway, than leave the search to Amy.'

'Lord, yes! Silas doesn't even know that she *exists*. I'll have to break the news, hope it's not too much of a shock, and somehow persuade him to agree not to breathe a word about wanting to get rid of her.' Maria wiped her eyes on her sleeve, having worked through the whole packet of tissues Kate had kindly provided. 'And even if that works – and it's a big "if", I assure you – Amy may still be disappointed when she meets him in the flesh. I mean, she's so high-powered herself, she might not have much sympathy for a man who always got by on his wits.'

'That was way back in the past, though. He might have settled, years ago, for a nice safe job in banking or insurance.'

'That's as unlikely as an elephant flying.'

'So how did he actually live?'

'Well, he had such charm and confidence, people were like putty in his hands. He'd eat their food and borrow their flats and even cajole them into coughing up handouts. And, believe it or not, they never seemed to object, because he was just so charismatic. He looked the part, as well. He'd pick up amazing vintage clothes at Portobello Market. It was really cheap in those days – not like now. And he'd gatecrash snazzy parties and fill up on drinks and canapés and stuff.'

'Forget charismatic – he sounds a total shit!'

Maria braved a laugh. 'Amy said the same.'

'You should be spitting fire, not laughing – I mean, the way he used you when it suited him, then left you to take the consequences, seems quite disgusting to me.'

'I used him just as much, though, especially at the start. You see, I met him just as I was finishing my foundation year at the Cass and about to move to another art school. At that point, I was terribly vulnerable – scared of the upheaval, and already daunted by the prospect of eventually losing the security of college altogether and trying to make it as an artist on my own. So Silas became my life-raft. He invited me to share his flat – a little place in Tufnell Park he'd borrowed from a mate – and he gave me a sense of purpose in life, very much tied to his own. He was so sure of himself – so sure of everything – and I needed that to make up for my own wimpishness.' Whatever Kate or Amy might think, it was essential for her self-respect that she didn't damn her lover totally, but retained something of the great romantic idyll.

'Well, wherever he is and however he lives, we'll have to go and dig him out. I can drive you, if you like, if he's moved a long way away.'

'But why the hell should you, Kate? I feel bad enough already, turning up on your doorstep in such a hysterical state and expecting you to drop everything for me.'

'Don't worry – I was only tidying Polly's room, which she ought to do herself. And, anyway, I do actually believe that Amy's right in wanting to find her father. But let's not go into all the details till we have more idea of where he lives or whether he's alive at all. What matters at the moment is to make some sort of peace with her. And, you know, whatever the rights and wrongs of any argument, I feel it's the mother, not the child, who should be prepared to make the first move. I've learned that with my own daughters, and I'm sure it applies even more to grown-up kids. It doesn't really matter who's to blame. What's essential is to try to patch things up. And Amy's pregnant, don't forget, so she may be a bit hormonal, and perhaps secretly worried about how she's going to manage motherhood on top of everything else. And she's probably missing Hugo, too.'

'Yes, you're right. I should have been more understanding, especially about the Hugo thing. It must be quite a strain for her, him being away and all the hassle in Dubai, added to his normal pressures. And she's worried about Chloe, too.'

'Who's Chloe?'

'Oh, one of her friends from way back. She's expecting twins and much further on in her pregnancy than Amy, so she's suffering with backache and leg-cramps and what-have-you, and stuck at home a lot of the time. Amy feels bad about not popping in more often, and also scared, I suspect, that she'll develop all those symptoms herself. In fact, the more I think about it, the more I feel I should do what you suggested and write her a note of apology. And, if I did it right away, I could head straight back to her office with it, and maybe leave that lovely baby shawl as well – you know, as a peace offering.'

'Perfect! And why not add a line saying the shawl is for Mother's Day, because Amy's the best present any mother could have?'

'Oh, Kate, that's brilliant!'

'Hang on a sec – I'll fetch some paper and a pen.'

While she was gone, Maria sneaked a quick glance in her handbag-mirror, recoiling at the sight of her swollen eyes and tear-stained face. She looked an utter wreck and also felt distinctly awkward at having wept all over Kate and burdened her with the whole tangled story of her past. Never had she revealed such things to her friends back home, despite the fact she had much more in common with Carole, June and Jacqueline than she did with wealthy Kate. Not only had she known them years, but they, like her, were shabbyish and poorish, and more used to digging cars from snow-drifts, rounding up stray hens or nursing orphan lambs than attending opera galas or swilling champagne at the Carlton Club. Yet, for all their differences in lifestyle, it was Kate she felt a bond with – and that had led her to confide all the pangs and perils of her early, fated love affair.

She tissued off the streaks of smudged mascara, then leaned back in her chair and tried to cheer herself by soaking up the atmosphere of this bright, convivial kitchen, with its poppy-printed china and sunshine-coloured walls. Her eye was caught by Polly's drawings, Blu-Tacked to the fridge: a three-humped camel, a stripy horse and a lopsided yellow castle. Her doll's pram stood in one corner, while Clara's skateboard was propped against the wall. She relished the thought of Amy's kitchen bearing this same evidence of children in just a few years' time.

'Sorry I was so long,' Kate called, sweeping back in with paper, pen and envelope, and also a glass of something amber. 'I was trying to hunt down Paul's brandy. Here,' she urged, 'drink this. It's best vintage cognac – guaranteed to make anyone feel better!'

'Oh, Kate, I shouldn't, honestly.'

'You're always saying you shouldn't, but why not, I'd like to know? Most people in my circle assume they have a natural right to every perk and privilege on offer, but *you're* completely different, Maria, as if you feel you don't deserve a thing. Have you never heard the slogan "because I'm worth it"?'

The very phrase seemed blasphemous. A strict Catholic upbringing did little to inculcate feelings of self-esteem. 'Lord, I am not worthy,' she had repeated at every Sunday Mass, and the nuns had taken a relish in pointing out that it was the sins of their small charges that had nailed Christ to the cross. She had always felt personally responsible for the Passion and the Crucifixion, despite the fact that her childhood sins were mostly peccadillos.

She took the glass uncertainly, but the warm kick of the brandy felt restorative and comforting as it trickled down her throat. Perhaps it was time she broke with all that early conditioning. Apart from anything else, it was totally out of kilter with contemporary society. During the student protests last year, she had particularly noted the stress on rights, not duties, and the contrast with herself as a student, when powerlessness and privation seemed just a normal state. On the other hand, too much sense of entitlement could make one irresponsible and lawless, as she had seen three days ago, when the TUC anti-cuts march had erupted into mindless, thuggish violence. Torn, as usual, between two opposing viewpoints, she took refuge in her brandy. 'Where's *your* drink, Kate?' she asked.

'I don't need one. My life's been a bed of roses compared with yours. I was spoiled rotten from the start, indulged by two doting parents who saw me as a super-child – a future Einstein, Florence Nightingale and Margot Fonteyn all rolled into one! Whereas you had endless years of being dragooned and criticized by a strict religious mother.'

'It was *nothing* like that, Kate! My mother saved my life. I was really ill for months and couldn't do a thing, but she was there for me a hundred per cent. She had to give up her secretarial job and do boring work at home – addressing thousands of envelopes for soulless mail-order companies – but she never once complained. Then, after Amy was born, I more or less fell to pieces – mentally, this time – but she still continued to support me, financially and every way, *and* looked after the baby. She even took my side against the gossips. She'd look them straight in the eye and say, "The father isn't with my daughter because he had to go abroad."' The words stumbled to a halt as she struggled with more guilt. That semi-truth she had relayed to Hanna and embroidered over the years was now set in stone back home; everybody speculating where the mysterious man had gone and why he'd disappeared.

'You mean he doesn't live in England anymore?' Kate was obviously surprised.

'I'm not sure,' she mumbled, settling for a fudge. 'But, look, returning to my mother, you probably don't quite realize what a lifeline her religion was. In fact, I doubt she could have managed without it. The Church rallied round to help, you see, when she was widowed and pregnant with me, and then, when *I* came home in disgrace, they were incredibly supportive again.'

Kate gave a cynical grin. 'Relieved you hadn't had an abortion, I suppose?'

'Well, yes, of course, but it went much further than that.' Maria raised her voice above the stutter of a police helicopter circling overhead. 'We were part of a real community, with the priest on hand to help, and a definite sense of belonging. That's important for rootless people, Kate. OK, you may find it hard to imagine, coming from your large and stable family, who've all lived here for generations, with not an outcast or a foreigner amongst them.'

'I'm sorry, I shouldn't have spoken. It's just that I worry about you, Maria. I mean, forgive me for asking, but how are you coping financially?'

'Fine. I'm living rent-free, in luxury, and Amy pays all the bills, even my food bill and phone bill. And of course she'll give me a proper salary once I'm working as a nanny. In fact, she keeps trying to insist that I take it right away – and backdated to the day I first arrived – but I wouldn't dream of such a thing.'

'Why not? She was the one who asked you to come so early, so I reckon it's your due.'

'It isn't, Kate – you're wrong. I'm not doing a thing at the moment – well, a bit of ironing, maybe, and cooking the occasional meal. You see, they already have a cleaner and, in any case, they're out so much the house stays clean and tidy.' She took another sip of brandy, enjoying the sensation as it tingled through her empty stomach. 'Besides, I have my pension, don't forget, and some savings stashed away – not a lot, I admit but—'

'And what about your expenses back home – council tax and car insurance and train fares when you return for visits?'

'I can manage, honestly. I'm used to things being a bit of a struggle.'

'But you *shouldn't* be – that's my whole point. In fact, it makes me feel ashamed. Paul earns a good whack and my parents left me money and I've never wanted for anything. For instance, just last week, I blew two hundred pounds on a haircut and barely gave it a thought.'

Maria all but gasped: £200 had been more than enough to keep her and Hanna in food for a month. And they had always cut each other's hair – well, until her mother's dementia. Even here in London, she had discovered a local salon with a special rate for pensioners on Mondays: a trim for just a fiver.

'But, listen, talking of money, did Silas ever give you any – at least for the abortion he seemed so mad keen you should have?'

Maria shrugged. 'I told you, he was penniless. He did ask his friends for the cash, but, despite his famous charm, they all declined on that occasion. Maybe they didn't like the thought of being mixed up with such sordid stuff.'

'I still don't see why he couldn't have got a proper job.'

'Oh, he claimed that would be selling out, or compromising his art. Anyway, let's change the subject. I must have bored you rigid by now.'

'Of course you haven't. A man like Silas is hardly boring. But,' she added, with a glance at the clock, 'I'm afraid I'll have to get my skates on. I need to leave soon to collect the girls from school. I'd invite you to come with me and join us all for tea back here, but I'm taking them on to a ballet class, and then to—'

'Oh my God!' Maria exclaimed.

'What's wrong?'

'I've been so fixated on Amy, I've clean forgotten Felix.'

'Felix?'

'The guy who runs my life class.'

'But I thought the class was on Friday.'

'It is, but he's asked me to... Look, forget it, Kate – you're in a rush.'

'No, tell me what he asked. I still have ten minutes before I have to go.'

Suddenly, and against her better judgement, Maria began relaying the whole Felix saga, too, as if, having started in confessional mode, she couldn't stop. Yet there was a huge relief in sharing the story with someone unshockable and non-judgemental. 'I can't possibly see him tonight,' she concluded, 'not in this awful state and, anyway, I ought to stay home, so as to be there when Amy gets back.'

'No, I don't agree. She'll need time to simmer down. Once you've delivered the note and the shawl, she's bound to feel heaps better, but I wouldn't push things, if I were you. Leave it till tomorrow. In any case, it'll do you good to have a bit of male company.'

'But that's what scares me, Kate. If Felix does take things further, I'm so out of practice, I'll be like a virgin again.'

'Well, as far as I can gather, most men find virgins the most fantastic turn-on, so Felix will be in clover!'

'I doubt if virgins in their sixties have quite the same appeal.'

'Do stop going on about age. My Aunt Agnes embarked on a wild affair when she was only a year off eighty and she swore it kept her young. You're never too old for a lover – that's what *I* say. Of course, it used to be tricky for men – you know, losing their erections, once they'd passed a certain birthday, but now we have Viagra the whole thing's so much easier.'

Viagra? She was so naïve, it hadn't crossed her mind. And the thought of Felix needing a little blue pill to perform didn't fit her ardent fantasies. Shouldn't passion be the spur?

'And, whatever else, Maria, make sure he uses a condom – or you risk landing up in the STD clinic!'

She willed Kate to change the subject; couldn't bear to think of Felix struggling with a condom, or infecting her with some ghastly disease. In fact, if sex was so unromantic, she wasn't sure she wanted it at all – or only in her head, at home.

Fortunately, her friend began darting round the kitchen, collecting up her keys and bag, now clearly pressed for time. 'Look, go for it tonight,' she called, as she went to fetch her jacket from the hall. 'And finish up your brandy – that'll give you courage!'

Maria rationed herself to one more consoling sip. She needed a clear head to deal with the two tricky situations – her daughter and her tutor – and ensure that neither went from bad to worse. First and most important, she must try to make her peace with Amy, write her the most loving note conceivable and emphasize the fact that she felt no shred of resentment – never had and never would. But once note and shawl were delivered, she *would* keep the date with Felix, insisting, however, that they returned the relationship to strictly friendship only. The kiss, she would explain, had been an aberration – one she now regretted and which mustn't be repeated. Perhaps they could have supper together instead. It would certainly help her to recover from the highly stressful last few hours, if they could enjoy a leisurely meal and discuss non-threatening subjects such as their favourite painters and writers. And, if he couldn't cook, well, *she* would. At least her culinary skills were in good working order – more than could be said about her bedroom ones.

Chapter 12

'MORE, MORE – YES, *more!*'
Not her voice – couldn't be; not that insatiable, primeval cry of need. Normal self left far behind, abandoned by the bed, with the pile of crumpled clothes. All the emotion, passion, wild desire, suppressed and denied for decades, pouring out in a white heat of lust; all those terrifying sins, denounced by the Church – intemperance, licentiousness, concupiscence – now changing to intoxicating pleasure. Anger, too; a reckless energy possessing her, as she raged against her past: the closing down of prospects; the loss of independence; her timid, craven celibacy in those long years of stagnation. Anger not another sin, but simply part of lust; a ferocious and ecstatic part, as Felix thrust against her, in tune with her, in time with her, fused with her and one with her; no boundaries, no his-and-hers.

'Go *on!*' she shouted, glorying in the rhythm; the sudden, savage impetus as they pounded to a close – one body, inextricable.

'My God!' he gasped, slumping down, exhausted, breathless, spent.

His weight hunkered on her body, his heat and sweat flowing into hers. Couldn't speak; wouldn't even look at him; refused to leave this new, unchartered world. The only thing that mattered was the moment, these rapturous sensations of skin against bare skin; warm hands on startled breasts; semen leaking out of her; no condom; no restraints.

'Maria ...' He twined his fingers through her tangled mane of hair, long since fallen from its neat, obedient chignon. 'That was just ...'

She closed her ears. Words would only bring her back to guilt or shame or worry, and it was essential to stay longer with this new, outrageous self. Neither must he move, or she would lose that sense of fusion: belly pressing belly; limbs interlocked, conjoined.

'I hope you realize, woman, you're the most amazing fuck.'

Those words she *did* allow: the crude thrill of 'fuck', and that unceremonious 'woman', which made her fiercely female; rebellious Eve, not virginal Maria.

'I adore the noise you make. It's so utterly abandoned, like you couldn't give a toss if the whole of London heard! You seem to be two people – one dutiful and prudish, and the other a tornado.' He broke off, suddenly, levered himself up on his elbows, so he could look at her more closely. 'What's wrong, Maria? You haven't said a word.'

Reluctantly, she opened her eyes, feeling a flicker of surprise to see grey hair and jowly face. Where was her impetuous young lover? *She* had been no age at all during the last tempestuous hour; every stage and segment of her life – infant, child, student, sinner, mother, adult, carer – streaming out in one curdled tide of remorse, relief, release.

'I hope your back's not hurting. It actually suits me to sleep in the studio, but these pull-out beds are fiendishly uncomfortable. Or maybe the smells are getting to you? Jesso and white spirit are hardly the most seductive scents!'

'Felix,' she said, still unwilling to speak, but clasping him tightly, so he wouldn't feel rejected, 'nothing's wrong in the slightest.'

'But you seem so quiet – I mean, compared with how you were before. I'm worried you might be having second thoughts. After all, when you first arrived, you told me even a kiss was forbidden.'

'And I meant it,' she whispered, 'honestly.'

He couldn't suppress a smile. 'Well, it didn't take much to change your mind.'

'Don't say that, or I *will* have second thoughts.'

'No, they're strictly banned. But I'm dying for a drink, aren't you? How about some orange juice? Or another glass of wine?'

'Orange juice would be lovely.' How banal it sounded but, if he left the room a moment, she could savour, in silence, this extraordinary sense of liberation; the fact that all her onerous past, even her current problems, had wafted away like thistledown. She lay, eyes open, the unfamiliar surroundings gradually coming into focus: the two half-finished paintings on the two adjacent easels; other pictures stacked against the walls; the three mismatched wooden chairs; the four rows of shelves, holding brushes, paints and varnishes, all tidily arranged; the contrasting savage chaos of his latest composition, a huge canvas hanging opposite the bed. Its plunging verticals and violent brushstrokes seemed to capture her own mood, as did the jolting colours – not docile Virgin-Mary blue but seditious scarlet, heinous black.

Felix strode back in, still naked, a glass in either hand. 'I'm still worrying about that bloody bed. The mattress has seen better days and—'

'Felix, the last thing on my mind was the comfort or discomfort of the bed!'

'Are you sure?'

'Well, d'you imagine I was faking all that noise?'

He laughed. 'Hardly. But you *are* two people, you know, and I suppose that rather threw me. Although I reckon, this is the real you – I mean, lying here, with your legs apart and your voluptuous body on show.'

'*Fat* body, don't you mean?'

'Not at all. I loathe skinny women – the sort who go straight up and down, and are always dieting. As far as I'm concerned, proper women are curvaceous and celebrate their appetites.'

More words to relish: voluptuous, curvaceous. All her life, she'd been plump: a chubby baby, a podgy child, a teen eiderdowned in puppy-fat, a bosomy adult and, now, an overweight grandmother-to-be. Yet Felix had changed the categories.

'And I love your bush. It's so wonderfully dark. Where do you get your sultry looks?'

'From my Hungarian grandfather, so I'm told. Apparently, my father was blue-eyed and fair, so I'm nothing like him in appearance.' Her pubic hair had kindly maintained its colour, rather than gone the way of her head-hair; its once-dramatic black now stippled grey.

'Have you always slept in your studio?' she asked, embarrassed by his scrutiny. He was still gazing at her body, as if they were back at the life class and he had selected her as model.

'No, only since I moved here and had less space than before. Frankly, it's a waste of a room to keep it just for sleeping and, in any case, a bed destroys a room.'

The thought jolted her, yet maybe it was right. Amy and Hugo's bed – a ruffled, white, giant meringue – *was* a shade absurd.

'Besides, sleeping in my studio seems to give me useful dreams. Sometimes, if I'm stuck on a painting, I'll dream the solution on an imaginary canvas and, however hard I might have been struggling during the waking hours, everything falls into place in the dream. So, the minute I wake up from it, I jot down the shapes and colours I've seen and, when I start work the next day, I use it as a memory jog, which means I can focus on the dream again and make it a reality.' He leaned across and placed the glass of juice in her hand. 'But that's enough about work – we're meant to be off duty. Drink this up and I'll fetch us something to eat.'

'Can I help?' she asked, surprised by her avid thirst as she drained the glass.

'No, it's hardly haute cuisine, just croissants and cheese and stuff – oh, and those strawberries you kindly brought.'

'I'll get dressed, then,' she said, swinging her legs off the bed.

'What for? I presume you're staying the night.'

'Felix, I can't possibly! My daughter will be worried sick if I don't come home tonight.'

'Well, give her a ring and explain.'

'I, er, can't. Things are a bit tricky at the moment.' Amy might still be furious and, in any case, what could she 'explain' – that she was staying the night with a lover, so they could continue their blatant antics till dawn?

'Surely you don't let her dictate your movements?'

'No, of course not. But please don't press me, Felix. I have to be back tonight – no argument.'

'OK, but it's only five to nine, so no need to rush off now. Let's have our food, then I'll walk you to the tube. But don't you dare get dressed! I want to enjoy your body as long as I possibly can.'

Basking in his approbation, she made a supreme effort to stop obsessing about her daughter again. Not easy, now the subject had come up.

However, Felix's presence helped. He returned with a loaded tray, which he placed on the upturned wooden box that served as a bedside table. Then, having coaxed her to loll back against the pillows, he began feeding her mouthfuls of croissant, along with cubes of cheese.

She gave a sudden laugh. 'Do you realize, Felix, it's Lent, which means I should be fasting, not gorging, let alone indulging what the Church would call my baser passions.'

'Bugger the Church!'

She gasped at the blasphemous words; almost scared that Hanna had heard them from her presumably high place in Heaven.

'I've no time for all that stress on fasting – and Ramadan's even worse than Lent. All these religions do is try to control us; damp down our vital life-force so we won't have the energy we need to lead a full, instinctual life.'

Strange, she thought, that both Silas and Felix should be so hostile to religion, when, in all other respects, they were totally unalike: the one tall, dark, Byronic and flamboyant; the other shortish, greyish, ordinaryish – although not ordinary in the slightest when it came to making love.

He was feeding her again and a few flakes of greasy croissant fell between her breasts. Immediately, he tongued them up, his tongue so lingeringly sensuous, she closed her eyes to block out all else. The scenario she had envisaged for tonight was a far cry from this indulgent lovers' feast. She had seen herself concocting a meal in the kitchen, which she and Felix would eat, fully clothed, at a table, and engaging in high-minded conversation.

It was time for her to feed him in her turn, although she was sadly aware that she didn't have his erotic expertise and so couldn't add those beguiling little refinements. But he seemed happy just to eat, licking a drool of butter from her fingers and scooping up the fragments of crumbly cheese that had fallen on the bed. They continued feeding each other until the croissants were finished and he reached out for the fruit.

'These are very singular strawberries. Look at their weird protuberances!'

She flushed. She had bought them half price in the market and hadn't even noticed their asymmetry.

'I really like these lumps and bumps – much more original than regular-shaped strawberries.' He held out a three-pronged fruit, for her to see. 'This is my favourite. It's curvaceous, like you, but with three breasts, instead of two!'

'Well, if that one's female, this one's definitely male,' she said, showing him another, with a distinct but diminutive phallus at each end.

'And here's a Henry Moore in miniature – the same satisfying curves. Although miniature's not the word – it's the biggest strawberry I've ever seen in my life. Here, have a bite.' He held it to her mouth and, having nibbled off its swollen tip, she offered it to him, and they alternated, bite by bite, until there was nothing left but the little frilled green stalk. Instead of discarding it, he used it to trace the outline of her lips, the sensation tickly cool. Then he slipped his little finger into her mouth and gently grazed it across the tips of her teeth; the tiniest, subtlest pressure that seemed to kindle her whole body. Maybe she could learn from him all these inventive techniques, as she was learning the refinements of drawing, at the class.

He was still gazing at her intently, as if following his own advice: any artist worth his salt must observe in the closest detail. 'You have very interesting eyebrows, Maria.'

'I hate them! Eyebrows should be meek and unassuming, and mine are almost fierce.'

'Which is exactly why I like them.' He knelt astride her, leaned down and kissed each brow, then, moving his mouth to her lips, he kissed them in the same galvanizing fashion, and continued inching his mouth down the entire length of her body, as if it were a table, laid with sweetmeats, every one of which he must lick and sip and taste.

'Look,' he said, raising his head from the arch of her foot, 'you're turning me on again.'

She stared, intrigued, at his penis. The only one she had ever seen was Silas's – apart from a few in the life classes at art school, which had embarrassed her so much, she had deliberately averted her eyes and drawn only the male models' chests and torsos. But now she gazed in wonder at the glistening, stiffening insolence of this, in Felix-parlance, 'cock'. She had to admit she found those slang words arousing, although she would never use them herself. Indeed, neither she nor her mother had ever referred to the male member under any appellation, slang or anatomical, during the whole course of their lives. Hanna had even been uneasy about words like 'breasts' and 'bottom'.

Felix's penis seemed much younger than the rest of him: vigorous and sturdy and clearly in its prime. Kate would probably attribute that to Viagra, but she refused to allow so pedestrian a thought. Surely it was more to do with the organ's essential character – an assertive, bumptious individual, not willing to be thwarted, as she had found an hour ago.

Having flung the strawberry cartons off the bed, he lay back, reached out his arms. 'You on top this time.'

'Felix, I *can't*! I have to leave.' However strong his inducements, she had to set a limit and also keep a strict eye on the time. Her second self – the responsible and dutiful self – was still hovering somewhere, warning and restraining.

'Not yet.' He drew her down towards him, locked his arms across her back, keeping her his prisoner. 'That's tutor's orders, and tutor's orders have to be obeyed!'

Chapter 13

AS THEY DAWDLED to a halt outside the tube, Felix gave her a last, lingering kiss. 'Why don't I come with you – see you right to your door?'

'No, I'll be fine. It's not that late.' His bodily presence wasn't necessary, since he'd be with her anyway throughout the journey home; his hands still on her breasts, his tongue still in her mouth, their lungs inhaling with one breath …

She descended in the lift, its five other occupants all wired up to iPods and seemingly unaware of any world beyond their earphones. Nonetheless, she ached to impart to each of them how totally transformed she felt, from greenhorn to adventuress. And, when the train rumbled into the station and she grabbed an empty seat, it was all she could do not to broadcast to the carriage that tonight had been a watershed, a vital rite of passage.

The man beside her was reading the *Standard*, but the grisly headlines – famine in Ethiopia, a fatal stabbing in Peckham – made no sense at all. The planet *she* inhabited contained only euphoric news. The tube itself seemed airborne, winging from station to station, with no bumps or rattles or delays, and when she changed to the Victoria Line her feet barely touched the ground, as if she were swifter, lighter, livelier than the other plodding passengers. She stood waiting for the next train, entranced by everything she saw: the witty posters and willing benches, the stretch of shining rails.

She skittered out at Pimlico and floated up the escalator. The homeless chap she often saw was hunched in his usual pitch, with his begging bowl and mangy dog, despite the fact it was almost eleven.

'Spare some change.'

She showered a cascade of coins into his bowl, glad they were mainly pound coins and not measly fives and tens, and feeling so expansive tonight she was tempted to give him the entire contents of her purse.

The air was refreshingly cool as she sauntered along Lupus Street, smiling at the passers-by, who seemed unaccountably surly on such an enchanted night. Once she had turned the corner into Amy's road, she stopped a moment to gaze up at the sky, which was dark and overcast. Recalling the brilliant stars back home, she longed to strip them from the vast Northumbrian sky and send them in glittering shoals to cluster over her lover's house.

Only when she had let herself in did she prang to earth with a hideous crash. Amy had already gone to bed, leaving no note or message – nothing in response to her own long and loving letter and, suddenly, her former wild elation seemed totally inappropriate. Indeed, if her daughter were to discover how she had spent the evening, she would assume it was a repeat of Silas – an act of irresponsible abandon – and become even more resentful. And it *was* a repeat, in some ways: the same bewitchment, the same besotted state, but at least with Silas she'd had the excuse of youth. Now, such excessive transports were surely a sign of arrested development.

Miserably, she crept up the attic stairs and stood a moment, surveying her granny-flat, which seemed bare and stark compared with Felix's treasure-house. But her lover had no place here – although, even as she undressed, wayward memories of him unfastening her bra and easing down her jeans kept lasering through her body.

Having switched off the bedside light, she slipped between the cold, unfriendly sheets and lay staring at the luminous dial of the alarm clock. Never had it ticked so slowly; every minute from 11.30 to midnight seeming more like an hour. And even by half past one, she was still fidgety and restless.

Well, if sleep eluded her all night, that was a fitting punishment for the harm she had done in depriving her beloved daughter of a live-in, loving father.

Six penises, each erect and each pointing in her direction. With penises so rare in her life, it seemed extraordinary to see so many, at one and the same time. But, peering closer, she realized they were door-handles, one for each of a row of six black doors – doors that could only be opened if she grasped those stiff and slippery appendages. She glanced around for help or explanation, but she was utterly alone and, since she had no mobile phone or means of transport, there was no chance of either escape or communication.

Yet doors, she thought, might mean rooms beyond – maybe other people; even hopeful possibilities – so, gingerly, she crept towards the largest door and reached out for its swollen penis-handle. But, just as her hand made contact, the entire row of doors collapsed and she opened her eyes to a finger of dawn-light, wavering through the curtains.

She sat up with a start, surprised to see familiar surroundings: the square-shaped attic window, the small abstract painting opposite the bed. Her first thought was of Felix and she gave a sudden hooting laugh, imagining his reaction to the dream: 'That's greed, Maria, pure and simple! Most women are content with one cock; *you* want half a dozen!'

But, as she reflected further, she was aware of the darker aspect of the dream: that sense of being cut off and out of contact was obviously related to the situation with Amy. In her daughter's eyes, she was a mature and sober grandmother-in-waiting; not an artist's mistress. And, because she couldn't admit to the sex, she would be forced to live a lie; the secrecy a barrier between them. She was cut off from Amy anyway, in that her daughter had rejected her overtures. She had expected a few scribbled words, or a brief text on her mobile – at least something in response to the gift of the shawl. Maybe Amy had rung Hugo in Dubai and, because of his stress about the court case, he had overreacted and urged Amy to harden her heart.

She checked her watch: 6.20 – over an hour before her daughter left for work, which meant she could have a word with her and try to sort things out. Normally, she left the pair to themselves. They didn't want her under their feet and she had learned long ago not to offer to make breakfast. Hugo grabbed a bacon sandwich on site, while Amy's PA fetched her coffee and a croissant later in the morning. Coffee and a croissant seemed a far-from-nourishing breakfast for a woman twenty weeks pregnant but, again, she mustn't interfere.

Croissants reminded her of Felix and a frisson of excitement displaced the worry and remorse, if only momentarily. As he'd said, she seemed to be two different people and the sudden shifts between the two were as disconcerting for her as much as for him. But her first duty at the moment was to get dressed and go downstairs, in a bid to end the hostilities.

She felt distinctly apprehensive as she stepped into the shower; running the water as hot as she could bear, to wash off the last traces of her second, sexual self. And she deliberately chose frumpy clothes, suited to a grandmother, and coiled her hair into a severe, unflattering bun.

Even so, it wasn't easy to venture down the attic stairs and, halfway down, she dithered to a halt. Amy was always busy at this time: washing her hair, applying blusher and lip-gloss so as to look the part in the office, checking texts and emails before she had to leave.

She turned on her heel and began walking back the way she'd come. Best to wait until this evening and hope by then –

'Mum!'

She wheeled round to see her daughter, fully dressed and made up, darting up the stairs in her worryingly high heels.

Amy sprang towards her and enfolded her in a hug. 'I'm so *sorry*, Mum! I just don't understand how I ever said those awful, hurtful things. I'm worried you won't forgive me, or—'

'But didn't you get my note?' Maria's voice was muffled in the embrace.

Amy disengaged herself. 'What note?'

'I left it at reception, in your office, yesterday.'

'Oh Lord! I had to go to Clerkenwell the minute I got back in. And from there I went on to—' She broke off with a frown. 'Actually, Rebecca did phone me – I remember now – and said something about a delivery, but I'd no idea it was from you.'

'Yes, I left a present, too – something for the baby.'

'Oh, Mum … And I thought you were still furious.'

'And I thought *you* were!'

They hugged again, Maria's reaction veering between tears and laughter.

'Mum, have you got a second? There's something I want to say.'

'I've all the time in the world. It's *you* who's in the rush.'

'No, I'm not – for once. I deliberately got up earlier than usual because I didn't want to go to work without seeing you.'

Knowing how much Amy valued sleep, Maria felt genuinely touched. 'Well, come on in and I'll make you some tea. Or how about a boiled egg?'

'Mum, let's not go mad! You know I never eat this early. And no tea either, thanks. What I'm going to tell you is important, so I don't want you fussing around with kettles and cups.'

Mystified, Maria ushered her into her mini-sitting-room and offered her the sole armchair, while she perched on the window ledge.

Crossing her long, elegant legs, Amy leaned back with a sigh. 'I should have said this years ago – which only goes to show what a selfish git I am.'

'I'm sorry, I don't follow.'

There was a sudden awkward pause, then Amy spoke in a rush. 'I want to tell you – a bit late in life, I admit – how much I appreciate everything you did for me. All my life, you've put me first – praised me and supported me, made me feel good about myself. Whatever I said yesterday, you're actually the best mother in the world. No, don't contradict me. In fact, you're not to say a word until I've finished. You may think I never twigged how hard things were for you; how you had to go out to work, to pay for my clothes and shoes and hockey boots and all that sort of stuff. In fact, you were like my dad, as well as my mum – earning the money, but also making my school lunches and sewing party frocks.'

'Yes, but your Grandma did as much as—'

'Mum, don't interrupt! I'm not talking about Grandma – I'm talking about you. Take holidays, for instance. You never went abroad, but you scraped the cash together to send *me* on foreign trips: school excursions to Paris and Brussels and even a fortnight's skiing. And remember that big Youth Pilgrimage to Lourdes? You paid for me to go on that as well, yet you couldn't afford to go yourself, like most of the other mums did.'

'Who'd want to go to Lourdes?' Maria interjected, with a grin.

'*I* did! I was mad keen to see a place where amazing cures might happen, and where I could buy miraculous medals and bottles of Lourdes water and all that pious tat. Oh, I know it sounds unlikely, but when you're only thirteen … But, look, we're going off the point, Mum, so let me have my say, OK? When I was older, several of my school friends had parents who divorced and then shacked up with other partners, so there were all these messy relationships with step-parents they hated, or with stepkids they saw as intruders. You never put me through that. I had your total attention and devotion.'

'But Grandma was the one who—'

'Not another word about Grandma! I haven't finished yet. D'you remember that time when Carole's daughter, Becky, had a baby – the summer of 1991, I think it was – and Carole asked you to look after him, while she and Becky spent a week down south? I'd finished at Cambridge, so I was staying with you till I started my new job, and I've never forgotten how loving you were with that baby. "Tender" was the word that kept coming into my mind – the way you handled him and fed him, and how patient you were when he kept sicking up his milk – and I realized then that was how you must have been with *me*.'

Maria's first instinct was to shout a vehement '*No!*'; to come clean about the fact that she had been anything but tender – at least for the first two years. But something stopped her – and it wasn't only shame; more an overwhelming need for Amy to feel secure.

'I was twenty-one at the time and not thinking of having kids myself for at least another five years, but I knew that when I did have them I wanted you to *be* there, and be thoroughly involved, so you could treat them with the same … yes, tenderness.'

Maria sat in silence. Why spoil a precious moment with superfluous words?

'So I hope you'll forgive my outburst yesterday. Put it down to stress. I didn't tell you at the time, but the client I was seeing had really dropped me in it and—'

Maria got up from the window ledge and crouched by Amy's chair. 'Darling, the things you said were completely understandable. In your situation, anyone would feel the same. And you're absolutely right in needing to know more about your father. *I* was at fault, for not having acknowledged that an age ago. But, as I told you in my note, I intend to do my best to track him down. In fact, I'll make a start this morning and try all the things you suggested, so with any luck you should be able to meet him long before the baby's born.'

'Oh, that's fantastic, Mum! But why don't you let me help? I'm more computer-savvy than you, so it would probably take me a fraction of the time.'

Maria moved to the window and stood looking out at the morning light: uncertain still, and murky grey. 'Amy, you need to understand that this is a very emotional business, for me as much as for you, so, if you don't mind, I'd prefer ...'

The sentence trailed away. How could she admit her two overwhelming fears: first, that Silas might have died, which would be shock enough for Amy and, second, if he *were* alive but Amy located him first, he might let slip something about the presumed abortion. No way must her poor daughter stumble on either of those disastrous facts with no warning, no support.

Whatever she herself discovered – hopeful, tragic, or worryingly ambivalent – she must digest it first, somehow come to terms with it, and only then relay it to Amy with the utmost tact and, yes, tenderness.

Chapter 14

'NO, NEVER HEARD of the fucker!'

Maria winced at the aggressive tone, well suited to the pugnacious fellow confronting her in the doorway. With the solid build of a boxer, and his red, veined face suggesting an addiction to the bottle, he seemed unlikely to cooperate. Nonetheless, she stood her ground. 'Are you absolutely sure? He lived in this house for seven years, according to the records, and only moved out in 2009.'

'How the hell d'you think I'd know, then? We didn't come here till last December and the house was sodding empty.'

'But it must have been owned by someone. Could you possibly tell me who you bought it from?'

'Listen, madam—' The man raised his arm in a threatening gesture, on a par with the contemptuous 'madam' '—I don't want you, or anyone, poking their nose into my private affairs.'

Seeing he was about to close the door in her face, she pressed the full weight of her body against it; a resistance fuelled by desperation. 'Look, the last thing I want is to pry. But I'm extremely anxious to track down this Silas Keegan. It's a vital family matter, otherwise I wouldn't dream of—'

He cut her off mid-sentence. 'I couldn't give a fuck! And if you don't shift your arse, I'll thump you.'

Maria turned tail and ran. It would hardly help the search if she landed up with a broken jaw. Amy was already fretful that a full month had gone by with, as yet, no clue as to Silas's whereabouts, although she had impressed upon her daughter the hours spent on the computer, while hushing up the ever-mounting costs. She had been obliged to raid her savings to pay for the credits, search fees and numerous other charges. Google, Twitter, Facebook and MySpace all had offered leads but, once followed up, the Silas Keegans they had yielded were invariably too old, too young, in improbable professions (an osteopath, a banker, a ballroom-dancing instructor), or lived in unlikely places.

And, certainly, this dreary Tolworth street seemed eminently wrong for a man who had always loathed the suburbs and insisted on being close to London's cultural highlights. Yet a Silas Keegan of exactly seventy-six had apparently lived in this cramped and shabby house until a mere two years ago. No doubt, the trail would go cold again and if she did eventually track him down he would prove to be not *her* Silas but simply someone of the same name and age. However, she couldn't afford to ignore even the slightest chance of finding him, so she unlatched the next-door gate – number twenty-five – hoping the aggressive man she had just encountered might have more helpful neighbours.

She walked up the weed-flanked path and rang the doorbell loud and long. Whatever else, her assertiveness had increased over the last few frustrating weeks, especially on the phone. Having cold-called scores of people, her tone had gradually changed from apologetically tentative to confidently forceful – not that a single one of the calls had led her to her quarry.

The door was finally opened by a small, oriental-looking man, who shrank back in obvious fear to see her standing on his doorstep. Before she had uttered a word, he began vigorously shaking his head, as if denying all complicity in some crime or misdemeanour.

She gave him what she hoped was a reassuring smile. 'I'm just trying to hunt down a friend, a Mr Silas Keegan.'

He shook his head still harder, letting out a few indecipherable words.

Enunciating each syllable distinctly, she asked if he spoke English, but her question only elicited another unintelligible babble. However, she had learned persistence as well as boldness, so she raised her voice and all but shouted, 'Is there someone else I could talk to?', hoping a wife or grown-up child might be alerted by the noise and put in an appearance. But it only seemed to frighten him still more, so, to prevent causing any further distress, she was forced to relent and retreat.

Perhaps number twenty-one would prove more fruitful – a lucky number, after all. At least the gate was less wobbly, the path less weed-infested. A woman opened the door, this time – and a woman who spoke English.

'Oh, you must be the new health visitor. Do come in.'

Maria accepted the invitation and stepped firmly over the threshold, knowing she was less likely to be sent packing once she had a foot in the door. 'My name's Maria,' she explained. 'I'm afraid I'm not the health visitor, but I'm trying to trace a friend who—'

Her spiel was interrupted by a sudden wail from a baby; the noise issuing from a room upstairs and increasing in both volume and intensity.

'Oh, God – he's started again! I'm at my wits' end, what with the other one playing up, as well, and….'

The sentence hung suspended as the woman dashed upstairs, leaving the front door ajar. Maria stood a moment undecided, wondering whether to offer help. No, best leave that to the health visitor, who was obviously expected soon. Having closed the door, she walked back down the path. Never had she imagined that her search for Silas might result in personal injury or involve damage to an unattended child.

She persevered, however, crossing the road to number twenty-two. By now, she was so keyed up, it was almost an anti-climax when her repeated shrills on the doorbell brought no response whatever. She had an unnerving feeling that the bruiser in the house opposite was poised behind his net curtains, watching her every move. Too bad. She was doing nothing illegal and refused to give up now.

At number twenty-four, a cheerful-looking woman actually gave her a smile of welcome and, once she had grasped the situation, invited her into the kitchen and even offered her a cup of tea.

'No, please don't bother, I'm fine. I just need some information.'

'Well, I've lived here donkey's years so I should be able to help. Take a pew. I'm Ruby, by the way.'

Glad to take the weight off her feet, Maria was also encouraged to hear that the woman was a long-time resident. Ruby looked about her own age, with wiry grey hair and attractive grey-green eyes.

'I didn't know Silas personally,' she began, sitting opposite Maria at the battered kitchen table. 'And he didn't own the house. He just rented a room from the Johnsons. I shouldn't really say this but they were down-right standoffish, that couple – thought themselves a cut above the neighbours, which included me, of course – and didn't want to mix with people they saw as social inferiors. As for their "gentleman lodger", as they called him, he kept himself to himself. But then,' she added in a confidential tone, 'that's typical of this whole street. No way could you call it friendly.'

Maria nodded sympathetically. If this were a Northumbrian village, everyone would know everyone else within a five-mile radius. She was determined to keep to the point, however, and not get side-tracked onto the subject of suburban unsociability. 'But,' she asked, 'even if you didn't know him, I presume you saw him sometimes?'

'Well, yes, occasionally.'

'Could you give me some idea of what he looked like? You see, I have to be sure this is the same Silas as the one I used to know.'

Ruby rocked back on her chair. 'Well, he was very tall and thin – angular's the word I'd use. And he had very dark eyes and thick, black eyebrows.'

Correct on both counts. Maria allowed herself a flicker of hope.

'I noticed the eyebrows particularly, because they seemed odd on an old, balding chap.'

Although the thought of Silas being old and balding was utterly abhorrent, she ignored her personal feelings in an attempt to discover more. 'What I'm trying to find out is where he might have moved to.'

'Well, I remember *when* he went – it was the spring of 2009. You see, a month or two before that, Mrs Johnson actually deigned to speak to me – told me they didn't like the area, so they'd decided to sell up and move much further out.'

'And was Silas going with them?'

'Oh, no! Apparently, they didn't like him either.' Ruby gave a contemptuous laugh. 'But that's no reflection on your friend,' she added, hastily. 'They'd have probably hated Christ Himself if He happened to be their lodger. And if He'd started turning water into wine, He'd have been out on His ear, damn quick! They were strict teetotallers, the pair of them.'

Maria smiled politely, before pressing on with her questions – despite the awkwardness she felt about subjecting this poor woman to such an inquisition. 'Did they say what he planned on doing?'

'Gosh! It was so long ago, it's hard to remember much. But let me think. Yes, I seem to recall she said he'd found a flat.'

'Can you remember where?' A definite town or region would narrow the search considerably.

'Lordy – now you're asking! Lewisham, perhaps. Does Lewisham ring a bell?'

'I'm afraid I've no idea. I lost touch with him ages ago, which is why I'm bothering you. But do forgive me. You're being wonderfully patient and you're probably very busy.'

'Far from it. I've nothing to do and I'm only too glad of the company.'

As Ruby embarked on a protracted tale of her divorce, followed by her remarriage and then widowhood, Maria tried to balance sympathy with a keen desire to return to the subject in hand. She waited – at length – for a pause in Ruby's detailed account of her late husband, Graham's, funeral.

'I'm deeply sorry about your loss. It must be terribly hard. But, look, going back to Silas, you said he might have moved to Lewisham.'

'Did I?'

Maria suppressed a sigh.

'Well, in that case, it must be right. I mean, why else would I have come up with Lewisham, when I don't know a soul there myself?'

'But obviously you don't have an address.'

'Good God, no! As I said, I hardly knew the fellow. Graham met him once – bumped into him at Waterloo and travelled on the same train back to Tolworth.'

'And did they talk?' Please God, she prayed, let Graham have discovered some useful fact or detail.

'Not that he ever told me, but then my hubbie wasn't the world's greatest conversationalist! In fact, knowing Graham, he'd have probably said a brief hello, then buried his head in a book.'

As Ruby embroidered on her late husband's reading habits, even listing his favourite authors, Maria gave a covert glance at her watch. When the woman paused for breath between James Patterson and Wilbur Smith, she quickly put a word in, saying she would have to make a move soon. Ruby, she realized, might be all too happy to reminisce about her husband for the remainder of the afternoon. but since the unfortunate departed man could shed no light on Silas, it was crucial to steer the conversation back to more productive channels. 'Look, before I go, maybe you could put me in touch with the Johnsons, then I could get my friend's address from them.'

'Sorry – can't help there, either. We never kept in contact. Frankly, I was glad to see the back of them.'

'Well, just their first names would help.' If she had to embark on another search, Johnson was a depressingly common surname.

'I never knew the husband's first name and even the wife's escapes me. She's more or less a blank now, to be honest. Hold on a minute, though, and I'll try to get my brain in gear. In fact, if you could stick around, Maria, and we had more time together, I'm sure the name would come. And, even if it doesn't, we could have that cup of tea I promised and a good old natter about life in general.'

Life in general was not her interest at the moment. Her focus was narrowed to Silas and Silas alone. 'I'm really sorry but I'm rather pushed for time. So if you could have just one last think about Mrs Johnson's name …'

Ruby screwed up her face with the effort of recall, but nothing appeared to be forthcoming. Maria leaned back in her chair, trying to hide her growing frustration, but as she glanced around the small, poky room, with its depressing view of assorted wheelie-bins, she couldn't help but feel despondent. How could Silas have landed up in a downmarket suburban semi, a mile or two from a station that had only a slow, infrequent train service to London? Tall, angular men with black eyebrows and dark eyes weren't particularly rare, so the Silas who had lived here might be someone else entirely.

'I'm sure it began with an A.' Ruby started rehearsing names to herself. 'Angela ... Alice ... Annabel ... No, nothing as fancy as Annabel. Maybe just plain Anne. Yes, it could have been Anne, I suppose.'

Anne Johnson – there'd be millions.

'I couldn't swear to it, though. I may be muddling her up with an Anne I used to know from church.'

'Well, look—' Maria finally rose to her feet '—why don't I leave you my phone number, then if you do suddenly remember something, maybe you'd be kind enough to ring me.'

'Yes, of course.' Ruby reached for Maria's hand and clasped it firmly in her own, as if hoping to hang on to her for longer. 'Or perhaps you could visit anyway. I'd love to see you again, so we could get to know each other. I'm nearly always here, and nearly always on my own, so any day would suit. I could show you all the photos of Graham and the funeral and everything. It's a funny thing, you know, but the minute you showed up on my doorstep, I felt this sort of ... bond with you. Don't ask me to explain – it was just a mysterious feeling that you and me were *meant* to meet.'

Maria found herself at a loss for words. Her natural instinct was to respond to Ruby's overtures, yet the last thing she needed was any new relationship. The search for Silas was all-consuming – so much so that she was even neglecting Felix, and hadn't yet found time to go back north and check on the car and cottage. On the other hand, Ruby might recall some vital piece of information and thus it was imperative they stayed in touch.

Gently withdrawing her hand from the woman's eager grip, she wrote her phone number on a piece of paper, torn from her 'Silas' notebook. Amy had insisted that she keep a strict record of all the sites she'd signed up to, all the steps she'd taken so far, all the leads she'd followed up, all the calls she'd made. And every evening, she shared her progress – or lack of it – with her increasingly impatient daughter, who kept offering to take over the search herself; insisting she would do it so much faster and more thoroughly. Unlikely. Amy had a full-time job, and this *was* a full-time job and, indeed, the demands would be still greater if she had to make space for exacting personal friendships on top of everything else.

'Do you have email, Ruby?' she asked. A brief email or two would save protracted phone calls.

'Lord, no! I can't make head or tail of computers. Graham had one, mind, but after he passed away, I couldn't bear to have the thing in the house. It brought back such awful memories – you know, of him sitting there, fit and well, not knowing he'd … he'd …'

As Ruby broke off, close to tears, Maria felt torn between her own selfish concerns and Ruby's obvious needs. Was she a callous brute not to stay and offer comfort to this apparently friendless widow? And what about the frantic mother at number twenty-one? Perhaps she ought to pop back there, to ensure the health visitor was safely ensconced and neither child at risk. Yet she was overcome by a wave of sheer exhaustion. She had barely slept last night; too keyed up about this expedition and the sobering – indeed, frightening – thought of actually possessing Silas's current address. How naïve she had been to imagine that the present owner of the house would simply hand it over, without some complication.

She gave Ruby an affectionate hug before passing her the sheet of paper.

'Great!' Ruby snatched it like treasure. 'I'll ring you anyway. Will you be in first thing tomorrow?'

'Yes,' she answered, wearily – at the computer, most like, extending her search to Lewisham and the Johnsons.

As she trudged back up the road, she almost resented the serenely smug weather for being so out of tune with her mood. The sky was a cloudless blue and conceited daffodils trumpeted their yellow perfection in the small front gardens that weren't choked with weeds or filled with junk. For her, the suburbs were unknown territory, having spent all her life in a small rural village – and less than three months in central London. However, if Tolworth was typically suburban, then she couldn't say she was enamoured of its characterless streets and boringly identical houses.

But there was no hope of going home yet. She still had to make enquiries at all the shops adjoining Tolworth station and, firstly, at the newsagent's on the corner of this street and the small café next to it. If her Silas *had* lived in this area, then someone might remember him or even know his present whereabouts.

The window of the newsagent's displayed a prominent Royal Wedding poster. With the event just two days away, the hype was building up: souvenirs on sale; pre-wedding colour supplements in newspapers and magazines. As she gazed at the loving couple, she felt her usual pang of regret that she herself had never had a wedding. Forget the dress, the flowers, the cake – those were fripperies – it was the lasting vows she craved; the incredible security of having someone to support her in health or sickness, poverty or wealth. Her mother had been there for her, of course

– and in that she was extremely blessed – yet, to her lasting shame, she'd been greedy enough to crave sex as well as support.

Thoughts of sex rekindled scorching memories of her last passionate encounter with Felix. But that was ten long days ago and he couldn't understand why she was suddenly so busy and rationing their meetings. For a variety of reasons, she had refrained from mentioning Silas – even his existence, let alone her search for him – and it hadn't escaped her notice that he, too, seemed reticent on the subject of his past. The third time they'd made love, they'd lain talking afterwards and, although he'd said he was divorced, he had supplied no details of either the marriage or the wife. He had also admitted to a grown-up daughter, but said he very rarely saw her, because she lived in New York and was tied to a demanding job. Deliberately, she hadn't probed, feeling it was better that they respect each other's privacy when it came to past mistakes, and try to enjoy the present rather than dwell on former relationships that had brought them only pain.

She stepped into the newsagent's, although the only news she wanted was some definitive word of Silas. If he had opened an account here, they might have his name on record still, or one of the staff or paper-boys remember him. In the sixties, he had never actually read the papers, damning them as 'capitalist lies', but that view had probably changed now.

Having waited a good five minutes in the long queue at the counter – a single Asian trying to deal with all the customers – she decided to try the café first and come back later on. In any case, a strong coffee might revive her; renew her flagging energies. Indeed, once she saw the menu, with its cheap, substantial dishes, she was tempted to order a proper meal. She sat debating between fried fish with mushy peas or corned-beef hash and chips, but eventually rejected both: all her available funds had to go towards the search, not be frittered away in cafés. Amy had offered repeatedly to shoulder the costs herself, but it seemed unfair to add a financial burden to the existing emotional one – not to mention all her daughter's stress about the contention in Dubai, still a source of deep anxiety. Besides, Amy already paid the phone bills, which were increasing substantially, now that every possible Silas Keegan had to be rung and checked.

'A white coffee, please, and a round of toast.'

The waitress seemed a friendly type, so Maria delayed her a moment to give a brief description of Silas, repeating his name, in the hope the girl might recognize it.

'No, it doesn't ring a bell. But then we don't get many regulars – more just passing trade. And, of course, I meet so many different people, it's hard to remember individuals.'

'He's very tall and thin,' Maria reiterated. 'And the one thing you'd notice are his extremely dark eyebrows.'

The girl shook her head. 'I can't recall anyone like that. But I'm terribly unobservant, so my mother says. She reckons Lady Gaga might wander in one day and I wouldn't even notice!'

Maria forced a smile, although she was beginning to wonder if this whole day was just a waste of time. After all, there was no real proof, as yet, that Silas was even alive. His name had failed to come up in her extensive searches through a variety of death records but, since none of those records extended to the present, there was no way of knowing if he had died in the last few years.

Although she could barely admit it, even to her herself, let alone to Amy, one shameful part of her couldn't help wishing that he *would* turn out to be dead. At least it would spare her the ordeal of having to meet him, face to face, when he had several well-founded reasons to be angry: her pretence at being on the Pill, her lies about an abortion she wouldn't have contemplated in a thousand years, and her breaking of a solemn vow never to contact him again.

'Do you want jam on your toast?' the waitress asked, returning with a small, chipped plate and a watery-looking cup of coffee.

'No, thanks.' At school, they'd been exhorted to refuse any proffered treat, be it sweets, or cakes, or jam, because of the constant need, encouraged by the nuns, to make retribution for one's sins. And, since her transgressions against Silas had been indefensible, no way must she indulge herself today.

So, as she sipped her sugarless coffee and swallowed a mouthful of flabby toast, spread thinly with low-grade margarine, she tried to take pleasure from the fact that, for once, she was tempering her greed.

Chapter 15

'M UM?'

Maria jumped at the tap on her door. She was still in bed, half-dozing, and certainly hadn't expected Amy to be up so early on a Bank Holiday. 'Yes, come in, darling,' she called, praying it wasn't some emergency. Her daughter was doing far too much, rarely found time to rest and hadn't yet enrolled in any antenatal classes.

Her anxiety redoubled as she saw Amy pale and dishevelled in her nightdress, looking stricken, tense and close to tears. 'What's wrong?' she asked, springing out of bed.

'It … it's Chloe … Nicholas rang late last night. I didn't tell you because you'd already gone to bed, but he was absolutely distraught.'

'What's happened?' Aware her daughter should be sitting down, Maria steered her towards the bed.

'Well, she went into labour yesterday but there was some sort of complication so she had to have an emergency Caesarean, and … and one of the babies died and the other's in intensive care.'

'Oh, my God, how awful!' Maria clasped her hand in sympathy. 'But what on earth went wrong? I thought she had one of the country's leading obstetricians.'

'She does – she did – but I suppose even the top guys have their off days. Nicholas didn't give me any details and I didn't like to press him, when he's so worried about Chloe. She needed a blood transfusion and she's still incredibly weak.'

'Is there anything we can do?'

'No, she's not allowed visitors, except Nicholas, of course. He's staying at the hospital until things are a bit less fraught.'

'Is the surviving twin in danger?'

'No, thank God. He's very small, but basically OK and they say he should be fine, once he's reached his proper weight. It's Chloe I'm concerned about. Having a baby die when you've carried him for thirty-eight weeks must be quite unbearable. In fact, I feel so gutted, I don't know how I'm going to get through today.'

'Do you *have* to go?' Maria asked, annoyed that, even on a Bank Holiday, Amy was expected to be on duty. 'Couldn't you explain the situation and say you don't feel up to partying?'

'No way! Jonathan's my most important client.'

'Yes, but if it's a great big bash, there'll be crowds of other people flocking around, so surely he'll let you off.'

'Mum, he expects me to be there and that's an end to it. And, anyway, it's *not* a great big bash. His house is on the Royal Procession route, so half of London's been angling for an invite and he's had to restrict the numbers to, mainly, the top brass.'

Maria sat in silence for a moment, trying to judge the situation. Maybe attending a glitzy champagne brunch would be better for her daughter than staying at home and brooding all day long. 'Well, actually, it might be a good thing, you know. At least, if you go, it'll take your mind off Chloe. Besides, if you cancel so late on, you'll only fret about that, too.'

'Yes, Hugo said the same.'

'Well, there you are – great minds think alike! But, seriously, why not try and enjoy it? Oh, I know it's basically work, but it *is* a special occasion – one you can brag about to your grandchildren!'

'Yes, it'll certainly be a splendid affair, but it seems so crass to be partying when poor Chloe's in such a state.'

'Darling, there's nothing you can actually do to make things any better for her – not at the moment, anyway. In fact, the more I think about it, the more I feel you should stick to your plan and be there for Jonathan. So what I suggest is you go back to bed for a couple more hours and try to catch up on your sleep, then you'll have some energy to put on a good show. That's the most important thing right now.'

'Oh, Mum, you sound so calm and sensible, and you're right – I know you are. It won't do any good at all if I let everybody down.'

'Well, off you go and get some rest. I'll see you later, OK?'

Once alone, Maria stood by the attic window, feeling anything but sensible and calm. If an eminent obstetrician at one of London's finest hospitals couldn't prevent so dire an outcome, what hope for Amy on the NHS? And Chloe hadn't worked for at least the last three months, whereas the pressures on Amy seemed continually to increase. The night before last, she'd been involved in a client presentation and hadn't got home till ten. And two weeks ago, she'd stayed late again, for what seemed a ludicrous reason: she personally had to inspect the canapés and petits fours ordered for a VIP reception to be held at her office the following day. Batches of each item were actually made up in advance, so they could receive her imprimatur before the final order was sanctioned. But then, if you were entertaining some of the highest paid toffs in the land, presumably even the garnish on a canapé or the glaze on a petit four was a matter of the utmost seriousness.

The thought of food made her hungry, so she mooched into her kitchen and raided the biscuit tin, yet even whilst guzzling ginger nuts her mind refused to shift from Amy. At twenty-four weeks, the baby was now technically viable – an important milestone, they'd assumed – yet Chloe's baby had died at a much later and safer stage, so obviously there was no certainty in anything. The thought of a similar tragedy happening to her daughter was all but unendurable.

She made a determined effort, though, to banish gory images of waxen infant corpses or post-partum haemorrhages, and to remind herself that Amy was remarkably fit, the baby growing well and that, in any case, there was far more risk with twins. Rather than resorting to comfort-food, she ought to get showered and dressed, then she could busy herself with the continuing search for Silas.

However, once sitting at her laptop, her mind veered off to another problem: Felix. Impulsively, she dialled his number, only to get his answer-phone – again. She suspected he was deliberately avoiding her after their recent argument. That argument – the first they had ever had – was entirely her own fault. Admittedly, he had rung at the worst possible time, when she'd just got back from Tolworth and was feeling tired and low, but that was no excuse for her negative response. His only crime had been to suggest that they escape the Royal Wedding and spend the day together in Brighton, but, instead of accepting with alacrity, she had snapped at him and said she hadn't time. And, when the poor man asked her why she was so suddenly so busy, she'd hesitated, stalled and finally said she couldn't tell him, which had upset him even more.

Well, serve her right if he had found another woman – someone decades younger, far less tense and tetchy, and not busy on a mission she was unable to divulge.

She jabbed the keyboard irritably, aware of the ironic fact that, although she'd pleaded busyness to Felix, she had completely lost her concentration and was unlikely to achieve anything today. In truth, she was growing weary of the task. She had tried several different sites now – not just Tracesmart, but Find-A-Person, People-Finder, Lost Amigos and Friends

Reunited – yet seemed no further forward, despite the fact she'd decided, quite some time ago, to limit her search to London, since expanding it countrywide, or worldwide, was just too overwhelming. Yet, even with that restriction, she continually drew blanks. In light of which, she must be mad, if not masochistic, to have opted for the unlikely hope of finding shadowy Silas over the certainty of a happy day with alluringly substantial Felix. And with the usual Friday class cancelled on account of the Bank Holiday, and Kate away in France, there was little chance of any other distraction.

All at once, her mobile shrilled. *Felix*, she prayed, ready to apologize and say she could leave immediately for Brighton – or even John O'Groats. But instead of Felix's throaty tones, Ruby's shrill and eager voice vibrated in her ear.

'I know it's the crack of dawn, Maria, but you did say you're an early riser, and I've just had a great idea – why don't you come down to Tolworth and watch the Royal Wedding with me on television?'

Maria mumbled something about having other plans. Having listened to Ruby yesterday, at length – a monologue centred on Graham: his job, his hobbies, his fear of water, his passion for Man United, his preference for bitter over lager – her patience was wearing thin. In fact, if she watched the wedding with so garrulous a woman, she doubted if she would hear much of the commentary. It would be less Kate and Will than Graham, Graham, Graham.

'Oh, what a shame! You see, I'd also planned to give you some good news – I've thought of a way we might track down your friend, Silas.'

Maria rallied instantly. 'Couldn't you tell me now?'

Ruby also seemed to brighten at the prospect of a longer conversation. 'Actually, I can't think why it didn't occur to me before. But sometimes these things just pop into my mind, when I'm miles away, doing something else. So, there I was, cleaning my teeth this morning, when I suddenly remembered a girl in the road called Barbara, who used to go out with the Johnsons' son. She was only eighteen at the time, but there was quite a thing between them, so she was often in the Johnsons' house. Well, she must have seen your Silas sometimes – that's obvious, don't you think? And it's just possible she knows his present whereabouts. And even if she doesn't, she'll definitely have the Johnsons' new address, so maybe she could ask them on your behalf.'

'Oh, Ruby, that's fantastic!' Maria was tempted to cancel her mythical plans and scoot down to Tolworth straightaway to seek out this miraculous Barbara. However, she certainly didn't want a wasted journey. 'Would she be in today?' she asked, warily.

'No, 'fraid not. I met her mother yesterday in Sainsbury's and she said the whole family were off to Sussex – you know, taking advantage of the four-day break. The lucky things own a little country cottage, although it beats me how they afford it when the husband's only a glorified clerk. She told me they're having a big street-party in the village, which is more than *our* street would ever think of doing ...'

While Ruby elaborated – again – on the unfriendliness of Tolworth, Maria tried to work out whether to let her make the preliminary enquiries, or to go down in person, as soon as Barbara was back. She opted for the latter, partly because it was so important, and partly to satisfy Ruby, who was still pressing for a date for the pair of them to meet.

Once she'd rung off – a feat in itself – she decided to start a new painting. She had recently ventured into oils, and needed much more practice in what, for her, was a challenging medium. And, anyway, there wasn't much point in pressing on with the Silas search until she had gleaned more information from Barbara and also tried to ascertain if this particular Silas was the one she actually sought.

There was no escaping Felix, though, since it was *he* who had given her the oil paints, insisting they were 'spares', despite the fact the tubes looked almost new. Their vivid colours – burnt umber, cobalt, alizarin crimson, viridian, French ultramarine – seemed to echo the flamboyant brilliance of his love-making. Miserably, she wondered whether she would ever go to bed with him again and, when her mobile rang, she was torn between distaste for a second dose of Ruby and a longing to hear her lover's voice. She reached for the phone with the utmost caution, ready to tell Ruby she was just dashing out of the house, but then saw Carole's name flashing up on the screen.

'Hi, Maria. I knew you'd be up early so I thought I'd ring for a chat before you have to set off for the abbey!'

'If only! Though, actually, I doubt my bladder would be up to it. The guests have to be in situ two or three hours before the service even starts.'

'You'll be going to see the sights, though, I presume?'

'Well, no, I hadn't planned to.'

'For heaven's sake, Maria, you're right on top of everything! I'd give my eye-teeth to soak up all the atmosphere in person, instead of having to watch it on the box.'

'I'm not that bothered, to be honest. Princess Diana's wedding was enough to last me a lifetime.'

'Oh, yes, remember that wonderful street-party we had, with Amy and Becky dressed as fairy-queens and Eddie in charge of the bar? And I'll never forget Hanna's cakes. She must have baked enough for the county!'

Maria felt a sudden pang for her home, her former life. In 1981, Hanna had been fit and compos mentis, and Amy just a child of nine, with few concerns about her father and no real pressures on her save to win a place in the netball team. 'Are they doing anything similar this time round?'

'Well, nothing on that scale, but there will be a celebration in the village. I've been cooking up a storm – Hanna would be proud of me! And as well as all the cakes, I've made cardboard crowns for the grandkids and a Prince William mask for Eddie, to hide his jowls and crow's feet!'

For a crazy moment, Maria considered travelling up for the day and being part of the whole jamboree. But Bank Holiday trains were bound to be infrequent and by the time she had hung around at Hexham for the second, slower train, and waited even longer for an unreliable bus that trundled round the side roads to her village twenty miles away, any celebration would be over. Besides, she needed to be here when Amy returned from the reception, in case she was still upset over Chloe.

'So when are we going to see you?' Carole asked, as if she had tuned in to her fantasy of a day-trip to Northumberland.

'Soon, I hope.'

'You've been saying that for ages, yet we never get a glimpse of you.'

'I know. It's just there's so much going on.'

'Oh, the lure of London life! I reckon we've lost you, Maria. You'll never want to come back to the sticks.'

'You're wrong. I miss it – miss you all. Give me another couple of weeks and I promise to make a date.'

'Good. I'll keep you to it. Meanwhile, don't worry about the cottage. I go round and check it regularly and everything's hunky-dory – no problems, inside or out.'

'You're an angel, Carole. Thanks.'

'Well, happy Royal Wedding! And, for goodness' sake, go and join the crowds in The Mall, then you can report back to your benighted country cousins.'

She had no intention of going anywhere – well, unless there was a sudden call from Felix. She must work on her painting – in fact, do it for Felix specifically, so that when she next saw him (*if* she next saw him), he'd be so impressed, he would immediately ditch any rival female angling for his attention.

Thoughts of such a woman – mistress, muse, nymphet, even another student in his class, or, worse, one of the voluptuous life models – resulted in such extremes of jealous fury, she exploded into action, sloshing paint on the canvas with frenzied, jabbing brushstrokes. Next, she seized a palette-knife and applied more paint impasto, swatting at the canvas, as if poking out her rival's eyes, or buffeting some fatuous female face. Never before had she worked so fast, or with such new, unwarranted confidence, and, as she layered crimson over cadmium orange, and violet over French ultramarine, she knew already this *would* be her best creation.

'Bye, Mum!' Amy followed Hugo out of the front door, frantically waving her hands about to try to dry her nail polish.

'Goodbye,' Maria called. 'I hope it all goes well.'

All at once, her daughter doubled back and joined her in the hall. 'You do understand, Mum, don't you? We'd love you to come with us, but I couldn't really expect Jonathan to—'

'Don't be silly – I wouldn't dream of coming. Why on earth should the poor fellow have to include his friends' ancient mothers?'

'You're *not* ancient and, anyway, I don't like leaving you alone on what's meant to be a special day.'

'Actually, I thought I'd be useful and do some housework for you, since Sumiah won't be coming in today.'

'Mum, that's absolutely forbidden! And she's coming on Tuesday, anyway. Besides, I want you to watch the wedding on our television. It's miles better than that tiny thing in your flat, and we should be back to join you, for some of it, at least. One good thing about a morning do is that we won't have to hang about too long.'

'Amy!' Hugo shouted, already a few paces down the street. 'We're going to be frightfully late.'

Maria noted his querulous tone. He had just returned from Dubai, having spent the Easter break attending a pre-trial briefing, and the strain of the court case was telling on him, obviously.

As the couple turned to wave goodbye, she blew them both a kiss, but once she had closed the door she felt distinctly spare. Her painting was completed, done in record time, but it had taken so much out of her in terms of energy and concentration she felt too drained to attempt another work, even the briefest sketch. In fact, she had changed her clothes and scrubbed her paint-stained fingers, as if preparing for some outing, yet the reality was a long day on her own.

Well, best follow her daughter's suggestion and watch the proceedings on the big wall-mounted TV in the sitting-room.

Kate's mother, Mrs Middleton, is just leaving the Goring Hotel. Doesn't she look supremely elegant in that beautifully tailored coat and matching dress? And her hat is the exact same shade as...

She fidgeted on the sofa. The plummy tones, the perfect frocks and purring cars roused only irritation. It wasn't yet 10.30 and she dreaded the prospect of sitting here all day, watching endless replays of cutesy little bridesmaids, frothing seas of lace and tulle, and daft designer hats.

And now the Princess Royal is alighting from her state car... Her floral outfit, in lilac and pale green, is brilliantly attuned to the English country-garden theme of the abbey's decoration ...

On an impulse, she sprang up from the sofa, ran upstairs to fetch her bag and jacket, then let herself out of the house. Carole was right – it *was* a tad pathetic to live so close to the abbey yet see nothing of this historic occasion, except second-hand, on screen.

Sutherland Street was deserted. She tried to imagine a street-party in full swing, but junketings and bun fights seemed unlikely in so exclusive and unsociable an area. And, as she trudged up Warwick Way and crossed into Rochester Row, there were still very few people in evidence and an air of almost stagnation hanging over the shuttered houses and mainly empty shops.

Yet only minutes later, as she turned into Great Smith Street – now a mere 200 yards from the abbey – she suddenly found her way completely blocked by a huge, seething crowd, marshalled by police. She craned her neck to try to see over the mass of serried heads what, if anything, was happening, but the only view was of backs, and backs of heads. Although she waited behind the mass of people for a good ten or fifteen minutes, there was no sign of any movement, so she decided to change her plan. Best take a different route and cut through the side streets to Buckingham Gate, then at least she would see the royals arrive at the palace once the service was over.

She retraced her steps along Great Peter Street, stopping at a stall to buy a Union Jack baseball cap – not exactly flattering headgear but a way of getting into party mood. She also bought a flag, since they were clearly *de rigueur* judging by the crowd she'd just seen, where they seemed to flutter from every hand.

Then, continuing on, she crossed Victoria Street, into Broadway, pleased at her unhampered progress and pausing only for two seconds when a girl in Tetley Tea rig, distributing samples of 'KATE-TEA', gave her a couple, free, which she pocketed for *her* Kate. However, at the junction of Broadway and Ermin Street, she was forced to halt once more, her way blocked this time by an even greater throng. The road had been closed off with two lines of metal barricades and huge numbers of police were patrolling the whole area. Again, she stood stationary behind a mass of jostling bodies; again her only view that of people's backs and assorted festive headgear. Her feet began to ache and someone's rucksack was digging into her shoulder but, suddenly, there was the sound of horses' hoofs, accompanied by rousing cheers from the crowd.

'What's going on?' she asked the woman beside her, who, despite her ample girth, was attired in a pink princess-dress and a gold cardboard crown, studded with fake gems.

'No idea,' the woman replied, no hint of warmth in her tone.

'It's the Household Cavalry,' the man with the rucksack remarked, his voice all but drowned by the still-enthusiastic cheers and the still-clattering horses' hoofs.

By standing right on tiptoe, she managed to see the very top of one of the rider's plumes – and tried to be grateful for small mercies.

A larger mercy ensued, however, because, once the cavalcade had passed, the police removed the barricades, freeing the crowd to move. She joined the eager scrum as it swarmed along Buckingham Gate in the direction of the palace; some younger folk streaking past her, running at full pelt. Opting for a slower pace, she tried to take in the scene, so she could report the details to Carole: flowered, beribboned hats; feather boas in red, white and blue; children in fancy dress; two near-naked teenagers, attired in skimpy, matching bras and briefs, made from Union Jacks.

Almost no one was on their own, she noticed – most in pairs or family groups, and not a soul had spoken to her, as yet. Back home, any crowd of people would naturally start conversing, or even strike up friendships, and certainly wouldn't regard each other as 'strangers' who had first to be introduced before they could exchange the briefest greeting.

Still, she was now within a stone's throw of the palace, which must be one of the best vantage points in London. So she approached the end of Buckingham Gate with definite new hope – until, all at once, she encountered another blockage. The movement forward had stopped, trapping her between two crowds: one in front and another one building up behind, the latter pressing her uncomfortably against the first. She was sweltering in her clammy rainproof jacket. A cool, showery day had been forecast so she had dressed appropriately but, in the centre of so large a mob, she would have done better to wear a sleeveless cotton top.

Time ticked slowly on as she stood hot and claustrophobic. The service would have started long ago, yet she had seen nothing of the slightest interest. And, when the royal procession finally arrived here, there would be no chance of spotting even the top of a top hat, or the jewels on a tiara. The view would be the same as now: a swarm and huddle of anonymous bodies, and the tallest branches of the trees. Perhaps all these people were incomers and tourists, because surely genuine Londoners would know a better route, rather than spend the morning stalled in three separate bottlenecks?

Maybe wiser to cut her losses and return to the house in time to see the procession as it wended its way down The Mall. At least, then, she could watch it in close-up and from the comfort of Amy's sitting-room.

But trying to squeeze her way out of the crush was easier in theory than in fact, and she received angry looks and muttered curses as she struggled to extricate herself from the huge, congested mass. Even when she'd succeeded, she had to duck and dive between new groups of hopefuls still streaming towards her in the direction of the palace. Should she warn them that all they faced was a large, frustrating blockage? No, best keep quiet and simply smile her apologies as she bumped into pushchairs or collided with wailing toddlers.

Once back in Victoria Street, the crowds had thinned considerably, apart from a few odd clusters of revellers, decidedly the worse for drink. All the pubs had put on a good show and were strung with bunting and draped with flags. The Greencoat Boy, in particular, was so bulbous with great bunches of balloons it looked as if it had changed its shape. She was tempted to pop in for a glass of wine, but, as a single woman in a crowded bar, she would feel even more alone. So she carried on towards home, only stopping at the sight of a poor homeless chap huddled in a doorway on Vauxhall Bridge Road.

'God bless you,' he droned, as she gave him a handful of coins, then called after her in a husky croak: 'Which day is the Royal Wedding?'

'Today,' she said. 'It's happening now.'

'No.' He grimaced, displaying blackened teeth. 'I think it's next week. But God bless you anyway.'

Reflecting on his plight – dentist-less and homeless, with no access to the news – she wondered what, if anything, the Westminster Cathedral Protest had actually achieved. It was now six weeks since she and scores of others had lain prostrate on the piazza pavement, but had the soup-runs been reinstated; were the sandwich shops permitted to give away their unsold food? She was guiltily aware that she should have joined the campaigners' Easter vigil, instead of spending Easter helping Amy part with huge amounts of money buying state-of-the-art baby gear. The cost of the pram alone would have kept a brace of pavement-sleepers in food and drink for a month.

Yet those four days with Amy on her own had been a precious treat, notwithstanding their worry over Hugo, forced to spend his rare time off work closeted with lawyers in Dubai, their main aim to ensure that everyone involved in the case was as well prepared as possible and could agree on a general strategy. Knowing how overwrought her daughter was about the whole alarming mess, she had deliberately put her first, despite Felix's enticing suggestions of various Easter outings. However, she could understand his annoyance, now that she had turned down Brighton as well.

Once back at the house, she went straight into the sitting-room. She should be just in time to view the succession of landaus clip-clopping down The Mall, escorted by the Household Cavalry and, with any luck, should see rather more than one horseman's fluttering plume.

But, no – again she was thwarted. It appeared she had missed the entire procession by a matter of mere minutes, and that nothing of particular note was due to happen until the royal kiss on the balcony, almost an hour from now. Slumping on the sofa, she shrugged off her heavy jacket, first removing the two teabags from the pocket. Those flimsy little objects, badly creased and flattened, seemed to symbolize her day. And all she could hear, in place of triumphant wedding marches or jubilant church bells, was sirens screaming down the street and police helicopters complaining overhead.

It was hard not to feel dejected as she resigned herself to fifty-seven minutes on the sofa before she caught a glimpse of the much-heralded wedding dress. It struck her that this whole occasion was little more than an attempt to swathe grim reality in a carapace of ostentatious pageantry. Kate was joining herself to a prince who must surely be affected by his sadly dysfunctional childhood, and to a family whose marital failure rate exceeded the national average. And, in the midst of a major recession, with widespread unemployment and savage welfare cuts, today's extravaganza had troubling echoes of Marie Antoinette.

'Oh, for God's sake, don't be so pompous!' she muttered to herself, still listening with half an ear to the television presenter. He was doing his valiant best to fill in time; burbling on about the royal reception currently in progress: the Pol Roger champagne; the wild mushroom-and-celeriac *chausson*; the eight-tier wedding cake and the second, McVitie's-biscuit cake, specially requested by the bridegroom, as one of his childhood favourites.

A sudden idea propelled her to her feet: why not make a replica of that second chocolate-and-biscuit cake, which happened to be Amy's favourite, too? And she would be following Hanna's example, because her mother had made an exact, although miniature, replica of Princess Diana's wedding cake, much to Amy's delight. If she went out right away, to purchase the ingredients, she could have it ready in time for Amy and Hugo's return, two or three hours from now.

Relieved to have a plan, she left the presenter talking to himself and headed off to Sainsbury's, pausing for a moment at the corner of the street to watch the sun struggle through the clouds and fling a golden finger across the drab grey pavement.

Perhaps the gloomy day would brighten, in all senses.

'Mum?'

'Oh, I'm glad you've rung, Amy darling. I was getting rather worried.'

'I'm sorry. The thing went on much longer than we thought.'

'It's not good for you to stand so long – the midwife told you to rest, remember. But thank heavens it's all over now, so you can take the weight off your feet.'

'I'm afraid it *isn't* over, Mum. Well, the champagne brunch is, of course, but we're all going on to Inn the Park.'

'To where?'

'It's a restaurant in St James's Park, with marvellous views from the rooftop terrace.'

Maria checked her watch: 4.30. 'But surely there's nothing more to see, is there?'

'Well, no, but—' Amy lowered her voice to a whisper '—I can't really get out of it. Jonathan's mad keen to go, which means I must show willing.'

'If *he* was twenty-four weeks pregnant,' Maria began, indignantly, 'he'd jolly well—'

'Mum, I'm frightfully sorry, but I have to ring off, OK?'

'When do you think you'll be back?'

'No telling. But, for goodness' sake, don't make supper. We've been guzzling the whole morning on caviar and quails' eggs and by the time we've eaten lunch or tea, or whatever we're having next, we'll be completely and utterly stuffed.'

'OK,' she said, deliberately not mentioning the cake. 'But promise me you'll try to sit down.'

'Yes, promise, Mum. Love you!'

Maria wandered into the dining-room and surveyed her 'Royal Wedding' table, which boasted not just a cake but a Union Jack tablecloth, with matching serviettes, a 'Kate-and-Will' fruit-pie, two coffee mugs printed with the slogan 'Thank you for the free day off' (hardly applicable in Amy's case), and a Royal Wedding sick-bag she'd hoped would make

Hugo laugh. The shopping and the cooking had taken time and trouble, but her efforts now seemed pointless. Even the cake itself was ill-advised, since her daughter wasn't meant to gorge on high-fat, high-sugar foods and, in any case, she and Hugo were off again tomorrow, and away for the whole weekend, so they would have no chance to eat it. Felix, she knew, would love so rich and chocolatey a confection, but Felix hadn't rung and maybe never would again. And as for demolishing it herself in a bid to drown her sorrows, that would be the height of greed and would make her feel worse still.

So, having cleared the table and put everything away, she wrapped the cake in several layers of foil, hardly caring that she had squashed her laborious piping: the initials 'W' and 'K' surmounting a royal crest. She was about to put the thing in the fridge when she had a sudden brainwave: why not take it to the homeless chap she had seen on Vauxhall Bridge Road? And maybe also make him a flask of tea, to keep him warm tonight. The sun might be shining still, but by dusk it always turned cold.

She found the man in the exact same spot, although half-asleep and befuddled. He accepted her offerings with an expression of mingled suspicion and disbelief, and no words beyond a few incoherent grunts. He might have shown more interest, of course, if she had given him a bottle of hooch, rather than distribute unwanted largesse.

She trudged back home, annoyed at her folly on several different counts: for failing to catch even a glimpse of the wedding; for wasting time on the cake; for trying to play Lady Bountiful to a vagrant who'd probably prefer to be left in peace and, most of all, for alienating Felix.

In Clarendon Street, her mobile shrilled and she stopped to answer it. It was bound to be Ruby, who had promised – threatened – to ring again but, hungry now for conversation, she would be glad to speak to anyone.

'Oh, Felix. Good heavens! It's *you*!'

'What do you mean, me? Were you expecting another of your lovers?'

She laughed, dizzy with relief to hear his jokey, non-judgemental tone. 'I'm so pleased you've phoned, because I owe you an apology.'

'What for?'

'Being grumpy and unreasonable. And horribly ungrateful when you suggested going to Brighton.'

'Well, I did miss you – terribly. In fact, once I'd got to Victoria, I was tempted to take a detour and drop in at your house, to see if you'd changed your mind.'

'Oh, I wish you had. I've been trying to ring you all day.'

'I'm sorry, darling. I deliberately left my mobile behind. There was a warning on the news, you see, that petty thieves and yobs might be on the make today. Anyway, I'm back now and why I phoned is to invite you somewhere else, so don't you dare refuse!'

'I shan't, I promise. So where are we off to this time?'

'Not far, don't worry. Remember I told you about my friend, Scott, the only one of our circle who's become ultra-fashionable? The lucky dog can charge a fortune for anything he does. Well, on May 12th he's having a private view at a trendy Mayfair gallery. From all I've heard, it should be rather splendiferous. Two of my other artist friends are coming down from Suffolk for it and I'd love you to join us, too, so I can show you off to everyone.'

Show her off! And she'd imagined he was furious ....

'And afterwards we can go back to my studio and work off all that lovely food in bed. It's less than two weeks from now, so I hope you won't be madly busy still.'

Busy? No way! If the newly created Duke and Duchess of Cambridge asked her to dinner on 12 May, she wouldn't have the slightest compunction in declining, due to an infinitely more pressing engagement. 'Felix,' she said, her smile so exultant she suspected he could feel it vibrating down the phone, 'I can't wait!'

Chapter 16

FELIX SQUEEZED HIS way through the crush towards a tall, balding man in jade-green cords and a natty blue bow-tie. 'William,' he said, 'meet Maria – a fantastically talented artist.'

She didn't contradict him. Indeed, she was beginning to believe him, now that he'd been broadcasting her talent half the evening. And, with him as her shepherd and chaperone, she felt remarkably at ease in an ambience that would have otherwise been intimidating.

'So what's your main field of work?' William asked, raising his voice above the buzz of conversation.

'Well, at present, I'm exploring colour more than anything – mainly abstract stuff, in oils.'

'And what do you think of Scott's work?'

'Oh, it's incredibly original! In fact, I plan to come back tomorrow and study it in much more depth. It's not easy to do justice to it with all these people milling around.'

'You're telling me! I keep getting side-tracked by friends from long ago, who involve me in long, nostalgic chats about the old days. Or some beautiful girl—' He smiled at a young waitress, in a black mini-skirt and a frilled white apron, approaching at that very moment '—insists on refilling my glass.'

As the bubbles fizzed into her own glass, Maria couldn't help reflecting that, for once, she was rivalling her daughter: swilling Moët & Chandon and surrounded by the glitterati in one of Mayfair's leading galleries. Of course, during the years she'd worked at various galleries in the north she had helped to run many private views, but those had been extremely modest affairs. No famous names, no art critics or other art-world luminaries, no pinstriped city types, complete with bulging wallets, and certainly not this extensive range of skin colours. Even in the eighties, she couldn't recall a single black or Asian ever turning up.

William gave a distracted wave, as yet another fan or friend spotted him from yards away and began semaphoring wildly. 'Oh, Lord!' he hissed to Maria. 'That woman over there is poison, pure and simple! I just have to give her the slip. D'you mind if we move into the other room?'

She glanced in Felix's direction and, seeing he was deep in conversation with a peculiar-looking gent, sporting pince-nez and a Charlie Chaplin moustache, she eagerly agreed. 'Yes, Scott's earlier works are mostly in that back room and I'd really love to see them.'

'OK, let's go – quick march!'

'Quick march' was hardly the term to describe their stop-start motion, as they tried to weave their slow way through the crowd. William was obviously well known, judging by the number of people who buttonholed him and, unfortunately, the 'poisonous' woman caught up with them and tugged rudely at his sleeve. Ignoring Maria, she then began haranguing him, the words 'neglect' and 'betrayal' featuring prominently.

Embarrassed, Maria backed away, all but colliding with one of the bevy of young waitresses, who was advancing towards her with a large silver platter of sushi. She stammered her apologies, relieved to see that the sushi were still intact.

'No harm done,' the girl said, offering her the plate. Each fishy morsel was a work of art in miniature, and exotic orchid-heads had been decoratively arranged all round the edge of the plate – an idea she'd pass on to Amy for her next office party, perhaps.

As she was just finishing her mouthful, a glamorous but hard-faced female teetered up to her, unsteady on four-inch heels. 'Hello, I'm Eleanor Kingsley.'

As the woman went on to explain that she ran her own Bond Street gallery, Maria felt somewhat daunted, yet also glad of Eleanor's company, since William was still preoccupied. His persecutor had vanished but he was now being interrogated by an intense young lad, incongruously dressed in elegant black-velvet trousers, teamed with a lurid T-shirt, proclaiming I'M A GENIUS!

'How long have you known William?' Eleanor asked.

'About five minutes! I'm actually here with Felix Fullerton.'

'Really? I've always liked his work. And, of course, he and William were at the Hornsey together, weren't they? Not that I've had a chance to say hello to him – or to Scott, for that matter. But then it's hard to get anywhere near Scott, with all those fans paying homage! He's being lionized tonight – and rightly so.'

Maria peered across to where the star of the evening was standing amidst a circle of admirers, his head thrown back in a guffaw, his iron-grey hair dishevelled, his shabby jeans looking out of place amidst the snazzy suits. It must be a mark of success, she mused, not to have to bother to dress up. She herself had gone to quite some trouble, having found a rather special dress on the sale rack in a charity shop: a silky, swirly number in a purple-and-scarlet print.

As Eleanor moved away to talk to someone else, Maria continued to watch Scott, who seemed enviably relaxed, in marked contrast to the artists at the Northumbrian private views. Some of them, she recalled, were barely known outside the local area, and often desperately nervous, wondering if anyone would actually show up, let alone buy a painting. And the only food and drink on offer had been paper cups of bargain-bin wine and a few plastic bowls of crisps and nuts. And, of course, *she* was the one responsible for buying the refreshments, sending out the invitations, cleaning the glass on the paintings and vacuuming the whole place before the show. And, on the night itself, she was expected to act as waitress (whilst trying to stop the artist getting drunk) and also as clearer-up, next morning.

'Sorry to have left you on your own.' William returned to her side, at last. 'That poor young sucker,' he added in a whisper, 'is due to finish art school this July and was asking me the secret of success. Damned hard work, I told him, for at least twenty or thirty years.'

'Lord, you've probably put him off for life!'

'That's no bad thing, Maria. There are far too many of us artists as it is.'

Us artists – she relished the phrase, and the thrill of being bracketed with a painter as eminent as William. All thanks to Felix, of course, whose passionate kiss was still jolting through her body. He had met her outside Green Park tube and, regardless of the rush-hour crowds, had embraced her with such ardour, the kiss deserved a plinth and a glass case. But she was happy to be with William, just at present, because Felix needed time on his own, to chat up agents, talk to potential buyers, and also put out a few feelers, in the hope of being taken on by a new gallery. He'd been telling her, just yesterday, about the deficiencies of his own gallery, which had apparently hung his last show badly and done pitifully little in the way of any publicity. But, with her clinging to his side, he'd had no chance to network yet.

After a few more interruptions, she and William finally succeeded in reaching the back room which, mercifully, was far less crowded and allowed them to study the pictures properly.

'I have to say,' William remarked, as they moved slowly from painting to painting, 'I admire Scott's versatility. If you compare these works with the later ones, you'd hardly know they were done by the same artist.'

'And this is quite a contrast to the rest,' Maria observed, stopping in front of a large oil-and-acrylic entitled 'Near Horizon', which seemed to dominate the room. 'It's much bigger, for one thing, and he appears to be using colour in a very different way. It's more lucent, don't you think? More austere and restrained? In fact, it makes me realize how much I have to learn.' Stepping closer, she scrutinized the brushstrokes, trying to take in every detail. 'Those gradations in shade are so subtle – from steel-grey, to pewter, to oyster-shell, then fading away into a sort of ghostly pallor.'

Before William could reply, two matronly women joined them in front of the painting and began discussing it in ringing tones.

'He's such an intuitive artist, don't you think? Deeply spiritual, I'd say.'

'Yes, though I reckon he's a tortured soul, judging by his themes of vulnerability and isolation. There's certainly a strong religious dimension to his work, so perhaps he's seeking comfort from a higher sphere. In fact, in almost all his paintings, he seems to be exploring man's relationship with God.'

Once the pair had moved away, William nudged her in the ribs. 'If Scott heard that, he'd die laughing! He hasn't a religious bone in his body and as for being a tortured soul, nothing could be further from the truth. If he seeks comfort anywhere, it's down the pub, with a double scotch!'

'Maria!' Felix exclaimed, suddenly appearing in the doorway. 'I've been looking for you everywhere. And if you're planning to run off with William, I'm afraid you've left it too late! I've come to spirit you away.'

'What, leaving so soon?' William reproved. 'The party's hardly begun. And, anyway, aren't we all going on for dinner somewhere afterwards?'

'Sorry – can't do. Maria and I have another engagement.'

'Really? Where are you off to?'

Felix reached for her hand and moved his thumb in slow, suggestive circles, round and round her palm. To bed, he didn't say.

'Let's pretend you're still a virgin, darling. I want you to be just eighteen and strictly Roman Catholic and I'm your priest who's been sent from Rome to counsel you.'

She froze.

'Well, my child,' he said, adopting a patrician tone and switching his expression to one of lugubrious solemnity, 'having given the matter much deliberation, this is my conclusion, as your spiritual adviser. For many years, you've said your prayers and regularly attended Holy Mass, but now it's time for a radical change of direction. And, as a man of the flesh, as well as of the cloth, I feel I'm eminently suited to initiate that change and teach you the pleasure of carnal delights in place of heavenly ones.'

As he moved his mouth to her breast, she pushed him off; sat up.

'What's wrong?' he asked. 'I thought you enjoyed our fantasies.'

'Not that one.'

'Why not? It really turns me on to think about you then – so naïve and inexperienced and probably rather submissive.'

She hugged her knees, wincing at the adjectives: exactly how she had been with Silas. 'Felix, there's something I haven't told you ...'

'What, you *really* had an affair with a priest?'

'No,' she said, aware she had gone too far already, in light of her decision to conceal her murky past. Yet was that decision right? Felix was her lover, after all, so shouldn't she allow him access to her mind, as well as to her body?

'I ... I had an affair with an older man I met just after leaving art school.' Suddenly, it was all pouring out: the pregnancy, the baby, the break-up of her first and only relationship.

'Oh my God – you poor love! That must have been incredibly tough. But why on earth didn't you tell me before?'

She shrugged. 'Oh, lots of reasons,' Shame, embarrassment, concern about his reaction. 'It wasn't a very happy time, so I suppose I prefer to keep it quiet. Don't forget, illegitimacy carried a real stigma then. And a priest *was* involved, in fact, not to initiate me into carnal delights, but to urge me to do penance for what he saw as a serious sin.'

'Sex isn't a sin,' Felix exclaimed, indignantly. 'It makes me mad the way priests and Popes get everything so wrong.'

'The Church does have a point, though, in only allowing sex within marriage. If you look at the statistics, they all tend to show that children with two parents do far better than those of lone mothers. And I know Amy suffered from not having her father around. Which is why,' she explained, 'I've been so busy recently, trying to track Silas down. I'm getting closer, at last, thank heavens, and I reckon it's only a matter of days now before I lay eyes on him.' Last week, she had gone to Tolworth again, to meet Ruby's neighbour, Barbara, and actually been given an address, obtained by Barbara from her former boyfriend, Ian Johnson. Unfortunately, neither Ian nor his parents had heard any word of Silas since they had sold their Tolworth house and ejected him as lodger, so in the ensuing eighteen months he might have moved on somewhere else.

'You intend to *meet* him, Maria?' Felix exclaimed, cutting across her thoughts. 'What's the point, for Christ's sake? If he didn't want to be lumbered then, why the hell should he have changed his mind?' He sprang off the bed and began pacing round the studio, stark naked still, but with no trace of an erection now.

Startled by his vehemence, she wondered what had prompted it. Could he possibly be jealous, or simply annoyed by further demands on her time? 'I don't have any choice. I promised Amy I'd try to persuade her father to take an interest in her, and nothing would make me break that promise.'

'I'm sorry but I just can't see it working. Frankly, I'd let the bastard rot!'

She bit back a furious retort. How dare he be so negative, or judge Silas so harshly without ever having met him? 'I shouldn't have told you – that's obvious,' she said, in her frostiest tone.

'Yes, you should. I hate you having secrets from me. In fact, I can't understand why you had to hush it up at all.'

'Well, you *ought* to understand,' she countered, angrily. 'We're roughly the same age, so you can't have forgotten the social climate in the early seventies. OK, men often got away with fathering a bastard child, but it was completely different for women. Girls were banished from home for getting pregnant, or sacked from their jobs, or forced to give up their babies for adoption, however much they longed to keep them.'

'Not in the art world they weren't.' Felix turned to face her, his voice still querulous. 'Most artists see sex as a natural instinct and one very closely linked to creativity.'

'Bully for them,' she snapped. 'Unfortunately, I didn't come from that milieu. My mother regarded art as an insecure profession, and artists as unreliable and invariably self-indulgent.'

'Well, *that* was nice, I must say,' Felix jeered, 'when her own daughter trained as an artist.'

'So now you're attacking my mother, are you?'

'I'm not attacking anyone. I just want you to see sense.'

'Meaning you're the fount of wisdom and I'm seriously deluded?'

'Well, actually, I do think the way you live is somewhat misguided – your obsession with economy, for one thing, never splashing out and spoiling yourself. It's part of the whole Catholic thing – renunciation, self-denial ...'

'That's nonsense!' she retorted, incensed on her forebears' behalf: Theresia first orphaned, then penniless; Franz-Josef jobless after his imprisonment; widowed Hanna forced to scrimp and save. 'It's nothing to do with religion; it's to do with basic finances. My family never had money and I'm not exactly rolling in it myself. Just because you're loaded, you assume everyone else can splurge.'

'Come off it, Maria! You know nothing about my finances.'

'Well, judging by the treasures in this flat, you're not exactly short of a bob or two.'

'That's not the point. It's a question of attitude. Your Church taught you all these so-called virtues that happen to be negative.'

'I'm not so sure they *aren't* virtues – at least compared with nowadays, when everyone's fixated on conspicuous consumption. Yet people are actually more miserable – dissatisfied and envious, because, however rich they may be, there's always someone better off than them. Frankly, I'd rather live my own way than spend my time having to accumulate possessions and—'

'But why go to extremes? We don't have to be either out-and-out materialists or Gandhis in loincloths, begging for our daily crust. All I'm suggesting is that you throw off some of the baggage you seem to have inherited from a succession of frugal killjoys.'

Stung, she leapt to her feet. 'Look, if you're so dammed judgemental about me and my whole family, what am I even *doing* here?'

He said nothing more; just slumped down on the bed, his back towards her, while she stood, shaken, by the door. Despite her residual annoyance, it slowly began to register that he might, in fact, be right. Hadn't Kate said much the same, and even Amy criticized her penny-pinching?

As the silent minutes ticked on, her sense of shame increased; horrified that they were quarrelling at all, when normally their relationship was so blessedly harmonious. Worse, they were ruining the evening – an evening he'd wanted to make magical, purely for her sake. He had gone out of his way to boost and support her; introducing her to everyone; ensuring her glass was filled and that she never felt out of her element.

Tentatively, she approached the bed, touched his shoulder, coaxed him to turn round. 'Why are we arguing,' she whispered, lying back full-length again and drawing him towards her, 'when we have much better things to do?'

In place of an answer, he let his hand move slowly down her body, lingering over her breasts, caressing her belly and the inside of her thighs and, finally, running teasing fingers through her bush.

And, all at once, their argument was over.

'Oh, Felix, I just can't tell you how that felt. It was like I'd moved into some extraordinary realm where I'd left my normal self behind. I suppose it was such a relief to have told you about Silas and not to have to hide things any more, it seemed to ... sort of release me. I'm sorry, I'm not explaining it properly, but I don't seem to have the words.'

'You don't need words.' He smoothed her hair where it lay tangled on the pillow. 'I felt it myself. It was our best time ever, I'd say.'

She closed her eyes, wanting to concentrate on the sensations before they slipped away: the slight stinging of her face from the graze of Felix's chin, his touch still sparking her body, the warm wetness between her legs, and that sense of having moved beyond her conscious self, into a state of raw, uncomplicated being, where nothing else existed except her body under his. Even the smells seemed part of the experience: turpentine and varnish mingling with the last vestiges of the musky perfume she'd bought at Tachbrook Market for tonight. Her senses were so heightened that, when a car zoomed down the street, the sound shuddered through her bloodstream, and the stumbling notes of an out-of-tune piano, leaking through an open window, seemed to transmute into a lovers' serenade.

Felix, never good at silence, suddenly knelt up on the bed, but she kept her eyes tight shut and refused to be distracted. Nothing must dissipate this rare and blissful state. Somehow, she had managed to transcend the pettifogging sphere of everyday concerns; leave behind the nervy trivialities that often clogged her mind.

'Now I have something to tell *you*,' he announced, speaking with such eagerness she had no choice but to surface. 'Not a confession, Maria, my sweet, but a possible plan for the future.'

'What, you intend to become Pope and change all the Church's rules?'

'Well, yes, that, too – all in good time. But, first, I'm thinking of moving to Cornwall.'

The words jolted her into a state of total alertness; aghast at the thought of him being hundreds of miles away.

'It's only a vague idea, as yet, but I do need a bigger studio and London's fiendishly expensive. And I have this really good mate who lives there – a guy called George I first met when we were at the Hornsey together. He and a group of fellow artists left London ages ago and bought an abandoned farmhouse, with all its adjoining outbuildings. It needed a hell of a lot of work before any of it was habitable, but they were all young and fit and keen then, and eventually they turned it into a flourishing concern. Two families with children now live in the farmhouse, but George bagged the big old barn for himself and shared it for years with his partner, Tony. Sadly, Tony died two years ago, but quite recently George linked up with another guy – a much younger one called Daniel. I met him last time I stayed there and I can tell you he's a really pretty boy!'

'Oh, I see, you stay with them?' She was struggling to show some interest whilst quietly dying inside.

'Yes, I must have been down at least half a dozen times and it's certainly an idyllic spot – a few miles north-west of Fowey, but much less touristy than Fowey itself, or somewhere like St Ives. For all their charm, those places become more commercial every year, whereas George chose somewhere a bit off the beaten track. Anyway, over time, he and the others have built up a real community of painters and sculptors and craftspeople, who all encourage and support each other and arrange joint shows and suchlike. And they have regular studio open-days, when the public can visit and view the work-in-progress. Well, he's been nagging me for ages to buy a place close to his and become part of the local scene. Oh, I know Cornwall's corny – if you'll forgive the pun – and definitely a cliché, but, cliché or no, the landscape *is* sensational and the light is quite unique. A decade or so ago, I used to do a lot of landscape painting and I feel this urge to return to it.'

She searched for something positive to say, knowing her voice would betray her and sound despondent and flat. 'I've never actually been to Cornwall,' was all she managed, at last.

'You've never been to Cornwall?' he exclaimed. 'Well, that's a lack we must remedy at once. I'm going there in two or three weeks' time, just to have a recce and a brief look at properties. I was going to ask you to come with me, except I knew, if we went together, I wouldn't view a thing except your gorgeous body. Never mind – I'll gladly trade the most fantastic bargain on the books of every estate agent in Cornwall for the sake of having you in bed with me a whole night! I hate the way you always rush off home, and get up and dress, each time. In fact, it'll be four or five whole nights, because I intend staying several days.'

As yet, they had never spent a single night together, so she couldn't help delighting in the prospect. However, mixed with her elation was a harrowing awareness of what his long-term move would mean for her: a return to celibacy; no one to give her confidence and compliments; no enthusiastic fellow artist to encourage and appraise her work.

'If I do decide to join them, George offered me the converted pigsty, which happens to be free. I suspect that was a joke, though, and, anyway, I'm not wildly keen to live right on top of the others. But, as long as I find a place within a few miles, I'll be near enough to gain all the advantages, without the risk of losing my privacy. And, of course, there'll be much more chance in Cornwall of being taken on by a decent local gallery. The London art scene's becoming just too money-oriented; more in love with celebrity than talent. Recently, quite a few galleries have dropped the artists who've been with them for years, and now deal in minor doodles by bankable Big

Names. But things are slightly less venal in Cornwall and, anyway, I feel I can start again there, with a new style and real new energy.'

He appeared to be slipping away from her into an exhilarating venture that would totally exclude her, apart from the initial exploratory trip he'd just proposed. Was there any way she could change his mind, she wondered desperately, already dredging up a raft of reasons why he shouldn't, *mustn't* go. Whatever the lure of a new start, would that really compensate for losing all his London friends; giving up this enchanting London flat; having to stop tutoring his classes? And he would be exiled from the dizzy whirl of London's cultural life and its whole sense of innovation and excitement.

Slowly, she sat up, as another option occurred to her: couldn't he settle for *renting* a Cornish cottage, somewhere close to George, just for short breaks and holidays, rather than buy a permanent place and sever all links with London? Perhaps, when they were away together, she could implant that idea in his mind; work on him subtly but compellingly, whenever a chance arose. And, if she had to use her sexual powers to supplement her persuasive ones, well, what was wrong with that?

Chapter 17

MARIA DARTED INTO a doorway to shelter from the sudden shower; peering out at the graffitied walls, boarded-up shops and general air of desolation. Lewisham, she had blithely assumed, would be a pleasant, leafy sort of place, given its proximity to Greenwich and Blackheath, yet this particular part of it seemed unutterably bleak.

Once the worst of the rain had eased off, she ventured along the street, head down, trying to dodge the puddles. Despite the dismal late-May weather, she had worn her best clothes and shoes, since it seemed crucially important that Silas didn't judge her as an unfashionable old crone. Not that she could actually count on him being at this address. Since he was bound to be still single, with no ties, he could live as a nomad, if he chose, continually moving on.

Yet, refusing to lose hope, she made her way to the faceless block of flats and stood gazing up at the small, mean windows, ugly metal grilles and dingy concrete façade. This was worse than Tolworth, which at least had small front gardens and a variety of paint colours for windowsills and doors. Here, everything was uniformly grey, as if the building was simply too dejected to sport brightly coloured paintwork or even a few green plants.

The rain suddenly increased in force, so she dashed inside, shook off the worst of the wet, and rummaged for her handbag-mirror to ensure her lipstick hadn't smudged and that her hair was reasonably neat. Both lifts were out of order so, having found a door to the emergency stairs, she began toiling up to the seventh floor. The concrete steps were stained, the whole stairwell chill and desolate, and it seemed totally unjust that a man of Silas's talent should have to call this place his home, while *she* had the good fortune to be living in a large, ultra-stylish house. In fact, in light of Felix's comments about her obsession with economy, perhaps she *should* be less abstemious, since she was basically secure, with no heating, lighting or housing costs.

However, her awareness of inequalities had sharpened since she'd moved to London. In a small northern village, there weren't the flagrant contrasts between billionaire bankers and hapless down-and-outs. But at least, in just the last few days, the Westminster Cathedral Protest had achieved a minor victory: the ban on rough sleeping had been lifted and indoor soup-runs were now allowed.

Once she reached the seventh floor, her initial apprehension escalated to a sense of almost panic. Would Silas even recognize her and, if he did, might that prompt some furious reaction? Some people *did* bear grudges for a lifetime, so, for all she knew, he might slam the door in her face with a string of accusations. If only she didn't have to face him on her own, but although Amy, Felix, Ruby and Kate had all offered to accompany her, each of them, for different reasons, was likely to hinder rather than help her mission.

Nonetheless, it required a supreme effort on her part actually to ring the bell. As she heard it shrill inside, she was aware of her tight chest and sweaty palms. No one came. She rang again, sick at the thought that, after all the build-up, all the stress and fear and speculation, she might have to trail back home, with nothing achieved. Ruby had advised her to write to Silas in advance, but that seemed self-defeating. Warned, her quarry could well flee, or hide.

Of course, he might have just popped to the local shops, so perhaps she should calm down and simply wait for his return. But supposing he was out for longer, or had gone away on holiday? She could hardly camp out on his doorstep for a week, or two, or three. Indeed, a couple of people had already passed her in the corridor and glanced at her suspiciously and if she lingered here too long they might report her to Security. Perhaps her fears were right and he *had* moved on elsewhere, or even died some time ago, so if no one answered her third ring she decided to give up.

As she stood with her finger on the bell-push, the door was opened, suddenly, and she came face to face with Silas – the first time in over thirty-eight years. It was all she could do not to let her expression reflect her sense of shock. His former emphatically dark hair, falling thick and glossy to his shoulders, had always been his defining feature, making other men's hair seem meagre and anaemic in comparison. Yet now he was completely shiny-bald.

'What the hell do you think you're doing,' he barked, 'making such a racket? I was trying to take a nap and—' He broke off in mid-sentence, the angry grimace fading as a look of astonished recognition slowly dawned on his face. 'Maria!' he exclaimed, clinging to the door-frame as if her presence was so startling it had actually knocked him off-balance. 'Is it really you?'

She gave a nervous laugh. 'Yes, back from the dead!'

'I can't believe my eyes! Last night, I dreamt about you – which I haven't done in decades – and now you're here, standing on my doorstep. Is that just pure coincidence, or was the dream some sort of …?'

His voice tailed off again, although she was barely listening anyway, still focused on the appalling change in him: the jowly face and saggy skin disguising his once-distinctive cheekbones; the stooped, round-shouldered posture a total contrast to the old days, when he had always stood as tall and straight as a mast. And what had happened to his dress sense: those stylish clothes in offbeat or brilliant colours, which had allowed him to flaunt like a peacock amidst a flock of dreary sparrows? She had never seen him dressed so badly, in baggy tracksuit bottoms and a crumpled off-white sweatshirt.

Aware of her scrutiny, he shrank back in distrust. 'Are you sure I'm not still dreaming? I mean, it seems so odd that you should turn up after all this time. And, anyway, how on earth did you know where I lived?'

She explained her odyssey to Tolworth and subsequent meeting with Barbara, wondering all the while if he intended to invite her in – although she could understand his wariness. If *she* were shocked, how much greater the shock for him: a ghost from so long ago, materializing in the flesh. 'Well, aren't you going to ask me in?' she said, deciding she had better take the initiative.

Still he hesitated. 'The place is in an awful mess. I wish you'd warned me you were coming, then I could have tidied up a bit.'

'Silas,' she said, with a disarming smile, 'I've come to see *you*, not your flat.'

'But *why* have you come? What for? I still don't understand.'

No way could she explain the purpose of her visit whilst standing on his doorstep so, forced to dissemble, she mumbled something about wanting to get back in touch and catch up with his news. After all, her duty was to Amy, first and foremost.

Reluctantly, he ushered her in to a small and ill-lit sitting-room, bare in terms of furniture but with a tide of flotsam littering the floor: battered files, old newspapers, dirty cups, tomato-stained pizza boxes and empty McDonald's cartons. When she'd first met him, he couldn't so much as boil an egg and now, it appeared, he lived on takeaways. Had he ever learned to cook, she wondered, in the intervening years?

'Do sit down.' He gestured to the sole armchair; a dilapidated thing, covered in rough brown fabric.

Picking her way between the clutter, she felt distinctly over-dressed in this cramped and shabby room.

'Can I get you a cup of coffee? You do look rather wet.'

'No, honestly, I'm fine.' Having not seen him for close on forty years, she had no wish for him to disappear, even for five minutes.

He sat opposite, on the only other chair, a swivelling vinyl one that looked as if it had come from surplus office supplies.

'Well,' she said, knowing she must gain his trust before presenting him with unwelcome news, 'tell me what's been happening all these years. Are you still writing poetry?'

He gave a hollow laugh. 'I lost heart, Maria, years ago. My work's always been misunderstood. It was ahead of its time – that was the basic problem - and most critics were too blinkered to appreciate its worth.'

As a young girl in her twenties, she had accepted that as true; now it seemed an excuse for failure.

'Poetry's a mysterious process. It requires a gift, even a certain genius, I'd go so far as to say. But most run-of-the-mill people fail to recognize true genius, even if it's right in front of their nose.'

Over the years, the word genius had made her increasingly uneasy. She had come to realize that any form of art required years of work and a long, dedicated perfection of one's technique. But, way back in 1970, she too had believed in Silas as a genius. After all, he appeared to breathe the same rarefied air as those he read and talked about – Rimbaud, Nietzsche, Sartre, Ginsberg, Mailer, Burrows, Kerouac – and she had seen him as their equal, if not their superior.

'But the sole concerns of editors and publishers are money and commercial appeal, and both of those are the kiss of death for poetry. So, in the end, I just gave up the struggle.'

Her eyes strayed to the cluster of pill bottles ranged along the single bookshelf, and, hanging above it, last year's calendar. 'But how did you earn your living, keep the wolf from the door?'

'Well,' he said, defensively, 'I did meet another woman – soon after you walked out, in fact.'

'Walked out' was hardly an adequate description of what had actually occurred, but she let that go, more concerned with the woman in question. If Silas had fathered other children, that might have some important bearing on Amy's situation.

'A gorgeous girl called Camilla, who believed in my talent one hundred per cent and was more than happy to support me – pay the bills and so on. Her parents were loaded, so it wasn't any hardship. We lived in her snazzy flat in Primrose Hill for more than eleven years, but then it all broke up. She betrayed me, the cow, as people always do.'

Everything he was saying took her directly back to the past. Then, too, he would damn those very folk who had befriended and supported him – once their patience or their bounty had run out. At the time, she had failed to see that Silas had a pernicious habit of pushing people too far and demanding just too much. 'Did you have children?' she dared to ask, although unsure whether a 'yes' or a 'no' would bode better for Amy's purposes.

'God, no. Camilla didn't want them, thank Christ! *I* was her main project in life, which, of course, made it all the worse when she two-timed me.' He frowned in irritation, as raucous music from a neighbouring flat all but swamped his words. 'That cretin drives me insane! He's nothing better to do all day than play his ghetto-blaster. What I was *trying* to say—' He raised his voice above the din '—was that, after the bust-up with Camilla, I did have a stroke of luck. I succeeded in landing a job on a small poetry maga-zine, and, although they only paid me a pittance, I managed to survive. Not that it was easy. The editor was a pain and treated me like shit. And, after I'd slaved out my guts for him for a good five years or so, he sacked me, would you believe? It was totally his fault, of course, but *I* was the one who got the push.'

All at once, the music stopped and, with a histrionic sigh of relief, he resumed the story in his normal tone of voice. That, too, had changed, she noted; no longer exuberantly confident, but a cowed, complaining whine.

'I was on the dole for a while, but they made me take these sod-awful jobs. Well, demeaning work like that kills the poetic instinct stone-dead and, eventually, the stress took its toll and I went down with a series of illnesses. Then, to cap it all, I was diagnosed with bowel cancer, seven years ago.'

'Oh, Silas, I'm terribly sorry.' For all his pretentiousness and self-decep-tion, all his sponging off other people, she did feel genuine pity. No one could deny he looked a broken man. He had always been skinny, but now he was near-skeletal; his complexion porridge-grey, and dark circles etched beneath his eyes. His eyebrows alone seemed healthy – still dark and fiercely thick – but their very vigour only emphasized the pallor of his face.

'You've no idea how humiliating it was. I even had a colostomy-bag at one stage and, before that, chronic diarrhoea. It got to the point where I didn't dare go out, for fear of being caught short.'

Mixed with her compassion was a distinct feeling of revulsion. This was her one great love, for God's sake – her Byron, Shelley, Swinburne – but romance simply couldn't co-exist with diarrhoea and a colostomy-bag.

'I lost my hair, of course and, although it grew back, it was thinner and much greyer. And then, just as I dared hope I was in the clear, the cancer returned, last year. So I was back to the horrendous round of chemo and radiation, and it was much worse, second time around. Apart from anything else, not a single hair has regrown, as you can see.' He touched his bald pate with an expression of disgust. 'In fact, I'm surprised you recognized me. I did try a wig, but it was hot and itchy and I was terrified it might fall off.'

Byron in a slipping wig! Her sympathy was tainted with a sense of crushing disillusionment. She was even beginning to wonder if she had ever been in love at all, or just mired in self-deception, on a par with his. Or perhaps she'd simply mistaken excitement for love. There *had* been a definite thrill in being swept into a different world by an older man who scorned religion and convention and all her former values. Despite her years at art school in so-called swinging London, the sixties had passed her by entirely and she had remained devout, naïve and timid, until Silas exploded her into life.

Aware that he was still talking about his illness, she forced her mind back to the present. 'But how are you now?' she asked. 'What's the current prognosis?'

'Well, they say I'm in remission but ... but ...' As he fumbled for the words, an expression of fear suddenly flickered across his face. 'I mean, they could find another tumour any time. I just have to live from day to day.'

In the ensuing silence, the rain drummed against the window with callous mockery, as she sat, wrestling with her conscience. She could hardly expect a hopeless invalid to take an interest in a child he didn't even know existed. Yet she was spending tomorrow with Amy, for another of her antenatal check-ups, and how could she possibly admit that she hadn't so much as broached the subject when her daughter was expecting a full report?

As if in reproach, a baby started crying somewhere in the block, the noise barely muffled through what must be cardboard-thin walls. Again, she felt a surge of guilt that Silas should be living in such inadequate surroundings, but then it suddenly struck her that he had failed to ask how *she* was, or put a single question to her about her own life and circumstances. For all he knew, she too might have been diagnosed with cancer, or sacked from a job, or living in a dump. Did he even care? Had he ever cared about anyone except himself and his non-existent talent? She'd been so dazzled by his charisma at the start of their relationship, so grateful for a saviour and a life-raft, she had simply clung on to him blindly; ignoring his narcissism, his self-absorption, his belief that other people existed only for his benefit.

'Silas,' she said, abruptly, abandoning her plan of a gentle, tactful build-up to the subject of their child, 'there's something I need to tell you – something you won't like.'

His eyes narrowed in suspicion. Too bad. In fairness to Amy, she had to keep her promise. 'You can't have forgotten that when I "walked out", as you put it, I was pregnant with your child.'

'Yes—' His voice rose in anger '—a child you tried to trick me into having, although you knew damned well I didn't want kids.'

'That was wrong, I admit it, but please don't interrupt, because there are other things you *don't* know.' She was still scared of his reaction and only managed to continue by fixing her attention on Amy and her needs. 'You see, despite all your insistence, I didn't have an abortion. I went ahead and had the baby – a daughter who's now nearly thirty-nine.'

He stared at her a moment, clearly needing time to register her words. Then, as the unwelcome news hit home, he jumped to his feet, his face contorted with rage. 'I can't believe what I'm hearing – that you gave birth to my child, completely against my wishes or even knowledge! That's another betrayal – an act of base deception. No wonder I feel bitter. There's not a soul in the world I can trust. In fact, now I come to think of it, you've betrayed me twice over, because you made a solemn vow never to contact me again. Oh, I realize why you've come now – you're going to dun me for maintenance, backdated thirty-nine years. Well, I'm afraid you're in for a shock, woman! I don't *have* any cash, except my pension, which is barely enough to live on.'

'I don't want a penny from you,' she retorted, incensed by that demeaning 'woman'. 'My daughter happens to have a very good job and doesn't need your hand-outs. But, actually, I thought you might feel some shred of interest in her. You haven't even asked her name, yet she's flesh of your flesh and carrying your genes. In fact, that's the reason I'm here. She's expecting a baby herself and the hospital need to know your medical history. And before you interrupt or object, I want you to understand that I did my absolute best to keep my promise to you. Amy's almost middle-aged, for God's sake, and not once did I come near you, or breathe a single word about her existence. Yet, all her life, she's longed to know who her father is and to lay eyes on him at some stage. Can't you imagine how diffi-cult that was for me, always having to say no to her and deprive her of a father's love and interest? Well, now it's different, I'm afraid, because it's a matter of hereditable diseases that could threaten the health of her child.'

'Life itself is an inheritable disease,' he interjected, virulently, pacing round the tiny room like a lion enraged by the confines of its cage, 'as I've come to see it, anyway.'

'There's no need to be so bitter.'

'*You'd* be bitter, if you'd suffered as much as I have.'

'And how do you know I haven't? You're so eaten up with self-pity, it hasn't even occurred to you to find out how things have been for *me*. Surely, out of simple good manners, you should have asked me how I am.'

He had the grace to look shame-faced and slumped down in his chair again. 'Well,' he said, although grudgingly, 'how *are* you?'

'Well, things weren't too brilliant in the past, but I'm OK now and what matters at this moment is our daughter. I deliberately say "our", Silas, because she is your daughter, whether you acknowledge it or not.'

'A daughter I didn't want, as I've told you twice already.'

'Can't you be less self-centred and try to see things from her point of view? She's not to blame in all this and what she dearly wants is recognition from you and a chance to meet you, before it's too late.'

'It's already too late. I can't cope with any more problems in my life, let alone responsibilities.'

'No one's asking you to be responsible for anyone. Amy has a perfectly good husband and I shall be the baby's live-in nanny. All she wants from you is just a couple of meetings, so she can tell her child about—' The sentence stumbled to a halt. *Would* Amy actually want that, in these new, unfavourable circumstances? Might it not be wiser to allow her to preserve the image of a talented, handsome, decent sort of father, rather than a selfish wreck? She could always emphasize the cancer and persuade her daughter how impossible it was to make demands on a dying man. Yet part of her was maddened by Silas's sheer intransigence. Perhaps he was so resentful at not having published a single poem, or made any contribution to culture or society, he was blind to any further possibilities.

'Listen, Silas, there are other things in life besides poetry and fame. Many people settle for a quite different type of immortality, through their children and their grandchildren, by passing on their genes and leaving them with memories of who they were and how they lived. You can do that, too. You still have time to get to know your daughter *and* your grandchild, and create some new relationships.'

'I don't want relationships. I'm in no fit state to get to know anyone, let alone some shrieking brat. There are quite enough of those round here, all with useless parents who let them caterwaul all night. Nor do I have the slightest wish to be saddled with strangers who'll expect me to cough up. In fact, I'll have to ask you to leave, Maria – *now*. All this has been incredibly upsetting for me and I need time to rest and recover.'

'Fine!' she yelled, sarcastically, marching to the door. Typical of Silas to fail to see that this encounter had been 'incredibly upsetting' for her, as much as for him, and would be even more 'incredibly upsetting' for their frustrated and still fatherless daughter.

Chapter 18

SEEING AMY REAPPEAR at the door of the waiting-room, Maria jumped up from her seat and went to join her.

'Sorry, Mum, we're not done yet.' Amy gave a shrug of resignation. 'The midwife says my blood pressure's a bit high and my haemoglobin's too low. She needs to discuss the results with the doctor, but he's busy with another patient, so she told me to come back here and wait.'

'Oh, darling, I'm so sorry.'

'Don't worry, it's nothing serious – just a damned nuisance coming on top of everything else.'

Coming on top of *Silas*, Amy hadn't said, but Maria picked up the subtext, knowing how desolate her daughter was at the news of an outright rejection. 'I'm sure you're doing far too much,' she added, as they returned to their former seats, 'which alone might account for the blood pressure.'

'It's only slightly raised, Mum. The midwife thought—'

The sudden shrieks of a toddler cut across her words. Several other under-fives were waiting with their pregnant mothers, adding to the general hubbub. Every so often, a nurse would come to the door to summon a patient, but, for each one that left the room, another took her place and there was now barely a free seat.

'All the same,' Maria said, once the toddler's yells had subsided, 'I do think you ought to rest more. Isn't there any chance you could start your maternity leave earlier?'

'Mum, for goodness' sake, don't fuss! I've arranged to stay until 22 July and I can't just change my mind and let them down. Anyway, that gives me four whole weeks before I'm due, which should be quite enough rest. You don't seem to understand that I'm in the middle of really tricky negotiations for one of my top clients, which are likely to go on for at least six or seven weeks. And then there's my lead candidate for the CEO job in Hong Kong – he's sticking out for more share options *and* a bigger bonus. The chairman thinks he's simply being greedy, so I'm caught between the two of them.'

Maria also felt caught – between her desire to reduce the pressures on her daughter and her instinct that she shouldn't interfere. 'But suppose,' she ventured, warily, 'you stop work on the 22nd but take longer than three months off? I thought six months was more the norm, in fact, or even a whole year.'

'Not in this present economic climate, with people being sacked right, left and centre. I can't afford to be away too long or they might start thinking they can manage fine without me! And, anyway, I lose all my bonuses while I'm on maternity leave and that money will come in handy for the baby.'

Maria refrained from saying that the baby, however precious, didn't actually need the £500 cot Amy had ordered last week, or the cashmere babygros recently sent by Hugo's parents. Didn't Beatrice realize that cashmere was a devil to wash and that the child, not even born yet, already had a wardrobeful of clothes? An infant could thrive perfectly well wrapped in an old cardigan and put to sleep in a drawer. But, of course, Amy lived in a different world from most of the women here. She only had to look around and see their casual, comfy clothes to realize that Amy's elegant suit and sleek designer briefcase put her in a class apart.

'And even Hugo can't count on really well-paid work once the Olympic project's finished. I suspect the issue of his future is preying on his mind, along with the whole Dubai thing, of course. The legal wrangles seem to be dragging on forever, with constant emails back and forth, and sometimes phone calls in the middle of the night – which really isn't on. They seem to forget the time-difference, or perhaps they all work twenty-four/seven! I can't help being anxious, though, because at the start he was pretty certain his old firm would win, but now he's getting jittery, which really is unlike him. And when I try to probe, he's strangely reticent, as if he's hiding something.'

'But surely he'd be frank with *you*?'

'Well, he always has before, but I get this feeling he's somehow on the defensive.'

'When will he know the outcome?'

'God knows! They're forever changing their minds and, anyway, corruption's rife over there, so you're never quite certain how things will pan out in the end. And, when it *does* come to the trial, he's bound to be nervous, poor darling. He's never appeared in court before and he doesn't know the language. And translating from the Arabic often leads to misinterpretations, with all the regional variants and suchlike. The culture's entirely different from ours, so, what with nepotism and face-saving and the whole religious thing, it could be a bit of a minefield.'

'I'm terribly sorry, darling. It's the last thing you need at the moment. But, court case apart, do you think Hugo *misses* Dubai – maybe even wishes you'd never left?'

'Oh, no. I can't imagine bringing up a child there. And we'd both had enough of living in high-rise apartments, so we're much happier in our London house. And he actually prefers his current job, although he's no less busy, unfortunately. I mean, take today – he arranged to have the morning off, so he could come with me to this—'

'I hope I'm not a poor substitute?' Maria interrupted.

'Mum, of course not! In fact, he's much less patient than you are, so he'd probably be getting grumpy by now, having to wait so long. But, going back to Dubai, our three years there seemed exactly right and, businesswise, taught me a hell of a lot, but now we're in a new stage of our life. I just wish we could draw a line under the whole court case thing, instead of being involved in all this hassle. Wow, the baby's kicking like crazy! It's probably picking up my stress. Here – feel it, Mum.' Amy reached for her mother's hand and laid it across her stomach.

'Lord, it's going bananas! You'd better take some deep, slow breaths to calm the poor thing down.' She felt privileged to touch Amy's 'bump'; feel it heave and bulge; be in such intimate contact with her grandchild.

Amy laid her own hand over her mother's, as if bonding the three generations. 'You know, I can hardly bear to think of Chloe – how close she must have felt to Simon, long before he was born, and then to lose him at the end.'

'Try *not* to think of it, darling, if only for the baby's sake. You need to send it good, positive vibes and believe everything will be all right.'

'Yes, but even the surviving baby, Sam, looks so frighteningly small and he's all wired up to tubes and things.'

'Do you think you ought to have seen him? Neo-natal intensive care is enough to frighten any pregnant mum.'

'I had to, Mum, and anyway, she was really pleased to have me with her at the hospital, if only for an hour or two. Apart from anything else, it must be an awful strain for her, having to *live* there, more or less. Of course, she needs to be with Sam as much as possible, but even so—'

'Perhaps I could pop round to her house one morning before she leaves and see if I can help in any way – maybe cook a meal for Nicholas or something?'

'Yes, great idea! Forget the cooking, though. I think what she'd really like is someone older to talk to. Neither she nor Nicholas has any parents to hand and she's obviously quite shell-shocked at the moment. In fact, is there any chance you could make it fairly soon, Mum, because I feel she needs a boost right now – maybe even a shoulder to cry on?'

'Yes, no problem. I'll drop by tomorrow morning.'

'Great! I'll phone her and let her know.'

'Mrs Talbot?' The nurse had returned and was scanning the room for Amy.

'Want me to come with you?' Maria asked, as Amy rose to her feet.

'No, I'm fine. Read a magazine or something. You must be sick of waiting.'

Impossible, she thought, to read any magazine, with so many problems weighing on her mind – not just Amy's, but Chloe's and Hugo's, too. In fact, her former blithe assumption that her daughter had broken with the family tradition of suffering and sadness seemed less certain now, what with these new health concerns, the continuing worry over Dubai and, most of all, her bitter disappointment about being unable to meet her father.

And she herself was gutted by the fact that she had left her bag behind in Silas's flat. Fine to march out in fury – not quite so clever to leave her credit cards, her mobile and her free travel pass in his possibly vindictive hands. Only when she was halfway down the stairs had she stopped in horror and realized what she'd done, but although she'd instantly dashed back and rung his bell repeatedly, he had refused to open the door. All evening, she had tried to obtain his phone number, but had drawn a blank with Directory Enquiries, and then with Tracesmart, Barbara and even with Ian Johnson. Finally, in desperation, she'd rung Felix and poured out the story, but he'd been so incensed with Silas he'd threatened to break the rotter's door down – which was hardly any help.

Although she'd had to use Amy's landline for the calls, fortunately her daughter hadn't heard them. She had no desire to explain the loss of the bag, since it would only highlight the dissension between her and Silas, which she had deliberately played down, concentrating mainly on his illness as the reason for his negative response. Even so, her daughter had reacted badly and, once she had kissed her goodnight and trailed up to her flat, she'd sat staring through the darkened window, brooding on the losses: Amy's loss of a father; Chloe's loss of a child, and her own much smaller loss of what nevertheless seemed vital possessions.

She shifted in her seat, wishing she still believed in saints like Jude and

Anthony, the patron saints respectively of hopeless cases and of finding mislaid objects, who had helped her as a schoolgirl if she lost her purse or broke up with a friend. These days, however, her faith was gossamer-frail and a month ago she had actually missed Easter Sunday Mass – a heinous sin in Hanna's eyes. And, as for her sex with Felix, her mother would be deeply shocked to think that the daughter she had raised to be devout and chaste could ever have sunk so low.

A heavily pregnant African woman, just summoned by the nurse, was trying to squeeze past her in the row. Maria gave her a distracted smile before returning to thoughts of Felix, which only prompted yet more worry. She was due to accompany him to Cornwall in just a fortnight's time, yet how could she disappear for three whole nights without explaining to Amy and Hugo where she would be? On the other hand, it seemed unwise and tactless to mention another man when her daughter was still shaken by the Silas debacle.

She was so absorbed in the dilemma, she jumped when her daughter touched her on the arm.

'Sorry, I didn't realize you were back. How did you get on?'

'Well, they want me to take iron for the anaemia – just a basic supplement, they said, from somewhere like Superdrug.'

'And the blood pressure?' Maria prompted, aware of the risk of pre-eclampsia, more common in first pregnancies *and* in older mothers.

'It's not high enough to warrant medication, so the doctor said. They'll just check it more often and also do more frequent urine tests.'

'But surely he told you to rest?'

'Well, yes, he did. And he also recommended a few nice, gentle walks in the fresh air – you know, to get some exercise. In fact, it's such a glorious day, let's not have lunch inside. Why don't we buy some stuff from that snack bar outside the hospital and picnic in Brompton Cemetery?'

'Picnic *where*?'

Amy laughed. 'Don't worry – I haven't developed a death-wish! It's actually more like a park, big and quiet and peaceful, with lovely old trees and squirrels darting about.'

Maria glanced at her watch. 'But how do we get there? Don't you have to be back in the office by two?'

'Oh, it's only a short walk from here, so I'll be getting my fresh air and gentle exercise, and we can even rest while we sit and eat our sandwiches, so what better way to obey Dr Wainwright's orders!'

*

'I can't believe we're in London!' Maria exclaimed, as she surveyed the vista stretching far ahead: a variety of trees – beech, larch, horse chestnut, sycamore – spreading their welcome shade across the path. On either side, a tangled undergrowth of brambles, ferns, nettles and convolvulus all but choked the ancient gravestones. 'There's not a soul around, so it's like a real oasis. Most cemeteries are boringly neat, but this one seems to have gone its own sweet way. And look – butterflies!' She watched two meadow-browns flit across the cow-parsley, then slowly come to rest on the powdery white flower-heads.

'The only thing that spoils it is the planes.' Amy winced as yet another jet droned over. 'But if you tune those out ...'

Maria stopped to study a carving on one of the tombstones. 'You know, I do miss Mama an awful lot. And this place reminds me I haven't visited her grave for – let's see – nearly four months. I must go back to the cottage soon and sort out things up there. And I'll need to order a headstone. Obviously, it'll take a while to erect, but, once it's done, perhaps we could have a little ceremony – all go up north together and lay a wreath or a bouquet of gorgeous flowers.'

'Good idea – except knowing Grandma's views on extravagance, she'd probably prefer a bunch of dandelions!'

Maria's thoughts returned to Felix: his dislike of her own obsession with economy. Yet economy was built into her DNA, as well as into her mother's and her grandmother's. However, she deliberately dropped the subject, not wanting to seem critical of Amy's spendthrift ways, or how they contrasted with her ancestors' frugality.

They wandered on, arm in arm, until they spotted a bench sheltered from the sun that seemed ideal for their picnic. Maria unwrapped the sandwiches and spread her handkerchief – a large but flimsy one of Hanna's – across Amy's pristine skirt. They both ate in silence for a while, Amy nibbling at the food in a half-hearted sort of manner. Maria guessed that she was tired, not only from the anaemia but because the baby's lively movements probably disturbed her sleep at night.

'By the way, Mum,' Amy said, throwing a crust for the pigeons, which were now flocking round their feet, 'the midwife said I should be thinking about my birth-plan, but I'm confused by all the options. What did *you* do, when you had me?'

'There were no such things as birth-plans then. You just lay on your back and did what you were told!' She forbore to mention how completely unprepared she'd been for the extremes of pain and ensuing waves of panic that had rollercoastered through her body, along with the contractions, or with the added stress of being left alone for such long and frightening periods. Her mother had been banished and, since the hospital was under-staffed, her screams and writhings went largely unobserved. In the end, she had lost control entirely and become near-hysterical, until the strict, censorious matron shamed her into silence.

'To tell the truth, I rather envy you your choices, Amy – birthing-pools and birthing-balls and being allowed to walk around and even listen to music.' *And*, she didn't add, a loving, supportive husband permitted to be present and expected to play an active part throughout. 'And all those new developments in pain relief.'

'Yes, but it's still hard to make up your mind. I mean, I'm tempted to go for an epidural, but apparently they can slow your labour down, or give you a raging headache, or leave you with backache afterwards, and I certainly don't fancy any of that. Still—' She shrugged '—let's not discuss it now. I need a break from all the baby stuff.' She fed her last crust to a squirrel, tame enough to take it from her hand.

'Hey, remember that picnic Grandma brought for my Cambridge gradu-ation, when I'd already booked a restaurant? I don't think she ever forgave me for spurning her home-made pasties and cheese scones. But after your long journey, they were decidedly the worse for wear.'

'She was so excited, though. We were both just bursting with pride. No one we knew had ever got into Oxbridge, let alone won a scholarship. I don't know where you got the genes from.'

'Silas?' Amy suggested, reaching for an apple.

Maria didn't contradict her. Having always stressed Silas's intellectual gifts, she had no intention of denying them now. All at once, she rummaged in the carrier she was using as a handbag, removed a small brown envelope and withdrew from it a photograph – an old black-and-white one, criss-crossed with strips of yellowed Sellotape. 'Amy, there's something I want to show you, but I'm not sure if I should or not. I mean, it might upset you, which I'd hate.'

'What *is* it, for heaven's sake?'

Still Maria hesitated, before finally blurting out, 'The only photo of Silas I possess.'

'But you always said you didn't have any,' Amy said, indignantly.

'I know. I'm really sorry. But I didn't feel I could share it with you because I'd ... I'd ripped it into pieces – you know, after he and I went our separate ways. But I'd barely finished tearing it up when I realized how precious it was, so I rescued it from the waste-bin and stuck it up again.'

Maria was still holding it, face down, on her lap, but Amy leaned across and took it. As she stared in silence at the handsome profile, the long dark hair and blazingly black eyes, she suddenly burst into tears.

'Oh, darling, I'm so sorry. I should have kept it private. I've been agonizing for ages about what was best to do, but when you said last night that now you'd never know what your father even looked like, I decided—'

'It's OK, Mum,' Amy sobbed. 'It's just that he seems so ... so special and I can't bear the thought of never having met him.'

Maria's guilt was so great there was nothing she could say. It was *her* fault Amy had no father, *her* fault Silas had refused to see his daughter, and the fractured state of the photo seemed to symbolize the relationship itself.

'It's worse for you, though,' Amy said, wiping her eyes on the handkerchief. 'I don't know how I'd manage being pregnant without Hugo around to help – let alone through all the years to come of being parents – yet you did it on your own.'

'Oh, I didn't, Amy. Grandma was there from day one. And, considering what a strict Catholic she was, it's a wonder she didn't show me the door. You can't imagine just how shameful it was to have a baby out of wedlock. One girl I knew miscarried and her family said it was the best thing that could have happened.'

'OK, give Grandma her due but, whatever you say, a mother's not the same as a husband. And, anyway, to have to lose a man like this ...' Amy was still gazing at Silas's proud, alluring face. 'He looks every inch the poet.'

Again, Maria failed to correct her. Some untruths were merciful.

'Oh, I realize he was about to go abroad and couldn't cope with a marriage and child, but even so ...' Amy retrieved her apple, as yet uneaten. 'I just hope he didn't leave you penniless.'

'No,' Maria lied. She had often wondered, since that time, if she should have taken a much tougher line. After all, he expected her to go through with an abortion, so shouldn't he have tried a little harder to raise the wherewithal to pay for it? That cash would have helped her mother with the expense of an out-of-work daughter and of a newborn baby without a cot or pram to its name. But to take money under false pretences would have been a truly serious sin, resulting in an avalanche of guilt. Besides, she was so far from being tough back then, the question was purely academic.

'Can I keep the photo, Mum?'

'Yes, of course.' Extraordinary that she should feel a pang at parting with it, yet, in light of her visit to Lewisham, this tiny, mutilated snapshot seemed the only remaining evidence that she had once loved a handsome poet, once been muse and mistress to a man of genius.

'And we'd better make a move. It's half past one already, but if we walk on to the Old Brompton Road, I can take a taxi back to the office and drop you off first at home.'

'No, I'm coming with you, right to the door of your office. This morning's been quite stressful for you, so you need your mum to hold your hand, OK?'

'OK. And listen, Mum – thanks for everything, including having *had* me in the first place. That took courage, I bet.'

Yes, she thought, gigantic courage.

'Goodbye, darling. Try not to stay too late.'

With a final wave, Amy shut her office door, leaving Maria to retrace her steps, back along the corridor, hung with expensive modern art. Then she took the mirrored lift again, down to the spacious reception area. She had been here only once before and had felt much the same unease at being in so daunting a place, with its marble floor, steel-and-glass coffee table and weirdly angled ultra-modern chairs. And no wonder Amy had to dress so well, when even the receptionist resembled a fashion model. She slunk past the snooty female, trying to make herself invisible. No one old or shabby or down-at-heel should surely be admitted to MacKendrick, Lowe and Partners.

As she walked briskly back to the house, her mind was still preoccupied with the problem of her handbag. She desperately needed money yet couldn't withdraw it without a bank card. Even getting back from Lewisham had proved something of an ordeal. She'd had to plead with the ticket collector to let her through without her travel pass, and repeat the exercise at Charing Cross. In fact, that second time, she'd actually broken down in tears before the chap relented. Mercifully, she always kept a spare £10 note in her flat, so now she had a small reserve of cash, but after today's expenses that was already down to a mere £4.35. Should she return to Silas's flat this very minute and ring his bell so loud and long he'd be forced to open up from sheer annoyance? No, that would only alienate him more.

Once home, she walked miserably up to her flat, although the sight of her mini-studio did lift her spirits slightly. A battered junk-shop trolley now held her art supplies – most of them gifts from Felix. She had graded the brushes by size in a row of empty jam-jars and arranged the tubes of paint side by side in an old cigar-box, while her bottles of solvent and varnish stood on the shelf above. She relished the fact that the place now looked professional and even smelled the same as Felix's studio. Poor pregnant Amy found the smells abhorrent, but to her they were consoling.

She picked up the finest sable brush, recalling the exquisite sensations when he had touched its tip against her nipples, then stroked her bush with the bristles of a badger-brush. Tomorrow, they would be making love again, immediately after the class – Felix had an engagement in the later afternoon. But, however pushed for time he was, maybe they could spend five or ten minutes, at least, working out a way to retrieve her missing bag.

Unable to settle to any painting, she went downstairs again, having decided to do some ironing for her daughter. It was pathetic to think that a few nicely ironed blouses or tea towels could compensate for Amy's lack of a father; nonetheless, she felt the need to make some tiny gesture.

As she was setting up the ironing board, the phone extension in the kitchen rang. She was about to let it click through to the answerphone, as Amy and Hugo preferred, when, suddenly, she heard Silas's voice, leaving a garbled message.

Racing over, she snatched up the receiver. 'Silas, I'm *here*! Don't ring off, I beg you. I must collect my bag. I'm completely lost without it.'

'Calm down – your bag's quite safe. In fact, I'm glad you left it behind, because otherwise I wouldn't have found your phone number and I need to speak to you.'

'Well, shall I come and fetch it right away, then we can talk in person?'

'Look, forget the bag for a moment. What I've rung to say is that I'm sorry if I overreacted yesterday.'

Sorry? Could she be hearing right? Silas had never apologized for anything in all the years she had known him.

'But what you don't understand is that Wednesday was a truly dreadful day for me. In fact, you couldn't have chosen a worse time to come. You see, when I got up that morning, I discovered a lump in my groin and immediately assumed the worst.'

'Oh, Silas, how ghastly! But why on earth didn't you tell me?'

'Well, however crazy it may sound, I felt that if I spelled out my fears to you, I'd make them a reality. And one part of me was still clinging to the hope that it might not *be* a tumour. All the same, I worked myself into such a state, I finally took to my bed, which is why, when you rang my bell, I didn't answer straightaway. Anyway, this morning I saw my GP and he told me the lump was a hernia and therefore totally benign. It will have to be repaired, he said, but there's no urgency about the operation and – far more important – no sign of the cancer returning. I was so relieved, I was able to eat, the first time since Tuesday evening.'

'That's really good news, Silas. In fact, if I came round now, we could have a drink to celebrate.'

'No, I'm afraid I'm due for an eye test in an hour. Anyway, I haven't finished yet, so will you listen, please? While I was sitting over lunch just now, I got to thinking that maybe I'd been too harsh – not just yesterday, but when you were pregnant, all those years ago. And it struck me, all of a sudden, that you were the only person who ever really cared.'

What about Camilla, she wondered, the gorgeous girl who'd supported him and housed him, stuck it out for ten whole years? 'Well, yes, I did care, Silas, and I'm glad you haven't forgotten. But about my bag,' she persisted, as he clearly didn't realize how inconvenienced she was without it. 'Could I fetch it after your eye test?'

'Sorry – I'll be too tired. This last day and a half has been the most god-awful strain and I'm ready to collapse. But how about tomorrow lunchtime?'

Tomorrow lunchtime was her life class, not to mention the post-class sex, and Felix was annoyed enough with Silas as it was. But perhaps she could go to Lewisham first thing in the morning. No – she had offered to visit Chloe then and would hate to let her down.

'I'm no great shakes at cooking, but I could buy a pizza or something and we could discuss the whole issue of your daughter.'

'You mean you've changed your mind?' she asked, incredulous.

'Let's put it this way – I have what I hope is a good idea.'

'Can't you tell me now?' she pleaded, daring to feel a grain of hope.

'I'd rather explain it face to face, so why don't you come for lunch tomorrow, as I suggested in the first place? I'll expect you about half past twelve, OK?'

He hadn't lost his former dominance, she noted, yet if there was the slightest chance of Amy meeting her father before it was too late, she couldn't afford to argue about dates or days or times. So, putting aside all thoughts of life-drawing and love-making, she accepted with a resolute, 'OK!'

Chapter 19

'I'M SORRY, MARIA, I've been moaning on for hours and you're probably sick and tired of me. But at least you understand now why I feel such a hopeless failure. I mean, first I lose Simon and then I'm useless with Sam. Every time I go to the hospital and see his pathetic little body, I just can't stop crying – which is no help to him or anyone. The nurses like me to talk to him, so he gets to know my voice, but all I seem to do is bawl my eyes out.'

Edging closer on the immaculate dove-grey sofa, Maria reached for Chloe's hand – although tentatively, as they were still comparative strangers to each other. 'You mustn't be so hard on yourself. It's only natural to cry – any mother would. And, remember, you've been through a huge upheaval and suffered a terrible loss. Heaven knows, *I* was blubbing all the time, after Amy was born, and with far less reason than you.'

'Honestly, Maria?'

'Believe me, I was a complete and utter mess. But it does get better, I promise. This is the very worst time for you, Chloe, because you're not only grieving for Simon, you're bleeding and sore and scarred, and still reeling from the shock of all that's happened to your mind and body.'

A shock manifest in Chloe's whole appearance: her eyes puffy from fatigue, her expression one of defeat, and even her posture awkward, presumably reflecting the pain of the Caesarean. 'Many women in your position would simply have collapsed, yet here you are, up and dressed and functioning.'

'I'm not sure about the functioning.' Chloe managed a weak smile. 'You see, when I'm with Sam, I keep feeling I'm not coming up to scratch. I'm meant to continue expressing my milk, but I've come to detest using that damn breast pump. It's not just uncomfortable, it reminds me all the time that I can't feed Sam myself.'

'But you will eventually – once he's strong enough to go home. And,

WENDY PERRIAM

meanwhile, think of the good it's doing him, even with the pump.' She had no intention of admitting her own sense of failure when it came to breast-feeding: the sore, cracked, swollen nipples, the tears streaming down her face – and the baby's – as she wept in pain and frustration. And her mother's obvious embarrassment about so intimate a subject had prevented them discussing it at all.

'You need to give yourself a few pats on the back for coping so well in such a difficult situation. You see, it's important that you keep strong enough and well enough to make those daily visits. And don't worry if you cry. The crucial thing is that Sam knows you're there and can feel your touch.'

'Hell, I should be with him now!' Chloe glanced at the mantel-clock: an elaborate antique one, with two gilded shepherdesses supporting an ornate dial. 'I'd no idea how late it was.' She stood up slowly and stiffly, as if she had aged a decade during the last few weeks. 'I'm usually at the hospital by ten and it's almost quarter to eleven.'

'Right, off you go, but try not to rush and tear. And,' Maria added, getting up herself, 'if there's anything I can do, you only have to say. Amy reckons I'm a dab hand at housework and ironing, so I could run round the house with the Hoover while you're at the hospital, or iron Nicholas's shirts and stuff. Or, if you'd both like a few dinners cooked, I can rustle them up in Amy's kitchen, then come back later and put them in your freezer.'

'You're an angel, Maria, honestly, but there's no need for any of that. Nicholas belongs to Shirt-Express, so they take care of his laundry, and we've signed up to a catering service, which delivers home-cooked meals each day. And, as for housework, our cleaner comes in daily. In fact, she should be here any minute.'

Maria felt almost foolish for having imagined such a wealthy couple would actually iron shirts, scrub floors or toil over a hot stove. Yet she was well aware that, for all their money, Nicholas and Chloe still faced a raft of pressures unknown to her at their age – or indeed, at any age: the necessity to look super-gorgeous, super-slim and super-groomed, to pursue super-successful careers, and possess super-stylish homes. All that took its toll. Indeed, earlier in their conversation, Chloe had been fretting about the weight she had gained in pregnancy, and saying she couldn't imagine ever feeling fit enough to return to her demanding job, even when Sam was back from hospital and the full-time nanny ensconced.

'Thanks for everything, Maria, including those croissants and peaches. I know I wouldn't have bothered with breakfast if you hadn't actually put

164

them down in front of me! I'm just sorry I was in such a state when you first arrived.'

'Don't worry. Amy told me you were feeling low.'

'She's jolly lucky to have a live-in grandma,' Chloe observed, as they walked to the front door together. 'My mother's a top barrister and so high-powered she's almost too busy to see us, let alone stay and lend a hand. And Nicholas's poor mother has been or less inoperative since she had her stroke.'

'Well, I can pop in any time you like and when Sam's well enough maybe you'd let me take him out in his pram. After all, I need some practice with babies.'

'I'd love that, Maria. In fact, you can be his honorary grandma, if you like.'

Maria gave her a hug, feeling mingled apprehension and excitement at the prospect of a relationship with *two* babies. At twenty-eight weeks, Amy's child had an 85 per cent chance of surviving even it if were born today and, by its due date of 16 August, Sam would be over three months old and, with any luck, a strong and healthy child. Perhaps she could bring her grandchild to Chloe's in its carrycot and wheel both babies round Regent's Park. She had already noticed the elegant twin-pram parked, sadly, in the hall.

Once she had left the house and set out towards the tube, her mind returned to Simon's tragic death, and to the item on the news last week, claiming the UK was a far riskier place for childbirth than most other first-world countries. Even if her grandchild was delivered alive and well, she still worried about how Amy would cope with the pressures Chloe was facing: the shock of the birth itself, the problems around breast-feeding, the constant pull between home and work and – most daunting of all – the frightening sense of responsibility for a new and fragile life, a responsibility so fiercely compelling it was as if the umbilical cord had never been cut. Sometimes, as a young mother, she had felt overwhelmed by the sheer temerity of having brought another person into the world, when that person faced the all-too-human risks of illness, addiction, depravity and despair.

In fact, the visit to Chloe had been sobering altogether and, although she was more than willing to help – indeed, ached to lessen Chloe's grief, she just had to clear her mind before the all-important lunch with Silas. It was essential that it didn't prove as disastrous as her first visit, so she decided to take a walk until it was time to leave for Lewisham. Perhaps today's serene and sunny weather would dispel her gloom and even leave her calm and well prepared.

Silas removed the pizza from the microwave and placed it on the stained Formica worktop. 'But what you never understood, Maria, is why I didn't want kids.'

'Yes, I did.' She was standing against the wall, since there was barely room for the two of them in the cramped and gloomy kitchen. 'You valued your freedom and hated being tied down. And you had plans to go abroad and—'

'Yes, all that—' He gave an impatient wave of the oven-cloth '—but something else I never divulged, although it was the main reason, actually. You see, my own childhood was so wretched, I vowed when I was just sixteen never to inflict that level of misery on anybody else. Safer not to have children if you couldn't guarantee them a decent sort of life. And, to put it frankly, I wasn't sure I could ever give any such guarantee.'

She stared at him, astonished. This was a very different Silas, concerned about others rather than himself. 'So what happened in your childhood? Weren't your parents there?'

'Oh, they were there all right, but useless. My father was a drinker and my mother suffered appalling bouts of depression. And, being the only child, I bore the brunt of my father's rages and my mother's constant mood-swings. But I'd rather not go into it. It was such a painful time, what's the point of raking it all up again? All I'll say is that it changed the way I regarded family life, which for me became abhorrent.'

She was not only jolted by the revelation; she also began to wonder if *she* had been as self-absorbed as him, by failing ever to consider that his intransigent adult character might have been forged by a traumatic childhood. Yet, mingled with her sympathy was a worry about the genes he might pass on to Amy's child: alcoholism, mood-swings and depression.

'Anyway, the pizza's getting cold, so we'd better have our lunch.' He cut two large slices and placed them on mismatched plates, which he carried into the sitting-room. He appeared to have no table, so they had to eat on their laps, and the only drink on offer was plain tap-water. His poverty distressed her, especially the contrast with her own situation: living in a house with a well-stocked wine cellar and a table seating twelve. Yet at least he had made an effort in sprucing up the flat. All Wednesday's clutter had disappeared and he, too, looked distinctly smarter, in a clean white shirt and decent tailored trousers. She was still surprised, however, by how conventionally he dressed these days, compared with in the past.

When she came to think of it, though, she too had changed in that respect. Her natural inclination back then had been to go for drably muted clothes, to avoid attracting any attention to herself. Yet, here she was, in her sixties, wearing a multi-coloured velvet top and eye-catching earrings, set with glittery fake stones – both charity-shop purchases, and both due to Felix's influence. He encouraged her to dress with panache and actually liked her to stand out in a crowd – the very opposite of how she had been in her youth. Her mind leapfrogged to the life class – the tuition she was missing; the sense of camaraderie with her lively fellow students; the kick it gave her to imagine their astonishment were they to see her, afterwards, disporting naked in the tutor's bed.

'It's a good thing I like pizzas,' Silas remarked, with a wry smile. 'They're usually two-for-one, and a couple last me for at least six meals, so you could say they're my staple diet.'

'And this one's delicious,' she said, politely, forcing her attention back to the food. In fact, bought-in pizzas were hardly economical, compared with cooking from scratch – and hardly healthy, either. Just as well she had brought some fruit for dessert, since she doubted if he could afford his five-a-day, even cheap, from a market. She was also struck by his cultural poverty. Where were the books, the records, which, even without a permanent home, he had lugged from one friend's pad to the next? And where were the challenging views on movies, music, theatre, art? So far, they had talked of little save the deficiencies of the NHS and the dire state of the economy. Yet, however narrow his present outlook, she acknowledged the debt she owed him in having widened her horizons and hugely stretched her mind. Without him, she might never have been introduced to a whole wealth of new opinions, provocative philosophies, daring writers, way-out jazz.

'Well,' he said, leaning forward in his chair, having finished his pizza slice, 'I asked you here to tell you my idea, so maybe now's the time.'

She looked up, encouragingly, determined to respond as positively as possible to whatever he might say.

'To put it in a nutshell, I've been reconsidering this business of our daughter. I admit I overreacted and allowed the past to carry too much weight. I should have moved on from my childhood by now, considering how long ago it was.'

She smiled approvingly. The obdurate Silas of Wednesday had changed beyond recognition. And the fact he had used the phrase 'our daughter' was nothing short of a miracle. 'So would you be willing to meet her? Of course, we'd make it as easy as possible – both come *here*, so you wouldn't have to travel, and choose a day and time to suit you.'

'Well, I wouldn't want just one meeting.'

'Oh, Silas!' she exclaimed, incredulous yet jubilant. 'Are you actually saying you want to be part of her life?'

'No, that's not quite what I mean.' He looked up and met her gaze. His emphatically dark eyes seemed to have burned two holes in the ashes of his face. 'I want *you* to be part of *my* life.'

Confused, she failed to catch his drift. Perhaps she hadn't heard right, on account of the noise from the flat above. Someone had started hammering and the sound echoed through the ceiling.

'You see,' he said, raising his voice to compete with it, 'yesterday evening, I began thinking back to those years we spent together and I realized they were the happiest of my life.'

Happiest? He had seemed anything but happy at that time; rather impatient and belligerent – not to her, admittedly, but towards the world in general.

He reached out a hand towards her – an old man's hand, swollen and blue-veined. 'Oh, I know it all went wrong because of the baby, but that doesn't mean we couldn't start again. And things would be easier this time, because we wouldn't need to keep shifting from pillar to post, as we did when we were young. If you moved into my flat, at least we'd have a place to call our own. And we'd both have our pensions, of course, and ...'

She was rendered all but speechless by so preposterous a notion. He was indulging in total fantasy – further depressing proof of his total self-absorption. Clearly, he hadn't given the slightest consideration to *her* viewpoint in this plan; that she might already have a relationship, for instance, or already made her own plans for the future. And how could he fail to see that the prospect of giving up a stylish and substantial house to move into a tiny flat with a man not far off eighty and facing a likely death sentence wasn't wildly attractive?

His words were still washing over her, but she was so appalled she could barely concentrate, until another mention of 'our daughter' focused her attention.

'Obviously, she could come to visit, although I wouldn't want the baby staying too long. That may seem harsh, Maria, but I'm just no good with babies.'

I, I, I, I, I ... What about *her*, for God's sake and – more important – what about Amy herself? He was talking about the flesh of his flesh, yet without the slightest interest in any child or grandchild, beyond restricting their hours of access. It was all she could do not to march out in disgust – except she had done that already, on Wednesday, and with disastrous consequences. Instead, she said nothing whatsoever; just clenched her fists in an effort to control herself, and let him maunder on.

'Oh, I admit I've let myself go, but with you here, Maria, I'm pretty sure I'd buck up. Of course, it wouldn't be like the old days, with a whole circle of my arty friends inviting us to gigs and poetry-readings and all that sort of stuff, but you and I could go to films and plays together.'

And who would pay, she wondered? Two seats in a West End theatre could set you back well over £100, and even movies weren't cheap.

As the tide of fantasy finally petered out, there was a sudden awkward silence in the room, but he probably hadn't noticed that she hadn't made a single comment yet.

'So what do you think?' he asked, putting his plate on the floor so he could move across and hover by her chair.

All at once, an image of Felix flashed into her mind, his incredulous, indignant face as she relayed Silas's proposal: to swap her ardent artist-lover for a monstrously selfish, clapped-out invalid and spend her days taking him for check-ups at the hospital, or eye and hearing tests and chiropody appointments. And, suddenly, to her horror, she felt a great, explosive guffaw beginning to well up in her throat. Desperately, she fought it. It would be insulting and unkind to laugh – in fact, completely unforgivable – and, in any case, would wreck all chance of Amy ever meeting him. So, with a frantic effort, she tried to turn the laugher into a dramatic, belching cough.

'I'm sorry, Silas,' she snorted, clapping her paper napkin to her mouth, as she struggled to suppress the slightest hint of mirth. 'There's a piece of pizza stuck in my throat and I just have to spit it out.'

And, dashing into the kitchen, she did indeed spit into the sink, as her guffawing coughs choked slowly to a halt, to be replaced by further resentment. It was as if she needed to spit out the last two hours, along with her fury, her distaste and her total bafflement as to how on earth she could respond to this new, abhorrent life-plan, while still retaining Amy's hopes of a meeting with her father.

Chapter 20

WHILE SHE WAITED for a train in the dingy underground station, Maria reviewed the life class she'd just left. The male model had provided a real challenge but, unlike her days at art school, she hadn't averted her eyes from his penis but studied it with zeal; its indolent limpness, the interesting blue veins snaking along its length. She had also managed to capture the sharp angles of the model's figure and brooding hauteur of his face. Felix was impressed – she was pretty sure of that – although he had deliberately tempered his praises, as he always did these days, to prevent any of the students picking up the slightest hint of their affair.

That affair was on her mind because of tomorrow's trip to Cornwall and, as she stepped into the carriage, she was anxiously aware that tonight was her last chance to mention the plan to Amy. Her daughter, she feared, was unlikely to welcome the news of an entanglement with another man when she was still distressed about the delay in meeting Silas. The problem was, Silas was still holding out for a personal relationship with *her* before he would agree to one with Amy – although he had at least accepted that she couldn't move to Lewisham on account of her commitment to the baby. Amy, however, was ignorant of all the tricky bargaining involved, and she could hardly explain her deep distaste for any such relationship, without damning him in his daughter's eyes.

Yet, as she alighted at Oxford Circus and changed to the Victoria Line, she burned with indignation at his blithe assumption that she would want to share his bed – further proof of his narcissism and total lack of interest in her feelings and situation. Was he even capable of sex, at the age of seventy-six and after all his cancer treatment? According to Kate, even Viagra couldn't work a miracle.

Not that she had seen her friend of late, with so much on her mind, but she decided to pop in now, on the way back home, so they could catch up with each other's news and discuss the Silas dilemma.

However, Kate seemed flustered as she opened the front door and began pouring out her own woes. 'Maria, forgive me if I don't ask you in, but you've caught me at the worst possible time. I'm at my wits' end, phoning all my friends, in the hope one of them can help. You see, Janet was meant to be collecting the girls today and keeping them till seven, but she's just let me down, would you believe, right at the last minute. And I've booked a Botox appointment specifically for today, because it takes a good five days to work and I just have to look my best for Paul's big do next Wednesday. Of course, I should have gone this morning, but they were fully booked and only fitted me in at half past three, as a favour. And, anyway, even if I'd cancelled it, I'd still be in a fix, because I'd arranged to go straight on from the salon to visit my aunt in hospital. She's not far off the end, I reckon, so I just can't let her down. Besides, I'd promised to bring her a—'

'Don't change a thing,' Maria said, interrupting the cascading tide of words. '*I'll* get the girls from school, give them tea and stay till you get back.'

'No, I wouldn't dream of asking you. I know you're off to Cornwall at the crack of dawn tomorrow and you'll need to pack and—'

'Calm down, Kate, I can do that later on. I'm perfectly happy to hold the fort, if it's any help.'

'Of course it's a help – it's bloody wonderful! OK, Botox isn't my top priority, but I do feel us women should be willing to put in the work. In fact, I see it as almost a moral duty to make the best of ourselves.'

Maria could think of more compelling moral duties. In any case, she would much prefer to 'put in the work' on her art than on eradicating wrinkles.

'Thanks a million, Maria. Come on in and I'll give you the keys. Oh, and I'd better phone the school and tell them it's OK for you to collect the girls.'

Once she'd made the call, Kate dashed around, collecting up her jacket, bag and sunglasses whilst issuing instructions:

'You know where the school is, don't you? And there's masses of stuff in the fridge for tea. Actually, they like to choose their own food, but do make sure they change first. Polly's a messy eater and I don't want her uniform covered in ketchup. And, as for homework – I warn you, you may need to nag.'

'No problem, Kate, I'm good at nagging! But I'd better get off pretty sharp myself. It's quite a long walk to the school.'

'Oh, take a taxi, for heaven's sake.'

'No need, if I leave now.' She waved away the £20 note Kate was holding out, almost hearing Hanna whisper, 'What shocking extravagance! Walking's cheaper *and* good exercise.' Although Felix, of course, would espouse the opposite view: why not enjoy a bit of luxury for once?

She and Kate left the house together, her friend hailing a cab, as usual, while Maria set out in the direction of Belgrave Square, hoping she would have a chance, when Kate returned, to discuss both Silas and Cornwall. It had been stupid on her part to have left it so ridiculously late to breathe a word about Felix to her daughter. Yet there was something about having an affair at the age of sixty-six that seemed not only inappropriate but also slightly distasteful. Or was she simply echoing her mother's prudish views? Kate herself approved, thank God, claiming age should be no bar to anything, be it deep-sea diving, or adventurous sex.

Only when she was halfway to the school did Maria suddenly realize that she was still wearing her old painting-smock – a shapeless garment covered with charcoal dust. She was also perspiring in the sultry mid-June weather, and just hoped the girls would forgive her if she turned up grubby and sticky.

What she hadn't reckoned with, however, were the intimidating mothers – stylish, Sloaney types, who looked at her askance as she joined them outside the school. Presumably, any parent who sent their child to this exclusive institution was expected to dress accordingly, so she placed a wary distance between the smart set and her discreditably scruffy self. Did all these females resort to Botox, she wondered, feeling her usual unease about such procedures, and not just on account of the cost. It seemed a form of cheating to remove all signs of age and, frankly, she would rather look a normal sixty-six, even fraying at the edges, than an enhanced and phoney forty-six. But maybe Botox would become so common that she and her gauche friends in the north would be the only ones with quaint, old-fashioned frown-lines. On the other hand, when would Kate and her ilk decide to call a halt – at seventy, eighty, ninety? – or would they soldier on with youthifying treatments even as doddery centenarians?

As the pupils began streaming out from school, she kept a careful lookout for Clara and Polly, who would be expecting Janet to fetch them and might therefore fail to see her in the crowd.

'It's not fair!' Clara wailed, once Maria had explained the situation. 'Janet promised to take us to Queen's.'

'What's Queen's?'

'Oh, it's this really fantastic ice-rink, where lots of famous people go, like Kate Moss and Robbie Williams. And the lights change colour while you skate – pink and blue and green and....'

'And,' Polly added, equally enthused, 'Madonna's son, Rocco, held his sixth birthday party there. I wish *I'd* done that when I was six.'

'There's a bowling alley, too. And Janet said, if we had time, we could bowl as well as skate.'

'I'm sure she'll rearrange it for another day.'

'Can't *you* take us, instead?'

Maria hesitated. She didn't have enough money on her to pay for three entrance tickets to some celebrity venue and, in any case, she knew she would only worry that the girls might fall on the ice and do themselves an injury. 'No, not without your mother's permission.'

'Phone her!' Clara commanded.

'I can't at the moment. She's busy.' Probably being injected at this very moment with the miraculous toxin that would freeze her lively face into a mask. 'But, tell you what, we could do some cooking instead.'

'Cooking's boring.'

'Not if we made some sweets.' Maria ushered both girls along the south side of the square and into Belgrave Place. 'Chocolate fudge? Coconut ice?'

'Yes!' whooped Polly.

'No,' Clara repeated, stubbornly. 'I want to go to Queen's.'

'Maria, your top's all dirty,' Polly accused, mercifully changing the subject, much to Maria's relief.

'It's not dirt,' she explained, 'it's charcoal.'

'What's charcoal?'

'Stuff you draw with. I've just come back from my art class.'

'We had art today,' Clara interjected. 'And I'm the best in the class.'

'I'm the best in the *world*,' her sister trumped.

Their extraordinary confidence, Maria assumed, must be the result of years of training in self-esteem, a concept unknown in her own fifties child-hood. Devout Catholic girls were expected to examine their consciences twice daily, which made them far more aware of their faults and failings than of any intrinsic worth. Indeed, being top in anything could inculcate the sin of pride and thus was best foresworn – a fact she had better not relay to Felix, if she wanted to avoid his ire.

'Polly, wait at the lights,' she warned, grabbing the child's blue blazer to stop her dashing ahead.

'Mummy lets us cross on red.'

'I'm sure she doesn't.'

'*Does!*'

Maria suspected she would be ragged by the evening, but she consoled herself with thoughts of tomorrow: strolling across a Cornish beach with

Felix, spending whole days and nights with him, which she had never done before.

'Tell me more about school,' she urged, returning her attention to the girls as she shepherded them across the road.

'At break I played with Gemma. She's my best friend. We played "my operation". I was the doctor and I cut her tummy open.'

'Gosh, that sounds pretty serious.'

'It was.'

'And what did *you* do, Clara?'

'The usual stuff.' Clara reeled off a list of subjects, with a world-weary expression, concluding with judo and Latin. 'Only the clever ones do Latin,' she added. 'I'm top of the class in that, as well.'

'And *I* got three gold stars,' Polly claimed, refusing to be outdone. 'And a sticker saying "Well done". I have loads and loads of stickers and gold stars – not just from school, but for being good at the doctor's, and not crying at the dentist.'

Again, Maria reflected on her own childhood and the nuns' extreme reluctance to praise anyone or anything, for fear their charges might forget that, basically, they were sinners. She wondered which was worse: to eradicate any sense of self-worth in kids, or to regard not crying at the dentist as an act of heroic valour, and praise every childish doodle as a work of art on a par with Michelangelo's?

'I want a drink,' Polly demanded, as soon as they were back at the house. 'Please!'

'It's boring to say please.'

'It's *polite* to say please.'

'Polite's boring.'

'When I was a child, we weren't allowed to say anything was boring.'

'That's boring, too,' Polly giggled.

'Anyway, no drinks or food until you've changed out of your uniforms.'

'I'm so thirsty,' Clara claimed, histrionically, 'I'll *die* if I don't have a drink.'

'I don't think that's very likely.' Maria was determined to hold her ground, despite more lengthy arguments, and ushered the girls upstairs, to keep a watchful eye on the proceedings. Their bedrooms never failed to amaze her: their sheer luxury and size, and the vast range of toys and gadgets strewn around, often duplicating those in the playroom. She and Amy had shared a bedroom until the child was ten, when a partition was erected to divide the already small room in half. Yet those ten years had been precious and, often, when she had woken in the night, she would look across at her sleeping daughter, curled up in the adjacent bed, and feel blessed to be so close.

'Sit here,' Polly ordered, indicating a small armchair, upholstered to match the hangings on her own mini-but-magnificent four-poster. 'I want to show you my new swimsuits.'

The garments in question turned out to be bikinis – surely inappropriate for a six-and-a-half-year-old, Maria couldn't help but think. Would it be make-up at eight, Botox at eighteen?

'These are for my summer holiday. I forget the place we're going, but it begins with an M and it's somewhere very far away, so we have to go on a plane for hours and hours and hours.'

Malibu? Maria wondered. Mombasa? The Maldives? 'How long will you be gone?'

'Oh, weeks and weeks,' the child said, airily.

'I'll miss you.'

Polly slipped her hand in hers. 'Why don't you come with us?'

'I'm not sure your parents would like that.'

'I'll tell Mummy I want you to come.'

Maria smiled, anticipating her role as grandma when, she hoped, she would be loved and needed like this, at least for a few short years. 'Right, I'll leave you to get changed, Polly, and see if Clara's ready.'

The elder child was already in the kitchen and, within minutes, Polly raced down to join her – although more arguments ensued over the question of their tea.

'You said we could have sweets – fudge and coconut ice.'

'No, we'll make those *after* tea. First, you need something healthy. How about an omelette, or a ham and chicken salad?'

Both girls screwed up their faces in distaste.

'Well, shall I make some sandwiches?'

'OK,' Polly conceded, 'but I only like white bread. And I don't want lettuce in them, or tomatoes. Tomatoes are all slimy. And I don't like ham or chicken.'

'Right, we'll have "nothing" sandwiches.'

'What are they?' Polly asked.

'Two pieces of bread with nothing in between – no butter, no filling, no ham, no cheese, no chicken.'

'Yeah, great!' the child carolled, even managing a smile.

'I don't want sandwiches at all,' Clara mumbled. 'I want waffles with maple syrup.'

'Sorry – not allowed. Something healthy, I said.'

'"Nothing" sandwiches aren't healthy,' Clara pointed out, with maddening rationale.

'You're right. Which means we have only two choices: either an omelette, or proper sandwiches made with ham or egg or chicken. So which is it going to be?'

Half an hour later, they were actually sitting eating; Maria vowed that her grandchild would be treated with less leniency and granted far less choice. She had seen Kate submit, in the past, when the girls refused to go to bed ('Bedtime's rubbish'), or to eat the food she had cooked ('stinky elephant-poo'), and had even known her drive thirty miles to buy some special toy or treat, despite the fact that it would be broken or discarded before the week was out. Whatever Felix's views about indulgence, it could be as dangerous as repression when it came to children's upbringing.

'Mummy says you don't have a husband,' Polly remarked, pushing away her plate, having left half the sandwich and all the crusts.

'That's right.'

'Did he *die*?' Clara asked, with relish.

'No,' she said, quickly filling in the pause to prevent further awkward questions. 'Talking of husbands, who would you girls marry, if you could choose any man in the world?'

'There's no one good enough for me,' Clara replied, with a shrug.

'I don't want to marry at all,' Polly said. 'And I don't want any children.'

'Why not?'

'Because you have to cook for them and wash their clothes. And, anyway, I might have a boy and I don't like boys, only girls.'

'Finish your omelette,' Maria instructed, seeing Clara also push away her plate.

'No, I don't want to get fat.'

The child was stick-thin, but Maria held her peace, having no desire to embark on the vexed subject of children dieting.

'*You're* fat,' Polly observed, gazing fixedly at her breasts.

Yes, she thought – fat and old and messy. Would her grandchild also damn her as unfashionable and overweight? Still, whatever the questionable joys of looking after children, at least it provided the perfect distraction from the pressing problem of what to tell Amy tonight. And, anyway, true to her entrenched belief that all pleasure had to be earned, the harder she worked now, the more she would be permitted to enjoy the break tomorrow.

*

'So, what I suggest,' Kate concluded, stretching one arm across the sofa-back, 'is that you make out it's more an artistic thing – you know, you're hoping to derive inspiration from the landscape and the light? And don't forget what I said – to keep stressing Felix's role as tutor, rather than mention any close friendship, let alone anything sexual. But, listen, Maria, you're an adult, for heaven's sake, so why let your daughter dictate what you do or don't do in bed?'

'Yes, you're right. And, even if she does twig, she's hardly going to read the riot act.'

'How long do you plan on going, by the way?'

'Only five days. I wish we could have left today, but Friday's the life class and, anyway, Felix already had something fixed for this afternoon. And we can't stay the whole week because I need to be back well before next Sunday. Hugo's parents are coming up for Father's Day and I promised Amy I'd do the shopping and cooking. But never mind all that. I want to talk to you about Silas – he's even more of a problem than Felix. I mean, how do I convince him that sex is out of the question, without making him feel spurned?'

'Tell him you're going through the most appalling menopause.'

'I'm a bit past that, at sixty-six!'

'No, actually you're not. Paul's Aunt Eileen started the change at fifty and had these really awful hot flushes and night sweats. Now she's almost seventy, but they're still as bad as ever. Thank God for HRT – that's what *I* say! I was put on it last year and I don't intend to stop it till I'm safely in my coffin.'

Maria thought back to her own tedious sweats and flushes which, fortunately, had stopped of their own accord a good ten years ago. But, even had they continued, she would never have resorted to drugs to halt the natural course of ageing.

'Poor Eileen.' Kate gave a rueful smile. 'She told me she's so dry down below she can't bear her husband coming anywhere near her, so, you see, that would be the perfect line for Silas.'

'Kate, I'd be far too embarrassed to mention things like being dry.'

'Why, for heaven's sake, when he told you all about his bowels, in grue-some technicolour detail?'

Suddenly, they both began to laugh, rolling around on the sofa, until they were near-hysterical.

Kate sat up and wiped her eyes. 'Oh, I just wish I could be there, when you confess.'

'*Don't!* I'll never keep a straight face. But, look, I'd better be going – it's almost eight o'clock. Thanks a ton for everything.'

'It's you who deserve the thanks.' Kate ushered her to the door, calling out to the girls, who came galumphing down the stairs to see her off. 'But I won't hug you, if you don't mind. After Botox, you have to be careful not to touch the treated area.'

Maria refrained from comment. The only difference she could see after this £500 procedure was a marked redness on Kate's forehead. And alcohol was forbidden for twenty-four hours afterwards, so while *she* had made serious inroads into a bottle of Prosecco, her friend had toyed with a fruit juice. However, the wine had certainly made her more relaxed and, as she walked the short distance to her house, she was still giggling at the thought of her non-stop menopause. She no longer even felt anxious, but determined to do as Kate had urged and enjoy the next few days. As for Felix, well, *he* was hardly likely to complain about her new-found hedonism.

Despite the late hour, neither Amy nor Hugo was back from work, so she went up to her flat and, having extracted her suitcase from under the bed, started on the packing. She spent some time selecting her most sexy bra and pants, and a couple of exotic tops; only breaking off when her mobile rang. Felix, probably – he'd said he would phone tonight, to confirm the final arrangements.

But it turned out to be Carole, ringing from Northumberland – to report on the cottage, no doubt, or on any village gossip or scandal. 'Hello. How are you, love?'

'Never mind how *I* am. I'm afraid I have bad news.'

'Not Eddie?' Maria asked, worried by her serious tone.

'No, Eddie's indestructible! Look, I don't know how to tell you this – in fact, I feel almost responsible. I mean, it *is* my fault in a way, for not having checked on the cottage since last weekend.'

'Why? What's happened?' she asked, with a prickle of alarm.

'There's … there's been a break-in, Maria, just a few hours ago. They smashed a window and got in round the back. They've taken your Kenwood Chef, I'm sorry to say, and the radio, and your mother's clock, and that lovely silver photo frame, with the photo of your dad. The worst thing, though, is they've made a god-almighty mess – peed all over the place, would you believe, and even pooed, the filthy buggers!'

Maria leaned against the wall, feeling sick and shaky to think of her mother's treasures stolen, her home defiled. Never mind the Kenwood – it was pretty old, in any case – but the clock had been her parents' only wedding gift, and the framed photo of her husband had meant more to Hanna than all her other possessions put together.

'I was about to clear it up, but the police told me to leave everything exactly as it was.'

'Oh, they've been already?' she asked, still finding it near-impossible to digest this shocking news.

'Yes, I called them right away and they were there within the hour. They suspect it's the work of a group of yobs who've been up to no good, apparently. Another house was burgled recently, and the police also found empty beer cans in a hide-out near the river, and needles for injecting drugs. Anyway, they want you to come up as soon as possible, so they can check what else might be missing from the cottage. Obviously, I couldn't tell them, as I don't know what's kept where. But I said it shouldn't be a problem because I knew you were intending to visit very soon, and that I'd ring you right away. So shall I tell them you'll be coming up tomorrow?'

Maria slumped down on the bed, beside the half-packed case; the sexy knickers and lacy bras seeming to deride her now. 'Yes,' she said, in a flat, defeated voice. 'I'll catch the first train in the morning.'

Chapter 21

THE POLICE OFFICER snapped his notebook shut and leaned forward in his chair. 'Right, Miss Brown, I've noted all the details of the items you've reported missing, but what I need to do now is—'

'No, wait,' she said, aware of the catch in her voice. 'There's something I haven't mentioned.' Desolate about its loss, she hadn't found the courage, yet, to put it into words. 'We … we called it our Treasure Box. It wasn't actually valuable, although it might have seemed so to burglars, because it was carved wood, painted gold, and looked very old and precious.'

The policeman picked up his pen again. 'And what did it contain?'

'All my … father's stuff – everything we had left of him. His Gallantry medal, his letters home from Normandy, photographs, and other letters …' She paused, fighting for control. She had so little of her father as it was, and had planned to keep the box as a keepsake for her grandchildren. 'Do you think there's the slightest chance we might get it back?'

The officer shook his head. 'I wouldn't hold out much hope, Miss Brown.'

Did *he* have a father? she wondered: a man who had been there since his birth, watched him grow up, maybe still lived close by; a father so substantial and secure, his son wouldn't need mementoes to prove he had once existed?

'Do call me Maria,' she said, suddenly wanting to dispense with the formality, crawl over to his chair and simply curl up on his lap. He looked so solid and dependable; a burly man, too big for the small sitting-room, with a weather-beaten face, strong, capable hands, and kind, blue, crinkly eyes.

'Well, only if you call me Glynn.' He gave a friendly grin.

'OK,' she said, although Glynn seemed wrong for him; too effeminate for his broad shoulders and brawny arms, the bristly-dark moustache.

'I'll keep in touch, of course, and let you know if we find the culprits –

or, indeed, the missing items. But, before I go, Maria, I must advise you about security. There are several things you could have done that might have prevented this incident, and which I urge you to do right away, especially as you plan to return to London and leave the house empty again. I suggest you invest in a couple of timers, one for the lights and one for the radio, and programme them to switch on and off at set times – that will give the impression somebody's at home. And I'd recommend some good, strong window-locks. You could also fix up security lights outside the property. It's quite lonely round here, on the edge of the village, which makes the place more vulnerable.'

His words induced another surge of guilt. It was her own carelessness and lack of foresight that had resulted in this outrage. Her mother might be dead but she could well imagine her horror and distress at the thought of the cottage ransacked – even used as a public toilet – and, worse, of Kenneth's intimate letters now in some vandal's hands.

Glynn replaced the notebook in his pocket and rose to his feet, his bulk blocking out the light from the small window. 'If you need any further help, don't hesitate to phone. You'll come through to the central switchboard, but just ask for me – Glynn Cunningham. Here's my card, and also an information pack on home and personal safety, which I'd like you to study once I've gone. And I'll jot down the crime reference number, too.'

'Thank you,' she said, ushering him to the door, which she opened to the full force of the wind, a boisterous south-westerly that swept in a flurry of debris: broken-off twigs, stray wisps of grass and straw.

'Wild weather for June,' he observed, with a smile, before striding out to his car; head down against the gale.

Wild, maybe, but apt for Pentecost. Tomorrow's Whit Sunday Gospel was nudging somewhere in her consciousness – *and suddenly there came a sound from heaven, as of a mighty rushing wind* – and it struck her, all at once, that perhaps the break-in was a punishment. After all, she had planned to spend the second most important Feast of the Church naked in her lover's arms, instead of attending Holy Mass.

Arrant nonsense, Felix would say, but it was impossible for him to fathom the depth of her conditioning; the way her mind was steel-etched with Catholic teaching; her calendar still imprinted with all the Church's Feasts, its Holy Days of Obligation and Days of Special Prayer, its alternating periods of penitence and jubilation. Still less could he understand her belief that every action had a consequence, and thus loss of faith, or extra-marital sex, were bound to bring retribution.

But why torture herself with thoughts of sin and punishment, when she was already tired and shocked? What she needed was a cup of strong, sweet tea, to help her through the remainder of this long, exhausting day.

As she walked into the kitchen, she was aware of how small and shabby it looked compared with Amy and Hugo's. Indeed, since her return here, a few hours ago, she had felt caught between two worlds; no longer seeming to quite belong in either. And the whole cottage brought painful reminders of her mother's Alzheimer's. Here, in the kitchen, the cupboards still bore the brightly coloured pictures she had put up years ago, to help Hanna, in the earlier stages of her dementia, remember what was where: a carton of teabags, a jar of Maxwell House, a can of soup, a biscuit tin – all cut from magazines. And she had raided mail-order catalogues to find similar pictures for the bedroom: photos of cardigans and petticoats, stockings, knickers, shoes, which she had stuck on all the appropriate drawers. But, as Hanna slowly deteriorated, even the pictures meant nothing and, later still, she became so frail and befuddled she could no longer enter the kitchen at all, let alone go upstairs. Yet, deliberately, she hadn't removed the 'signposts', for fear it might appear that she wished to oust her mother from the cottage and snatch it for herself. Now, though, she began ripping them down, preferring to remember Hanna in her prime, rather than in her dotage.

As the front door slammed, she tossed the crumpled pictures into the bin and went out to greet Felix, who looked dishevelled from the wind.

'The car's fine now,' he reported, putting down his clutch of bags, so he could give her a quick hug. 'I checked the tyres in the local garage, filled it up with petrol and oil, and gave it a good run. And, while I was about it, I stocked up with more food to keep us going for the next few days. I know Carole did the basic shopping, but I thought I'd treat us to some goodies. Oh, and I bought you these.' He rummaged in one of the carriers and drew out a sheaf of flowers. 'I'm afraid they're only cheap carnations, but I couldn't find anything better.'

'They're gorgeous, Felix, but, honestly, there's no need for flowers. You've done so much already, I just don't know how to thank you. I mean, coming with me here and having to change the plans, right at the last minute, and running all these errands and—'

'It's nothing,' he said. 'Anyone would do it.'

Not Silas, she thought. *He* would have gone to Cornwall on his own; left her to cope, alone. 'Well, the least you deserve is a cup of tea. I've just put the kettle on.'

'Fine, but it'll have to be a quick one. I'm off to Hexham next and I must get there before the shops shut. I reckon I can fix that broken window, so long as I find a glazier who can cut the glass to shape.'

'The only glazier I know of,' she said, taking the flowers into the kitchen, while he followed with the shopping, 'is usually out doing emergency repairs, and certainly won't be open on Saturday afternoon. But, don't worry, it's all in hand. While you were out, I phoned this builder's merchant – someone I've used in the past, who knew my mother well – and he's promised, as a favour, to have the glass ready if I fetch it before five. He's only a couple of miles from Hexham, so while I'm there I'll pop along to Argos and get some security lights and time-switches and stuff – you know, to prevent another burglary.'

'*I'll* get those – I'm an expert on security. My studio's so well protected, it's not far off a fortress! And I can pick up the glass, as well, if you tell me where to go. That'll save you a journey and I know you're pretty tired.'

'Felix, you're a saint, but why *should* you do all this?'

He put his arms around her; held her so close she could smell the soap on his skin and feel his prickly jersey pressing into her face. 'Because I love you, Maria,' he whispered through her hair. 'I know I haven't told you before, but I suddenly feel now's the time.'

Stunned, she was reduced to silence; torn between elation and dismay. With so many emotions already churning in her mind, love seemed too complex to add to the curdled mix. In any case, the experience with Silas, so early in her life, had left her almost scared of love; its irrational, all-consuming nature, its close link with obsession. Yet Felix was still passionately embracing her, presumably expecting her to say 'I love you, too'. Flustered, she kissed him on the mouth to prevent the need for words. Then, tenderly but firmly, she withdrew from his embrace and busied herself with warming the teapot and getting out the cups.

The awkward silence continued for a moment; broken only by the whistling of the kettle and the soughing of the wind, outside.

'Well, the place certainly smells better now,' he said, at last, moving bathetically from high romance to the mundane.

'Yes,' she said, seizing on the change of subject. 'Carole did a heroic job, but shit-smells tend to linger. So this time I used a really strong disinfectant, which has almost done the trick.'

'Mm, now it smells of pine *and* poo!' he laughed.

Thank God he was so amenable and showed no sign of being hurt by her failure to respond. Although she couldn't declare her love – not yet, anyway – she could express her gratitude and, once they had moved into the sitting-room, she poured out her thanks again.

'You've thanked me twenty times already but, honestly, it was no big deal. Naturally, George was disappointed, but he completely understood and just told me to reschedule any time that suits. Don't worry, darling, I intend to show you Cornwall one way or another!'

Relieved that they were back in safer waters, she unstacked the tea-tray and passed him his cup and the plate of shortbread fingers. 'God, it was so embarrassing, though, having to blurt out all my private life to Hugo. But I didn't have any choice. I mean, when he offered to drive me up north next morning, I just had to admit your existence and tell him you'd already booked the train tickets. And I'm still worrying about what Amy thinks.'

'But we went over all that on the journey, and I told you then, it's simply not her business. And, anyway, it still beats me why she should object to your having a sex life.'

Maria sugared her tea and stirred it meditatively. 'I suppose it's a mother-daughter thing. And also to do with my age. I mean, it must seem rather gross to her that I'm still … *doing* it at sixty-six. I just thanked my lucky stars that she and Hugo were both late back from work, so they were probably too knackered to wonder why I hadn't told them about you before. And, of course, the whole business of the break-in diverted their attention. It was a dreadful shock for Amy, though. After all, this *was* her home for twenty years, and she's obviously concerned about how safe it'll be in the future.'

'Well, tell her we intend to leave it as impregnable as Fort Knox!'

Maria nodded vaguely; still focused on her discomfiture last night. 'And then there was Carole, of course. I felt really awkward having to confess that I'd be coming up with a bloke in tow.'

'So you said on the train.'

'I'm sorry, Felix, I'm boring you.'

He put a conciliatory hand on her arm. 'It's not boring; it's unnecessary. I mean, that word "confess" makes you sound like a criminal, yet, as I've told you over and over, sex is perfectly natural and normal, regardless of your age. And, as for Carole, she couldn't have been friendlier when she met us at the station.'

'Yes, all she said on the phone was, "Good on you!", so I guess she can't have been that bothered.'

'Sensible woman! Anyway, here we are, safe and sound, despite all your fears and worries. Oh, I know there's a lot of practical stuff to do, but once it's sorted out we can still enjoy our mini holiday and make glorious love, as we planned.'

Again, she resorted to silence. He'd been so decent, so supportive, he deserved sex day and night, yet in point of fact she felt not the slightest spark of lust. And it wasn't just anxiety about Amy's disapproval; infinitely worse was the thought of making love in what was still her mother's house, and with her mother's shade hovering over the bed. Besides, the burglary itself had left her with a sense of violation, hardly conducive to desire. The reek of the vandals' faeces, still lingering in the air, kept reminding her of all she'd lost – not just her father's things, but the old, friendly mantel-clock that had ticked out every second of her life. Even her awareness of Pentecost added to her sombre mood. Indeed, the angry wind rampaging round the cottage seemed to threaten further punishment if she dared profane this sacred season with full-throttle, flagrant sex, whatever Felix might say about it being 'natural and normal'.

'There's no double bed, I'm afraid,' she said, at last, and limply.

'Oh, that won't put me off,' he laughed. 'We manage fine in my studio, so why not here as well? But I'd better get off now or Argos will be shut.' He jumped to his feet, leaned over her chair and kissed the top of her head. 'Keep the single bed warm for the minute I get back!'

'Will do,' she promised, feigning a smile to conceal her deep unease.

Grappling with the wind, Maria made her way round the back of the cottage, where Felix was still working on the window. His hair was tousled and there were flecks of putty on his hands, but he was whistling cheerfully as he smoothed the edges with the putty-knife.

'Felix, why not call it a day? It's already ten past eight, and you've been slaving since the moment you arrived.'

'It's almost finished – this stage, anyway. I'll paint the frame tomorrow, once the putty's dry. Tell you what, though – be an angel and open that bottle of wine I bought. This is thirsty work and I'm dying for a drink.'

Once he'd washed and changed, they settled themselves on the sofa, with the bottle of Shiraz and the home-made venison pie Carole had delivered earlier, to save them cooking supper.

'It's not often I eat venison,' Felix said, appreciatively. 'Carole's certainly done us proud.'

'Well, a friend of hers shoots roe deer on his land and keeps her well supplied and she makes pies for him in return, as well as for herself, of course. She had this one in the freezer, so she only had to defrost it. But, listen, Felix, however busy we are tomorrow, I insist on showing you something of the countryside. The forecast's surprisingly good. This wind should drop tonight, they say, and there'll even be some sunshine. So what I suggest is we start out on the Pennine Way, go up to the top of Hareshaw – where there's a really wonderful view – then make our way back down Hareshaw Linn. The landscape's pretty impressive, so I'm hoping it'll inspire you. You might want to make some sketches to develop into a full-scale work in London.'

'I'm already inspired by what I've seen so far, on the train from Newcastle and driving back from Hexham just now. The rape-fields looked as thick and yellow as butter, and there were swathes of unripe barley rippling in the wind, like an expanse of cool green sea. I was so absorbed in the play of light and shadow, I almost crashed the car! It felt rather weird to be driving again, at all.'

'I know you sold your car when you moved to your present flat, but where did you actually move from?' He was always extremely cagey about his past, and she was curious to discover more.

'Scotland.'

'Really? Which part? We're only twenty-odd miles from the Scottish border here, so perhaps you knew this area?'

'No, I was very much a townie. I need my fix of culture, so I deliberately chose to live near Edinburgh.'

'Was that with your ex-wife?'

With the briefest of nods, he began demolishing his slice of pie, as if to excuse himself from saying any more.

'So did your daughter grow up there?'

'Partly.'

Perhaps his marriage had been so dire, he preferred to blank it out. Nonetheless, she persevered. It seemed wrong to know so little about a man who had just declared his love for her. 'So when did you move away – as a family, I mean?'

He finished his mouthful, slowly. 'Well, I never felt I quite belonged in Scotland, so I was the one who left first. I was keen to return to London, you see, and I'd already been there a good few years, when my daughter also decided to relocate. She was offered a job in New York, which was her idea of heaven! But, going back to landscape painting, I wondered if it might interest *you* at all?'

'Not at the moment,' she said, noting the change of subject but finally accepting his reluctance to confide. 'I'd rather stick with abstraction for a while. I'm becoming quite high on shape and colour alone! Although I wanted to ask you, Felix, whether you think my colours are getting too theatrical and I ought to tone them down?'

'Absolutely not. You were forced to tone your*self* down, and I see your art as a way of getting through to your true, authentic self. I've noted recently that you're revealing much more turmoil in your work, symbolized by that raw, convulsive colour. Those paintings don't lie, I assure you. They show you breaking out of the straitjacket you've been encased in far too long. You were born *wild*, Maria, I'm sure of it, but you let yourself be tamed by your mother and the Church and—'

'You mustn't keep blaming my mother. Some grandmas *killed* their daughters' bastard babies rather than have them shame the family, yet Mama—'

'In the bad old days, maybe,' he interrupted, 'but we've moved on since then, thank God. And, as for the Church, it's always stressed pain and suffering, glorified its martyrs and—'

'I longed to be a martyr,' she said, interrupting him, for a change. 'It seemed the perfect form of death.'

'Well, there you are – proof of what I'm saying. If you'd grown up in a different culture, you might have focused less on pain and more on pleasure. I mean, that awful story you told me about the nuns replacing the windows in your classrooms with opaque, clouded glass to prevent you seeing out. That's abuse, in my book – all the more so for a would-be artist who should be using her eyes and looking at things in detail.'

She shrugged. 'I'm afraid they knew more about St Augustine than they ever did about art, and *he* came down very hard on any sort of curiosity. He called it "lust of the eyes" – something sinful that had to be strictly curbed.'

Felix gave a grimace of distaste. 'It really bugs me that girls should be taught such rubbish, and taught by women who hide their bodies, shave their heads, deny themselves all pleasure and take a vow of chastity. What sort of training is *that*, I'd like to know. If you'd been free to develop your natural instincts, and been presented with a more positive view of life, I'm sure you'd have avoided a lot of misery.'

As she topped up both their glasses, in an attempt to lighten the mood, she wished they had never become entangled in so controversial a subject. As she knew from past discussions, Felix could be as intransigent as Silas when on his hobbyhorse.

'Tantra, for example,' he continued, ignoring his glass in his determination to influence her views, 'regards sex as a gateway to the divine. Yet, for your nuns, it was the gateway to Hell.'

She tensed at another mention of sex. Despite the wine, she still felt strangely sober – sober in all senses – as if she had become, again, the chaste, submissive Catholic of the old days.

'So, because of their indoctrination, you were forced to live a narrow, celibate life. In fact, I find it hard to believe that a sensuous woman like you had to shun all other men after the Silas disaster.'

'That's nonsense!' she retorted, suddenly losing her cool. 'When I was working in the gallery, I mixed with men all the time. And I actually went out with a couple – one in the late seventies, and one four or five years later. Unfortunately, I eventually discovered both were married and had children.'

'And so your Church forbade you to see them, of course.'

'I'm not an automaton, Felix.' Angrily, she banged down her glass. 'I do have my own opinions and I personally feel it's gravely wrong to break up a marriage and maybe leave the kids without a live-in father.'

'OK, I respect your view. But, as for priests or Popes, they know next to nothing about marriage or relationships. The only thing they're good at appears to be child abuse.'

'That's a bit sweeping, isn't it? Why damn every churchman because of a few bad eggs?'

'A few!' he expostulated. 'Literally thousands were implicated, but, conveniently, it was all swept under the carpet. And some elements in the Church still try to make out that the whole thing was just a media conspiracy.'

'Look, I agree it's an appalling scandal, but …'

'And what bugs me even more is that those "bad eggs", as you call them, still assume they have a hotline to one infallible truth. However bafflingly complex the questions, *they* have the answers off pat. And it's been the same for centuries, of course. Anyone with an original idea was censored, excommunicated or tortured, even the most brilliant minds. Copernicus, Galileo, Spinoza, Voltaire, Kant … the list goes on and on. That kind of thought-control is worse than anything in Orwell.'

'Felix, I understand how strongly you feel, but now's hardly the time to …'

The sentence petered out and he, too, said nothing further; just finished his last mouthful of pie and sat, shoulders hunched, shredding his paper napkin between his fingers. A gulf had opened up between them, which she had to admit was her fault as much as his. She was the one who had riled him by shouting at him so fiercely, whereas any normal woman would be profoundly grateful that he had devoted the last twelve hours to helping and supporting her. And he must be disappointed, if not seriously frustrated, that she had resisted all his sexual overtures. Here they were, away together, with nothing more to do now but make the 'glorious love' he'd proposed, yet she had given him no encouragement, shown no glimmer of desire. For pity's sake, couldn't she stop agonizing, put her arms around him and just let what happened happen?

No, apparently not, because she continued to sit in tense, uneasy silence, watching the small stretch of sky, framed by the cottage window. The clouds were scudding along in an agitated fashion, chivvied by the restless wind – a turbulence echoed by the turmoil in her mind.

Suddenly, her mobile shrilled and, glad of the distraction, she jumped up to answer it.

Carole's cheery voice helped her relax a little. At least it wasn't Silas with an ultimatum, or Amy reporting a pregnancy scare or some further complications in the court case.

'Sorry to bother you two lovebirds.' Carole gave a throaty guffaw. 'But Pam's just rung and she's really chuffed to hear you're back. It's her birthday tomorrow, so she's suggesting we all get together for a pre-lunch drink at the Black Bull.'

Pam, a local farmer's wife, was something of a gossip-monger, so was probably less interested in celebrating her birthday than in laying eyes on the 'lovebirds' and relaying any spicy titbits to anyone who'd listen. However, she could hardly hide Felix from the village, so she told Carole to hold on, while she asked him what he thought.

'Great idea. I'd love to meet your friends. And tell Carole that's the best venison pie I've eaten in my life – although I can't say I've had very many!'

Once she'd rung off, he got up to join her, cupping her face in his hands. 'I'm sorry, darling, I've been a bit tense this evening, and that anti-Church rant was totally mistimed. I'm so tired, I guess, I'm forgetting what you've been through today.'

He had put her to shame by apologizing. It was she who should be making overtures. Instead, she seized on his word 'tired', longing to say, let's have an early night and go to bed to *sleep*. He might even suggest it himself, although the still radiant daylight outside countered thoughts of sleep. The longest day was less than a fortnight away, so there was no sign of dusk, as yet, let alone full darkness.

He slipped his hand between the buttons of her blouse and gently stroked her breast, feathering the nipple with his thumb. 'I know just the thing to rejuvenate us,' he whispered, 'some slow, sensuous Tantric sex. Tantra's perfect when you're tired, because it takes the stress off performance. There's no rush to reach a climax, and no need to prove yourself as the greatest lay since Cleopatra! In fact, you can prolong the whole thing endlessly; spin it out in a meditative sort of way, and that's incredibly erotic.'

How, she thought, dismayed, could she respond to endlessly protracted sex, when all she wanted was to become a leaf or cloud – something with no body and no mind?

Chapter 22

'HAPPY BIRTHDAY, PAM!
'Many happy returns!'
The twelve of them crammed around the corner table clinked glasses in a toast.

'You don't look a day over seventy!' Dave, her husband, joked, taking a large gulp of his Scotch.

Pam gave him a friendly punch. 'If I'm fraying at the edges, whose fault is that, I'd like to know? Anyone marrying a farmer needs their head examined.'

Yes, Maria reflected, many farmers' wives up here seemed to be still living in the 1950s, expected to cook substantial meals and do all the housework and childcare, as well as helping with the outside work, such as haymaking and lambing.

'I hope he's taking you out to dinner tonight,' Angie said, through a mouthful of nuts.

'Fat chance! I'm amazed he's torn himself away even for half an hour. Anyway, enough of me. I'm more interested in Felix.' Pam swivelled round to face him. 'It's an unusual name, isn't it? I've never met a Felix before.'

'Well, it means happy, fertile, fortunate and blessed, so perhaps most parents are scared their kids won't live up to all of that.'

'And did *you*?' Carole asked, raising her voice above the raucous group at the adjoining table.

'Oh, absolutely – well, except for the "fertile". I only managed one daughter, I'm afraid.'

'And is she an artist, too?' enquired Alistair, a Forestry Commission worker Dave had brought along, and the only one of the party Maria didn't know. Apparently, he had moved to the village only in the last few months, whereas most of this crowd had, like her, all been born and bred here.

'No, she works in advertising and, anyway, she, er ...'

'Talking of art,' Maria interjected, noting Felix's usual hesitation on the subject of his family, 'I'm taking Felix up Hareshaw this afternoon. He's hoping to get ideas for some new paintings.'

'I know nothing about art,' declared Alan, the small, sinewy fellow who ran the local shop, with his taller, well-upholstered wife, Louise. 'I was always bottom of the class at school and, to be perfectly frank, I can't see why people should go to all that trouble trying to put something on paper when they could just as soon take a photograph.'

'Yes, I tend to agree,' Felix said, jovially. 'But, you see, the only reason we're artists at all is because we're often pretty useless at any other line of work!'

As everybody laughed, Maria felt for his hand beneath the table and gave it a grateful squeeze. After a brief initial wariness, her friends had all accepted him; warming to his easy, jokey manner. She, too, felt distinctly better than when she had woken up this morning, disoriented, half-drugged from sleep, and alone in her mother's bed. The Tantric sex hadn't gone quite as planned; its techniques so relaxing that Felix had actually drifted off to sleep after only fifteen minutes. *She*, however, had lain awake, uncomfortably jammed against his body, in the narrow single bed, and becoming increasingly restless as the long, lonely night wore on. Fearing she might wake him, she had crept out of bed at 2 a.m. and slipped into her mother's room. There, she continued to lie sleepless for another couple of hours, vowing they would make love in the morning, however tired or disinclined she might feel. Yet, when she finally drifted off, she had slept so long and deeply it was almost noon before she surfaced – and nearly time to leave for the pub. So the sex had been postponed, again, till tonight. And, thank God, her former doubts and fears had abated, along with yesterday's gale; her mood today as sunny as the weather.

Pam was still quizzing Felix, clearly determined to find out all she could. 'So how did you two meet?' she asked,

Maria took her time in answering, wary of mentioning the life class in front of prudish Louise. But Felix came to the rescue, taking a jokey line again.

'Oh, I stood on her toe in the tube and you should have heard the fuss she made! So I more or less *had* to invite her out.'

More laughter. Maria knew that, if she brought Felix here in future, he would soon be part of their crowd. And, suddenly, it struck her that perhaps she could persuade him to move to Northumberland, rather than to Cornwall. After all, it was equally beautiful, in its own distinctive way; equally inspiring for a painter. He would still be miles away from London, of course, but at least not at the opposite end of the country from what, for her, was home.

'My round,' he said, pushing back his chair. 'Same again for everyone?'

'Count me out,' said Dave, also getting up. 'I really must get off now. One of my cows is poorly and I need to keep an eye on her.'

'See, what did I tell you?' Pam sighed histrionically. 'The cows come first, as usual. And, birthday or no birthday, he'll expect his lunch on the table on the dot of one o'clock. Which it certainly *won't* be,' she added, checking her watch with a shrug.

'Well, in that case, hadn't you better leave, as well?' Jacqueline gave Pam a sly nudge. 'Or the beef will be raw, the potatoes unpeeled, and *you'll* be in the doghouse.'

'No way!' Pam retorted, joining in the chorus of goodbyes, as her husband moved towards the door.

'Knowing Pam,' Sonia observed, 'she'll already have the joint in the oven, the potatoes in the roasting tin and the apple pie just waiting to be browned.'

'Same as me,' Angie nodded. 'It's no real hardship cooking Sunday lunch, so long as you're well organized.'

'Well, if you moved to London,' Maria put in, 'you wouldn't need to bother. From what I've seen so far, most Londoners eat out at weekends, almost as a matter of course. If I suggest to Amy and Hugo that I'll make them Sunday lunch, they always seem to be meeting friends in some wine bar or restaurant or other.'

'Frankly, I'd rather cook a million Sunday lunches,' Louise said, emphatically, 'than have to move to London. All that knife-crime and violence, for heaven's sake! And the noise and grime and traffic, and everyone pushing and shoving. I reckon if you were handicapped or blind, you'd be trampled underfoot.'

'Come off it, Louise, it's not that bad.' Maria ripped open a packet of crisps, making up for her lack of breakfast. 'Although I have to say I do miss the peace, and the sense of space and general friendliness. And, when I look at Amy and Hugo, I'm appalled by how hard they work and all the pressures on them – having to keep up with the latest trends and go to the right hair salon and all that sort of stuff.'

'I cut my own hair this morning,' Carole admitted, airily, 'and I don't think it looks that bad.'

Maria refrained from comment. Cutting one's own hair would be considered an unthinkable barbarity among London's smarter set. 'And I also miss little things like hanging out the washing. Yesterday, while Felix was in

Hexham, I washed all the fusty sheets and got quite a kick from seeing them billowing on the line. Amy has this state-of-the-art tumble drier but, in my opinion, it can't beat a boisterous south-west wind.'

'On the other hand,' Alan pointed out, 'it's mid-summer now, so things are at their best. It's a different story when you're faced with snowdrifts ten foot deep or lanes ankle-deep in mud.'

'True,' Maria agreed, also aware that, since her move to London, she would jib at the sense of living on the boundary of things, far removed from the pulse and pith of life. And, as she glanced around the crowded pub, she couldn't help but notice that the clientele was uniformly white; the nearest thing to an ethnic minority was a redhead at the bar. And there was none of London's vibrant mix of types – everything from Goths to drag-queens, with exotic outfits to match. Here, the standard uniform was jeans and a work-shirt, or cords and a fleece, mostly in drab colours.

'Sorry I was so long.' Felix returned to the table with a loaded tray of drinks. 'There was quite a crush at the bar.'

Sonia, current star of the local Amateur Dramatic Society, took her glass from him, clinging to his wrist with a decidedly coquettish air. 'You must come and see our production,' she coaxed. 'This evening's the last night of the run, so this is your only chance. One of the characters happens to be a painter, so it would be fantastic to have a real live artist in the audience.'

'I doubt,' Felix quipped, putting down his own glass, 'if I'll be either real or live if I drink much more of this! It's really got a kick to it. Is it a local beer?'

'Yes, it's made by Wylam Brewery,' Jacqueline informed him, 'which is getting quite a name for producing potent beers. Two of these and I'm under the table!'

'Do come to the show,' Sonia persisted. 'I can easily get you a couple of tickets. Are you busy this evening?'

'Yes, 'fraid so,' Felix said, much to Maria's relief. With so much to sort out – Hanna's headstone, probate, all the new security measures – it was only fair to Felix to keep their evenings free. She knew he would much prefer to be in bed with her than sit through some half-baked production performed in a draughty church hall.

'Maria!' a voice called from the door. 'Great to have you back!'

She swung round to see Desmond, now retired and nearly ninety, who had been something of a father to her when she was growing up. She dashed across to greet him and, as he pressed his whiskery face against her cheek, she inhaled his faint, familiar smell of diesel and old dog. The warmth of her welcome – not just from him, but from half this small community –

made her realize how deeply rooted she was here. She might have certain reservations about living in the sticks, but when she had first set foot in the pub, there had been greetings on all sides, drinks on the house and a touching sense of pleasure at her return.

'Let me buy you a beer,' Desmond offered, linking his arm through hers, as he made his doddery way across the room.

'Desmond, if I drink any more I'll be legless. And, anyway, I'm with a friend from London. He's keen to see the countryside, so we're about to make a move.'

Although not strictly true, she decided to make it so, suddenly wanting Felix to herself. Besides, they ought to set out on their walk before the fickle sunshine disappeared, and they still had to return to the cottage to change their clothes and make a picnic lunch. So, ushering Desmond towards their table, she informed the others that she and Felix were now departing for their walk.

'Be good!' Carole called, with a conspiratorial wink.

'Are you *sure* it's just a walk?' Eddie added, with a grin.

'I don't know what you're insinuating,' Felix retorted, with mock indignation. 'But I'll have you know Maria and I are just good friends and if anyone says different they'll have me to reckon with!'

'It's a stunning view,' Felix observed, shading his eyes against the fierce mid-summer light.

'Yes, you can see as far as Cheviot, and even Carter Bar – the border with Scotland. Oh, I know it's very bleak up here, but I like that, in a way.'

'Me too. I prefer a hint of menace in my landscapes rather than pretty-pretty scenery.'

'There used to be a village near here, but that was years ago. There's almost no trace of it now and the whole area seems deserted.'

'And it's so amazingly quiet.'

'Apart from the skylarks. And we should hear curlews, too. I must bring you here in the autumn, when it looks as if nature's on fire, with everything flaming and flaring.'

'D'you mind if we rest our bones? My muscles are beginning to complain. Anyway, I want to do a few sketches of these huge outcrops of rock.' He squatted on his haunches to examine the nearest one, rearing up, bare and rugged, not far short of his own height. 'In fact, I think I'll do a series of paintings, just on these alone. The textures are so interesting and I like their jagged shadows.'

She stood watching him a while. 'What I notice, Felix, is the way you look so intently at things, as if you're trying to devour them and digest them. I realize I've been looking only superficially, in comparison with you.'

'Well, for me it's a way of capturing the truth of a subject, by getting right to its core. On the other hand, when I'm actually painting, I like to move beyond that reality and trust much more to instinct. I suppose, as a painter, one's constantly trying to strike a balance between abandon and control.'

'A bit like in my life.'

'Oh, you're not there yet – still too much control and not enough abandon!'

'Well,' she laughed, 'it's ages since we stopped for lunch, so why don't we have a tea break and you can watch me abandon myself disgustingly to those lovely squidgy flapjacks you brought! But let's walk down to that dip. It'll be more sheltered there. Even on a calm day, there's always a breeze on these hills.'

Once they reached the dip, she spread the picnic rug across the springy bed of heather, and unpacked the flapjacks and the flask of tea. As they ate, she saw Felix's gaze travel slowly across the vista of greens and golds and browns, absorbing every detail. She, too, looked up, trying to see the landscape through his eyes: dappled swathes of sun and shadow, gradually melding into a bluish, blurry heat-haze on the horizon.

'I love these gently rounded hills,' he said. 'They remind me of your body – soft, voluptuous curves.' He pushed her gently back on the rug, knelt astride her, moved his lips towards hers.

The long, slow, smouldering kiss was like a switch, turning on every cell and organ of her body, yet she couldn't help but worry when he began unbuttoning her blouse. If some hiker or climber should come here, they would be open to public view. However, the thought of making love outside had always seemed enticingly erotic, although she had never actually done it, except in fantasy. Alone in the cottage, she had imagined being Manet's model for 'Le Déjeuner sur l'Herbe'; the artist so aroused, he had interrupted his work to ravish her on the dewy grass. Or she had been Botticelli's Venus, frolicking with the painter amidst playfully caressing waves, or seduced by a brazen Byron on some moonlit Grecian strand.

Byron, Manet, Botticelli; all were present and cajoling her. Nonetheless, as Felix slipped the blouse from her shoulders and began easing down her zip, she continued trying to restrain him. 'We *mustn't*,' she whispered, 'not here.'

He kissed away her objection, then, moving his mouth to her breasts, flicked his tongue-tip slowly back and forth against the nipples; the sensation so exquisite, her resistance melted like butter in the sun. His sense of urgency excited her, the frantic way he fumbled off his clothes and pressed his naked body so closely against hers, she could feel its bones, its warm and solid weight.

However, she forced him to lie still a moment, wanting to savour the sheer sensuousness of being in the open air: the tingle of the breeze against her skin; the hardness of the ground beneath, tamed by the springy prickle of heather; the plaintive cry of plovers; the faint, peaty smell of earth and still fainter whiff of sheep. The untroubled sky arched, vast, above, and, as she gazed up at the serenely languorous clouds, she felt part of something boundless.

Felix, though, was noticeably impatient, refusing to lie quiescent. He began to thrust against her and, within minutes, she was swept into his rhythm – a fierce, insistent rhythm that made her so much part of him, she soon lost all sense of which was him and which was her. All the restrictions of her mother's house – not just last night but throughout her adult life, when even solo sex was, of necessity, silent and furtive – were miraculously dissolving, as was any hint of disapproval from her daughter. Even Pentecost was no longer a source of guilt, but seemed to laser through her body in some new sexual sacrament: the rushing wind; the tongues of fire; the sense of stupefaction. She had left the normal world behind and was inhabiting some wayward sphere, where any distinction between earth and heaven, right and wrong, was completely overturned. Her sole duty was to surrender to that other, savage self; now inseparable from his. He alone directed her, while everything else hurtled out of control: the planets plunging from their orderly trajectories; the tides rebelling against the stern curb of the moon, thwacking and buffeting the shore; the seasons co-existing – burning autumn, skittish spring, keen winter, sultry summer, jumbled in a flagrant mix of hypnotic heat and jolting cold.

She could hear someone shouting – not her, some other woman, brazen and unbiddable. 'Go on! Go on! Yes, more, yes more!' 'No, don't come, don't come yet!' Unbearable to stop – she must continue this for ever – yet if she didn't climax soon, she would self-destruct, burn out. Then, suddenly, explosively – back arched, eyes closed, nails clawing down his back – all the tumult she'd suppressed for over thirty years broke like a summer storm across the hills.

He collapsed against her, panting, out of breath. 'I love you,' she said – the other woman said. Love and sex were one. If your lover took you beyond all normal boundaries, changed the physical structure of the universe, then you loved him, plain and simple. Their sex was now imprinted on this landscape and every time she came here, the ground would spark and thrill again, the clouds reel and preen, in awe. Slowly, almost reluctantly, she opened her eyes, surprised, as always, to see Felix's lined face. He had been a wild young colt just now – unbroken-in and wilful, galloping and bucking for the sheer, crazy hell of it.

'That was quite incredible,' he said. 'I loved the way you were shouting yes and no at once.'

'Was I?' she murmured, languidly. 'I can't believe I was asking you to stop!'

'No, you meant "don't come too soon". No wonder I call you greedy.'

She laid her hand on her breast; the nipples insolently hard, her heart still pounding frantically. 'It's you who makes me behave so badly. Just look at us – lying naked in a public place. We could be had up for gross indecency.'

'That's exactly why you need me – to help you behave atrociously. You were making so much noise, you must have scared the sheep for miles around!'

'But that's your fault, again. I don't know how you do it but you make me feel I'd shock anyone and do anything, and not give a damn. Is that *really* me, though?'

'Absolutely. You're a profoundly sexual creature, Maria. It's just that you don't acknowledge it. And I hope,' he added, smoothing back an unruly strand of her hair, 'that it was *really* you when you said you loved me just now.'

Suddenly, she recalled the message on her St Valentine's Day heart: *love is never impossible*. 'Yes,' she said, 'it *was* me.'

'Good, because there's something really important I need to ask you.'

'Hadn't we better get dressed first?' Already, she was moving from tumult to timidity; her cautious, straitlaced, other self was slowly creeping back and fretting about propriety – indeed, appalled by her casual sacrilege in sexualizing Pentecost. Felix would never understand such guilts, so she voiced, instead, a fear he could accept. 'I know it sounds ridiculous but I have this vision of Eddie and Carole coming up here, for some reason, and finding us stark naked. I'd die of embarrassment.'

'I imagine they're dozing in their chairs, digesting their Sunday lunch – but, OK, just to keep you happy.' He passed her her clothes, helped her put them on, then, once they were both decent, he coaxed her back beside him again.

'This is something I've been thinking about for ages, so I want you to take it seriously.'

She glanced at him, intrigued by his solemn tone, yet still torn between guilt and rapture, worry and abandon.

'As you know, I'm pretty set on moving down to Cornwall. In fact, when I spoke to George on Friday night, he said he'd found a place he's sure I'll love. You'll never guess what it is.'

'An abandoned copper mine?' she ventured, adopting a fake cheery tone, to hide the misery she felt about him relocating. 'Or an amazingly artistic cowshed?'

'Try again.'

'A tower? A cave? A railway carriage?'

'A chapel,' he said, laughing. 'Not Catholic, I'm afraid, but a charming little Methodist one, with solid granite walls and a slate roof.'

'Felix, you can't live in a chapel when you disapprove so strongly of religion.'

'Don't worry, it's deconsecrated. And skilfully converted, so it's already a home, not a church, but according to George a wonderfully original home, with a steep-roofed gallery that'll be ideal for a studio, he thinks. And it's perfectly positioned, only a few miles from his place, in a village called Tywardreath. Actually, I know it, because when I stay with George he always takes me to the pub there – a really friendly one, with a fantastic range of real ales. The village itself is a mile or two inland, and it's a self-contained community, with its own working population, which means it doesn't depend on the tourist trade. That's a great advantage, because so many places in Cornwall get overrun and noisy and frenetic in the summer.'

His exuberant tone only aggravated her dejection as again he began enthusing.

'And property's much cheaper there than in Fowey or St Ives. And, although it's such a peaceful spot, it's only minutes from Par station. Obviously, I'd buy a car if I moved there, but it'd be jolly handy to have a good fast service from London. The train goes all the way to Penzance, too, and you can also get to St Ives, with just one change.'

She lay crestfallen, unspeaking; all her former contentment shrivelling. How could she exchange their present gratifying closeness for a sporadic, long-distance relationship? However fast the train, they would still be achingly far away from each other. She couldn't even suggest he moved up here, instead of to Cornwall, when now, it seemed, he had found the perfect property in an ideal village, conveniently close to George's artist-friends.

'But I can't bear the thought of losing you – or at least seeing you only now and then. So I wondered if—' He stopped and shifted position; seeming to need the pause to find the exact right words '—if there's the slightest chance you'd come and live with me in Cornwall? And, before you object, it's not just a selfish wish. I feel it's really crucial for you to have a proper studio and be with someone like me, who'll do everything he can to foster your career. Despite your talent, you've never had the time or space to develop it. But if we were both in Tywardreath and part of George's community, you could exhibit your work along with the other artists and really blossom as a painter. And you needn't worry about money. I have enough for both of us and, anyway, given time, I'm sure you'll sell your stuff, once people see how special it is.'

She sat up on her elbow, thrilled, touched, aghast. And now it was *she* who paused; knowing she was duty-bound to refuse, yet not wanting to seem ungrateful when he had showed such generous interest in her career.

'And our fantastic sex would all be part of it. Remember what Picasso said about art and sex being so closely linked? Well, you're inspiring new ideas in me and new sources of creativity, and *your* work's changing, too; gaining in force and confidence, and becoming much more sensual. Right from the first life class, I noticed how you exaggerated the model's curves and size, and I saw in you this sort of voracious energy. Yet I also noticed how that very quality seemed to disconcert you, so you almost had to disown it. I do honestly think you need me, Maria, to help you, as both woman and artist, to accept your basic nature and glory in excess. So, you see, if we lived together—'

'Felix, darling ...' She had to stop him before he said another word. His plan was so enticing, it might fatally undermine her familial obligations. 'It's a wonderful idea but I'm afraid it's out of the question. I've committed myself to Amy and her baby. She's already thirty-one weeks pregnant and I can't just change the plan at this late stage.'

'But you devoted your whole life to her when she was a child. Surely that's enough. She's an adult now, with a husband and plenty of cash for a nanny.'

'It's not only a question of cash. I—'

'Isn't there a danger she's just using you,' Felix interrupted, 'ignoring your own needs?'

She pondered the question, aware that she had used Hanna, in her turn. It wasn't always easy for daughters to have insight into mothers' needs. 'Look, I *want* to be the nanny. And, anyway, I don't trust anyone else to look after the baby with the love and commitment that I'll bring to the task.'

'But you love *me*, Maria, too. Doesn't that mean anything?'

'Of course it does – it means a huge amount – but it still seems a selfish sort of love, compared with my duty to Amy.'

He gave an exasperated sigh. 'You're using your mother's terms, again, and the Church's. As I've told you so often, you've let those values rule your entire existence; always saying no to any sort of gratification because your stern God disapproves. But here's your chance to do a U-turn and say yes, for once, instead. In fact, I want you to say "an *enormous* yes"! That's actually a phrase from a Philip Larkin poem and, although I'm not a fan of Larkin, those words seem tailor-made for you at this particular juncture. Don't you see, Maria, you could change things radically; be the self you were born to be, not some life-denying self your religion forced you to adopt? All you have to do is take this opportunity to embark on a new life – one that includes sex and art and happiness, instead of guilt and gloom and restraint.'

She began twisting her hair into its former tidy chignon. 'An enormous yes' seemed an enormity itself, requiring a conviction and cupidity she simply didn't possess.

'And, before you object, I want to stress that it's *not* an indulgence to develop your inborn talents. Even Christ said that.'

'But He didn't mean at the expense of other people.' The hair fell back, dishevelled, round her shoulders. 'I've already done harm to Amy by depriving her of a father and if I cry off as nanny it would be – well, unforgivable.'

'Isn't it time you thought of yourself, though? You could leave behind a substantial body of work, your legacy to the world. Art isn't just a frippery, Maria. Gerhard Richter regards it as one of life's essentials, like bread, or love, or shelter; something that gives us hope and comfort and actually helps us to survive. I happen to consider Richter the greatest living painter in the world, so surely his views should carry some weight.'

'Yes, art's important – that goes without saying – but I just can't agree that it's more important than bringing up a baby. All the experts believe that what happens in a child's first five years is crucial in determining whether it'll be happy or not.'

'So can't Amy give up *her* job and ensure her own child's happiness?'

'No. They need two incomes to pay their hefty mortgage.'

'But surely she can't expect you just to sacrifice yourself?'

How could she explain that she saw it not as a sacrifice but more of a necessity; how express her deep desire to be intimately involved with her daughter and her grandchild, in order to break the chain of suffering the family had endured? Felix might dismiss that as some irrational whim.

'Listen, darling, I had this dream last week. I wasn't going to mention it but it may help you understand. I dreamt that Amy went through a dreadfully long and painful labour but, at the end of it, there was no baby – nothing at all. She was lying on the bed, her arms cradling empty air.'

He leaned forward and gently traced the curve of her cheek. 'That was just your daytime worries, my sweet, magnified into a nightmarish scenario, which is totally unlikely in reality.'

'I'm not so sure. Any labour can go wrong, and Amy's already had a few problems. And, of course, she's increasingly stressed about the whole Dubai thing, which can't be good for her health – or the baby's, come to that. And Hugo's in such a state, he's not being his usual supportive self so, honestly, Felix, she really does need me around.'

He sat frowning for a moment, as if trying to organize his thoughts. 'OK, I can see you have to be there until the actual birth, and maybe for the first couple of months, just to put your mind at rest. But that's no problem, actually, because it takes at least three months to buy any sort of property, and often a lot longer. Admittedly, the guy who owns the chapel is pretty keen to get it off his hands, because he plans to move to France, but even so I can't see myself signing a contract until October at the earliest. So, assuming all goes smoothly, say we moved in the late autumn, would that be easier for you?'

Confused, uncertain, she scrambled to her feet. 'Felix, I don't know what to say. This has all come as quite a shock and I need more time to think.'

She walked blindly across the heather; suddenly wanting to be alone and away from his persuasive pressures. What answer could she possibly give to so intolerable a dilemma? Of *course* she burned to be an artist; to become part of an artists' community and have people around to encourage and support her. And to be part of a couple was even more appealing – something she had craved since the seventies. And how could she not be tempted by the thought of having her own place, instead of being confined to a granny flat and dependent on Amy and Hugo? A converted chapel sounded wonderfully romantic and, if it were furnished with the same flair and originality as Felix's London flat, it would make a magical home. Yet, however much she longed to say 'an enormous yes' to sex and art and Cornwall, such self-dedication seemed an unjustifiable luxury, compared with her clear-cut duty to her daughter and her grandchild.

She stumbled on a tussock, not looking where she was going; focusing entirely on the turmoil in her mind. If it came to a choice between her happiness and Amy's, how could she put her own needs first? Yet, secretly and selfishly, she was just as avid for happiness as she was for sex. Indeed, the two were linked. Making love just now had flooded her with a wanton rapture nothing else could bring. But if Felix moved to Cornwall without her, he was bound to find another woman – someone free of ties – and she might never have sex again. A woman in her sixties was hardly likely to have lovers queuing up.

She stooped to pick a sprig of heather – heather for good luck. And, yes, she *had* been lucky to meet a man like Felix; a man who genuinely cared about her work; a man who didn't expect his partner to be twenty years his junior. Which made it all the more deplorable that the relationship might have to end after only a few short months, instead of becoming something permanent that could transform the rest of her life.

She broke into a run, stumbling on the rough, uneven ground; her thoughts now switching to Silas. She was obliged to keep in touch with him, to ensure he fulfilled his roles as father and soon-to-be grandfather. And, since he was lamentably ill-suited to such roles, she would need to see him regularly – impossible if she were almost 300 miles away. And equally impossible to explain a move to Cornwall without arousing his anger and jealousy – or to mention Silas to Felix, without unleashing the same emotions.

Lurching to a halt, she flung herself down on the heather, envying the sheep, dotted like white boulders across the grass. *They* weren't prey to agonizing conflicts; indeed, had nothing much to do except graze and munch and stare. Her attention was drawn to a ewe and her twin lambs, the pair so small and spindly, they had clearly been born late in the season. How sedate the mother looked, as she anxiously guarded her offspring, giving a bleat of alarm as she registered a human presence. At some distance from the trio was a larger and much podgier lamb, in no need of its mother, but still young enough to frisk around in a carefree fashion. As she watched, it suddenly leapt into the air; all four feet off the ground, as if exulting in its freedom, its perky joie-de-vivre.

'Maria! Where are you?'

She started at the sound of Felix's voice; swung round to see him further up the hillside but clambering down to find her. She sat stock-still; irresolute. He might already be expecting some decision on her part, but did she choose to be an encumbered mother-ewe, or a free and frisky lamb?

Chapter 23

'**K**ATE, ARE YOU busy?'

'Am I ever busy?' Kate laughed. 'But you look loaded down. Want to come in for a coffee?'

'Actually, I want to come in and sound off.' Maria stepped into the hall and deposited her clutch of Sainsbury's bags. 'I'm absolutely livid! I'd just done all this shopping when my mobile rang and it was Amy saying Beatrice and Tom had cancelled – right at the last minute, would you believe? They were meant to be arriving this evening, and now they want Amy and Hugo to flog all the way to Shropshire instead. The last thing Amy needs at the moment is a long, exhausting drive on top of a full day's work. And it's even worse for Hugo, because he's due to fly out to Dubai again, the very next day – the Monday. No wonder he's tense, with all that to-ing and fro-ing.'

'Have they fixed the date for the trial, then?'

'No. Now they're trying to reach an out-of-court settlement, which would obviously be better. But it'll still be incredibly stressful, what with everyone haggling and arguing and issuing threats and counter-threats. And, as well as everything else, his present employers are putting the screws on, too.'

'What, the Olympic project, you mean?'

'Yes. They're behind schedule, Hugo says, so they're getting fed up with his absences and he has to keep inventing excuses for being away again. But, listen, going back to Beatrice and Tom, it's thrown *me*, too, completely. You see, I'd promised Amy I'd take care of all the meals and now I'm landed with this load of fancy food I can't possibly finish up in one weekend.'

'Lord! I'm sorry.' Kate ushered her into the sitting-room and coaxed her to sit down. 'But why on earth did they change the plans?'

'Oh, a whole lot of footling reasons, Amy said. Apparently, Beatrice had promised to read the lesson at their local church on Sunday, and her new neighbours are dying to meet her son, and it's the weekend of the village fete and—'

'But with all that going on, why in heaven's name did they arrange to come to London in the first place?'

'God knows! Between you and me, I suspect Beatrice is agoraphobic. She always wants to stay on her home territory and dreams up endless reasons why she should. And this time she has the perfect let-out – it's Father's Day, so Hugo has to spend it with his father.'

'But I thought the whole point was they were spending it with *you*.'

'Exactly. And I've made a special Father's Day cake – stayed up late last night, so I could keep today free for shopping and cooking.'

'I do agree it's appallingly bad manners but, you know, it could just be a blessing in disguise.'

'A blessing, when I've missed the chance of going down to Cornwall? Felix will be on the train right now and if Beatrice had rung earlier – as any half-decent person would – I'd be sitting there beside him. Hey!' she said, springing to her feet. 'It's not too late, is it? If I threw some things in a case, I could catch the next fast train.'

'Honestly, Maria, I wouldn't recommend it. You've only just come back from Northumberland and, to be perfectly frank, you do seem in a bit of a state. I don't mean about Beatrice and Tom – that would drive anyone bonkers – but this whole Cornwall thing. And if you dash after Felix and try to make a decision on a property, he may pressure you into something you could well regret later on.'

Maria slumped back on the sofa with a sigh of mingled exhaustion and frustration. 'It's not his fault, honestly. He's not in any particular rush himself, but this wretched couple have appeared on the scene who are mad keen on the chapel. Apparently, they live close by and have viewed it twice already, so George is worried they may snap it up and pip Felix to the post. So *he's* the one who talked Felix into going down today.'

'Well, that's OK for Felix – it's *his* life and George is his friend – but you need more time to think.'

'Look, there's no way Felix would go ahead until I've seen the place for myself. But if I leave it much longer, there's a genuine risk we'll lose it.'

'Maybe so, but I still think it's extremely unwise to make a huge, life-changing decision when you've barely recovered from the upheaval of the burglary. Surely he must realize that you need a chance to simmer down a bit. What I suggest is that you take it easy this weekend and make the most of having the house to yourself.'

'Well, I must admit, it'll be almost a relief to have Amy and Hugo out of the way. Every time I see Amy, I feel an absolute brute for even thinking of letting her down, and Hugo's been quite snappy since I got back. Oh, I know he's very tense about the court case – in fact, he's forever on the phone to Dubai – but I keep worrying that he's also shocked about me having a lover.'

'Maria, honestly, you're nuts! You seem to think everyone's like your mother and sees sex as a horrendous sin.'

'Yes, that's what Felix says but, you see, Hugo's mother is pretty strait-laced too, so I must seem really flighty in comparison.'

'She may be straitlaced, but she's also damned selfish, messing everyone around like this.'

'D'you think Hugo plans to tell her?'

'Tell her what?'

'About Felix.'

'Oh, yes, I'm sure! Just as they're sitting down to a nice quiet sherry in the ancestral home, he'll regale her with all the details of your goings-on, en flagrante!'

Maria laughed, despite herself.

'That's better. You've been looking a real sad-sack. Let's go and have that coffee and you can tell me more about how you got on up north.'

'I'd love a coffee, but I won't talk about that, if you don't mind – or Cornwall. They both involve Felix and every time I think of him I feel more confused and torn. Anyway, I'd rather hear about *you*.'

'There's nothing much to tell, except Paul's managed to change his usual Sunday flight to one first thing Monday morning, which is great for Clara and Polly, because it means we can celebrate Father's Day. In fact, why don't you join us, Maria? At least you'll have some sort of celebration, then.'

'No, I'd hate to intrude on a family thing.'

'Don't be daft! The girls would love it. And they're planning a dance-display for their dad, so they'll be really chuffed to have you in the audience.'

'OK, but only if you let me do the cooking. It'll be the perfect way to use up all that food.'

'I wouldn't hear of it. Anyway, life's too short to cook so, knowing me, it'll be mostly shop-bought stuff.'

'Well, I insist on bringing the cake. Otherwise it will go to waste. And I'll make the girls some gingerbread-men.'

'You spoil them, Maria. Oh, and listen – I almost forgot – Paul wants to see some of your paintings. He's thinking of buying one for his office.'

'Really?'

'Yes, I was telling him about them and he seemed genuinely interested. I suspect he wants to impress his clients with a bit of real live modern art.'

'Or shock them, more likely,' Maria laughed, secretly elated at the thought of having a buyer – and a wealthy buyer at that. In fact, she felt a sudden urge to go back to her flat and start a new work, specifically for Paul. She wouldn't need to be untrue to her vision, just more restrained and reflective: no hectic colours or plunging diagonals, but a sombre, subtle palette. The idea was a definite challenge so, having drained her coffee and thanked Kate for her advice, she set off home in a distinctly better mood.

Having mixed Chinese white with Antwerp blue, she laid a thin, translucent wash across the ground of Payne's grey, then stood back to judge the effect. She was aiming for the colour of rain – an elusive, ghostly non-colour, austere and almost unearthly. No picture had ever taken her so long. Having worked on it most of Friday and all day Saturday, she had begun again this morning, at first light. She was no longer slapping on paint in her usual swift, impetuous fashion, but employing a more measured technique, slowly building up several thin, successive layers and allowing each to dry before adding the next. And the procedure had brought an unexpected bonus in that it seemed to calm and relax her, as if the unhurried pace and muted colours acted like a form of meditation.

However, she couldn't keep her thoughts away from Felix and the chapel, because of his phone call yesterday, when he had described the place as a gem, with tall windows and a high ceiling that made it wonderfully light and thus perfect for two artists. And the very act of painting reminded her how much she needed a proper, decent-sized studio, with room for all her materials, as well as wall space to display her work. And there would be no more need to worry about the smells of turps and oil paint seeping into the rest of the house and making Amy nauseous. Her daughter had enough to contend with; what with backache and leg cramps and her increasing apprehension not only about the birth, but about the number of tasks she had still to complete at work before she started her maternity leave in a matter of just five weeks. Yet those very problems only made her feel more selfish for even considering a move to Cornwall. Felix had simply no idea how hard it would be to say 'an enormous yes'.

Forcing her concentration back to the painting, she used her fingers to stipple the pale bluish wash with flecks of Flake white. Her mobile chose that moment to ring, so, before she could pick it up, she had to grab a rag and wipe her messy hands. But, despite the interruption, nothing could temper her exuberance at hearing her lover's voice.

'Darling, I know you're working and I'm disturbing you again, but I'm missing you so badly, I have to make contact every now and then, just to keep me going. And, anyway – great news! The other prospective buyers have dropped out.'

'What, the couple who were so desperately keen?'

'Yes, but all their plans have changed. The wife's mother's just had a stroke and, although she was lucky to survive, it seems she'll be permanently incapacitated and they've decided to move in with her, so they'll be on hand to help. It's rotten for them, but I can't help being relieved as far as we're concerned. You see, now they're out of the running, the owner's agreed to give me more time to make up my mind on the property. I told him I couldn't possibly come to a decision until *you'd* had a chance to see it – and the whole area, of course. So I want to bring you down here the minute we're both free.'

Instantly, the churning indecision flooded back. He was so loving and so decent, so concerned about her opinion, she could hardly admit that, were the matter left to her, she would put it in cold storage for at least the next six months. Already, though, he was pressing for a date.

'I'll be back in London on Tuesday and obviously I'll have to stay to run the Friday class. But suppose we left the minute it's over; went on straight from my flat to Paddington and—'

'No, Friday's Amy's birthday and we're having a little supper party to celebrate. I'll be at the class, of course, but I'm afraid I'm busy the rest of the day. How about Saturday morning?'

'Sorry, I can't hear you. I'm out on a walk and the reception's pretty dire. Tell you what – I'll wait till I'm further up the cliff-top, then try you again, OK?'

'OK,' she said, feeling close to panic at the thought of having to make a decision in less than a week's time. It seemed a betrayal of her daughter to agree to view the property at all.

Until he phoned again, she was unable even to pick up her brush and just stared down at her palette, trying not to think of all the personal and professional advantages such a move would offer.

At its very first ring, she clicked on her mobile, her voice tense and harsh, as if a stone were lodged in her throat. 'Actually, Saturday might be difficult, now I come to think of it. Could we possibly – Oh, I'm sorry, Silas, I thought it was—'

'You sound odd. Are you OK?'

'Yes, fine. Er, happy Father's Day!'

'That's exactly why I've rung. I've never even noticed Father's Day before – hardly knew it existed, to be honest – but this year I've been aware of all the cards in the shops and all the hype in general. And that's made me think more deeply about being a father myself, and it doesn't seem quite so daunting, to be honest.'

'That's great,' she said, with a sense of mingled elation and surprise, although still finding it hard to shift her mind from Cornwall.

'In fact, I wondered if I could see you today? It would be rather nicely appropriate, I thought.'

'I'm sorry, I'm tied up.' Why was Silas always so last-minute in his suggestions, as if it failed even to occur to him that other people might have prior engagements? 'I'm going to a friend's for lunch.'

'Couldn't you get away early and come on here straight after?'

'No, I've arranged to stay all day.'

'But we need to talk, Maria. You see, I've come to realize – in fact, just this very morning – that I've been a bit unreasonable, demanding so much in return, before I agreed to meet your daughter.'

Our daughter, she silently corrected, although amazed that he should admit to being in the wrong.

'As you know, I was definitely hoping we might resume the whole sexual side of things—' He gave an awkward laugh '—but, to be perfectly frank, I doubt if I'm actually capable these days. All that cancer treatment doesn't exactly do wonders for one's libido. And—' Another embarrassed laugh '—*you* may be past it, too, of course. From what I gather, women in their sixties do often lose the urge.'

'Yes, true,' she said, feeling a total hypocrite, as she suddenly recalled the feel of the damp moss beneath her naked body as Felix straddled her in a lonely part of Countesspark Wood. Their outdoor sex on Hareshaw last week had proved so wildly exhilarating they had tried it again, twice. And, in the wood, an indignant jay had begun screeching raucously, perhaps objecting to such unseemly goings-on in its usually unscathed territory – which had made them laugh, then start all over again.

'So what I'd like to discuss with you is a different basis for our relationship – less physical and more—'

'Could we discuss it tomorrow, Silas?'

'No, I'm afraid that's not convenient. I have a check-up at the hospital and they may keep me hanging around for ages.'

'OK,' she said, tersely, incensed by the fact that he always put his own convenience before that of other people. 'I'll come over this evening.'

'Maria, you know I hate evenings. You seem to forget I'm unwell and get tired by the end of the day.'

Little chance of forgetting, when he continually harped on his illness. 'Well, how about Tuesday morning, first thing?'

'You don't understand,' he persisted, 'that it's important I see you *today*. You see, I want to make a definite date to meet Amy, and Father's Day seems the perfect occasion to do so.'

Could she be hearing right? She had longed for him to say those words since their very first encounter. Yet there was no guarantee that he might not change his mind by Tuesday, so, whatever the inconvenience, she simply had to agree. 'All right, I'll leave Kate's straight after lunch and should be with you by half past three, OK?'

'Perfect. See you then.'

She rung off, fazed by all the conflicting emotions: delight that Amy could meet her father, at last, yet annoyance at that father's manipulation; concern about Felix's reaction if he ever got to know she was discussing sex with Silas; worry that Kate might think her rude if she dashed off after lunch, or the girls be upset if she missed their dance-display.

Well, she had better arrive dead on time to compensate – which meant stopping work on her painting and getting washed and changed. And if she had left the house before Felix rang back, that might actually be a blessing because, in her present frame of mind, she couldn't cope with any more pressures.

Having cleaned her hands with turps, she gave them a final scrub with soap and water, then, returning to her easel, tried to calm herself a moment by focusing on the serene, unthreatening colours. Whatever the turmoil in her mind and whatever might transpire later on at Lewisham, she intended to enjoy the time at Kate's, however short. At least the only conflict in that easygoing household would be which of the girls should sit next to her at table, and whether Kate would allow them to risk spoiling their appetites by eating the gingerbread-men before lunch.

She rang the bell again, so loud and long this time that, even if Silas had dozed off in his chair, the shrill crescendo would wake him – indeed, would wake the soundest of sleepers. But still he didn't appear. She shifted from foot to foot, annoyed to have dragged out here on a sluggish Sunday train and cut short the happy day at Kate's, all in vain, it seemed. Could he have forgotten she was coming?

No, that made no sense. He might have cancer but there was nothing wrong with his memory and, anyway, they had made the arrangement only a few hours ago. She rummaged for her phone and dialled his number – a pretty pointless exercise, since, if he hadn't heard the bell, why should he hear the phone? And, as he didn't own a mobile, there was no way of getting hold of him if he *had* slipped out for some reason. But why should he go out when he had wanted to see her so badly? They had agreed on half past three and she'd actually arrived at 3.37, but surely even Silas wouldn't stalk out in a huff because she was seven minutes late.

Or was she being too impatient? After all, he *was* an invalid and did suffer with his bowels. For all she knew, he might have been caught short and was trying to clean himself up in the bathroom, unable to face her until he had made himself presentable. Or perhaps he had suddenly felt dizzy, or unwell, and needed time to recover before he made it to the door. In any case, Silas was a law unto himself, so she must simply wait it out and trust he would show up sooner or later.

She paced back and forth along the shabby corridor, her thoughts returning to Kate and Paul. The latter was so affable and courteous, she couldn't help contrasting him with Silas. Apart from his frequent absences in Frankfurt – which, in any case, were due to end next month – he seemed the perfect father, and she only wished her own daughter had been blessed with such a loving dad. However, that made her all the more determined to persevere with Silas until they had agreed a date for him and Amy to meet. And the perfect time would be round about Amy's birthday – a mere five days away. So, whatever it took, and however long she had to stick around, either ringing his bell or searching this whole vicinity, she wouldn't rest until that date was in her diary.

Chapter 24

'HAPPY BIRTHDAY, DARLING!'

As Amy appeared at the kitchen door, Maria went to meet her and enfolded her in a hug – the sort of gentle, careful hug now necessitated by the increasingly prominent 'bump'. 'The last year of your thirties, so make the most of it!'

'Think of *next* year, though. I'll be a proper mother then, with a baby nearly ten months old.'

'You're a proper mother now,' Maria told her, fondly. 'And I'm glad you've let me cook you breakfast just this once.'

'Yes, I can highly recommend the scrambled eggs with smoked salmon.' Hugo waved his fork in their direction before scooping up another mouthful. 'Far superior to my usual bacon roll at work. But I'm afraid I'll have to be off in a tick. It's an early start this morning, so all celebrations later, OK? And Amy, darling, I'll give you your present this evening, at the party, if you can bear to wait that long!'

'The suspense will kill me,' she said, seating herself beside him with a smile. 'And, talking of the party, don't go to too much trouble, Mum. I know it's your life class day, so we're not expecting the fatted calf.'

'Don't worry, the class only lasts a couple of hours, so I'll have plenty of time to make dinner.'

'I'm so glad Chloe and Nicholas can come.' Amy helped herself to eggs and toast. 'In fact, we ought to make it a double celebration – you know, with Sam being discharged from hospital tomorrow.'

'They must be over the moon.' Maria had finished her own breakfast and was already washing the egg-saucepan, aware of her busy day ahead. 'After him being in intensive care for – what was it, eight weeks?'

'Yes, but they're also frightfully anxious – I mean, having to cope on their own, without a whole battery of nurses to hand.'

'Well, let's try and make it as relaxed for her as possible – relaxed for all of us, in fact.' Little chance of that for *her*, but she was determined to keep her worries to herself, since Hugo had enough to contend with; still jetlagged after last night's flight from Dubai and bitterly disappointed that the two warring parties had failed to reach a settlement. 'I know how hard you two have to work, so it'll be just a simple, laid-back supper, at a time that suits you both. When she phoned, Chloe said Nicholas won't be working late, so what shall we say? Half past seven? Eight?'

'Eight is safer,' Amy said, 'so long as that's all right for Felix.'

'Yes, perfect.' Maria felt a new ripple of unease. Amy had insisted on Felix joining the party, to 'make him part of the family' – something of an irony when *he* was the one urging her to put herself and her art before family or duty. Yet at least it seemed to show that Amy had accepted their affair. In fact, her disquiet on that score had been replaced by constant speculations about the rival claims of her lover and her daughter. She even found herself working out the best possible time to quit her post as nanny, should she so decide. Autumn was far too early, whatever Felix might say, but suppose she stayed on hand for the baby's first six months – including its first Christmas – and then joined Felix in late January? She had, of course, forbidden him to breathe a word about Cornwall. The whole matter was on hold until she had actually viewed the chapel – a visit she had managed to postpone until tomorrow week.

'More coffee, Hugo?' she asked, resolving to ignore the unpleasant churning in her stomach that inevitably resulted whenever her thoughts returned to Cornwall. If her son-in-law could conceal his apprehension beneath a cheerful demeanour, then she must do the same.

'No, I'd better dash. But thanks for breakfast.' He gave them both a kiss, before grabbing his car keys from the dresser. 'See you this evening, OK?'

'I ought to be off myself pretty soon.' Amy drained her orange juice, then forked in the last of her egg. 'There's an important client meeting at 8.30.'

'Have you time to open your present before you leave?'

'No, let's have presents this evening, as Hugo suggested. And, anyway, Mum, I gave you strict instructions not to get me a thing. You've been far too generous already, buying all that baby stuff.'

Was it generosity or guilt, Maria speculated? The more Felix stressed the advantages of Cornwall, the more monstrous she felt towards her daughter and grandchild.

While Amy went upstairs to do her make-up, Maria sat at the kitchen table, head in hands, reflecting on a still greater source of worry: that of Silas's whereabouts. She had been back to his flat every day this week, yet, exactly as on Sunday, there had been no answer to the bell and no reply when she phoned. Endless frightening scenarios had begun to play out in her mind: his cancer had returned and he'd been rushed to some specialist hospital; he'd gone out on the Sunday to buy something for their tea and been knocked down by a car; he was lying unconscious in some high-dependency ward. Yet she had checked on all the local hospitals, *and* on both branches of the Marsden, and none of them had admitted a Mr Silas Keegan.

Perhaps he had simply panicked at the thought of being a father and decided to lie low. The prospect of any commitment, however vague or occasional, might simply be too daunting for him after a lifetime free of any responsibilities. The uncertainty of the situation was beginning to wear her down, even giving her bad dreams. Last night, she'd woken in terror after a succession of bombs exploded through her sleep; she had been dreaming of her mother working in the munitions factory, way back in the war, when, suddenly, the factory suffered a hit and erupted in sheets of flame.

Of course, she hadn't said a word to Amy about her worry over Silas, let alone to Felix. *He* would be annoyed that she should be expending so much time and angst on a man he judged as worthless.

All at once, she came to a decision. However busy she might be today, she would trek out one final time to Latimer Court and if she drew a blank yet again she would report Silas's apparent disappearance to the Lewisham police. It would make her timings tight, but she just had to keep him as her number-one priority, otherwise she knew she couldn't concentrate on shopping and cooking for the party. Admittedly, it was a good hour's journey to Lewisham, each way, and she would also need a fair amount of time to discuss the matter fully with the officer on duty – which meant almost half the day gone. However, if she went straight on from Lewisham to the life class and left the class the minute it was over, she should be able to conjure up a decent birthday dinner well before eight o'clock. For once, she was glad the cleaner was due. Normally, she was embarrassed by the sight of poor work-worn Sumiah tackling the heavy chores and had to restrain her natural instinct to pitch in with broom and bucket.

'Mum, are you OK?' Amy had reappeared, briefcase in hand; her previously pale face now glowing with blusher and lip-gloss.

'Yes, fine,' she said, hastily sitting up.

'Well, you don't look fine, slumped over the table like that! You're obviously dead beat, so why not do a Chloe and *buy* the food for tonight?'

'Shop-bought food for my daughter's thirty-ninth! I wouldn't hear of it. Anyway, I'm perfectly all right. I was just thinking out the shopping list.'

'Well, that's a relief. I thought you'd keeled over at first. But, look, I'd better run now. Enjoy your day, Mum.'

'Will do,' she said, feigning a cheery smile. Whether she enjoyed her day or not depended totally on what transpired with Silas.

Nervously, she hovered outside the police station, feeling horribly alone and somehow unwilling to go in. Finally, though, she forced herself to enter and walked up to the reception desk, her outward show of confidence belying her jittery mood. Once she had explained the situation, she was directed to one of the daunting-looking booths, ranged along the side of the room and constructed of what appeared to be bomb-proof, bullet-proof glass. As she entered, the automatic glass doors closed noiselessly behind her, sealing her off in a claustrophobic space, and she felt almost like a prisoner being punished for some transgression.

'Can I help?' asked the female sitting behind another wall of glass – clearly not a police officer, since she was dressed identically to the receptionist, in a pale blue blouse, blue cravat and saggy navy cardigan. Nonetheless, Maria repeated her story, which the woman relayed by phone to, presumably, someone in authority. There followed a frustrating three-way exchange – the female frequently breaking off to check various facts and details with Maria – before finally saying that an officer would be out to see her shortly and would she kindly wait for him in reception.

As the automatic doors released her, she joined a couple of other people who also seemed to be waiting, yet looked enviably relaxed; one chatting on his mobile, the other leafing through the *Sun*. Too tense to sit down, she studied the police noticeboards, her eye caught by the headline: *DO YOU KNOW WHERE THESE PEOPLE ARE?* It required courage to scrutinize the half-dozen featured mug-shots, for fear of seeing Silas's face. Could he have been kidnapped, perhaps, by an enemy from his chequered past, seeking revenge or retribution, or even have committed some crime himself? No, she must restrain her wild imaginings; there was bound to be a simpler explanation.

'Maria Brown?'

She swung round to see a cheery-looking officer with a chubby, freckled face and hair an unabashed flame-red, who introduced himself as PC Michael Forrester.

'Do call me Mike. I like to keep things informal. And may I call you Maria?'

'Yes, of course.'

'Right, come this way, Maria.'

He showed her into a small, windowless room and, having motioned her to one of the chairs, seated himself opposite. 'Now, I understand you're worried about a Mr Silas Keegan. Would you like to give me more details – when you last met him, what happened on that occasion, and whether you've asked his friends and neighbours if they've seen him or not.'

She recounted the story – third time – including her futile attempts to question the people in the flats adjoining Silas's, as well as those above him and below, and also detailing the enquiries she had made at all the local shops, and her phone calls to a variety of hospitals.

Having jotted down all she said, he then asked her for a full description of Silas, so he could check his records and see if anyone on the Missing Persons Register answered to that description.

'Won't be long,' he said, although every second of his absence seemed to crawl and dawdle, as if the clock had contracted some degenerative disease.

'No,' he told her, on his return, 'there's no one on the register bearing any resemblance to your friend. But, look, if you're really concerned, I'll call one of my colleagues and we'll come round to the flat with you and see what we can find. Would you wait for us outside this building, by the entrance to the car park, and we'll pick you up in ten minutes or so.'

Once outside, she peered through the tall, blue, metal gates at the impressive array of police vans, cars and motorbikes. Eventually, Mike drew up in one of the BMW saloons and, as she got into the back, he introduced his colleague as PC Yvonne Prescott: a solidly built woman with a majestic bosom but no discernible waist. She chatted affably as they drove along the High Street, but Maria found it difficult to say much in reply. She was looking at the normal, carefree people wandering from shop to shop; wishing she could be even half as calm.

Having parked outside Silas's dingy block of flats, Yvonne and Mike escorted her up the concrete stairs and along the seventh-floor corridor. As Mike rang the bell loud and long, Maria had a sudden vision of Silas appearing in person on the doorstep, making her look a total fool in front of the police.

But no one came; not even when Mike shouted Silas's name and banged on the door with both fists. And Yvonne's enquiries at the adjoining flats yielded no information. In fact, the man at number 728 slammed the door in her face, after yelling, in a furious tone, 'How many more times do I have to tell the lady I ain't seen the stupid old bugger? Is she deaf or something?'

And, at flat 724, the same doddery old lady appeared, whom Maria had also questioned frequently; the last time less than an hour ago. The crone repeated her story: no, she rarely caught a glimpse of her neighbour and had long since written him off as a recluse.

'I'm afraid I'm going to have to force the door,' Mike said. 'So, if you hold on here with Yvonne, I'll go and fetch the enforcer from the car.'

While they waited, the woman made more small talk, although, with her mind fixated on Silas, it was no easier for Maria to engage in conversation than it had been earlier. If he were, in fact, deliberately avoiding her, he might be out now at the shops and would be incandescent with rage to come back home and find his flat violated, his front door wrecked.

When Mike returned, he was carrying something she recognized from television police dramas: a bright red metal object, about two feet long, with a handle on the top.

'Stand back!' he warned. 'There might be flying splinters.'

Yvonne led her out of harm's way, a few steps along the passage, yet, even so, she flinched at the sound of a splintering crash; watched the door fly open; saw the woman at 724 peering from her own door in astonished curiosity.

'Wait there, Maria,' Mike called, 'while we check things out.'

Yvonne followed him into the flat, leaving Maria on her own, apart from the nosy neighbour, still gawping and expostulating.

The minute she saw Yvonne emerge, Maria darted forward to meet her at the open door, recoiling at the stench wafting from the flat: a sharp, acrid, shitty smell – the smell of death, decay. 'Wh...what's happened?' she stuttered, screwing up her face against the nauseating reek.

Yvonne took her arm. 'I'm afraid it's not good news.'

Those chilling words, coupled with the fearful stench, could only mean one thing. The thought induced first disbelief, followed by choking panic. Could Silas be *dead*? But *how*? Last time they had spoken, he'd seemed reasonably well, even uncharacteristically upbeat. 'Y...you found his body?' she asked, surprised she could speak at all, so great was her distress, yet desperately needing confirmation.

Yvonne nodded. 'I'm very sorry, Maria. This must be a terrible shock. But you can leave everything to us, OK? What I suggest is that, while Mike deals with the formalities, I take you down for a brief walk in the fresh air, to settle your nerves and help you come to terms with the news.'

'No, I must see his body myself.'

'I'm afraid that isn't possible – not at this stage, anyway. It'll be taken to the mortuary and, since Silas has no relatives and you say you're his only friend, they'll need you to identify it formally. But that won't be until Monday, at the earliest.'

'It's important that I identify it *now*.' She knew she had to stand her ground. If Silas were dead – which still seemed beyond belief – it was imperative she proved that for herself; registered the appalling fact beyond all possible doubt.

'I'm sorry, but that's not our usual practice.'

'But I shan't be here on Monday. I'm going away – tomorrow.' Felix had persuaded her to catch a train to Cornwall first thing in the morning. Although such a trip was now completely out of the question, she had no intention of revealing that to Yvonne, since her overwhelming desire was not to abandon Silas to strangers.

'Even so, we still need to follow normal procedures, which include checking for any suspicious circumstances, or even a criminal element.'

'Look, Silas was seventy-six and he'd had cancer for seven years, so his death must have been from natural causes, surely.'

'We can't assume that and, anyway, we have to stick to the rules.'

'I need to see him *now*,' she repeated, politely but insistently, 'before I go away. He's the father of my grown-up daughter and I'm the closest person to him in the world.'

'But you'll find it extremely upsetting. The body's not a pretty sight. It's already started to decompose.'

Despite the surge of nausea rising in her throat, she made a supreme effort to appear composed. 'I can deal with that, Yvonne. I'm not someone prone to panic.' Panic already threatened to engulf her, but she strained every nerve and muscle to control it.

'Look, I'd better have a word with Mike, OK?'

As Yvonne went back inside the flat, Maria saw two more prying neighbours loitering in the corridor, clearly intrigued by the proceedings. Angrily, she turned her back, unable to bear their ghoulish faces.

When the officer returned, Maria was informed, although still with some reluctance, that Mike was willing to let her identify the body, since it was obviously so important to her.

Maria's courage almost failed, however, as she was led inside the flat and along to Silas's bathroom, where Mike was waiting for them. With every step, the vile stink increased, until she was coughing and retching in reaction.

The sight that met her eyes only increased her sense of shock. Silas was slumped on the toilet; his trousers drooping round his ankles; his body limp and lifeless; a sludge of mingled urine and excrement pooling at his feet; frantic flies already buzzing round the corpse. As she gazed, aghast, at the exposed genitals and grizzled pubic hair, she feared she might fall or faint, and had to clutch the officer's arm.

'Can you confirm this *is* your friend, Silas Keegan?' Mike asked, his kindly tone doing nothing to alleviate her mounting agitation.

'Yes,' she muttered, hoarsely, 'that's Silas.' More than just a friend; once, her lover; once, the man she had worshipped.

As soon as Mike received her confirmation, he radioed Force Control. 'We're at Latimer Court, flat number 726. Can you please contact the FME, Dr Tony Campbell, to attend and certify a death.'

FME? All sense and meaning were foundering as the normal world unravelled.

'Let's go into the kitchen,' Yvonne suggested, 'and I'll make you a cup of tea.'

In a daze, she let herself be steered into Silas's cramped, untidy kitchen. The waste-bin was overflowing; the draining board piled with dirty cups. Yvonne began searching for teabags, then checked the fridge, to see if there was milk. Yes, sour milk, which she sniffed with a grimace, then poured away down the sink.

'I don't want tea,' Maria said. If she drank a mouthful of anything, she knew she would instantly vomit. It struck her now, with horror, that Silas might have died as early as the Sunday, and shortly after they had spoken on the phone. Otherwise, if he were expecting her for tea, wouldn't he have bought fresh milk and washed the dirty cups, as he had done last time she'd visited?

'Are you sure, my dear? Strong, sweet tea can be helpful when you're shocked.'

Maria shook her head, still appalled by the fact that a man could expire so suddenly and with no apparent cause – unless something she had said on the phone might have precipitated a seizure or a heart attack? Maybe she'd been at fault all along, in trying to induce him to play a part in Amy's life, when he was old, ill and basically unwilling. Which meant *she* was to blame for his death, at least in part.

'Well, I think you should sit down, if nothing else. Shall we go into the living-room?'

'Living-room' seemed wrong. Nothing was living in this flat. However, she was grateful to have direction; a solid, motherly figure to support her shaky limbs, which seemed to have turned from flesh and bone to sawdust. She sank, trembling, into her usual chair, stroking the rough brown fabric and recalling Silas sitting opposite, tucking into his pizza and inviting her to live with him. Had she agreed, he might be still alive.

'Is there anything I can do to help?' Yvonne offered, still hovering by Maria's chair. 'Maybe phone a friend or relative, so they could give you some support?'

How could she tell a soul? A shock like this might threaten Amy's pregnancy, and Felix would be preparing for the class. In any case, she couldn't bear anyone to know the humiliating details of Silas's death. 'No, thank you. I'll just sit quietly.'

The silence and the stench seemed to coalesce into a curdled, miasmic layer. Phrases drifted through her head: dead silence; deathly hush; quiet as the grave; reek of putrefaction. She latched onto the words; tried to spell them out for a class of imaginary pupils. Any distraction was a life-raft, to save her from total collapse.

'What's an FME?' she asked, raising her head, at last, and almost surprised to see Yvonne still standing by her chair; substantial, busty, extraordinarily normal.

'It means forensic medical examiner – a specially trained doctor who deals mainly with prisoners in custody. Some do the job full-time, but most work on a contract basis and combine it with their other duties, as a GP, perhaps, or a hospital doctor. Fortunately for us, we found your friend's appointment card in the flat, and realized Dr Campbell is actually his GP, which makes him the ideal person to certify the death. He'll carry out a few tests and—'

'I want to be there when he does them.' She was surprised by her own request, yet it seemed crucial that, as Silas's only friend, she should remain with him right to the end; witness every process, however challenging.

'I'm sorry to keep saying no, but these things just aren't permitted.'

'Can't you ask Mike again? *Please*, Yvonne. This means a huge amount to me. And I assure you I can handle it,' she added, with less conviction than she felt.

Yvonne was gone for quite some while, but eventually reappeared to say that, since she seemed a calm and stable person, Mike had agreed to ask Dr Campbell's permission and leave it to *him* to decide.

She had never felt less calm and stable, and was worried that her nerve might fail if the FME were delayed. 'How long before he comes?' she asked.

'Well, they're usually here in under the hour and it's been half an hour already, so pretty soon, I'd guess.'

When she had waited at the police station, time had seemed to slow down; now it had speeded up. How could half an hour have passed? She was vaguely aware of having planned a schedule – hours ago, in some other, different life: attending a life class; shopping and cooking for a party. None of that seemed to register. There was only the horrendous smell; the sensation of being thrown off-balance, as if the earth had tilted on its axis and she was sliding off, plunging into nothingness.

'Are you sure you haven't changed your mind about the tea?' Yvonne enquired, in her usual soothing tone.

Again, she shook her head. Silas might have run out of teabags, or left a dirty spoon in the sugar packet. She didn't want him shamed; his domestic inadequacies revealed.

Silence ensued again, suddenly interrupted by the noisy fellow banging about on the floor above. She half-expected Silas to yell abuse at his 'cretin' of a neighbour, or even dash out from the bathroom and go thundering upstairs to bawl him out. Instead, she heard voices, footsteps at the door.

'Ah, that'll be the FME,' Yvonne said, as Mike came in, accompanied by a man in a smart, grey, pin-striped suit.

Having been introduced to the doctor, Maria stammered a hello, her attention distracted by his suave, well-groomed appearance, totally out of place in Silas's shabby flat. She had expected him to be wearing protective clothing, yet the dapper little fellow looked dressed for a directors' meeting in the boardroom.

'Maria is a close friend of the deceased,' Mike explained. 'And she'd like to be present while you certify death. How do you feel about that?'

Dr Campbell frowned. 'It's not our normal practice,' he demurred, echoing Yvonne's words.

Maria stepped forward purposefully. 'It means a lot to me,' she said, she too repeating her earlier words, 'and I assure you I can handle it.'

The doctor continued to look dubious and was clearly wrestling with his own misgivings. However, he finally agreed and also took the opportunity to express sympathy for Maria's loss.

She tried to return his smile, but her mouth formed only a grimace, as the four of them made their way to the bathroom. 'Stop!' she wanted to shout. 'I don't want anyone else to see him in this undignified position.' If only he could have died in his bed, or in the sitting-room; not trouserless on a stinking bog.

'This won't take long,' Dr Campbell said, kneeling beside the toilet bowl and opening his black bag. 'But could you stand well back, please.'

Maria pressed herself against the bathroom wall; glad, once again, of Yvonne's support. As the doctor placed a stethoscope on Silas's chest, she willed it to show some sign of life, however frail or weak. And when he picked up the limply dangling arm and felt for Silas's pulse, she found herself desperately praying, 'Let there *be* a pulse.' Finally, he lifted both the eyelids and, again, she begged Hanna's all-merciful God that Silas's eyes would flicker into life.

The doctor replaced his stethoscope, rose to his feet and reported tersely:

'I would consider your friend to have been dead for a matter of several days. As I said, you have my deepest sympathy, Maria. And, if you need anything to calm you down, I can write you a prescription straightaway.'

Politely, she declined. It was essential she was in full command if she were to see this through to its grim finale and ensure that Silas went to his rest with due respect. If she allowed herself to be sedated, she might fail him in his final hours.

As they all backed out into the tiny hall, Mike was already radioing Force Control. 'Can we please arrange removal of a body from Latimer Court, flat number 726?'

'Now's the time for you to leave,' Yvonne said, gently. 'Mike and I will remain here until the ambulance arrives, but it could take up to a couple of hours, so I'd advise you to go home and get some rest.'

Although tempted by this easy option, Maria refused to weaken. 'No,' she said, emphatically. 'I prefer to stay.' Two hours, three hours, four hours – time was of no consequence. All she knew was that she had to do her duty by Amy's father; not hand him over to people who would fail to understand that he was a gifted individual whose lifelong ambition was to make his mark as a poet.

When the men finally arrived to remove the body, again she was jolted by their appearance. She had assumed that those who did such work would wear white coats or overalls, whereas this pair was attired like undertakers, in sleekly formal black suits. They were trundling a strange contraption into the flat – a cross between a stretcher and a trolley – and although she had got up from her chair to meet them in the hall, the two officers tried to persuade her to return.

'This is not for you to see,' Mike warned. 'I'd like you to stay with Yvonne in the sitting-room, OK?'

'Silas would want me to be with him,' she said, determined, once again, not to be overruled, and thus adopting the same steely tone she had used with the FME. Without her present, they might handle Silas insensitively, or treat this solemn task as just routine.

She noticed Mike and Yvonne exchange glances with the men, then, after a tense pause, the four consulted amongst themselves in barely audible voices. However, her resolute, assertive stance must have reassured them, because she was led along to the bathroom, behind the undertakers.

As she saw the two men donning rubber gloves, she squeezed past them in the confining space and crouched by Silas's body. 'I want to say goodbye,' she told them, again speaking with authority and rigour, in the hope of being obeyed.

Taking Silas's unresponsive hand, she whispered under her breath, 'Thank you, Silas, for everything. You taught me so much; widened my whole world. And thank you most of all for Amy. Even if you didn't want her, you'd have been proud of her, I know, if only you could have met her.' It required all her self-control not to weep, not to retch at the overpowering stink, but if she showed the slightest sign of weakness, Mike and Yvonne might well insist she left. So she kept her voice as steady as possible as she pronounced her final goodbye. 'I'll never forget you, Silas, my first love. Rest in peace.'

Having kissed his hand, she rose to her feet, letting the undertakers take her place. With almost callous expertise, they positioned themselves, one at Silas's head and one at his feet; took him off the toilet and manipulated his body into a large, heavy-duty, zipped black bag.

'Look away,' Yvonne advised.

Ignoring the advice, Maria continued her silent witness, as Silas was lifted onto the stretcher and wheeled towards the door. She followed at a respectful distance, but deliberately turned her back before the trolley was manoeuvred through the door and out into the passage. She had no wish to see Silas's goggling neighbours inflate a tragedy into some vulgar tabloid drama.

'The body will be taken to Lewisham Hospital Mortuary,' Mike informed her, as he and Yvonne returned to the sitting-room. 'As it's Friday today, the post mortem may be postponed till Monday, or performed tomorrow, possibly. One of our officers who works for the coroner will phone you on the Monday, anyway, to introduce himself, then phone again a day or two later, to give you the result. I understand you'll be away next week, so be sure to leave your contact details with us.'

Away? How could she go anywhere? Cornwall seemed a mere diversion compared to this catastrophe.

'And what I suggest now,' Yvonne added, 'is that I take you back to the police station for a cup of tea or coffee. Mike will stay here until the premises are secured, but *you* need a chance to recover.'

What she actually needed was a chance to be alone. 'I'd prefer to go straight home, if that's all right.'

Home. My God! For the last few hours Amy's birthday simply hadn't featured in her thoughts, but now the whole scenario came whirling back in a turmoil of anxiety. How could she cook party food, or play her part in a joyous celebration, when she was sick with shock and grief? And if she mentioned Silas's death this evening, it would shatter the mood at a stroke. Yet how, in God's name, could she hush it up, when her whole demeanour was bound to reveal her frantic state?

But as she moved towards the still gaping door, some instinct seemed to tell her what to do: she must ignore her own emotions and carry on as planned, although perhaps with a few short cuts when it came to the actual cooking. Her duty was clear and simple: she must call on those reserves of strength that had got her through today and extend them into the evening – right on till midnight, if necessary.

Amy had lost all chance of meeting her father, so her mother must be there for her, whatever courage that demanded.

Chapter 25

'HIS DRAWINGS ARE SO varied – that's what strikes me most.' Felix moved in closer, to study a sketch of a lightning-blasted tree. And, according to this—' He waved the information-sheet '—he takes inspiration from artists as different as Gainsborough and Jackson Pollock, so that's probably why they're so eclectic.'

Maria could barely concentrate. Indeed, she wondered what she was doing here at all; struggling to show some interest in an exhibition by an unknown Latvian artist, in a more or less deserted East End gallery. In her present mood, she would prefer to be at home, sitting by the phone, in the hope of further news about Silas's funeral arrangements.

'And this one has a real sense of movement,' Felix continued, once they'd moved on to the next work. 'The lines almost seem to dance! In fact, it reminds me a bit of oriental calligraphy.'

She knew she ought to take an interest, if only for Felix's sake. Fortunately, the next drawing was a life study, which made it easier to comment. 'It's amazing how he achieves the effect of a solid, living body with just a few delicate lines. Actually, it reminds me of how Rosie draws, at the class.'

'Yes, it's a pity you missed the last two. She did some really stunning work, both weeks.'

'I could hardly come when I'd just found Silas dead,' Maria retorted, her annoyance mixed with jealousy. Rosie (pretty, blonde and fortyish) had joined the class a month ago – although, in fact, if Felix felt attracted to a younger, more attentive woman, she had only herself to blame, having more or less ignored him since Amy's birthday supper. Even her phone calls had been rationed, despite his frequent offers of help. In truth, she was baffled by her own behaviour, aware only at some vague and troubling level that she was acting self-destructively. On the other hand, it was surely wrong to involve her present lover in her past lover's tragic yet unpalatable affairs. 'And the following Friday wasn't much better.'

'OK, OK.' Felix sounded tetchy, too. 'Let's not go into all that again. I just hope you'll be there tomorrow.'

She gave a vague murmur of assent; knowing Felix simply couldn't grasp how much Silas's death had affected her. All the pain and sadness of her *first* loss, in 1971, seemed to have come flooding back again; along with the depressing sense that men never stayed around, be it Amy's father, or her own. Nor had she yet recovered from the hideous shock of seeing Silas's stinking, flyblown corpse. However, that was no excuse for treating Felix so unfairly, especially when he was always so supportive.

'It's just struck me, Maria, you might find it interesting to have a go yourself at this ink-and-wash technique. And maybe also aim to copy Petrov's spare, ethereal style. His use of monochrome and his blurred, amorphous lines are so different from your own full-blooded exuberance, I reckon it would make a good experiment.'

'Funnily enough,' she said, trying to engage with what he was saying, 'I did attempt something new in that painting for Kate's husband. When things have quietened down a bit, I'd love you to come round and see it. I think you'll be surprised by how restrained it is.'

'It's fantastic you have a paying client. That's more than many artists do, even when they've been slaving away for decades. I reckon, once you've established yourself in Cornwall, the buyers will be queuing up!'

She tensed at the mention of Cornwall. The subject was taboo, at least until lunchtime, when she would be forced to break her news, since she simply couldn't leave it any longer.

'I admire the way they've hung this show,' Felix commented. 'The pictures are well lit and properly spaced, which makes me all the more annoyed about the mess they made of *my* show. One great thing about Cornwall is that I'm sure I'll be taken on by a new gallery.'

Every reference to Cornwall increased her agitation about how to soften the blow, and the remaining works passed her by in a largely meaningless ink-and-wash blur.

'You seem tired,' he said, once they'd toured the whole room, she proffering the occasional lame remark. 'Or maybe you're just hungry? I'm ready for lunch if you are.'

She nodded; forced a smile.

'I noticed several places when we were walking from the tube. What do you fancy? Mexican? Italian? Or a nice, fierce vindaloo?'

'Not Indian,' she said. 'Anything else is fine.' She knew her stomach would revolt at any sort of curry.

They eventually opted for a starkly simple bistro, mainly because there was plenty of room for them to spread themselves at a table at the back.

'I think we're in need of some wine,' Felix said, looking up from the menu. 'White or red?'

'*You* choose.' She seemed incapable of even the smallest decision and, anyway, it felt wrong to be drinking at all, with Silas still in the mortuary. She'd been having literal nightmares at the thought of what his captive body had endured at the post mortem. Sometimes, she woke screaming at the image of some callous butcher slitting it from top to bottom, as if it were a lump of meat; maybe gutting it like a chicken – even whistling while he worked, for all she knew.

'Well, I intend to have a steak, so shall we go for the Shiraz?'

'Fine. And I'll have steak as well.' These last two weeks, she had lost her appetite but, having neglected Felix all that time, it was imperative to make an effort now. And she certainly wouldn't broach the subject of Cornwall until they were feeling more relaxed, after a glass or two of wine.

Once the waitress had taken their order, she glanced around at the sombre walls and ultra-modern chairs and tables. There was no hint of colour in this place – everything as lacklustre as her mood. And, like the gallery a few blocks away, it lacked any sense of buzz or bustle; being empty save for one old fellow huddled over his plate and eating in a furtive, almost guilty fashion. And she herself was hardly a lively companion. Normally, she was never lost for words with Felix, but today every topic seemed perilous: painting, Cornwall, Amy, Silas ...

It was he who broke the silence, reaching for her hand across the table and giving it a loving squeeze. 'This time on Saturday, we'll be on the train to Cornwall! I just can't wait, can you?'

Unable to meet his gaze, she stared down at her lap. He had pre-empted her; scuppered her plan of finishing their meal before she weighed in with bad news. 'Felix, I ... I'm terribly sorry. I don't know how to tell you this, but I'm afraid I have to postpone our trip again.'

'Not a *third* time?' he exclaimed. 'What the hell am I meant to say to George? He's already changed that supper party from last Sunday to this, and he only arranged it in the first place for you to meet the crowd down there. But forget the party – what's far worse is losing the chapel. The owner's getting ratty and says if the other prospective buyers make an offer, he's going to have to accept.'

'But I thought that couple dropped out.' The waitress had brought their starters, but no way could she eat.

'They did. This is a different pair and they have cash up front, apparently.'

'But why on earth didn't you tell me that, when I had to cancel our trip last week?'

'I didn't want to worry you when you were so upset and shocked and, anyway, what good would it have done? You couldn't go, so that was that.' He glanced down at his paté, as if surprised it had arrived. 'Look, you mustn't think I didn't realize how devastating the whole thing was, especially coming out of the blue like that. And I also understood that you didn't want to see me for a bit. But Silas died a fortnight ago tomorrow, so surely by now, you—'

'Felix,' she interrupted, 'I had simply no idea how long everything would take and what a hassle it would be arranging a local-authority funeral. I deliberately haven't told you much about it, but you need to understand how complex it is. You see, first they have to be absolutely sure that the dead person hasn't any means to pay for it himself. So they'll do a search of Silas's flat, looking for a will, and, if they find one, that's proof of an estate, so the council won't cough up. They also check every single scrap of paper – old bills, address books, letters, diaries – anything that might reveal the existence of surviving family members, who might have funds themselves. And, of course, they snoop around for valuables – a gold watch, or real gold cufflinks, say, which have to be sold, to go towards the costs.'

'But Silas didn't own things like that – or not from what you've told me.'

'No, but they're hardly likely to take my word for it. Anyway, what I'm trying to say is that it seems to take an age even to arrange the search. But it appears I'm getting somewhere, at last, because they phoned first thing this morning and informed me it's scheduled for tomorrow.' In fact, she hated the thought of heartless strangers riffling through Silas's possessions, and felt stricken that he should have no cash or savings; no family to foot the bill.

Felix sat silent for a moment, ignoring both his paté and his wine. 'Tomorrow's Friday, Maria, and there won't be any funerals over the weekend, so couldn't we go on the Saturday, as planned?'

Before she could reply, the waitress bustled up to their table. 'Is everything all right?' she asked, noting their untouched plates.

'Fine,' Maria murmured, wondering how to answer Felix. Yes, technically, they *could* go on the Saturday, but emotionally she was in no state to make a decision on a property that would affect the rest of her life. 'I ... I need to be here, on the spot.'

'But you said that last week, too. OK, you were in the thick of it, at that point, but what else is there to do right now?'

'Well, the death hasn't even been registered yet.'

'Couldn't you do that tomorrow morning? Or even this afternoon? We don't need to linger over lunch, and I'll come with you, if that would help.'

'No, it's not me who does it. I'm not allowed, by law, because I'm not an executor or a relative.'

'Who, then?'

'The same guy that does the search – an Access Benefits Officer, called Clement Codd, of all names! But it seems he can't register the death until he's completely certain there isn't any will, or any living family members.'

'I'm sorry to seem thick, darling, but if it's this Clement fellow's responsibility, why do *you* need to be around?'

'Because he may phone me over the weekend.' She wasn't even sure if that were true. There had been so many phone calls, she'd become increasingly confused: calls from the police, the coroner's office, the Access Benefits Office. Even a local journalist had rung, hungry for a story.

'Well, if you gave him your mobile number, couldn't he ring you in Cornwall? I mean, it does seem rather extreme that you can't get away just for two or three days. That's all it need be, Maria – enough time for you to see the chapel and the village and a good stretch of the coastline, so you can make up your mind about us living there.'

She took a spoonful of soup and forced herself to swallow it. That was the whole problem: making up her mind. Whichever way she decided, there would be guilt, regret and worry, and she couldn't face any more upheaval until all the grim procedures concerning the disposal of Silas's body were finally complete.

'Felix, darling—' This time she met his eyes; gripped his wrist in a gesture of almost desperate affection '—I just can't decide about the chapel, let alone socialize with George's friends, while all this is going on. Once I have the date of the funeral, I'll feel more settled altogether. But it may take a while to arrange, because if the council decide they *are* liable for the costs – which I'm pretty sure they will be – they'll probably put Silas right at the end of the queue. Obviously, if the crematorium's busy, the free funerals can't take precedence. Actually, I was tempted to pay myself. Oh, I know I don't have the funds, but I thought of taking out a loan or—'

'Maria, that's insane! It could cost you literally thousands. Silas never did a thing for you, so why bankrupt yourself for him?'

Because she wanted Amy's father and the baby's grandfather to be buried with a modicum of style; not palmed off with a pauper's funeral. However, Felix would hardly sympathize with that.

'Couldn't Amy pay herself?' he suggested. 'It's her father, after all.'

'Felix, she's never even met him! And, anyway, she's no idea how hard up he was. I've always wanted her to see him in as good a light as possible.'

Felix gave no answer beyond a grunt.

'Look,' she said, flustered by his attitude, 'I really do feel dreadful, messing you about like this. But everything's so uncertain at the moment, I feel I just *have* to cancel – or at least postpone the trip – until things have moved on a bit.'

'OK,' he said, tersely, making no attempt to conceal his disappointment. 'We'd better wait till you're ready.'

The rest of the meal was strained, although they both put on a pretence of normality; discussing Petrov's drawings, and the gallery scene in general, over their soup and paté. And, even after they'd finished their main courses, they continued the charade of having enjoyed the food.

'Excellent steak!' Felix's show of relish, as he swallowed his last mouthful, was very nearly convincing.

'Yes, and I liked those crinkly chips. Chips may sound simple to cook, but it's actually quite an art to get them crisp on the outside and soft and floury inside.'

'You'll have to teach me to cook. I can manage omelettes and fry-ups, but not much else.'

Glad of so unthreatening a topic, she promised to show him the secrets of some of her grandparents' native Austro-Hungarian dishes. 'When my mother first married, she was trying so hard to be English, she tended to avoid them – and even more so once we were evacuated. And, anyway, the war was on and everything was rationed. But, later in her life, she'd some-times try her hand at goulash and Wiener schnitzel and apple strudel and suchlike, although that wasn't really her style. On the whole, she preferred plain and simple food.'

Aware of Felix relaxing, at last, she elaborated on Hanna's baking skills and the cakes she made for every church bazaar, garden fête and village celebration. And it wasn't until they were eating cake themselves – having chosen the chocolate gateau for dessert – that he returned to the subject of Silas.

'This is just a thought,' he said, leaning forward in his chair, 'but are you absolutely sure you have to attend the funeral?'

'Oh, definitely! There wouldn't be a single mourner otherwise and I can't let Silas go to his grave without a soul to say goodbye.' She glanced at the old fellow in the corner, who was now slurping his tea and staring vacantly into space. Maybe *he* had no friends and family, and might breathe his last with no one knowing or caring.

'But I don't like the thought of you being all alone on such a grisly occasion. I know you don't want *me* there, but what about Amy and Hugo? Couldn't they go with you, or even go on your behalf? Surely you've been through enough as it is?'

'That's out of the question, Felix. Amy's thirty-four weeks pregnant, so I need to protect her as much as possible from any extra stress. In fact, I've deliberately played the whole thing down and given her a censored version, with none of the ghastly details about Silas being found on the toilet, or being dead for so long. I've let her think he died instantly and painlessly.'

'But perhaps he did, Maria.'

'Well, the post mortem wasn't able to confirm that – only the fact he suffered a heart attack. Anyway, Amy's upset enough already.'

'But you just said she never met Silas, so it's not like losing a father she knew and loved.'

'Yes, that's the whole point – she was desperate to know and love him, and now she's lost the chance. And, in any case, she's totally exhausted.'

'But you're tired, too.'

'Maybe so, but I don't have a full-time job. Her hours are quite horrendous and last night she wasn't home till really late. The first Wednesday of every month, they have these big marketing dinners – black-tie affairs, at Claridge's. They may sound grand but they're just another form of work. And, even when she did get in, she went straight to her desk to polish up some job-spec or other – said it couldn't wait, because she had to discuss it with her boss first thing in the morning. Yet she was up at the crack of dawn, today, as usual, although she didn't get to bed till half past one.'

'Well, Hugo, then. Couldn't *he* attend the funeral, to spare both you and Amy?'

'No, that would be completely inappropriate. Besides, he'll probably be away. You see, at long, long last, they've fixed the date for the court case in Dubai and, as he's one of the key witnesses, he's booked to fly there on the 20th. That's less than three weeks away and even if by some stroke of luck they managed to fit in Silas's funeral before then, I wouldn't dream of asking him to slog out to Lewisham for the sake of a virtual stranger. To be honest, he's even more stressed than Amy – incredibly anxious about the trial and having to prepare his witness statements, on top of all his other work.' She pushed her plate away, having lost all interest in the gateau. 'No, I'm the one who has to go – me and me alone – and, anyway, I want to. It's my final service to Silas, you could say, and, after that, I'll devote myself to *you*.'

'Oh, darling,' he said, taking both her hands in his, 'I'm sorry I've been pressuring you. I just didn't realize how fraught your life is right now, what with Amy and Hugo's problems, on top of all the Silas stuff. So let's forget Cornwall altogether, at least for the next few weeks. If we lose the chapel, we lose it, but it's not the end of the world. There'll be other properties. And when this is over and done with and you've had a while to recover, *that's* the time to reschedule.'

No, she mused, wretchedly, it most certainly was not. Amy's baby was due in just six weeks and it would be unthinkable to be absent during the last fortnight of the pregnancy. So, if Silas's funeral was seriously delayed, as seemed likely at the moment, there would be no chance of going anywhere before January next year.

'Hello. This is Maria Brown. Could I please speak to the Access Benefits Officer, Mr Clement Codd.'

'Hold on,' said the bored female voice, 'I'll see if he's around.'

Please let him be, Maria prayed, otherwise she might lose her nerve. It did seem an imposition to be pushing the poor man, let alone asking favours.

'Mr Codd? Look, I'm really sorry to bother you, but I'm in a bit of fix. It's a matter of some urgency that I go down to view a property in Cornwall, but I can't make any arrangements until I have some idea of when Silas's funeral might be. So, if it could be sooner rather than later, that would be a terrific help.'

'Actually, I was about to phone you to check on convenient dates. We completed the search last Friday, as you know, and found no will, or valuables, or any trace of living relatives. So I registered the death this morning and now I need to book a slot at the crematorium. The statutory funerals are always at 9.30 in the morning, but you do have some choice as to date. And, if you're keen to speed things up, the first slot I could offer you is Friday, July 22nd.'

She did some quick calculations in her head. Friday was the life class – the last one of the term and maybe the last one altogether, if Felix moved out of London – but, with such an early funeral, she could be back in time for it. The 22nd was also Amy's final day at work, since by then she would be thirty-six weeks pregnant. However, if she and Felix left for Cornwall immediately after the class, they could return to London the following

Monday or Tuesday. Surely Amy wouldn't miss her during so brief a spell, especially as the pressures would be enormously reduced once she had started her maternity leave. On the downside, though, Hugo would already be in Dubai and she jibbed at the thought of leaving her heavily pregnant daughter alone in the house. Irritably, she shook her head, as if to dislodge the conflicting requirements and priorities; near-impossible to balance, without upsetting one person or another.

'The crematorium's not actually in Lewisham,' Mr Codd was explaining, 'but just a mile or two away, in Hither Green. You'll need to take a train to Grove Park station, then catch the 284 bus, which stops directly outside. And we like you to arrive at least—'

'I'm sorry to interrupt, but I've just had another idea. Is there any chance I could go to Cornwall *before* the funeral – let's say this weekend?'

'That's entirely up to you, Miss Brown.'

'I mean, if I left on the 16th – Saturday – would you need me for anything?'

'No. Once I've confirmed the date as the 22nd, then everything else is down to the funeral director. He'll collect the body from the mortuary, prepare the coffin and arrange a minister to take the service. Actually, I'd like to give your phone number to the minister, so he can ring you for a chat, a day or two beforehand. But, as long as you're contactable in Cornwall, I can't see any problem.'

'Yes, I'll have my mobile with me – the same number you always ring.'

So, Saturday it was! And, considering all the complications, it was a definite advance to have actually found a date, and one that seemed devoid of any hitch. Even if they didn't return from Cornwall till the Wednesday, they would still be back before Hugo left, since he was catching a flight to Dubai that very evening. 'By the way,' she added, returning her attention to the phone call, 'I'm extremely glad to hear there'll be a proper service. I thought the free funerals might dispense with any ceremony.'

'Please don't call them "free",' Mr Codd reproved. 'The council defrays the cost, but that doesn't mean we do them on the cheap. On the contrary, we make every effort to ensure the whole experience is as dignified as possible. We even provide a floral tribute for the coffin and, if you couldn't attend the service, then *I* would go in your place, simply as a mark of respect.'

All at once, she felt close to tears: tears of gratitude about Silas's last rites; tears of relief that they could leave for Tywardreath in less than forty-eight hours. It was Kate she had to thank for changing her mind. Her outspoken friend had told her how unwise it was to risk her relationship with Felix – and all it offered in terms of companionship, security and passion – for the sake of a shit who'd deserted her an age ago, and was now a bag of bones on a mortuary slab.

Even Kate, however, couldn't make the trip a happy one – not with the funeral hanging over her, and the dilemma about the chapel. She was going more as a duty and out of love for Felix, but at least she had come to her senses in putting him first.

Chapter 26

'So are you a painter, too, Ben?' Maria asked, turning to the dark-haired man on her left. She'd been so absorbed in talking to the Croatian sculptor, sitting on her other side, she had more or less ignored Ben.

'No. I trained as a furniture-maker, but my main line of work at present is making wall-reliefs in wood. George was decent enough to buy some – you can see them over there.' He pointed to the opposite wall, where three reliefs hung side by side, each framed in a contrasting textured wood. 'I tend to use what I call "found and forgotten" timber – things like battered fence-posts and discarded lathes from roofs.'

'I'm afraid I'm too far away to do them justice, but after supper I'll study them in depth.' Maria shifted her gaze from the wall-reliefs to take in the whole barn – its soaring, high-vaulted roof and the huge open-plan space, arranged in three separate sections: an old-fashioned kitchen adjoining this living/dining area (the large oak table seating them all with ease) and, at the far end, George's studio, with two easels, a long trestle table and a cache of paintings stacked against the wall. The ancient wooden beams reminded her of a church – a church full not of silver plate but of unusual artefacts. Every wall was crowded with pictures – mostly done by George's friends – and the shelves held ceramic pots, along with small stone sculptures. And, on a low table near the sofa, was Daniel's collection of treasures washed in by the sea: a ship's lamp from a wreck, a broken Spanish guitar, half a dozen copper nails from some ancient galleon, and one sad, abandoned plimsoll.

Quickly, she returned her attention to Ben, aware he was still speaking.

'I like to use wood from a single, local source for each of my reliefs. You see, I'm interested in how timber responds to its environment; the way all its marks and blemishes are a record of its history,'

'How nice that you celebrate blemishes, immortalize them, even!'

He laughed. 'I don't see it quite like that, but it's an interesting idea.'

'Hey, Maria,' Emily called, from further down the table. 'George says you and Felix are thinking of buying some sort of chapel. Can you tell us what and where?'

'Oh, yes, it's in Tywardreath, and we went to view it yesterday, the minute we arrived. Actually, Felix had seen it already, about a month ago, and fell instantly in love with it. And I felt just the same. Then, first thing this morning, the owner showed us round again and we both think it's pretty near perfect.'

In her mind, she saw, once more, the simple, granite structure; the tiled slate roof and high-beamed ceiling inside, similar to this one, but on a much smaller scale. What appealed to her particularly was its solidity and character; the sense of prayer and history giving it an other-worldly atmosphere. 'It has a most unusual layout, with the two bedrooms downstairs, and a little spiral staircase leading to the upper floor, which is open plan, with a gallery, and light streaming in from the tall, arched windows.'

'And the original pulpit is still in situ,' Felix added, with a grin. 'The only problem is, Maria and I can't decide which of us will get to give the Sunday sermon.'

Everybody laughed.

'Well, I'll come and listen,' Emily promised, 'whichever one of you presides.'

'Do help yourselves to seconds.' Inelegantly, George shoved a couple of dishes along the table. 'I'm afraid there's no waitress service, unless Daniel wants to oblige.'

'Sod off!' Daniel retorted, although with undisguised affection. The two made an incongruous pair: white-haired George at least three decades older than his partner, who resembled a pageboy in a Renaissance painting, with his shoulder-length bob of flaxen hair and bright, distinctive clothes.

'And pass the wine round,' George added. 'There's plenty more, so don't stint yourselves.'

Maria had no intention of stinting herself on anything this evening. She owed it to Felix to make these few days special and enjoyable, rather than cloud them with her cares. And, much to her amazement, she had actually succeeded in clearing her mind of all her current anxieties. She could justify such uncharacteristic hedonism because, if she returned to London revived and refreshed, she would be better able to give of her best, first to Silas, at the funeral, and then to Amy, during the last weeks of the pregnancy.

'I'm planning a series of landscapes,' she heard Felix announce to Daniel. 'And I want to avoid all traces of romanticism. I regard nature as basically indifferent to us humans; going its own unfettered way and maybe sweeping us off the planet in a tsunami or an earthquake, and I hope to capture some of that bleakness in the work.'

Daniel paused with a forkful of chicken halfway to his mouth. 'But isn't landscape art more interesting if it contains some spiritual element, or even a sense of the sublime?'

As the others joined in the discussion, Maria felt she was almost back at art school, but a very different establishment from the one of long ago. Instead of feeling out of things, she had been totally accepted by this group of professional artists, who appeared to regard her as their equal. And it was definitely enticing to think this could be her own new world; these people her associates; her work included in their joint shows. She might even get commissions, if she used their contacts and drew on their long-established client base. And there were bound to be more friendly meals and gatherings; maybe even close friendships with one or two of the women. She had been feeling rather lonely of late, especially with Kate and family away for half the summer.

And, although she would never admit it, Amy and Hugo's stylish but arid house, with its *Homes and Gardens* atmosphere, had never really suited her, nor the company they kept: all middle-class, all thirtyish, all well-heeled business types. Here, in contrast, was every type and age of person, from the elderly Croatian, Ivan, to Lil, the baby-faced young ceramicist, with her East End accent and her patched and tattered jeans. And none of them seemed to waste their time keeping their homes spotless and uncluttered, or fretting about investments, or slavishly following fashion. She also liked the way that Gillian's three children had been permitted to stay up, rather than banished to their beds as an unruly element. Bored with sitting at the table for so long, they were now playing on the floor, and no one seemed to mind their giggles, squabbles or even occasional shrieks. She allowed herself to fantasize about bringing her grandchild here, if only for a week or so, and introducing it to the joys of community living, in the hope it might imbibe some in-depth knowledge about arts and crafts and culture.

Ben reached for the bottle of Chablis and offered her a top-up. There was no need to decline because, although she and Felix had hired a car for this trip, neither of them had to drive this evening, since they were staying on the premises – in the converted pigsty, of all things; still empty after being vacated by a print-maker. In fact, she almost *wanted* to get high, as it helped to keep the worries at bay; the pressing need for a decision, if not now, then soon.

'I thought landscape art was dead and buried,' the jewellery-maker, Frances, said provocatively, her hand-made enamelled bracelets jangling on her wrists. 'At least for serious artists. Don't they leave it to Sunday painters these days, or to the tribe of commercial crowd-pleasers?'

'How can it be over,' Daniel countered, 'when we're part of nature and live surrounded by it? In any case, each new generation depicts it in a different way.'

The argument continued, until Lil suddenly exclaimed, 'Hey! Look at that sunset,' and all eyes turned to the large window facing west. The sky was aflame with scarlet, gold, vermilion; the sun itself a fierce, fiery ball, causing everything around it to dazzle, blaze and glow.

'Let's go outside,' Emily suggested, 'and watch it from the garden.'

They all got up and trooped out; gazing past George's well-stocked vegetable beds to the rolling farmland beyond. With a great whir and flutter of wings, a cackle of rooks began rising from the fields and skittering home to roost and, soon, the line of ancient beeches by the farmhouse was black with tiny bodies, each trying to push another off a favourite branch or perch.

'Let *us* be rooks!' Gillian's youngest proposed, and all three children went flying down the lane, flapping their arms and cawing. Despite the hubbub, there was a sense of essential peace in the warm scented air and balmy summer evening; the sun burnishing the ripening wheat to a deeper shade of gold, and the radiant sky flaunting its flamboyant colours, like a work of art itself.

As Maria stood and watched, she felt a similar glow flooding through her body, not just because her mood had so magically transformed, but because she realized at this moment that all her life she had been seeking her natural element and now, at last, she had found it.

Chapter 27

'EACH TIME I see this place, I love it more.' Felix stood back to assess the chapel's austere and simple façade. 'Its very plainness is attractive, don't you think – nothing fancy or frivolous?'

'Yes, it appeals to my abstemious nature.'

'There's nothing abstemious about you, darling, except for your Catholic conditioning. And,' he added, as they slipped round the side of the building, to explore the former graveyard, 'I didn't see much trace of the good little convent girl last night. That sketch you did of my cock was utterly shameless!'

'Blame it on George's wine! Wasn't it exciting, though, going back from the party and drawing each other naked?'

'I'd say! I've never known you so brazen – scrutinizing every nook and cranny of my body, genitals included, without so much as a blush!'

'Yes, but watching you get bigger and stiffer really turned me on – all the more so because we knew we couldn't touch each other until we'd finished our sketches.'

'I've never worked so fast in my life,' Felix quipped, giving her a quick, passionate kiss once they were hidden from the road. 'Perhaps we should frame the drawings and put them up in the chapel.'

'Lord, no! Wesley would turn in his grave.' And *she* would be seriously embarrassed. Felix had penetrated so intimately with his pencil, he had made her seem audaciously available, so that anyone looking at his portrayal would feel like a voyeur. 'By the way, talking of graves, I'm glad they've got rid of them here. I'm not sure I'd like to live surrounded by the dead.'

'Oh, I don't know. A ghost or two might be interesting.'

Maria shivered suddenly, aware of Silas's ghost still haunting her, until his funeral in just four days' time. To distract herself, she inspected the window ledges, checking on the condition of the stone. 'It's a good thing the owner doesn't live on the premises or he might think we're snooping – I mean, coming back a third time, on our own.'

''Course he won't. He'll just know we're keen.'

Keen, most certainly; convinced less so. She had promised to give Felix her decision tomorrow evening, yet she still hadn't quite succeeded in banishing her scruples. 'Let's go for a walk to the sea,' she suggested, almost wanting to remove herself from the source of so much conflict. Never in her life before had she viewed a house for sale, or been consulted as to its purchase, and although the experience was empowering it triggered all her worries again.

'OK, we'll leave the car here and go on a circular tour – down to Par Sands and back. I should remember the way, because I did that walk when I came in June.'

They set off, arm in arm, towards the church, pausing to greet an elderly couple, approaching with their dog.

'This place was once on the sea itself,' he told her, once the trio had passed, 'with fishing boats and a ferry and a really busy harbour.'

'How weird! So where's it disappeared to?'

'Well, the estuary gradually silted up and, over the years, there was so much sand and muck and stuff, it was no longer navigable. There was also a big medieval priory, which stood roughly where this church does now. But Henry VIII dissolved it, along with hundreds more.'

'My mother detested the man! Not only for his immoderate number of wives, but because of all that destruction.' Although it was her father, not her mother, who was actually on her mind, as they stopped to look at the war memorial just outside the church. A heroic and unselfish man, who had sacrificed his life for others, might be deeply disappointed in a daughter tempted to desert her grandchild and embark on a life of self-fulfilment.

'Well, lecherous Henry apart, I have to say I enjoy living in a place with so much history. Tywardreath is mentioned in the Domesday Book, so George says. And it's directly on the Saints' Way, which means we're walking the exact same route as the early Celtic saints. They thought nothing of travelling from here to France with no map or compass, in a flimsy open boat. In fact, one of them sailed right across the Irish Sea on nothing more substantial than a leaf – or so they say! I've been reading up on all that stuff and it seems miracles were two a penny then. There was a hermit who lived on a self-renewing fish and every time he ate a slice for dinner the piece grew back, ready for the next meal. And a saint who calmed a raging sea just by making the sign of the cross over the fifteen-foot waves.'

'Felix, you're beginning to sound as pious as my mother!'

'Oh, I love that sort of thing – so long as I'm not expected to take it seriously.'

'And *I* love being in a village again. Everyone we've passed so far has stopped to say hello, whereas in London they'd look through you.'

'We're still foreigners, though, to them. Even George is still regarded as an incomer and he's lived here thirty years.'

'It's a bit like that in *my* village, but it doesn't mean we're not friendly. And I do relish the peace and quiet here – no planes or sirens or traffic.'

'Don't speak too soon,' he laughed, as a noisy tractor came chugging up the street. 'Wait a sec – I need to check this road ... Yes, it's Well Street, which leads into Tywardreath Hill, so we go all the way down to the bottom and that should take us to Par Sands.'

'I've been thinking,' she said, as they strolled along in the sunshine, 'about my mother's cottage. Or *my* cottage, I should say, now that probate's come through. If I do move here, what on earth should I do with it?'

'Let it?' Felix suggested.

'But that's such a hassle, and difficult to do long distance, if I'm living in Cornwall, five hundred miles away. Anyway, I'm not sure I'd ever get tenants, unless I spent a fortune first doing the whole thing up. Frankly, I'd rather sell it and put the proceeds into the chapel. In fact, I like the thought of having some real stake in it.' Guilt stabbed and stung again. Hadn't she planned to make the cottage a country retreat for her grandchild?

'Then, if you wouldn't mind,' she continued, as if attempting to excuse herself, 'I could invite Amy and the baby to stay for occasional holidays.' Couldn't the chapel be the new country retreat? It was far superior to the cottage, in terms of its amenities and size, and would also symbolize a complete new start; a break with all the sadness of the past. The south should be gentler and kinder than the north.

'Of course I wouldn't mind, darling. In fact—' He broke off as a car came speeding round the narrow bend of Tywardreath Hill, and quickly yanked her out of its path. 'I should have warned you, this is a dangerous road, what with no pavement and blind corners and crazy drivers like him!

'Don't forget,' he continued, as they proceeded, with more caution, down the steep incline, 'the chapel already has planning permission for a garage at the back, so if we need an extra bedroom and bathroom, those could be built on top.'

She gave a noncommittal grunt, cursing herself for having broached the subject prematurely. If she were planning to have Amy to stay, he would assume the matter was settled and that she had dismissed her former doubts. If only there weren't other people involved – not just the living, but the dead. She could almost feel her mother's disapproval at the very prospect of selling the cottage when it had been their home and sanctuary since 1946. And another continuing source of guilt was the loss of the Treasure Box. The police had failed to catch the perpetrators, let alone retrieve the stolen goods.

'Look ahead,' Felix urged, once they had crossed Polmear Road and turned onto a footpath, 'for your first glimpse of the sea.'

She gazed out at the expanse of deep-blue water; the foam-flecked waves glittering in the sun. 'Oh, it's beautiful,' she said.

'Well, you may be disappointed. There's a clay-works on the beach, although it's not visible from here, and also a rather hideous caravan park, but that's conveniently hidden by the dunes. Anyway, you'll see for yourself in a sec, because this path brings us straight onto the sands.'

Once they were facing the whole wide sweep of the bay, she felt no trace of disappointment. A lone horse and its rider were cantering along the shore; people walking dogs and flying kites, and a posse of gulls swooped and soared in the generously blue sky.

'I *like* the clay-works,' she said, as they swung along the sand in the direction of the tall white chimneys. 'They add a bit of character.'

'Well, we'll have a better view of them if we walk to the end of the beach. Then we can return to Tywardreath a different way and finish up at the pub. Hey, talking of pubs, Daniel said there's a new gastro-pub in Fowey, with pretty decent food. And, as tomorrow's our last night, I'd like to take you out to dinner there and maybe drive on afterwards to Readymoney Cove. Emily's doing a series of watercolours, with different views of the cove, and I'd rather like to see it for myself, especially in moonlight.'

'Felix, a moonlit sea is far too romantic for *you*, for goodness' sake!'

'Well, I'm sure I could make it suitably stark, if I decided to paint it myself.'

He stopped a moment, to look out at the sea, screwing up his eyes against the glare. 'See that ship, far out on the horizon?'

She looked where he was pointing, but it was hard to make out anything beyond a blurry shape, veiled by the shimmering heat-haze. Her future, she realized, was equally vague and indiscernible; nothing settled, nothing certain, only nebulous hopes, fluid possibilities, unresolved temptations.

Yet, when she switched her gaze to the sand, everything immediately shifted into focus: clear, distinct, substantial and gloriously bright. And she was suddenly aware how futile it was to waste these last two precious days on creeping guilts and uneasy speculations. She must enjoy the shining moment, as she had done at George's supper party, and leave her decision till the latest possible point, tomorrow night.

Chapter 28

'THAT GREAT SHINING path across the sea looks incredibly romantic. Even you can't deny that, darling!' Maria gazed out at the scene: the waves shimmering and rippling beneath an almost-full moon; their frills of foam embroidered with a silver sheen; light and darkness swirled together in the part-luminous, part-sombre sky. This cove was like their own private beach, deserted at the midnight hour; the dark hulks of sentinel cliffs rearing up on either side, as if to ensure that no intruder invaded its seclusion.

Felix turned her round to face him and looked deep into her eyes. 'Yes, it's wonderful,' he whispered, 'and tonight I'm a true romantic. I haven't brought you here to get ideas for my work, but to ask you, officially and solemnly, if you'll agree to share my life.'

Instantly, she tensed; her decision still not made. Was it even possible to make so difficult a choice, when whichever way she decided would involve heartache and regret? The soft sssshh-ings of the waves seemed to fill the silence with an uneasy, threatening roar, and it wasn't hard to imagine this sultry summer night suddenly being riven by a storm.

Slipping from his embrace, she tried to focus on the beach, if only to still her mind by noting tiny details, like the artist she was meant to be: the tangled skeins of seaweed festooning the murky sand; the two sets of footprints stretching back behind them; his larger and more emphatic than her indeterminate ones. Then, moving her gaze outward again, she looked beyond the pool of glittering moonlight to the ocean's furthest edge. It seemed jagged and serrated, as if it had ripped itself from the black seam of the sky, in a last bid to remain unattached and separate.

'Maria,' Felix prompted, approaching tentatively, yet linking his arms tight around her waist, 'I'm not asking you to marry me – that's far too conventional for a woman as unique as you. I'm asking you to live with me, down here, and commit to me, as I promise to commit to you.'

She could feel his chest pressing against her back; his warm, solid hands clasping her cold fingers. How extraordinary that, despite the warm night air, she should be shivering all over, as if battling through a force-ten wind.

He bent his head to her shoulder and spoke softly into her ear. 'I understand how difficult this is for you, so I've tried not to pressure you. But before we leave tomorrow, I'd like to put in an offer on the chapel, so you do really need to tell me, is it yes or no?'

All at once, she knew one thing at least: her answer had to be instinctive, to issue from her heart. She had agonized too long already; tried and failed to make a rational, measured choice. She also knew that whatever words might spring to her lips would somehow be the right ones – that she trusted totally – yet still she wasn't sure what form those words would take.

The pause seemed endless; no sound except her slight, nervous cough, as she tried to clear her throat, and the ever-insistent swish-swish of the waves. The sea didn't care which choice she made; the barren moon was utterly indifferent; the clouds more intent on their own languorous, nocturnal movement.

At last, she swivelled round to face him, about to speak in the same soft tone as his, but the words erupted in a triumphant yell – a yell so loud the whole Cornish coast must hear. 'Yes!' she shouted. 'My answer's yes – "an *enormous* yes", just like you wanted me to say. I'll live with you and share the chapel. Yes, yes, yes, yes, *yes!*'

Suddenly, she was racing towards the sea, he pelting in pursuit, the pair of them whooping and hollering like Gillian's madcap kids. And, even at the water's edge, they stopped only to kick off their shoes and tear off their clothes in a fever of excitement, before wading into the jolting cold. She caught her breath as the water, with its fierce caress, began creeping up her legs, fondling her thighs; lapping against her belly; lingering across her breasts; a skilled and sensuous suitor, exploring every curve and hollow of her body.

She, the greedy woman, who had opted for pleasure and excess over the leaden chains of duty, was now revelling in two simultaneous lovers: the icy grope and tingle of the sea and Felix's scorching bush-fire of an embrace.

Chapter 29

'AH, YOU MUST be Maria.' A tall, grey-haired man reached out his hand in greeting. 'I'm Richard Osborne, the minister.'

'It's good to meet you in person,' she said, noting with approval his well-groomed appearance and freshly starched white surplice. She had no wish for Silas's funeral service to be conducted by a slob. 'But it still seems disrespectful to call you "Richard" rather than....' Her voice tailed off. Catholic priests were 'Father', of course, and the vicar back home was unceremonious 'Ron', but 'Mr Osborne' was surely more appropriate for this grave, patrician figure.

'Richard suits me fine, as I told you on the phone.' He gave a cautious smile. 'But how are you feeling, Maria? I do realize what a shock this must have been.'

She could hardly admit that she felt shamefully upbeat – her elation over Cornwall still whooping and fizzing in her mind. But her sanguine mood wasn't purely selfish, because she had come to see that Silas's death could be for the best, since he was finally at peace; no longer prey to money worries, or fears about his cancer. And although Amy was still devastated about this final blow to her hopes, it could have actually been worse had she and Silas succeeded in establishing a relationship. Wouldn't his death have been more distressing then, than if they'd never met at all? And at least her daughter had been spared the disappointment of meeting a father she had always over-idealized. The discomfiting reality would have offended her high standards – of that there was no doubt.

Aware that Richard was still awaiting a reply, she murmured a few anodyne words, but was spared the need of further conversation by the arrival of the hearse, which nosed slowly along the drive and drew up outside the chapel. The first glimpse of the coffin was daunting. However buoyant she might feel, it wasn't easy to see Amy's father shut up in a box. Yet, as Clement Codd had assured her, all the outward trappings looked every bit as impressive as for any high-class funeral; the four bearers and the funeral director all impeccably turned out. Nor had the council failed to provide their promised floral tribute – a small spray of white carnations had been placed beside her own extravagant red roses.

After a brief word with the men, Richard turned back to face her. 'Would you like to come into the chapel with me, just ahead of the coffin, or walk alongside the bearers?'

She opted for the latter, wishing to stay as close as possible to Silas until the actual committal, when – she hoped – a sad chapter in her life would finally be concluded.

As the bearers shouldered their heavy load and began their solemn procession, she realized that the large, high-ceilinged chapel made the lack of any congregation all the more apparent. Yet even that could be regarded as a blessing; at least there was no one present who might rouse Silas's ire. Even in death, he was unlikely to be filled with the milk of human kindness.

Schoenberg's *'Erwartung'* was playing on the sound system – an unusual choice for a funeral, and one that brought her up in gooseflesh as the soprano's haunted voice echoed round the chapel. In truth, it had required a lot of effort to devise a ceremony for a man whose taste in music was untraditional, to say the least. A list of Britain's favourite funeral tunes had proved of little help. No way could Silas be buried to the strains of 'Over The Rainbow', or 'All Things Bright And Beautiful', and even the top classical choices – 'Nimrod', 'Ave Maria', Pachbel's clichéd 'Canon' – he would have dismissed with utter contempt. Indeed, the crematorium's sound system had been hard-pressed to find the pieces she had finally selected: not just the Schoenberg but Berg and Shostakovich.

As the bearers approached the altar, she slipped into the front pew while they continued slowly ahead and set the coffin down on the catafalque. It still took courage to look at it and she was torn between relief that her once beloved Silas had, at last, moved beyond suffering and pain, and a deep sadness for his wasted life. In fact, the time and care she had lavished on the details of this service had been her way of making amends. The choice of poetry had been as taxing as the music. Unfortunately, she couldn't remember any of Silas's own works well enough to recite, and the poets he liked – Swinburne, Burroughs, Ginsberg – were totally unsuitable.

In desperation, she had spent half yesterday closeted in the public library, searching through anthologies, wanting something hopeful for Silas as compensation for all he had endured. But she had to avoid facile optimism, which she knew he would simply deride. Finally, she had decided on a poem called 'Begin', by the Irish poet, Brendan Kennelly; warming to it immediately, yet still worried it was too sanguine. But time was ticking on, so she'd had to make a decision – even an imperfect one – to give herself a chance to rehearse her reading.

Richard was already standing at the lectern and, once the bearers had withdrawn, began intoning the words of the service in his deep, melodious voice. 'We brought nothing into this world and we take nothing out.'

Well, that was true of Silas, although she felt distinctly uneasy at the many subsequent allusions to God, the resurrection and, yes, the heavenly life to come. But she had been forced to strike a balance between his fiercely atheistic views and Richard's role as minister; here to conduct what was, after all, primarily a religious service. She joined in the responses only warily, half-expecting Silas to rise up and rebuke her.

'Lord, you have been our refuge, from one generation to another....'

The words swept her back to Hanna and Theresia. God *had* been their refuge – and probably that of all Radványis. She herself had been the first one in the family ever to harbour serious doubts about the mercy, or even existence, of such a deity. Nonetheless, she still half believed; still craved to share their certainty of a life hereafter, where she would meet her father, at last, and all her other lost relations – which was the reason for her choice of poem, with its stress on a new start. Although Silas had no shred of belief in any sort of afterlife, she longed for him to live on in some fashion – however inexplicable – rather than be reduced to dust. And, after all, Felix had once told her that the world was so mysteriously complex, no mere human could ever comprehend it, which meant, in fact, that one couldn't rule out anything, despite it seeming unlikely or arcane.

Richard was just concluding the Epistle – her cue to take his place at the lectern. Clearing her throat, she tried to copy Silas's deep, declamatory tones when he'd read his own poems to her.

'*Begin again to the summoning birds,*' she recited, still feeling apprehensive, because the poem was so rooted in the material, secular world. Yet it pulsed with a stubborn persistence that seemed to say there were always possibilities, however great the problems or disasters. Was it too absurdly fanciful to imagine Silas, in some as yet undreamed-of sphere, becoming the distinguished poet he had always felt himself to be?

'*Every beginning is a promise....*' That phrase she liked in particular; its hopefulness well balanced by the sadness further on: '*Begin to the loneliness that cannot end.*' Poor Silas had known loneliness for the last twenty years of his life.

Her voice gained in strength and confidence as she reached the concluding lines, which reiterated hope again.

'Though we live in a world that dreams of ending
that always seems about to give in,
something that will not acknowledge conclusion
insists that we forever begin.'

And, as she returned to her seat, her former devout Catholic self sent up an unspoken prayer that Silas's end might become a new beginning in another, better – if admittedly unfathomable – life.

'I'm so grateful, Richard. You made it a beautiful service.'

'We both did,' he said, with a smile. 'But I'm afraid I have to leave now. Can I give you a lift to the station?'

She thanked him but declined. Having just watched Silas sink down, down, down, on the catafalque, soon to be burned to ash, she needed a chance to recover, especially as she was going on to the life class, where the mood would be joltingly different. (Felix had bought champagne for them all, to celebrate the end of term.)

Walking slowly round the Garden of Remembrance, she was glad of the serene and sunny weather. The balmy air and deep blue sky helped to lift her spirits, as did her constant memories of Cornwall; some of them blushingly inappropriate for a crematorium. Indeed, she had to repress an unseemly instinct to broadcast to the silent dead Tuesday night's cavortings in the sea; that electrifying blend of midnight dark and moonlit bright, of fiercely cold and blazing hot. However, sexual thrills apart, what afforded the most profound relief was having come to a decision, at last. Readymoney Cove would now always be more than just a beauty spot; it had become their marriage bed and wedding chapel.

She stopped to read some of the inscriptions on the plaques, but even they had no power to upset her, as they would have done just days ago.

Love is forever …

Being loved by him has enriched my heart …

Beloved husband and devoted father …

No way could such sentiments apply to her and Silas, but at least now she could accept the fact, accept that no one was to blame – it was simply a matter of malignant Fate. And even Fate itself had become benign, as proved by Carole's phone call last night. Her friend had rung to say that, against the odds, the stolen Treasure Box had actually been retrieved; found by a local farmer, stuffed into a hedge, all its contents miraculously intact.

And surely, Maria thought, as she sauntered towards the crematorium gates, that symbolized an important change in her fortunes, from loss and privation to abundance and fulfilment. In fact, she halted in her tracks, with a jolt of mingled pleasure and surprise, as she realized it wasn't only Silas who was finally at peace.

Chapter 30

A S SHE ALIGHTED from the train at Charing Cross, she made a conscious effort to leave Grove Park behind. Her ties with Silas were cut now and her future lay with Felix, yet the new life they planned together wouldn't need to exclude her daughter. After her six-month stint as nanny, Amy, Hugo and the baby could come down for frequent holidays in Cornwall, and her grandchild – maybe grandchildren – could be introduced to George's community and imbibe a little art and culture, along with the sea air. The only thing still troubling her was how to persuade her daughter to see the plan in a positive light and not as a defection.

She was still wrestling with the problem as she descended to the underground. Probably best not to bring up the subject too soon. If she left it for a week or two, Amy would have recovered from the shock of Silas's death – to some extent, at least. And she would certainly be more relaxed and thus more receptive to the news, yet they would still have plenty of time to make arrangements for a successor.

A train was already standing in the station. She dashed in through the closing doors and, as it rattled on its way, sat musing on the dilemma of how to find a first-class nanny without it costing a fortune. Suddenly, however, she was distracted by her reflection in the window opposite. The smart black outfit she had worn in Silas's honour was hardly suitable for the life class, but since there wasn't time to go home and change, she would have to rely on Felix to provide some sort of cover-up to protect her from the charcoal-dust.

She suppressed a smile of pleasure at the thought of them making love this afternoon. Although forced to be on their best behaviour during the actual class – no meeting of each other's eyes, or exchanging meaningful glances – the minute the others had left, they instantly stripped naked and passionately embraced. And their passion was still greater now they had made a solemn commitment to each other.

The train lumbered into Oxford Circus, where a crowd of people pushed into the carriage, making the already oppressive stuffiness still worse. One man in particular, perspiring in his business suit, gave an audible sigh as he slumped into a seat, then immediately began working on his laptop. His tense, frowning face reminded her of Hugo, and she couldn't help but feel relief that her son-in-law was in Dubai. His bad temper had increased of late, on account of the implications of the court case, which appeared, worryingly, to reach far beyond the financial. Amy had dropped further hints that he had been personally involved in some oversight or even outright negligence, which he feared would come to light.

Despite her deep concern about the matter, she was enjoying the fact that she and Amy had the house to themselves. And, of course, they would have more mother-and-daughter time throughout the whole of Amy's maternity leave. She intended to make that period as special as she could, as a tiny compensation for the fact she planned to leave in February. Although, actually, for all she knew, Hugo might prefer a proper professional nanny; someone he could treat as a subordinate, rather than feel a need to relate to, purely for his wife's sake. Sometimes, she suspected he had never wanted her to live with them in the first place, but simply gone along with Amy to avoid the risk of argument. So, when she left for Cornwall, he, at least, might be secretly relieved.

But she had spent long enough on the problem. The rest of today was devoted to pleasure and, as the train pulled into Maida Vale and she emerged into brilliant daylight from the tube, she felt something of the sun's own skittish exuberance as it flung its golden beams on pavements, houses, shop-fronts. She might be wearing black but, strolling the short distance to the studio, her mood changed to rainbow-coloured.

She was surprised to see a woman standing right outside the house – not one of the students, but someone considerably younger than most of those in the class, and much more stylishly dressed.

All at once, the girl stepped out in front of her; deliberately barring her way. 'Are you Maria Brown?' she demanded.

'Well, yes, but—'

'Right, we have to talk.'

Maria stared at her, astonished. How did this stranger know her name? Or *was* she a stranger? The woman's features and face-shape did seem vaguely familiar. 'Do I know you?' she asked, mystified.

'No, and I'm not exactly keen to further the acquaintance. But I *do* need to speak to you – now!' The voice was harsh, peremptory; the whole manner overbearing.

'I'm sorry, I'm due at a class and—'

'Oh, yeah, I know all about your classes. That's just the half of it, of course, but—'

'Look, I'm sorry,' Maria interrupted, 'but I've no idea who you are and I don't intend to be late for my class unless you can give me some explanation, or at least introduce yourself.'

'My name's Felicia Fullerton. Does that mean anything?'

It took a moment to register. Felix's name ... Felix's name twice over, the feminine equivalent.

'I'm Felix Fullerton's daughter,' the girl said, in confirmation.

Maria felt a shiver of unease, and also felt somewhat disconcerted, having assumed his daughter would be a woman in her forties, not a girl of twenty-five or so. But she could see the likeness now: the same grey-blue eyes and square-jawed face.

'I know full well what's going on between you two. There's just one tiny problem. My father happens to be married.'

Maria was unable to suppress a gasp. '*Divorced*,' she corrected, almost pleadingly.

'No, married,' the girl insisted. 'But we can't talk here, in public. There's a recreation ground just round the corner, so I suggest we go there, OK?'

Maria made no move, torn between shock and disbelief. 'I ... I thought you lived in America,' was all she managed to blurt out.

'I do. And I'm thoroughly pissed off at having to keep flying back and forth. If it wasn't for my father ...'

Felicia broke off as Barry and Rosie arrived arm in arm, for the class, stopping when they saw Maria.

'Are you coming in?' Barry asked.

'Er, yes ... In a sec.' No way must any of the students overhear some compromising discussion, so she allowed Felicia to steer her along the road, in the opposite direction from the studio. Once they reached the recreation ground, it looked even less private than the street, being crowded with boisterous children on holiday from school. But Felicia walked purposefully towards the furthest end, found an empty bench, some distance from the swings and slides, and, with barely suppressed resentment, pulled Maria down beside her on the bench.

'Right,' she said, 'you need to know the situation. But we haven't time to waste, because I'm flying up to Scotland early this afternoon.'

'Scotland? But I thought you said—'

'My mother lives in Scotland,' Felicia cut in. 'Dad moved her up there, ages ago, because he was keen to join some damn-fool artists' community.

The place was completely wrong for Mum, but Dad's twenty-one years older, so he always makes the decisions. Anyway, to cut a long story short, he buggered off when I was nine – shacked up with another woman, an older one this time.'

Maria gripped the arm of the bench. Felix had never divulged the fact that he had deserted his own daughter when she was still so young and vulnerable.

'Mum just fell to pieces and *I* was pretty shell-shocked, too, but I did my best to help, even at that age. And I resolved to stick around until I'd finished university, so she wouldn't be alone. But once I'd graduated, I was offered my dream job, at one of New York's top advertising agencies. Fortunately, Mum was OK with that, especially as I paid for her flights over, so she could visit quite a lot. Anyway, it was all going pretty well until, three years ago, she was diagnosed with breast cancer. Dad just didn't want to know – especially once he'd heard she was having a mastectomy. Damaged goods, I suppose he thought.'

The malicious remark only caused Maria to spring to his defence, despite her perturbation and reeling sense of shock. 'I'm sure he wouldn't think that and, anyway, if he'd left your mother all those years ago and was living with someone else, then—'

'He wasn't. The woman he ran off with didn't last that long, and neither did the next two. He's not exactly marvellous at commitment.'

'I'm sorry, but I still don't follow. He told me, several times, that he's divorced.'

'He *was* divorced when he met Mum, but that was thirty years ago. I reckon he was simply trying to fool you; deliberately hiding the fact that he married again and is still married to this day. That's typical of Dad! In fact, I think it actually *suits* him to stay married, because it gives him the perfect let-out if any girl he meets wants him to settle down, or – worse – make babies with him. He's not the world's best father. He gave me his name, but not much else.'

Maria's overwhelming instinct was to take to her heels and run, to prevent her having to hear another word. Yet the insistent, rancorous voice kept her there, a prisoner.

'In fact, after he'd walked out on us, we very rarely saw him and even when he did visit he'd sometimes have a woman in tow. I mean, how cruel was that to Mum? My loyalty's to her, and always has been, so when she had the cancer, it was me that held the fort, even though it meant giving up my job *and* my snazzy apartment in Manhattan. I spent eighteen months as her carer, and I can tell you, Maria, it wasn't exactly a picnic, so when the doctors said she was in remission I felt I'd done my bit and was free to leave. My firm agreed to take me back, thank God, so things were pretty good until just this month, when Mum found another tumour. Of course, I'm absolutely gutted, but, however rotten I might feel, I simply can't be there for her this time. I've already flown over twice this month, but if I stay in Scotland for the whole course of her treatment that's the end of my job. I can't expect any more favours from my boss, especially in a recession. It's Dad's turn now to help. He doesn't even *have* a job, for Christ's sake – apart from his so-called art. He put that first in 2008, so he needs to get his finger out and put Mum first this time. I mean, what about those vows he made – "in sickness and in health", and all that stuff?'

Maria sat in silence, her outward stillness concealing a fierce inner agitation. Felicia's phrases were stinging in her mind: *keen to join some damn-fool artists' community … shacked up with yet another woman … not exactly marvellous at commitment … deliberately hiding the fact he married again.* Could this be the Felix she knew; the one who seemed so decent and supportive? Yet, although appalled to have her idyll shattered, she was still not sure if Felicia could be trusted. It did seem peculiar that, having travelled all the way from the States, the girl had made no attempt to see her father; had actually stood outside the house where he was teaching, yet failed to go in and find him.

'I have to say—' Maria adopted a cool and distant tone '—I dislike the way you've sneaked behind your father's back and tried to blacken him in my eyes. And I still don't understand why you're talking to *me*, instead of him. Can't you have this out with him directly?'

Felicia all but snorted. 'Anything I say is worse than useless. Once he's involved with a woman, he's like a man possessed. Frankly, I find it disgusting, at his age. But I suppose he's desperate to prove his virility; brag to his mates that he's still capable of pulling girls, even though he's ancient. Admittedly, *you're* not a girl, Maria. In fact, if you don't mind me saying, you look years older than most of his other women. But, as far as I'm concerned, that gives me a bit of hope. Because I want you to break it off with him, and you're more likely to listen to reason than some ditzy babe who's too selfish to think of anyone but herself. My mother needs help – and badly – so his duty is to her now, not to you. And *I'm* in a fix, because I have to be back at work by next Monday at the latest. Which means Dad must get himself to Scotland at least a day or two before that, so I can be absolutely sure there's somebody around when Mum comes home from hospital.'

Maria was struggling with a maelstrom of contradictory emotions: compassion and resentment for the mother; a tangled snarl of pity, guilt and anger towards Felicia herself; splenetic rage with Felix – rage tinged with shaming lust. 'Look,' she said, trying to control her voice, 'I do understand how worried you must feel, but if your parents have lived apart for so long, it does seem a bit unreasonable to expect Felix to return now and pick up where he left off. Doesn't your mother have any relatives?'

'None that could actually help.'

'Well, friends, then?'

'Of course she has friends, but that's not the point. Dad's her legal husband, so he bloody well *should* be there!'

'Well, I doubt if he'll agree. I happen to know he's just put in an offer for a property in Cornwall.'

Felicia gave a derisive laugh. 'Oh, Cornwall is it now? Yeah, great – that figures! He chooses the furthest possible point from Edinburgh and imagines he can hide away and no one will track him down.'

Maria could feel the broken slats of the bench, uncomfortable and hard beneath her silky skirt. *Everything* was broken; splintering and fraying; smashed beyond repair. Yet suppose Felicia was vilifying her father simply out of spite? She certainly sounded bitter and vindictive. And there were several things in her account that didn't quite add up. If Scotland was so wrong for the mother, why had she remained up there for years, and wouldn't she herself, the abandoned wife, have sued for a divorce once Felix had upped and left? There was also the issue as to how she managed financially. As a cancer patient, she was hardly likely to work, so perhaps Felix still paid her maintenance. Most baffling of all, however, was Felicia's claim that he had deliberately stayed married, to excuse himself from subsequent relationships, since he had shown no hesitation in inviting *her* to share his life.

A hundred questions churned and seethed in her mind, but she was so overwrought she couldn't seem to put them into words. 'How did you find out about me?' she asked, at last, and lamely, 'Or know I'd be at the class?'

'The father of one of my friends is a close mate of Leo McCann – you know, the guy who loans Dad his studio on Fridays.'

'But Leo hasn't the faintest idea that—'

'You'd be surprised who knows. The art world's quite a small one. But we're going off the point. I'm appealing to you, Maria, for my mother's sake. She's only forty-six. Dad met her when she was barely out of school – took advantage of her, I wouldn't be surprised. But that's another story.

What I'm trying to say is you've *had* your life – she hasn't – and if you get out of my father's hair, there's just a chance he may come to his senses. I mean, he's not likely to meet any *more* women – not at sixty-seven. So if you break it off with him now, he may finally realize he's past it and—'

Felicia interrupted herself by glancing at her watch. 'Shit! Is that the time? I'll be late for my plane if I don't get off this instant.' Rummaging in her bag, she withdrew a business card and scribbled something on the back. 'That's my number in Scotland,' she said, springing up from the bench. 'I'm relying on you to phone me, once you've discussed this with my father, so you can tell me what he says.'

'Felicia, it's *your* responsibility to speak to him, not mine. I've no wish to be involved in all this private stuff.'

'But you *are* involved. When I spoke to Leo, he said Dad's besotted with you. You're just his type, you see – OK, maybe not as young as he'd like, but dark and arty and curvaceous. All his women were like that. Mind you, it's only the sex he's after. Sex is a sort of obsession for Dad, so unless you break that obsession by removing yourself from his bed, there isn't a hope in hell he'll ever see sense.'

'Look here, Felicia, I do seriously object to—'

'Sorry – gotta go! If I miss that flight, Mum will be—' And, breaking off in mid-sentence, Felicia strode off across the grass, dodging dogs and children as she dashed towards the gate.

Maria lacked the strength even to get up. But was that any wonder? She was *old*, like Felix – run to seed, moribund and 'past it'; 'disgusting' creatures, both of them, even to consider sex.

Muffled shouts and laughter were rising from the swings and slides – normal mothers with normal lives supervising their carefree kids, enjoying the beneficent summer's day. Only she could see the storm-clouds; the dark, oppressive weather threatening floods and landslides. She stared down at the grass, examining each blade, observing its specific shape and texture, its particular shade of green – all the things they were advised to do at the class.

The class! She had already missed a good half-hour. Felix would be worried; wondering where she was. Or maybe he'd assume she had been delayed at the crematorium. Did she even care what he thought?

Yes, passionately she cared. All very well for Felicia to order her to break off their affair. It was so much more than an affair: a new start; a whole new future.

Or was it? If she were just one of a string of women – Identikit women, all dark, curvaceous and arty – what future could there be, with a man useless at commitment? Even the artists' community seemed merely a tired repeat.

She leapt up in fury – fury with Felix; fury with his daughter; fury with her stupid, gullible self. How utterly pathetic that she had let herself be duped again, despite her firm resolve not to repeat the Silas debacle, or embark on another relationship unless it seemed completely foolproof. But, for all her caution, the entire thing had blown apart.

Yet some tiny, tiny part of her still dared to hope there might be some explanation that would exonerate her lover. Maybe Felicia was seriously disturbed, even psychopathic; perhaps inventing a whole tangle of lies, to wreak revenge for past neglect. Before she damned Felix, she had to hear *his* side of the story, which meant going to the class, however overwrought she felt, because the minute it was over she was determined to have it out with him.

Limping across the grass, past the happy, laughing children, she suddenly stumbled to a halt as recognition dawned. If Felicia was right, this could mean the death-blow to her own rare and precious happiness.

As she rang the bell, she heard footsteps coming down the hall and Barry appeared, disgruntled, at the door.

'Why are you so late?' he asked, annoyed at having to let her in midway through the class. 'I mean, we saw you outside a good half-hour ago.'

'I, er, ran into a friend – someone I haven't seen for years, so I couldn't just say "hello, goodbye".'

Fortunately, he probed no further, and they both slipped into the studio, as quietly as they could, although the others were so absorbed in their drawing they didn't even bother to look up. Except Felix, of course, who made his way towards her.

'Are you OK?' he whispered, in his formal 'tutor's' voice.

'Yes,' she muttered, tersely, finding it hard to even look at him. 'But I need some sort of overall.'

He disappeared a moment, running up to Leo's bedroom and returning with a voluminous man's over-shirt.

Only once she had put it on, found a seat and sorted out her drawing materials did she focus on the model, despite the fact that the woman was strikingly, flagrantly old. Although Felix used a variety of models, to provide practice in drawing different body types, never before had he engaged one quite so ancient. Yet, even given such a challenge, Maria found it impossible to draw. Not only was her mind in turmoil, but, as she gazed at the wrinkled flesh, the dangling flaps of breasts and sparse grizzle of pubic hair, she recognized that when *she* had reached this age – become a pitiful, pathetic creature destined for the grave – there would certainly be no lovers paying court. Indeed, it was extremely unlikely that there would be any after Felix. And thus she was strongly tempted to turn a blind eye to his duplicity (if duplicity it were) for the sake of being wooed and desired, this one final time – yes, even if the relationship proved to be ephemeral.

'Thirty seconds left,' he told the class.

She glanced at his untidy hair, his sensual mouth and muscly, paint-stained hands – hands that explored every secret crevice of her body. Did she have to return to celibacy after so blazing an initiation into those supremely erotic refinements?

'OK, Meg, could you take up a different pose now, please.'

The model moved with excruciating slowness; struggling up from the sofa and leaning on the padded arm, back turned.

'We'll keep this a very short pose, to save you any strain, Meg.'

Whatever else, he always showed consideration for his models and, indeed, for most people, so could he really be as selfish and unprincipled as Felicia made out? Could *any* man be kind and devious, caring and disloyal, passionate and unfeeling, all at once?

'OK, everyone, keep your pencils moving, please. Some of you need to free up a bit. And try to get the whole figure in, even in the quickest sketch.'

Maria struggled to focus on the task in hand; to capture the scrawny buttocks and forlornly drooping shoulders; the misshapen, bony back. Yet, already, her mind had veered off on a different tack: it wasn't just a matter of there being no lovers in extreme old age – what was far more crucial was that, by that stage, she would be facing imminent death; maybe even judge-ment and damnation, if her former faith was correct. So, the way she had lived her life would become of supreme importance. And no one could deny how gravely wrong it would be to deprive a lawful wife – a woman little older than Amy, battling a second bout of cancer – of her husband's care and presence.

Aware that Felix was looking at her anxiously, she made an effort to sketch the pendulous folds of flesh sagging from the model's upper arms. But, all at once, the charcoal jerked to a halt as an utterly shameful thought flashed, unbidden, into her mind: she wanted the wife to *die* – actually hoped the cancer would kill her – in order to free Felix from his ties.

Appalled by her callous selfishness in putting her own trivial sexual pleasure before another's woman's very health and life, it seemed the height of hypocrisy to rebuke Felix for *his* transgressions. Yet, in less than two hours' time – after a mockingly ironic champagne celebration – that was exactly what she intended.

Chapter 31

'WILL YOU GIVE me a straight answer, Felix – are you divorced or not?'

The pause seemed to last forever, until finally he said, 'I'm divorced in all but name.'

'What's that supposed to mean? You're being utterly devious. Hell, I remember actually telling you about those two men I met, years ago, who turned out to be married, so I had to give them up. Yet even then you didn't have the guts to admit *you* were married, too.'

'Look, I do feel really rotten about—'

'Instead, you've let me think, all this time, that you haven't any ties, yet now I find—'

'I intended to tell you – I swear I did. But you've had so much on your plate – all the Silas stuff and your dilemma about the baby – so I decided to wait till things were easier.'

'Until you'd bamboozled me, you mean, into uprooting myself completely and coming to live with you in Cornwall under false pretences. What hurts most, if you really want to know, is the way you trotted out that romantic line about me being so unique and special, it felt wrong for you to propose conventional marriage. Yet, the sordid truth is you weren't free to marry anyway.'

'I didn't want to ruin things – that's all. I mean, we were so amazingly close and—'

'*Close?*' She spat the word. 'How the hell could we be close when you were concealing so much about yourself? I feel utterly betrayed.' All at once, her mobile rang and, angry with it, too, she switched it off and flung it back in her bag, before some piffling call could interrupt her. 'And, of course, now I see why you were so opposed to us living in Northumberland, instead – a bit too close to Scotland for you, wasn't it, whereas Cornwall was as far away as you could possibly be.'

'Maria, believe me – I just didn't see it like that. Cornwall is where my friends are and where I felt you'd blossom as an artist. And, anyway, I'd no idea my wife's cancer had come back, or that Felicia was involved.'

'Yes, Felicia – let's talk about her. She seems to think you were hopeless as a father, not to mention a serial philanderer.'

'Maria, listen, *please*. If you keep hurling accusations at me and refusing to take in a word I say, you'll never understand.'

'What *is* there to understand?' Maria slumped into a chair. So far, they'd been standing facing one another, like two contestants in a boxing ring. 'Frankly, I don't see how you can defend yourself, but if you think you can....' With a shrug, she let the sentence peter out.

He, too, sat down. The circle of students' chairs was still in place; the remnants of the party littering the surfaces: empty champagne glasses, plates littered with crumbs and cheese-rinds. Normally, he was punctilious about clearing things away, but the minute the last student had left she had deliberately confronted him, to prevent him disarming her with what she would now regard as totally inappropriate kisses.

'I'd better start at the beginning, and what you need to know is that I only married Alice because she was pregnant with my child. I knew the marriage was wrong – not only because of the age gap, but because we had absolutely nothing in common. But she refused to have an abortion, and I felt she was far too young and vulnerable to manage on her own.'

Maria was stunned into silence. A repeat of her own history yet, in contrast to Silas, Felix appeared to have done the decent thing.

'The problems began even on our wedding day and became fifty times worse once the baby was born. Felicia didn't sleep through a single night until she was almost three. The strain was horrendous, especially as Alice was never cut out to be a mother, and I was teaching full-time, as well as trying to do my own painting. What I didn't know was that Alice had been mentally ill long before I met her – in fact, she was having treatment while she was still at school. OK, so it wasn't her fault she couldn't cope, but where she *was* to blame was in hushing it all up. Neither she nor her parents ever breathed a word about all the psychiatrists she'd seen and the drugs she'd been prescribed. I suppose I should have realized, but she was so young and pretty, I was blind to everything else. Well, I paid for my folly – and dearly. Every day was a nightmare and, even when I finally found the courage to get out, I felt tremendous guilt and worry. And what made it worse was that Alice spent the next few years deliberately turning Felicia against me. Everything was *my* fault: her moods and depressions, the fact she couldn't hold down a job, even—'

'But, Felix, why on earth didn't you *tell* me all this – ages ago, I mean?'

He crossed his legs; uncrossed them; sat staring at the floor. 'It seemed so – you know – disloyal. I just didn't want to rubbish her and, anyway, I knew I was partly to blame. I was the one who got her pregnant, and completely failed to see that she was far too neurotic ever to cope with a child.'

Barely able to digest this whole new raft of information, Maria felt torn between compassion and suspicion. If the mother was so seriously disturbed, how had she managed on her own once her daughter had left, or coped with the stress of frequent flights to New York? Besides, wasn't it odd that Felicia should champion so useless a mother against a father who appeared to have done his best? 'Felix, your daughter never said a word to me about any mental illness. How do I know you're not inventing all this, to justify yourself?'

'Well, Alice's medical records are big enough to fill a book, but I can hardly show you those, so you'll have to take my word for it. And perhaps my daughter also failed to tell you that I supported them both, financially – Felicia until she left home, and my wife right up to now. I've always paid Alice maintenance and I don't intend to stop. It meant I had to work all hours and take on soulless commercial jobs, on top of my teaching and painting. But the whole situation changed with my parents' death. They left me their house – a big, old place in Sussex, which I sold at the height of the housing boom, so it made a pretty tidy sum. And then my pension matured and, after thirty years teaching at a variety of art schools, it wasn't inconsiderable. I've told you, Maria, I'm not short of cash, which means I can afford to hire a carer to help Alice through this new bout of cancer.'

'But Felicia expects you to do the caring in person.'

'That's out of the question! Nothing would induce me to go back.'

'Yet you didn't seem to mind leaving a little girl of nine with a mentally unbalanced woman, whom you admit yourself was a lousy mother.'

He had the grace to look shame-faced, although still endeavoured to defend himself. 'Well, Alice's sister didn't live too far away, so she'd invite Felicia over, when she could, and even took her on holiday each year.'

A few odd visits and holidays would hardly compensate for an absent father and inadequate mother. 'I'm sorry, Felix, but, aunt or no aunt, your daughter seems to think she was pretty much neglected as a child. She told me that, once you'd left home, you hardly ever visited.'

'Yes, because, if I *did* go, there'd only be tears and tantrums. And, anyway, Felicia sees everything in black and while. She's determined to cast me as the baddie, who can never do anything right. She even blamed me for Alice's cancer, would you believe!'

Felix got up from his seat and crouched by Maria's chair. 'Listen, darling, I'm desperately, desperately sorry to have involved you in all this. I realize now it *was* my fault, for not telling you before. In fact, I feel a bit of a hypocrite – I mean, blaming Alice, a moment ago, for hushing up important facts, when I've done just the same. But I did try to broach the subject – honestly I did. I kept screwing up my courage, but somehow I'd always chicken out. That was cowardly – I admit it – but I was just so scared I'd lose you, and losing you seemed utterly unbearable.' Springing to his feet, he took both her hands in his. 'Let's not ruin everything between us. We've both had difficult pasts – both made mistakes and suffered for them, but isn't this our chance to start again?'

Suddenly, he was kissing her – a kiss so wild and frenzied, she tried to pull away; half-frightened by his vehemence. Yet his tempestuousness as a lover was part of this whole imbroglio. Could she really expect so passionate a man to have lived tamely and conventionally, without misjudgements, blunders, negligences? Besides, how could she take the moral high ground, when – as he'd just pointed out – there were similar errors in her own past? She had tricked Silas into becoming a father; neglected her own baby for its first two vital years, expecting her poor, widowed mother to drop everything and cope. And she, too, had concealed from Felix how profoundly disturbed she had been back then. Perhaps it was only human to suppress the more reprehensible aspects of one's character. Nonetheless, she still burned with anger.

Clamping her lips to his again, she kissed him with the same ferocity and violence; biting his lips, even drawing blood. Still locked in the embrace, he steered her into Leo's bedroom, flung her on the bed and began tearing off her clothes.

There were no preliminaries. She was in no mood for tender kisses; gentle, lingering foreplay. And *she* would take charge, for once. Struggling up from under him, she shoved him onto his back, sat astride him and responded to his thrusting with something more like rage than passion – rage with him for his deviousness, for his neglect of a wife and child, for all the casual women in his life, for his crafty disingenuousness on that moonlit Cornish beach. And rage with Silas, too, for wanting their child aborted; rage even with her father for dying before she was born; rage with the Church, for outlawing greed and pleasure, forbidding sex outside the bonds of marriage.

Only a sharp cry from Felix made her realize she was biting his shoulder almost through to the bone; not from a deliberate desire to hurt him, but from sheer intensity of passion. She seemed to have become an animal – a jungle-beast, baring its teeth, emitting barbarous sounds and moving with such violence she might snap a tendon or twist a limb and it would hardly even register.

Releasing his shoulder, she clawed her nails across his chest, again impelled by the same animal-force. Yet any pain he might have felt appeared only to spur him on, as he thwacked against her with equal vehemence. Was he goaded by a similar rage – rage with Alice, with Felicia, with *her*, for finding him out?

She didn't care; had moved beyond all guilts and worries; left normal bounds behind. All that mattered was the moment and their two plunging, pounding bodies.

They climaxed at the exact same time – suddenly, convulsively – but barely had she caught her breath when her whole mood changed entirely and, as she slumped against his chest, she was racked with shuddering sobs, like another sort of orgasm. She was weeping not just for herself, but for all the losses inflicted on her grandparents and parents, and on every Brown and Radványi who had ever striven, suffered, lost; grieving for Alice and Felicia; for all parents of all war-dead; for all broken, damaged things; for all false promises, false people.

While she sobbed, Felix lay completely still, making no effort to console her; the sheen of sweat on his body damp against her skin. She felt achingly alone, because such outrageous extremes of feeling cut her off from normal women – women like Kate, or Carole, who wouldn't dream of turning an act of love into one of vengeful aggression. She feared she might be cracking up; all the strain of the past few weeks threatening a repeat of her unbalanced state when Silas threw her out. No one could deny that she was seriously overreacting. Women had been betrayed throughout the course of history, so why make such a fuss about a few distortions of the truth?

Raising her head, she saw the marks her nails had left, scored across Felix's chest, as if he were branded with her dangerous lust. 'I'm sorry if I hurt you,' she said, her voice ragged, faltering.

'I hurt you, too.' He shrugged. 'In any case, there's no need to apologize for what's part of your basic make-up. You've suppressed your dark, instinctive side so long that, when it does explode, it's like a force of nature, almost cataclysmic. I really feared you'd do yourself an injury just now – maybe even murder me. But, actually, it turns me on! I've never been attracted to half-hearted, tepid women. For me, females must be passionate, and you're the most passionate one I've ever met – and, believe me, I've met a few!'

Abruptly, she got up. He was confirming Felicia's words that there'd been *strings* of tempestuous women, all discarded in their turn, and probably all deceived. She was just a 'female' now, and one of many. 'I have to go,' she said, tersely. 'It's Amy's last day at work.'

'But surely she won't be home yet? It's only twenty to four.'

'Maybe not, but I'd still prefer to leave.' She needed to be alone; needed to recover before she faced her daughter. Her throat was sore and parched; her whole body hurting and trembling, as if someone had wrenched it out of shape.

He, too, got up and stood facing her. Their sweaty, unwashed nakedness now seemed vulnerable, pathetic; their recent sex a chimera.

'Maria, you're in no state to go anywhere. Look at you – you're shaking! Anyway, we need to talk.'

'We've talked enough.' He would only pressure her again; insist they went ahead with purchasing the chapel, despite his wife's cancer and Felicia's predicament. Should she concur with that, leave the wife and daughter to cope as best they could, or break with him, not just from duty and decency, and respect for a broken family, but for fear of future heart-break? She simply didn't know; couldn't wrestle any longer with impossible decisions. 'I'm too tired to even think straight, Felix, what with the funeral and—'

'You're right – you need to sleep. Leo's out till late, so why not stay here, in his bed, and rest for a couple of hours. Then I can order you a taxi and you'll still be home in time for Amy.'

Whatever else, he was kind. Nor were his skills as lover in doubt, or his generous, caring nature. Yet he was also a practised liar; maybe a philanderer, and clearly an irresponsible father. She couldn't deal with all the contradictions, any more than with decisions; couldn't even argue any more.

She sagged down on the bed and put up no resistance when he tucked the duvet round her shoulders; simply turned onto her front, as if to block him out. Her eyes were closing of their own accord; her ears registered vague rustling noises, as if he were getting dressed, then the sound of footsteps creeping to the door. But, once she had heard the click of the handle and more footsteps going down the stairs, everything went silent, as she sank into a near-coma of a sleep.

Chapter 32

'LOVELY EVENING,' THE taxi driver commented, pulling up at the lights. 'July's not been bad at all.'

Maria made some vague response, hoping he wouldn't talk all the way to Sutherland Street. She had too much on her mind to indulge in idle chit-chat; seesawing as she was between desire and doubt, longing and suspicion, as regarded any possible life with Felix. If he had abandoned his own family, was he likely to stick with *her*? And, if Felicia was right and he'd turned up with another woman when visiting his wife, that was surely callous and insensitive. But suppose the daughter had inherited some element of the mother's mental illness, she could well be distorting the facts. Besides, considering the amount of anti-Felix virulence she must have imbibed from Alice, she could hardly be counted as an impartial witness. And, in any case, was it really fair to blame him for events that had happened long ago?

A sudden stretch of bumpy road jolted her out of her reverie but within seconds she was back, reflecting on Felicia's accusations. It was certainly untrue that the only thing Felix cared about was sex; he was as passionate about her art as he was about her body – a passion echoing her own. Maybe they *did* belong together and she *should* embrace her wilder side. On the other hand, how could she build her own happiness on the suffering of a wife and daughter, when her whole upbringing and education had stressed the sacred bonds of marriage, and the virtues of duty and service? Nor could she suppress the distressing thought that, had Felicia failed to waylay her, Felix himself might never have revealed his marital situation and simply established her in Cornwall under false pretences.

'Traffic's bad.' The driver gave a shrug, as they slowed to a near-halt. 'Always is on Fridays.'

His remark brought her back to Amy – her last day at work before she started maternity leave. It was high time she stopped obsessing about Felix's daughter and thought about her own. Perhaps she'd cook a celebratory supper, although first she'd have to check with Amy that she hadn't made arrangements to go out with her workmates for a farewell drink or dinner.

Switching on her mobile, she was surprised to see six missed calls. Why the sudden flurry, unless they were all from Felix – whom she had left a mere ten minutes ago – trying to persuade her, once again, that Felicia's account of things was biased and unreliable.

Mum, where are you? Please pick up. I think I've started labour!

Mum, help, for heaven's sake! Something really awful's going on. I'm bleeding now and –

Mum, please answer. I've rung Dubai, but I can't get hold of Hugo, and Chloe's out and I'm all alone.

Mum, I'm really worried. I've had to call an ambulance. The minute you get this message, come straight to the hospital. I need you, Mum – please come!

Barely able to control her agitation, Maria tapped on the glass partition. 'Driver, I've changed my plans. Take me to the Chelsea and Westminster Hospital – and as quickly as you can.'

'We can't go nowhere quickly.' He raised his voice above the noise of a pneumatic drill. 'And we're in trouble here, to start with. But I'll turn off down the next side street and try to avoid these roadworks.'

His words barely registered, as gruesome images of Chloe's dead twin shuddered through her mind. If Amy had suffered a haemorrhage, she too might have lost the baby. Or was it fighting for its life in intensive care? It would be premature at thirty-six weeks and, even at thirty-*nine* weeks, you couldn't rule out a tragedy, as Chloe's case so sadly proved. Besides, Chloe had rested far more than Amy, whose recent workload had been even more pressured than usual, as she prepared to hand over to her successor. As yet, she hadn't attended a single antenatal class, or even made a birth-plan, leaving all such matters till the last month of her pregnancy. Now, it seemed, there wouldn't *be* a last month.

With unsteady hands, she dialled her daughter's mobile, only to get the message-service. Deliberately calming her voice, she said she was on her way, then phoned the hospital direct. However, despite being passed from person to person, no one seemed to know if a Mrs Amy Talbot had been admitted or not. Perhaps she was still in the ambulance, battling through the same heavy rush-hour traffic. Or maybe the baby had been born en route; delivered by some inept paramedic and already dead or damaged.

Hurry, she urged the driver, under her breath; cursing every red light, every build-up of traffic, cursing London itself for being so invariably congested. If only the hospital were near a tube, then she could go by underground, but even the closest one was quite a trek away. She would never forgive herself if she arrived too late to help Amy through some unspeakable crisis. And it was her own fault entirely, for indulging in that shaming sex; that inexcusable sleep. If she hadn't been so focused on her own petty personal problems, she would have been home with Amy at the first sign of any trouble and could have taken charge immediately and provided some support.

More alarm bells began sounding in her mind as she recalled the shockingly high stillbirth rate in Britain and the chronic shortage of midwives, with its alarming link to maternal deaths. The mere thought of Amy dying made her sweat and shake, as if the cab had been involved in a collision and she'd been seriously hurt. And, if such a disaster should happen, however would she break the news to Hugo?

She snatched up her phone again. She must ring him anyway; say nothing more at this point than that Amy had gone into labour four weeks before her due date, so he must catch the next flight home. He was her designated birth partner and should be with her at this instant.

Pick up, pick *up*, she pleaded. It was late evening in Dubai, so surely he couldn't be in court still. Perhaps he had switched off his phone and simply collapsed into bed, shattered by the strain of the last few days' interrogation by hard-nosed prosecutors.

She left an urgent message, then tried Amy's number again, but there was still only the disembodied voice telling her to press the hash-key once she had finished her recording.

As she pressed it, she suddenly recalled her dream: Amy going through a protracted, painful labour, but with no baby at the end of it. Had it been a sinister omen? Even the fact she was wearing black – black for a funeral – seemed a disturbing portent.

She longed to speak to someone, just to dissipate her panic. If only Kate weren't on holiday, she might have agreed to meet her at the hospital; helped her through this emergency. Felix would help – that she knew instinctively – and, despite all the recent problems, her whole mind and body still craved him, like a drug; a drug that might be dangerous, yet nonetheless offered ecstatic highs. But phoning him would only increase her turmoil – the last thing she needed at present.

In her isolation, she found herself praying – desperately, instinctively. There *had* to be a God: a merciful and powerful being who could save precious daughters, precious babies. But, if He existed, why had He failed to intervene when Chloe's Simon was born dead, or when that mother on the news last night died on her way to an out-of-town maternity unit, because her local one had closed its doors to any new admissions? At least that wouldn't happen at a large, well-established hospital like the Chelsea and Westminster – would it?

'Dear Lord,' she begged, 'I'll do anything you ask, if you'll only spare Amy and her child.'

The driver took a sudden jerky turn into Drayton Gardens. 'This'll bring us out on the Fulham Road, and then it's only another hundred yards to the hospital.'

The minute he stopped, she leapt out of the cab, pressed Felix's three tenners into his hand and, without waiting for the change, ran towards the entrance; only slowed by the revolving doors. There was a queue at the reception desk, where she fumed, first, behind a sharp-faced woman giving vent to a vociferous complaint, and then a doddery old fellow with very little English, trying to make himself understood.

Once it was her turn, she explained the situation, but the receptionist didn't appear to know whether Amy would have been taken to the Labour Ward, or A & E, or – God forbid – had been removed to some other ward where women who had lost their babies were cordoned off from newly delivered mothers.

'I suggest you ask at Maternity Reception – third floor, Lift Bank C.'

Maria knew those lifts from previous visits. You could wait an age for one to come and, even when it did, there were often long delays, as patients in wheelchairs or on crutches struggled in or out. Among the group of people waiting was a mother with a pushchair, containing a child who looked gravely ill. His skin was grey and waxen, his eyes closed and purple-lidded, and he lay unnaturally still. Yet at least he was alive, Maria thought; had survived beyond his infancy, beyond a few brief hours.

The lift ascended ponderously, but, having positioned herself close to the doors, she was able to dash straight out when it reached her floor.

The girl on Maternity Reception confirmed that Amy had been admitted and directed her to the Labour Ward. But, as she stood waiting at the reception desk, hoping to speak to a midwife, a patient on a trolley-bed was suddenly wheeled from one of the rooms and rushed along the corridor, accompanied by a posse of grim-faced doctors and nurses, all scurrying at a frantic pace.

Maria clutched the edge of the desk, her legs turning to tissue paper. Was that *Amy* in the bed, being sped to theatre with another haemorrhage? Or might she have developed pre-eclampsia – a life-threat to both mother and child, and always linked to high blood pressure? As long ago as May, Amy's blood pressure had been highish, and the shock of Silas's sudden death might have pushed it up to danger level. Yet, despite constant advice from the midwives, she had failed to take things easy during the last two stressful months.

Maria shifted from foot to foot, feeling invisible in the current crisis. The air of tension was palpable: midwives darting to and fro; the receptionist urgently phoning for yet another doctor. And the situation wasn't helped by the agonizing shrieks echoing from another room further down the corridor – some poor soul in labour, maybe all alone.

Hours seemed to pass before, finally, a skinny woman approached and gave her the ghost of a smile. 'Hello. I'm Jean, the midwife looking after your daughter.'

'Is she … she all right?' Maria stammered, barely able to form the words.

'Yes, but we've kept her in.'

What sort of answer was that? Hardly informative or reassuring. Still, at least Amy wasn't in theatre, or bleeding to death. 'Well, can I see her?' Maria spoke with all the authority she could muster.

'First, I'll have to check with your daughter whether or not she wants that.'

Maria bit back a retort. After six desperate messages, begging her to come, wasn't it obvious Amy needed her?

Jean was gone an unaccountably long time, causing Maria to worry on a different count. Perhaps Amy was so distraught she couldn't face even her own mother. And why had Jean said nothing? Was she hiding some ghastly problem?

Once the woman reappeared, she led her along, with still barely a word, to a single room which, although large and light, looked bare, austere and clinical. Amy was lying on a high-tech bed, clad in a hospital gown and hooked up to some machine or other. Her face was pale and drawn, and tendrils of her long, dark hair, escaping from the chignon, lay dishevelled on the pillow. But the only thing that mattered was that her 'bump' was clearly visible – which meant she *hadn't* lost the baby.

Her relief was so vast, she darted across to her daughter and enfolded her in an euphoric hug.

'Oh, Mum, thank God you're here!'

Maria prolonged the embrace, exulting in the fact that no calamity had occurred. Amy was living and breathing; still miraculously pregnant.

'I need to check some blood results,' Jean informed them, moving to the door, 'so I'll leave you two alone, OK?'

'Yes, fine,' Maria said and, as soon as she heard the door close, asked Amy to explain the frantic phone calls.

'I'm sorry if I worried you but I was in a terrible state because, when I saw the blood, I thought I was losing the baby. I mean, I was having pains and everything, so, naturally, I imagined the worst. What made it really awful was that it happened in the office. Fortunately, no one realized, or I'd have died of embarrassment. I was in the loo, at the time, and I immediately called a taxi and went home. But when I couldn't get hold of you, or Hugo, or anyone, I really started panicking.'

'I feel dreadful, darling, not picking up your calls.'

'It's not *your* fault, Mum. This all came on out of the blue. And I realize now I overreacted, stupidly. You see, when I arrived here, they took me straight to Triage and a midwife examined my knickers and said there was hardly any blood at all, only a brownish discharge, and it was just a harmless "show" and not a haemorrhage.'

'So you're not actually in labour, then?'

'Yes, I am. I've seen the doctor, too, and he gave me an internal and told me I was two centimetres dilated. So there's a hell of a long way to go yet. In fact, most women would be sent back home at this stage and asked to come back later. But because I'm only thirty-six weeks, that's classed as a "high-risk" delivery, so they need to keep me in. And I have to be wired up to this damned monitor all the time, so they can keep a check on the baby. And the minute it's born, they'll need to call a paediatrician – you know, to make sure it's all right. They also gave me a steroid injection, which helps mature the baby's lungs.'

Any relief Maria might have felt instantly capsized. A cot was standing by the window, prepared with sheet and blankets, but would her grandchild ever lie there, or be whisked off to intensive care with undeveloped lungs? 'What's that noise?' she asked, aware of a sound that resembled a galloping horse, which she had instantly noticed on entering the room.

'It's the baby's heartbeat.' Amy moved her gown aside and pulled irritably at the monitor's two straps: one positioned just above her 'bump', one lying tautly across it. 'This lower strap is picking it up, which I suppose is reassuring in a way. But I can't stand the feeling of being tied down, as if I'm in a straitjacket or—' She broke off, all at once, clutching Maria's hand in a vice-like grip.

'God, another contraction!' Baring her teeth in a grimace, she shifted on the bed in a vain effort to get comfortable.

'Try to relax through the pain,' Maria urged, wincing as her fingers were all but crushed.

Amy said nothing more until the contraction had faded, then slumped back on the pillows with a groan. 'Relax? You must be joking! I've never felt less relaxed in my life. The last few hours have been a nightmare. Even when I arrived here and was lying in Triage, my waters suddenly broke. The sheet was absolutely soaked and I felt completely gross.'

'It's just a normal part of labour, darling.' Maria was worryingly aware that Amy was so fastidious, she was bound to find it difficult to accept the earthier aspects of childbirth, without balking at their 'grossness'. And, since she had continually postponed any antenatal training, this crisis had caught her woefully unprepared.

'And, of course, I'm terribly concerned about the baby. I mean, suppose it's born deformed or something? Or pitifully weak, like Sam. I can hardly bear to think about it.'

Despite her similar fears, Maria tried to take her own advice and at least *look* relaxed, however far she was from feeling it. She settled herself in the bedside chair and decided to let Amy talk, since she was clearly still over-wrought. If she could get things off her chest, perhaps she would settle down and focus on handling her labour in the most constructive way.

'And I'm really gutted that Hugo isn't here. I can't even get hold of him on his mobile, although I've tried half a dozen times.'

'Yes, I tried, too, but I presumed he must have gone to bed. The strain of the court case must leave him pretty drained.'

'But he *wasn't* in court – not today. It's Friday, remember, so all the courts are closed. He did ring me late last night – which was the early hours in Dubai – said he couldn't sleep, because he was so het up about an emer-gency meeting arranged for today by his lawyers A big, important one, he said, with all the agents and assistants there, and a lawyer from the PI insurers – oh, and Stuart Smith, that friend of his who's also involved in the case. Then he rang again in their lunch break and sounded just as fraught; said the afternoon session might drag on quite a while, and he wouldn't be able to take any calls. Of course, I told him not to worry, because for me it was only eight in the morning and, at that stage, I was perfectly all right. But it's a different matter now. I need him here, beside me, yet he can't possibly get back in time. Even if he caught a flight this instant – out of the question, obviously – it would still be a good ten hours before he got here. And, anyway, he's still not answering his phone. I've rung his hotel, too – in fact, just before you turned up, but they said he wasn't back.'

'But the meeting must be over by now. It's nearly eleven at night, his time.'

'I know. I can't understand it. I mean, he's usually—' She broke off as another contraction held her in its grip and she lay ramrod-stiff, until it passed, gritting her teeth in pain.

'You need to breathe through them, darling. I'll breathe with you, if that would help.'

'Oh, Mum, you are a sweetheart!' Once the pain had passed, Amy even managed a smile. 'Rather than offering to help, you've every right to say "I told you so!" I mean, all those times you tried to persuade me to go to relaxation classes and I didn't take any notice. But, you know, it wasn't just a question of being short of time; it was more …' She paused and frowned. 'This may sound crazy, but the whole prospect of labour seemed completely unreal. I knew all about it in theory, of course, but I'm only beginning to realize now that theory's no damned use.'

Again, Maria concealed her unease. Amy had always taken an over-intellectual approach to life, which didn't bode well for the next twelve hours or more. Her own labour had lasted twenty-four hours – an ordeal she had never forgotten. 'Well, at least *I'm* here, my love, and I'll help you all I can. And if you give me the hotel number, I'll keep checking with them, to see if Hugo's back. He's bound to turn up sooner or later, and I'll make absolutely sure he catches the next flight out. If I take care of that, *you* can concentrate on what's happening in your body and try to blank out everything else.' Was that even possible, Maria wondered, when Amy was so used to being in control and would want to make the calls herself?

The midwife returned at that moment and, having checked the monitor, jotted a line or two on Amy's notes. 'I know you haven't made a birth-plan, my dear, but have you given any thought to the type of pain relief you may want?'

'Well, I'm tempted by an epidural, but also pretty scared, because I've heard awful things about them.'

'That's surprising,' Jean said, 'because they're actually very popular with patients. Although, admittedly, there *are* certain risks I need to spell out, before you make a decision. Firstly …'

Before Jean had reached the third risk, Amy was already shaking her head. 'I don't like the sound of any of that. And anyway, I read about a case where they couldn't get the needle in, and it all went horribly wrong. And, after four failed attempts, the woman was screaming in agony.'

'Well, that kind of thing is exceptionally rare, and the staff here are—'

'Even so,' Amy interrupted, 'I don't want to take the risk. The woman in question was still having problems a whole year later, and that would be disastrous for me. I have only three months' maternity leave, so I simply must be fit enough to return to work in late October.'

Amy was still focused on her job, Maria realized with dismay. Indeed, if she'd had to leave the office mid-afternoon today, there were probably things she had failed to complete, which might be preying on her mind. 'From all I've heard,' she put in, aware her daughter might not cope without some powerful analgesic, 'an epidural can really help. There's always a worst-case scenario but, if Jean says that's so unlikely, are you sure you won't change your mind?' She herself would have welcomed an epidural had they been available in 1972. Instead, drugless, hopeless and frantic, she had shrieked so loud they must have heard her up in Scotland, and actually attacked the midwife who had come running to her aid.

However, Amy's 'no' was so vehement, Maria desisted from saying any more; knowing she mustn't interfere.

'Well, we can give you Pethidine and gas-and-air,' Jean said, 'but not at this early stage.'

Amy let out a cry; gasping for breath at the pain of another contraction.

'Amy,' Jean said, firmly, seating herself in the second chair, 'if you tense up all your muscles, your breathing becomes fast and shallow, which only makes things worse. So I'm going to show you a breathing drill that'll help you handle the contractions. And, if you could learn it, too, Maria, that would be a bonus, because you can encourage your daughter to keep it up. I, or one of my colleagues, will stay here most all the time, although I may have to pop out occasionally. But, once you've established a good technique, Amy, you'll feel much more in control.'

As Jean began to demonstrate the breathing, there was a tap on the door and in walked a statuesque woman in a different, darker uniform. 'Hello, Amy. I'm the senior midwife, Harriet, and I've just come to introduce myself. How are you feeling?'

'Much better with my mother here. But worried, obviously.'

'Try not to be, my dear. We're monitoring you and the baby very closely and everything seems to be going well so far.'

Maria pondered that 'so far'. Did Harriet envisage problems further down the line?

Harriet murmured something to her colleague about needing her a moment, which made Maria start worrying again. Perhaps that patient rushed to theatre had died during a Caesarean, in which case, they *would* need extra help and, if they happened to be short-staffed, Amy might be neglected.

'Amy, I shan't be long,' Jean told her, 'then we'll resume the breathing practice. Just press this buzzer if there's anything you need, OK?'

'Anything I need,' Amy repeated, ironically, once they were alone again.

'I rushed here in such a state, I didn't bring so much as a toothbrush.' Suddenly, she giggled – a most welcome sound to Maria. 'You should see the list of stuff one of the online sites tells you to pack for your labour – video equipment, a CD of your favourite tunes, a laptop with computer games, jigsaw puzzles, playing cards—'

'For heaven's sake,' Maria interrupted, laughing now herself. 'It sounds more suited to an over-sixties cruise!'

'They even suggest you bring a rolling pin.'

'What, they imagine you'll have time to rustle up an apple pie?'

'No, it's for your partner to give you a nice, firm massage, in case you develop backache.'

'Well, I'm not sure I'd find a rolling pin in the Fulham Road, at this hour, but I could nip out and buy you a toothbrush.'

'Never mind a toothbrush – what I would like, Mum, is some orange juice and Lucozade. I haven't had a thing since breakfast, so I'm feeling really empty, but I'm not allowed to eat – only drinks, Jean says. Could you be an angel and go and fetch me some? The café may be closed by now but there's a drinks machine in the basement. Hurry back, though, please. I know it's quite pathetic, but so long as you're here, I don't feel half as panicky.'

'Don't worry, my sweet, I intend to stay and see this baby born! And I'll be back in two ticks, I promise.'

Once she returned to Maternity Reception, with a good supply of drinks, she paused only for a moment, outside the double doors, in order to summon all her strength. Amy needed her – maybe more than ever before. In Hugo's absence, she had become her daughter's birth partner, and thus was utterly determined to offer every possible help and encouragement it was in her power to give.

Chapter 33

'Mum, get *off*!' Amy snatched the cool flannel Maria was just laying across her forehead and flung it to one side. 'I don't want you fussing.'

The midwife exchanged a sympathetic glance with Maria. Cheery, chubby Linda had taken over from Jean at eight o'clock and, although it was now midnight, her genial good humour showed no sign of cracking, despite Amy's angry outbursts.

'I'm sick and tired of everyone! I wish you'd all—' The rest of the sentence foundered in a shriek as she was gripped by another contraction. Maria sat, impotent and silent, willing to take on this labour herself, if only that could spare her daughter.

'All I want is the pain to stop,' Amy muttered, once she was able to speak again.

'Well, in that case, my love—' Linda paused a moment and made an addition to the maternity notes '—I suggest we give you a Pethidine injection? That'll make you more relaxed.'

'What are the side-effects?' Amy demanded, tetchily.

'It's perfectly safe, given at this stage – first, let me assure you of that. It can make you feel a bit nauseous, and also rather dozy, but sometimes a little drowsiness can be a good thing.'

'Not for me it wouldn't,' Amy retorted, in the same peevish tone. 'I've told you already, I need to be in control.'

'You *will* be in control, but just a lot less tense.'

'It's a type of morphine, isn't it? I suppose you're just trying to dope me, because I'm not the ideal patient.'

'Not at all,' Linda said, amicably; her supplies of patience apparently inexhaustible. 'Many women find it very beneficial. But you might prefer to try some gas-and-air instead. Unlike Pethidine, that's out of your system in just a couple of minutes, so if you don't like the effects, you can stop immediately.'

'And what *are* the effects?' Amy still sounded deeply suspicious.

'Well, again, it may make you feel a bit sick, but only if you over-breathe. And if I show you how to use it, there's no great danger of that.'

'Why not try it, darling?' Maria urged, wanting to cooperate with Linda in any way she could.

Amy turned on her in fury. 'Stop interfering, Mum!'

Maria tried to disguise her sense of hurt. For the first few hours, Amy had welcomed her help – indeed, seemed supremely grateful for her presence – but now every suggestion she made was either rejected or derided. She was beginning to feel useless and expendable and, in the absence of any practical role, her fears kept creeping back: suppose Amy's panicky state was damaging the baby in some way? And what the hell had happened to Hugo? Despite her frequent calls, there was still no answer from his mobile, and his hotel insisted he wasn't back yet, despite the fact it was 4 a.m. in Dubai. Had he had some dreadful accident? Was Amy about to be widowed, on top of everything else?

The next contraction brought such piercing yells, Maria could feel the pain lasering through her own body, as if she were re-living her own labour. Certainly, she would never forget that mounting, racking, relentless escalation of the pain. If only she could hold her daughter's hand again, kiss her forehead, stroke her hair, as she'd been doing up till now, instead of slumping doltish in her seat.

'I've changed my mind,' Amy announced, in the lull between contractions. 'I can't take any more of this, so I *will* have gas-and-air.'

With another of her sunny smiles, Linda unhooked the apparatus from the wall above the bed and handed it to Amy. 'Breathe in through this mouthpiece, Amy, when you feel the next contraction starting. Take three or four good lungfuls, then let it go, as the pain dies down.'

All went well until Linda instructed, 'OK, now let it go.'

Ignoring the midwife, Amy continued to gulp down ravenous mouthfuls, like a desperate famine-victim.

Linda adopted a firmer tone. 'Take your mouth away now, please. You mustn't over-breathe, Amy.'

'I'm scared to stop,' Amy panted, freeing her nose and mouth for a grudging couple of seconds, 'in case I start too late for the next contraction.'

'You won't, my love, if the two of us co-operate.' Linda seated herself close beside the bed. 'If I place my hand on your stomach, like I did before, then I can feel your contractions and—'

'No!' Amy snapped, cutting her off in mid-sentence. 'I don't want anything else on my "bump". The straps are bad enough.'

'In that case,' Linda concurred, compliant as ever, 'why don't you give me a sign as each contraction starts, and I'll say, "Right, breathe in *now*"? That'll be your cue to take in a few deep breaths, then, when the contraction eases off, you release the mouthpiece and breathe normally. Shall we give it a try?'

Amy nodded, clutching the handle so tightly her knuckles showed white with tension.

'Right, breathe in *now*!'

Maria felt the effort in her own lungs as Amy took a frantic, gasping breath.

Yet she saw her daughter visibly relax, so it must be working, thank God.

'Amy,' Linda prompted, after a couple of minutes had passed, 'the contraction must have worn off by now, so please let go of the mouthpiece.'

Again, Amy took no notice, continuing to snort in gas-and-air at a voracious, frenzied rate, only breaking off with an anguished wail. 'Shit! I'm going to be sick.'

Linda was ready with a bowl and, having mopped Amy's face, asked Maria to give her some water while she emptied the bowl and cleaned up. More than ready to help, Maria held the glass to her daughter's lips, then settled her back against the pillows.

'This really is gross,' Amy muttered, screwing up her nose against the smell.

That word again. How, Maria, wondered, with an increasing sense of dismay, would her stylish, squeamish daughter ever endure this gruelling process to its end?

'It's important to ration yourself,' Linda said, returning to Amy's side, 'or you *will* be sick, and also feel dizzy and light-headed. And you need to do what I say, because that'll make things easier for all of us, OK?'

'I'm sorry, I'm sorry.' Tears streamed down Amy's face. Suddenly, she seemed defeated; her former fury subsiding into deep distress.

'Your mum and I are here to support you, so try to draw on that support instead of fighting it, OK?'

This time, Amy co-operated and actually succeeded in establishing a regular breathing pattern; becoming noticeably more relaxed.

'Brilliant!' Linda encouraged. 'You're doing really well. In fact, now you've got the hang of it, I'm going to leave you with Mum for just ten minutes or so. If you tell her when the contractions start, she can encourage you to breathe, and remind you to release the mouthpiece, just as I've been doing. Is that all right with you, Maria?'

'Yes, fine.' Maria feigned a confidence she was very far from feeling. If

Amy panicked, or vomited again, would she be able to re-establish the procedure without Linda at her side?

'It's very simple, actually, but if you need me, just buzz.'

Maria positioned herself beside the bed, feeling ridiculously nervous, as she awaited Amy's next contraction, signalled by a harrowing groan. 'Right, breathe in *now*!' she said, copying not just Linda's words, but her calm, authoritative tone.

To her surprise, everything proceeded smoothly; Amy following her instructions and even letting go of the mouthpiece every time. After a few contractions, she even dared relax, relishing the fact that, once again, she had a useful role.

However, as Amy inhaled at the start of the next contraction, Maria suddenly realized, to her horror and alarm, that the sound of the baby's heartbeat had inexplicably cut off. The monitor was now eerily silent; the only noise that of Amy's panting breath. Oh my God, she thought, the infant heart must have stopped. Had the gas-and-air affected it? Had it lost its frail grip on life?

Frenziedly, she pressed the buzzer. No one came. She tried again, so hard it hurt her finger, yet still there was no response. Perhaps Linda was helping out in yet another emergency and thus deaf and blind to this one.

She leapt to her feet, giving Amy what she hoped was a reassuring smile. Her daughter, thank God, was concentrating so deeply on the breathing, she appeared unaware of the crisis. 'Back in a sec,' she said, casually, although her pounding heart belied the offhand tone.

'Don't leave me, Mum!' Amy cried, immediately losing her concentration and returning to her former fractious state.

Torn between her daughter and the baby, Maria knew she must get help. 'I just need to ask Linda something,' she said and, without stopping to argue, barged out into the corridor and ran full-pelt to the desk. 'Quick, come *now*! The baby's heartbeat's stopped!'

There was no sign of Linda, but a different midwife rushed back with her to Amy's room and went straight over to the monitor. While she checked it, Maria could feel her own body pumping with adrenaline, her palms damp with perspiration. Would the last eight months prove so much wasted time; the prelude to an infant's funeral?

'Don't worry,' the new midwife assured them – a petite and pretty Asian, in a dark blue headscarf that matched her uniform. 'The baby's moved a bit lower down, that's all. It tends to affect the monitor, but it's no cause for alarm. Everything's just fine.' She readjusted the straps and, instantly, the galloping noise was restored.

Maria's relief was so colossal, she wanted to kneel at the woman's feet. An expert and professional was infinitely superior to some bumbling, nervy mother like herself.

Amy, however, seemed distinctly thrown and, even after Linda returned and took over from her colleague, continued groaning and complaining. 'Can't you let me off this bloody thing?' she wailed, pulling against the straps. 'I can't stand it any longer.'

'It's important for the baby,' Linda reminded her, patiently, 'as I explained to you before. We need to keep a constant check on how he or she is doing, right up to the birth.'

'And when will *that* be?' Amy asked, sarcastically. 'Next week?'

'You're doing great,' Linda soothed. 'In half an hour, you're due for another internal, and I reckon you'll be six centimetres dilated.'

'That's nothing.' Amy gave a sigh of mingled exhaustion and despair. 'I've still got ages to go.'

'Yes, but every contraction brings you nearer the moment when you'll hold your son or daughter in your arms.'

Amy's only response was a grunt, followed by a gasping shriek, as she fought the next contraction.

Her gown was rucked up in the effort, affording Maria a glimpse of her daughter's naked belly. It looked so huge and solid, she longed to crack it open like an egg and release the baby simply, swiftly, without these hours of pain.

'I'm bloody hot,' Amy protested, once the contraction had passed. 'And getting disgustingly sweaty under these straps. Why do I have to have my baby in fucking July?'

Maria felt embarrassed by the swear words, which Amy never normally used. But, as she recalled from her own experience, labour made you foul-tongued and hysterical. She wrung out the flannel in the coldest possible water and sponged her daughter's sweaty face and hands. Expecting a rebuff, she was inordinately pleased when Amy squeezed her hand affectionately instead.

'Right,' said Linda, 'let's get back to the gas-and-air, in time for the next contraction.'

Leaving Linda to cope, Maria moved to the window, still needing to recover from the recent shock. She pushed aside the curtain, but the frosted glass blanked out any view and all she could see was murky, clotted darkness, pressing against the pane. Wasn't that like the present situation: everything sombre, blurry and uncertain – and, as Amy had just pointed out – no prospect of any light until much more time had passed? Yet, whatever it required in terms of patience and endurance, she knew she had to be there for her daughter and – please God – for the baby, if it *did* survive.

'Hi! I'm Dr Herbert, the doctor on duty tonight. I've just come to say hello.'

Maria murmured a greeting to the tubby man in blue scrubs – a genial-looking character, with a shock of ginger hair and joltingly scarlet socks. Amy, however, barely opened her eyes. The change in her was remarkable; no longer irascible and overwrought, but relaxed and even dozy. Three hours ago, she'd become so distraught, she'd changed her mind about the Pethidine injection – suddenly grabbing Linda's arm and screaming at the top of her voice that she'd swallow a *ton* of morphine, if only it would dull the pain. Not only had the opiate worked; its effect had been dramatic.

'I hear you've been a tower of strength,' the doctor remarked to Maria, once he had checked the monitor and exchanged a few words with Linda.

A tower of strength? A ruined shack, more like it. Her back ached, her legs were cramped, her stomach rumbled audibly, but with Amy still in labour it seemed reprehensible to think about herself. Yet she couldn't help wondering how long she could continue to play a supportive role while she felt so tired and drained. Her watch said 4.15, but time seemed suspended, as if she'd been confined to this room for days or even weeks.

Once the doctor had left, Linda put a hand on her shoulder, as if picking up on her thoughts. 'That Pethidine injection will wear off pretty soon, so why not take the chance, while Amy's quiet, to give yourself a break? You do look really weary, and I think you need to stretch your legs and get something to eat and drink. You'll find vending machines on the ground floor and the lower-ground. They're not that marvellous, to tell the truth, but at least they'll fill the hole.'

'Good idea. Thanks so much. In fact, thanks for everything.' In contrast to her own state, Linda was still her serene and energetic self, despite the fact she had been on duty for eight-and-a-quarter hours. 'You've been an absolute saint.'

The midwife shook her head in deprecation. 'You save your thanks for when the baby's born. I'm due to go off duty at eight, but I hope I'll get to deliver this baby we've all been waiting for!'

'You mean Amy's less than four hours away from the birth?'

'Yes, roughly that, I'd say. In three-quarters of an hour, I'll give her another internal and I reckon she'll be almost fully dilated.'

Linda appeared to assume there would be no major problems, yet she herself dared not be so confident. Not only was the baby premature, but a whole raft of things might go wrong in the course of the actual delivery.

As she made her way out of the ward, she passed other labouring mothers; some walking up and down, hugely pregnant and supported by their partners. She willed them to have their babies soon, and safely; to be spared too much pain or trauma, or – God forbid – any defect in the child. And she was suddenly aware of all the mothers giving birth in every country in the world; despairing, desperate ones, maybe, squatting in shanty-towns or hovels, concerned about their ability to feed yet another mouth. She sent up a silent prayer for each and every one, whatever their hardships or their situation: 'Let all those infants survive. Let the mothers manage, somehow.'

Once in the lift, she pressed the button for the lower-ground floor, as if needing to hide away for a while; an exhausted creature creeping down to the shelter of its burrow. And it did prove restful in the quiet, deserted basement, where the usual harsh hospital lights were mercifully dimmed, and no one was scurrying about, trying to deal with patients in crises.

She traipsed along to the vending machines and, having found one that sold ice-cream, decided to treat herself to three tubs of Ben and Jerry's. OK, it was greedy, but she needed strength and sustenance to help Amy through the birth. However, before she ate or drank a thing, it was imperative to ring Hugo again.

Perching on one of the uncomfortable metal seats adjoining the machines, she rummaged for her mobile, hardly daring to imagine the extent of her anxiety if, still, he failed to answer.

'Hugo, you're *there*! Thank God. But where on earth have you been? We've—'

'Never mind where *I've* been. What the hell's going on with Amy? I've only just picked up her calls.'

Maria heard the note of panic in his voice. 'Don't worry – she's OK.'

'You mean she didn't lose the baby?'

'No, she went into labour early and she's only a few hours off the birth now, but she's in the best possible hands. We're just praying everything will be all right.'

'I still don't understand what happened. Can you fill me in?'

Having explained the last twelve hours, Maria added, as tactfully as possible, Amy's intense concern about the fact that her husband and birth partner had been out of contact all night.

'Christ! I'm sorry, Maria, but yesterday's meeting dragged on much longer than anyone expected and—'

A note of embarrassment, even a certain defensiveness, had crept into his voice.

'We were so shattered by the time it broke up, Stuart suggested we went on to his Yacht Club, to recover – just the two of us. There was quite a crowd in the bar, including some of my friends from the old days, and – you know how it is – one drink led to another and then we started playing snooker and I just lost track of time. I also totally forgot to switch my mobile back on.'

'But we rang your hotel, as well, and they said you hadn't been back.'

There was a pause before he replied.

'No, I spent the night at Stuart's place. He was keen for me to see his new pad. It's only minutes from the club, you see, and, once we were there, he opened a bottle of bubbly, to celebrate his house move, and then embarked on a great long saga about his latest girlfriend. And, by that time, it was so late, we just crashed out.'

Both of you pretty pickled, Maria refrained from saying.

'In fact, I only surfaced five minutes ago and, of course, the first thing I did was listen to my messages and—'

'Amy's frightfully keen you get here,' Maria cut in, aware that time was of the essence. 'Her labour's been quite gruelling and this final stage will be more so. So can you get to the airport as soon as you possibly can?'

'Hold on a minute! It's already nearly nine here and by the time I've washed and shaved, got back to my hotel to pick up my passport, taken a cab to the airport and hung around for a flight, I couldn't possibly reach London in time.'

'Well, obviously you'll miss the birth, but at least you can see the baby on its birthday and can spend the evening with Amy.'

Another pause.

'Maria, I'm sorry, but this simply isn't on. I have to be in court first thing tomorrow morning. Sunday in Dubai is like Monday in the UK – the beginning of the working week – so there's absolutely no way I could fly to Heathrow and back again, and be here in time for the start of the court proceedings.'

'But surely, if you've just become a father, they'll let you miss a day or two.'

'It's not a question of "letting" me – it's a question of how it might look to the prosecution. They'll use it as a weapon in their case and make out I'm running away.'

'I don't follow. What do you mean?'

The longest pause of all.

'Maria, I didn't want to tell you this and, for God's sake, don't mention it to Amy – not until she's stronger – but I'm in pretty serious trouble. The only thing that matters at this moment is not whether I see the baby tonight, or in a week or so, but whether I'm able to make any sort of life for it in the future. I just have to stay and fight my corner, or I could lose my present job, my livelihood – even our house, for God's sake!'

Despite the heat of the hospital, Maria felt a sudden chill shudder through her body. How could her solid, dependable, upright son-in-law be facing dishonour and insolvency?

'I'm sure it won't come to that,' he added, obviously trying to reassure her, although the casual tone sounded decidedly fake. 'Our lawyers are pretty damned good and, at the meeting yesterday, they came up with a new strategy that could save the situation. But it would be suicide for me to leave at this critical juncture.'

'I see,' she said. She *did* see. But it didn't prevent her being furious, on Amy's behalf, as well as on her own, that, once again, a man should be absent, unavailable and devious.

'What I suggest,' Hugo continued, with the same feigned nonchalance, 'is that you take some photos of the baby, as soon as it's delivered, and send them straight across to my mobile.'

'Yes, of course I will. Good idea.' How could photos be a substitute for holding your own baby in your arms; introducing yourself as its father?

'And tell Amy I'll phone her as soon as she's able to take calls. But not a word about all this, remember.'

'Look,' she said, sharply, 'Amy already knows you're pretty deeply implicated.'

'Yes, but since she and I last spoke, things have … changed – and changed for the worse.'

'Don't talk in riddles, Hugo. I need to know what's going on, so could you please be straight with me.'

'Well,' he said, impatiently, 'the protective coating applied to the steel cladding was considerably cheaper than the one in the actual spec and—'

'Which I already know,' she interrupted, refusing to let him get away with prevarication. 'But it doesn't explain why you're in "pretty serious trouble", as you call it.'

'OK, I was at fault – that I can't deny. But I was so tied up with the purchase of our London house, it was all too easy to cut corners and lose focus. At the time, I was negotiating long-distance with a singularly inept estate agent in London, so the pressures were enormous. And, in the circumstances, I admit I let things slip through, because I was relying more on the contractors than I should.'

'Forget the contractors. Let's stick with *you*, OK?'

'Maria, you don't understand – it was the contractors who fouled up and, by the time I'd discovered they'd used an inferior coating, it was too late to start again from scratch. And, of course, to save their own skins, they were keen for me to hush things up. But the client happens to know I was a bit strapped to raise the deposit on the property, so he's making out that I benefitted from it personally.'

'And did you?' she demanded, determined to put him on the spot.

No answer.

'Hugo, I'm asking you, is there any truth in what the client claims?'

'Well, I suppose you could say the contractors made it, er … worth my while to turn a blind eye.'

'Are you telling me you took a bribe?'

'No,' he said, instantly defensive. 'I see it more in terms of a fee – you know, for solving their problem. They had their reputations to protect so, in a way, I was doing them a favour.'

Disgusted by his weasel-words, she sagged back in her seat, trying to come to terms with the fact that it no longer seemed a matter of negligence and oversight, but of downright fraud and corruption. And what if he were concealing more transgressions? Might he even land up in gaol?

Yet, when she tried to probe further, he suddenly clammed up, as if regretting everything he'd said so far.

Angry at his resort to silence, she returned to the attack. 'It seems pretty clear to me that, however you try to present it, it was still basically a bribe.'

'Maria, for heaven's sake, you're focusing on just one single aspect. What you don't appear to realize is the huge financial implications of not completing a project on time. If we hadn't complied with the contract programme, we'd have incurred cripplingly heavy penalties – and I'm talking as much as fifty grand a week. So, if I'd taken a strong line and insisted on removing the existing coating and applying the correct one, it would have delayed the programme fatally and left the contractor severely out of pocket. Then the firm would have been accused of mismanagement and all hell would have broken loose.'

'But what about the trouble you're in *now* – not to mention your legal costs?'

'Well, I admit that could be a problem if the firm hold me personally responsible and insist I engage my own lawyer. But, should that be the case, I'll make sure I find a really resourceful chap, who'll come up with a strong defence and claim mitigating circumstances.'

'I shouldn't have thought,' she countered, icily, 'that buying a house was an excuse for taking a bribe.'

'I've told you – it *wasn't* a bribe,' he snapped. 'You don't have a clue what you're talking about, so I refuse to discuss it further.'

Never before had her son-in-law addressed her in so rude and hostile a tone. Yet never before had he ever dreamed of confiding in her – actually admitting blame in the court case, at least to some extent, and notwithstanding his pathetically flimsy excuses. But, whatever he might have done, and however seriously implicated he might turn out to be, it was essential that they didn't quarrel; he was her precious daughter's husband, the father of the baby.

'OK,' she said, struggling to sound calm and friendly, despite her deep dismay. 'It *is* all very complicated, so I grant you I may not understand the technicalities. And, anyway,' she added, 'I'd better get back to Amy. She's pretty close to delivery.'

She registered the relief in his voice, as he too adopted a far more peaceable tone.

'I have to say, Maria, I'm damned glad you're holding the fort. And you're probably doing a far better job as birth partner than I ever would. Just between you and me, I wasn't exactly thrilled by the prospect! Amy's such a perfectionist, she might have felt I hadn't come up to scratch.'

Again, it was a shock that he should permit her to see a far less confident side to him than the self-assured outer shell he had always presented previously. Was he still hungover, she wondered, or had the stress of these last few days undermined his usual coping strategies? Yet she couldn't help reflecting that it was hardly any wonder he saw Amy as a perfectionist if he himself was prepared to let his own financial needs overrule high professional standards.

'Well, give her my special love and let me know the minute the baby's born.'

'Of course I will.' At least they'd managed to re-establish a cordial relationship, but, the minute she rang off, she sprang up from her seat and paced to and fro in an agitated state, unable to return to Amy until she had tried to calm the turmoil in her mind. Had her daughter any notion of how Hugo operated? Had he 'cut corners' on previous assignments; pocketed other backhanders?

Exhausted as she was, she could barely take in all the ramifications this latest bombshell threatened for the future. Having been up all night, her mind seemed out of service. The only breaks she'd had, so far, were two trips to the toilet and a brief stroll along the third-floor corridor, shortly after midnight. Yet, whatever the state of her grey cells, her chest and stomach had registered the news: one uncomfortably tight, the other churning with nerves, which made it impossible to eat or drink.

Hardly aware what she was doing, she found herself dialling Felix's number, not caring that he would be fast asleep at this hour of the morning. However, when he answered, sounding drowsy, she immediately felt awkward, recalling their recent row, the violent sex and her equally violent sobbing. Indeed, he too seemed constrained; expecting another attack, maybe.

'What's wrong?' he asked, warily.

All at once, and without even an apology, she began pouring out the whole saga since she had left his flat, from Amy's missed phone calls and pre-term labour, to Hugo's recent revelations.

'My God!' he exclaimed. 'And there I was, hoping you were enjoying a good night's sleep. Look, why don't I call a cab and meet you at the hospital, right now? I know there's nothing much I can do to help, but at least you wouldn't feel so alone.'

His kindness and his steady voice instantly made her feel less stricken. 'Felix, I wouldn't dream of putting you to all that trouble and, anyway, there'd be no point, because I have to get back to Amy pretty soon. But it's sweet of you to offer. In fact, I'm feeling better already, just offloading some of the stress.'

'Well, from what you've said, it's obvious you're doing a fantastic job. You stick in there, Maria, and try to focus on Amy's labour rather than worry over Hugo. I know that's easier said than done, but the birth of the baby is the most important thing – and more than enough to occupy your mind. If you start fretting about the court case, too, you'll dissipate your energies. In any case, Hugo must have professional indemnity insurance, so—'

'Yes, but if the insurers smell a whiff of fraud, they'll drop him at a stroke. In fact, they may have done so already, for all I know. Amy will be devastated if he loses his job *and* the house. And, as for his reputation, it'll be totally destroyed, if it should ever come to light he took a bribe.'

'Maria, the culture's entirely different over there. I once knew a chap who'd worked in Dubai and he said money changes hands as a matter of course and it's not really seen as bribery; more a way of oiling the wheels. Besides, if everyone else is doing it, I guess you have to join in, to get anywhere in business.'

Although she couldn't agree, she kept her scruples to herself. 'Well,' she said, wearily, 'whatever else, it puts the final kibosh on any thought of my

288

moving to Cornwall. Apart from all the other issues, like Alice and Felicia, I couldn't possibly leave poor Amy in this mess.'

'Maria, it's not your responsibility. *Other* people manage without four-storey houses and mega-salaries. I've told you, over and over, your life shouldn't be one long sacrifice. You're there for Amy now, and you'll be with her for the next six months but, after that, it's time you made a fundamental change of direction.'

'To be honest, I can barely think at all, with all this going on.'

'That's hardly surprising but, as I said, you're doing bloody well, and my advice is concentrate on Amy and leave everything else till later, when you'll feel less tired and stressed. And, anyway, things may turn out OK in the end. You told me how super-crafty Hugo's lawyers are and, of course, a big prestigious firm like his would obviously use the best ones in the field. So they may well swing things in his favour.'

'Yes, but once they realize what he's done, they'll refuse to defend him and make him use his own lawyer, which could cost him literally thousands.'

'Look, don't assume the worst. He's bound to appoint someone equally astute, and a really ingenious legal man can convince a judge that black's white, or vice versa.'

Again, she found such deviousness distasteful, yet Felix's own certainty did offer a grain of hope. 'Oh, Felix, I'm just so glad you're *there*! Who else could I ring at this ungodly hour without them complaining about the fact I woke them up?'

'Maria, I love you – don't forget that – so I want to help in any way I can. And I shan't go back to bed, then you'll know I'm here if you need me.'

'I can't tell you what that means, darling. To be perfectly frank, I was feeling close to the edge.'

'Well, phone me any time – you promise?'

'No, I'm afraid I can't – not with Amy so close to giving birth. In fact, I really ought to get back to her.'

'OK, fine. But ring me once the baby's born and you feel you're free to leave. I presume Amy will need to rest then, and you will, too, by the sounds of it. So come over here and I'll put you to bed – and I mean bed to *sleep* – nothing else! And, for heaven's sake, don't struggle here on the tube. Take a taxi and I'll pay the cabbie when you turn up at my door.'

Generous, thoughtful, loving, caring – even Felicia couldn't deny his sterling qualities. And, although he had bad ones, too, wasn't that true of most of humanity? Suddenly, in the gloom of the basement, it no longer seemed to matter what he had or hadn't done to Alice and Felicia. Even if all his daughter's accusations turned out to be true, they belonged to the past, whereas now, in the present, he had transformed her mood; offered total support and proved himself a tower of strength, to use Dr Herbert's phrase.

Even her stomach had calmed down and she knew Felix would advise her to make sure she ate and drank, rather than go back parched and starving to the ward. So she settled for one ice-cream – not three – and a bottle of orange juice. Returning to her seat, she deliberately relished the tastes: the tang of the juice citrusy and sharp against the smooth, bland creaminess of Madagascar Vanilla. As Felix continually said, why *shouldn't* she have pleasures; indeed, even a new life? In Cornwall, they'd bought Mr Whippys; nibbling each other's chocolate flakes off the top of the cones, and kissing between each mouthful, like besotted young lovers. How blithely normal those days seemed now – eating, talking, lazing, sketching – compared with this present Limbo of uncertainty and pain.

Once she'd finished her mini-feast, she made her way to the ground floor, deciding to grab a few lungfuls of fresh air to dissipate the stuffy, frazzled feeling in her head. It was now fully light outside, although the Fulham Road was uncharacteristically quiet; just a couple of nurses coming into the hospital and a lone bus rumbling past. It struck her, all at once, that whatever horrors Amy and Hugo were facing, the everyday world was still functioning as usual: buses running to time; policemen on the beat; milk and newspapers soon to be delivered; *babies* being delivered. She had to hold on to that blessed sense of order; to believe and hope that Amy and even Hugo – and, yes, Alice and Felicia, too – and she herself, of course, would somehow come through all the problems.

Maybe she was being too censorious about her son-in-law. If everyone took bribes in Dubai, was it really so heinous for him to have pocketed the odd sweetener or two? Her own strict sense of right and wrong was still revolted by that notion, but perhaps, as Felix always claimed, it was only *Hanna's* standards she obstinately upheld, rather than working out her individual views on questions of morality.

Before returning to her daughter, she glanced up at the sky, which was now suffused with glowing pink and blazing gold. The fervour of the sunrise, reflected off windows and buildings, constituted a striking contrast to the murky darkness last time she'd looked out. And it brought to mind the brilliant sunset they had all watched at George's place, and her deep contentment at being in her element. Perhaps the glittering prize of Cornwall might actually be feasible once more, if she made an effort to think in Felix's terms, rather than those of her mother, or of a restrictive Church stressing only self-denial. And she also had to emulate his optimism about the outcome of the court case, rather than instantly assuming it could result only in disgrace and ruin. She must stop being so pessimistic and try to see the very radiance of the sky as a hopeful portent that, despite Felicia's revelations, despite the appalling crisis in Dubai, the future could be similarly bright.

Chapter 34

'**M**um, I'm going to *die!*'

Amy's voice did sound so weak and wavering, Maria feared she had reached the limits of her energy and strength. 'Not long to go now, darling,' she said, unsure if that were true. The ordeal had lasted fourteen hours already, and she couldn't help recalling gruesome tales of forty-eight-hour labours. Yet the only kind of time that really seemed to register was the frequency and length of the contractions.

'Please take me home. I want to go home.'

Maria held the glass of water to her lips. (Even Lucozade and juices now made her daughter nauseous.) 'You'll be going home *with* your baby, in just a day or two.' Despite her words, she was beginning to doubt that there would be a positive outcome. Just last week, a headline in one of the tabloids had trumpeted the fact that one in every hundred-or-so babies died at, or soon after, birth. And, more horrific still, one woman died in pregnancy or childbirth every single week, in the UK.

She got up to refill the glass, as a pretext for exchanging a word with Linda, who was washing her hands at the basin. 'Is she going to be all right?' she whispered.

Linda nodded. 'She's in what we call the transitional stage, which can be very challenging. The hormones are changing, you see, and that can make a woman begin to doubt herself, or even feel like giving up entirely.'

'Is there anything I can do to help?'

'Just continue what you're doing – making sure she's not dehydrated and sponging her down with a nice cold flannel.'

Amy began to gasp and struggle through yet another contraction; her lips twisted into a silent howl; her body bucking and writhing. Linda returned to the bed, to help her with the breathing drill, while Maria laid the flannel against her daughter's forehead, first pushing back the sweaty strands of hair plastering her face.

'My back's agony,' Amy moaned, once the contraction had dwindled.

Linda moved her onto her left side, readjusted the straps, and showed Maria how to massage her back.

'Does that help at all?' Maria asked, worried she might be making things worse still. Suddenly, she recalled their earlier laugh about the rolling pin, but any world where it was still possible to laugh had long since disappeared.

'Yes, Mum, thanks. Your hands feel wonderfully cool.'

The relief was short-lived, however, since another contraction followed within a couple of minutes and, again, Amy tensed and shuddered, breathing like an asthmatic, despite the midwife's instructions. Even after all this time, she hadn't mastered the techniques, and the whole room seemed filled with her pain: an unstoppable, jangling, merciless pain – stabbing, searing, insistent.

'I've told you,' Amy panted, in the ever briefer lull between contractions, 'I can't take any more.'

Maria, too, had almost reached the limit of what she could endure, although with far less cause than her daughter.

'Just hang in there, my love. You're doing really well and, anyway—' Linda's next words were lost in Amy's cries, which seemed to rend the room apart.

Maria experienced each one as a shrill reproach, a jarring accusation. What use was any mother if she couldn't kiss a daughter better; assuage her agony? She got up again, to run her hands under the cold tap, so they would remain suitably cool for the back massage.

'Don't go, Mum!' Amy cried. 'I can't do this without you.'

Maria darted back to the bed and clasped her daughter's hand. 'It's all right. I'm here. I'm not going anywhere.'

'But you seem so far away. I feel cut off from everyone, like I'm in a different world.'

Maria looked directly into her daughter's eyes; hoping a concerned and loving gaze might make her feel less alone. There was so little she could do – mere crumbs and grains of comfort, when bushelsful were needed. Amy's eyes were the same black-molasses shade as Hanna's and her own: Radványi eyes, with a touch of Hungarian gypsy about them. Would the baby inherit them, too, or be more like Hugo, with fairer, English colouring? This child was a complete unknown, as yet. Girl or boy? Talbot or Radványi? Highly strung or placid? Clever or just average? Healthy or deformed?

Would there even *be* a baby?

'Amy, you're *not* alone,' Linda insisted, wheeling over the sphyg-manometer, so she could check her blood pressure again. 'We're here and helping you. And soon you'll deliver your beautiful baby.'

'I don't *want* a baby. I don't give a fuck about it!'

Maria hid her sense of shock. Already, she was troublingly aware of the infant's struggle to be born; the walls of the uterus compressing it and squeezing it; closing tighter, tighter; soon to expel it into an unfathomable and glaring world. Would it be too small to cope; its lungs too undeveloped to take that first, all-important breath?

Amy's voice cut through her anxious thoughts. 'I'd rather top myself than go through any more of this.'

Linda stayed completely calm. 'Try and remember what I told you and just take one contraction at a time.'

'I can't! They're coming so fast.'

'Yes, but you still have the chance to relax between each one. Use the slower, rhythmic breathing I showed you earlier. That's better! Good. Much better.'

All at once, Amy began to shake; her legs trembling and twitching, as if she had lost control of them. Maria did her best to massage them, worried by her daughter's feverish heat. How could someone be both burning hot and shivering?

'Don't worry,' Linda told them. 'It's perfectly normal to tremble a bit, at this stage. It's just a temporary thing, due to those hormonal changes I mentioned.'

'Christ!' Amy gasped, suddenly clutching Linda's arm. 'I feel I want to push.'

'Resist the urge, please, just for a moment. I need to check you're fully dilated.'

Maria went to stand by the window, as she had done for each internal examination, knowing Amy would hate to be seen with her legs spread wide apart – a position she regarded as blatant and undignified. Her daughter's howls of pain sounded even louder as she was rolled onto her back again, like a wounded creature trying to struggle free of a trap.

'My back's breaking in this position.'

'*Breathe*, Amy, as I told you,' Linda urged.

'I can't. Your hands feel like broken glass inside me.'

'I'm almost done, my love, and, yes, you're ready to push, which means now you can play a more active part in the birth. But I'd like you to wait till you feel the next urge to push. So hold on just a sec, OK?'

As Maria resumed her role as birth partner, she felt her chest tighten with a strange mix of fear and excitement. Would she see her grandchild soon, or would there be some tragedy, even at this late stage?

'You may find pushing easier than just lying passive and putting up with the pain,' Linda said, moving Amy back onto her side. 'But it's very important that you follow my instructions. When you feel you want to push, bear down hard, as if you're opening your bowels.'

Amy instantly tensed. 'But suppose I … soil the bed?'

'It doesn't matter. Nobody will know.'

'*I'll* know – and so will you.'

'I'm not bothered, I assure you.' Linda smiled. 'I've seen it all before – poo, wee, blood, vomit. They're simply part of our job.'

'For me, they're quite repellent.'

'Amy …' Linda's voice was firmer now. 'You *must* do what I say. It's crucial that you work with me, not against me. And I want you to do what your body tells you, instead of fighting it, so, if you feel the urge to push, then give it all you've got.'

Amy recoiled, however; clenching her fists and screwing up her eyes in an effort *not* to push.

'Amy, listen to me, please. When the next contraction starts, take a few deep breaths and, as it peaks, take another breath and push as hard as you can. Really go for it, OK?'

'I can't. I don't want to push.'

'You just have to help yourself, darling,' Maria chimed in, feeling increasingly anxious at Amy's refusal to co-operate. 'And help the baby, too, of course. Remember, every push brings you nearer to the birth. Then all this pain and effort will have been worth it.'

'Go away,' Amy shouted. 'Fuck off, both of you!'

Amy continued to swear and struggle, now losing the last vestige of control and screeching so loudly Maria feared that everyone in the ward must be flinching at the uproar. Linda went over to the door, put her head out and called to someone in the corridor to fetch Ruth, the senior midwife now on duty. While waiting for her colleague to come, she valiantly continued giving Amy advice, obviously still hoping to overrule her objections. 'Don't push with your upper body, but focus on a point just below the navel. And try to relax your face.'

Considering Amy's taut, resistant state, the word 'relax' seemed wildly inappropriate – although it was unlikely that she'd heard it, since she was still yelling and screaming and trying to throw herself about. Just as Maria was wondering if the baby might be affected by such extremes of behaviour, there was a knock on the door, heralding Ruth's arrival: an older, grey-haired midwife with a definite air of authority. Within seconds, she had taken charge, and was gloved and in position.

'Amy,' she said, sternly, raising her voice above the yowls of pain, 'you're not helping yourself or your baby by carrying on like this, so will you kindly calm down? We need you to co-operate, because if you don't make an effort and push this baby out, it may become distressed. So I expect you to do exactly what I tell you. Is that absolutely clear?'

Her imperious tone was little short of miraculous. It was as if Amy had met her match in this determined, no-nonsense woman intent on taking control, as Amy herself insisted on doing in most aspects of her own work.

Fortunately, Ruth could praise as well as reprimand. 'Well done, Amy! That's excellent. You see, calmness and control work better than blind panic, don't they? And, now the contraction's over, take the chance of a brief rest. Breathe very slowly, and let go all the tension from your groin and legs. Perfect! OK, now push again, and fix your whole attention on your breathing.'

Amy's only reply was a series of effortful grunts. Presumably no longer able to speak – or scream – she was, at last, co-operating.

'Good. Great. But go on, go *on*, keep going! I know it's tough, but just one more. That's beautiful! OK, now rest again.'

Maria offered her a sip of water, but Amy waved away the glass. Instead, Maria held her hand and kept whispering words of encouragement; hugely relieved to see her daughter more amenable.

As she watched the two midwives working together calmly and efficiently – and solely in the interests of Amy and her child – she was suddenly struck by the importance of their job. Whatever high claims Felix might make for art, how could any painting or sculpture possibly compare with safely delivering babies and saving vulnerable mothers? And his championing of 'excess' now seemed hollow, maybe dangerous, and clearly had no place in the lives of midwives and doctors or, indeed, in most professions. And, even in one's personal life, it could result in damage or abuse. If her mother, for example, had been wedded to excess and self-indulgence, rather than to control and moderation, would she have bothered to care for her child and, later, her grandchild, or simply left them to the vagaries of fate?

'If you changed position,' Ruth suggested, 'and got down on your hands and knees, it would make the pushing easier.'

'I'm not an animal,' Amy retorted, with some of her former acerbity, despite the effort it required to speak. 'I don't even like lying on my side.' She struggled onto her back again, despite her earlier complaint that it was unendurably painful. 'All positions are useless, as far as I can see. I mean, I'm bloody trying – doing all you said, but nothing fucking happens.'

'It *is* happening – I assure you.' Ruth straightened her up on the bed and ensured the straps hadn't slipped. 'But stay in control, please, Amy. You mustn't lose your concentration. I want you to relax into the process and let the baby come.'

'It'll *never* come,' Amy gasped, as, again, she tried frantically to push.

'Yes, it will – that I can guarantee. And you're doing brilliantly. It just takes a while, that's all.'

Amy closed her eyes, as if to block out any reference to further prolongation of her labour. Her head and hair were drenched in sweat; her face pale and almost haggard; her expression one of near despair.

'This baby doesn't feel like flesh,' she panted, in the next brief lull. 'It's like a piece of jagged metal splitting me apart.'

Maria was sweating with her daughter's effort; pushing *with* her, to all intents and purposes; feeling every grinding pain; every bulging sensation, as the baby made its slow descent down the birth canal.

Hearing a rustle of paper, she saw Ruth tear open a package and extract a large green sheet and some instruments, which she laid out neatly on a trolley. Linda, meanwhile, was supervising the delivery and suddenly announced, 'I can see the top of the head! And you'll be able to feel it, Amy, if you lean down and put your hand between your legs.'

Amy's only response was a violent shake of her head.

'Well, if you have no objection, my love, perhaps Mum would like to come down this end and take a look herself.'

'Is that OK with you, darling?' Maria asked, fearing the answer would be an emphatic no. Wouldn't Amy regard it as 'gross' or 'blatant' for her mother to peer up at her private parts?

But Amy gave a distracted nod. She was now so absorbed in puffing, blowing, pushing, groaning, she appeared not to care either way.

Softly, Maria stood up and tiptoed to the foot of the bed, standing to the side of the two midwives. As she glimpsed her grandchild's dark, wet head, she was swept by a tsunami of emotion: joy, wonder, crazy jubilation, terror, disbelief. The hair was fiercely black – Radványi hair; a world away from Hugo's blondish crop.

'OK, Amy,' Linda instructed, 'stop pushing for a minute. We need to ease baby's head out very gently, so I'd like you to change your breathing now and pant. Imagine you're blowing out the candles on a birthday cake, and that'll slow things down a bit.'

Amy panted with a sort of desperation, as if drawing on her last reserves of strength.

'Good. Very good! Keep panting. Now another little push.'

With the head appearing any moment, Maria yearned to stay where she was and watch the whole amazing process, yet she feared the midwives might object. Indeed, Linda had every reason to be tetchy, since she had been due to go off duty almost an hour ago. Far from showing any annoyance, however, she seemed eager to see her task through to the end, displaying, in the process, genuine love and dedication.

Maria was about to get out of the way when she suddenly remembered Felix saying, '*Ask* for what you want, rather than assume you don't deserve it.' Thus encouraged, she said, tentatively, 'Would it be OK if I watched the whole birth?'

'That's fine with us,' Linda assured her, 'but how do you feel, Amy?'

'I don't care,' she moaned. 'Please yourself.' With her eyes still closed, she seemed to have entered some dark, private world, where the baby was just a distraction, or an afterthought.

Maria longed to share with her daughter this life-changing event, but at least she could describe it to her later, when Amy was more receptive. Fixing her whole attention on the slowly emerging head, she could barely contain her anxiety as Linda guided it carefully out. 'Please God,' she prayed, 'let the baby be all right – not damaged or deformed.'

Once the whole head was born, the shoulders slithered out, and then, rapidly, the rest of the body – messy, purplish, blood-streaked – but with no missing limbs or parts, as far as she could see. Yet the infant hadn't made a sound. Surely all normal babies would yell in shock or indignation when confronted with bright lights and alien hands? So why was this one silent; why looking so inert and stunned? Could her grandchild be deaf or dumb – even mentally retarded?

The thought clamped her in a vice of dread, as if she, too, were paralyzed. She had no idea how long she stood, ears straining to hear the faintest, slightest cry – anything to prove that the infant lungs were not seriously impaired. Perhaps it was only thirty seconds, yet they were the slowest-moving seconds she had ever had to endure.

Then suddenly, miraculously, a howl of protest burst upon the air – a veritable hosanna to her ears. Her relief swelled like yeast in dough, as she watched the child seem to come to life before her very eyes – now kicking, struggling, bellowing; its features no longer impassive, but expressing mingled anger and surprise.

'Congratulations, Amy! You have a gorgeous little girl.' Linda made to deliver the baby directly onto Amy's stomach, but Amy pushed away the slimy, squirming bundle and turned her face to the wall.

'Amy,' Ruth prompted, 'wouldn't you like to hold your daughter, skin-to-skin?'

Amy's refusal was so violent, neither midwife made any attempt to persuade her; only to assure her all was well.

'Your baby seems absolutely fine, and a good size for thirty-six weeks – around six pounds, I'd guess. Of course, as she's premature, we'll have to call the paediatrician, but only for a routine check. I'm pretty sure there won't be any need for special care. As I said, she looks exceptionally healthy.'

Amy appeared to have closed her ears, in addition to her eyes, and made no response whatever. Maria's elation, however, arched like a resplendent rainbow across the whole of London – no, across the whole enchanted British Isles. Tears of relief streamed down her face, yet she was smiling with such lunatic abandon, it was the most brilliant, bumptious birthday-smile in the whole history of the world. All the joy and excitement she had failed to feel when Amy was born was now flooding through her body.

'Can *I* hold her?' she pleaded, knowing she had to make this precious child feel wanted, loved and needed.

'Yes, of course, so long as Amy doesn't mind.'

'I've told you, I don't care. Just leave me alone, *all* of you.'

That was clearly impossible, since the cord needed clamping and cutting, then Amy had to be given an injection, to facilitate the expulsion of the placenta, before being cleaned up, checked and monitored. But, since she was in skilled hands, Maria felt free to focus on the baby, watching in awe as it was dried with a towel, wrapped in a blanket and placed gently in her arms.

'Welcome to the world, my sweet.' She slipped her hand underneath the blanket, so she could feel its damp, warm skin; feel it breathing – triumphantly alive. Had God answered her frantic prayer in the taxi, to spare her daughter and her grandchild? She would never know; might never know if God was even *there*. Yet, for all the drawbacks of her old religion – its narrow dogmas, its stress on sin and Hell – its chief commandment of love had never seemed more important. Henceforward, the only 'excess' in her life would be to love this child to excess.

As she supported the fragile head, it seemed to fit so perfectly into the crook of her arm, it was as if they were two pieces of a jigsaw, now slotted indissolubly together. Like its mother, it had its eyes tight shut, but when she shaded them from the overhead light they opened wide and studied her with intense preoccupation. As she met that earnest gaze, it seemed totally out of the question to desert her long-awaited grandchild after a mere six months. How could she tear herself away and entrust this precious being to the care of some casual minder?

Yet, within a second, the full implications of that thought pierced her like a stab-wound. If she became the permanent nanny, she would lose Felix, Cornwall, their plan for a shared life. It would also be a betrayal of her lover; all the more injurious, in light of his recent kindness and support. Pain replaced elation as she imagined the horror of their break-up; the wrench of separation as they went their different ways. And, if she was no longer in his bed, he would find another woman – that she knew, indubitably.

The prospect induced such a pang of desolation, she struggled between two life-choices, in an agony of indecision. A mere day ago, she had been mourning her first lover; was she now forced to mourn her last; mourn the end of love altogether; the end of her ambition as an artist? Enticing snapshots from the last five months began flashing through her mind in tumultuous succession: she and Felix naked on the moors, a coquettish breeze caressing her bare skin; she and Felix embracing in his flat, he tonguing her exultant body, from her astonished eyelids to the tingling soles of her feet; she and Felix feeding each other strawberries, then kissing so ecstatically they were catapulted into a sensuous sphere beyond any she had ever known. And it was much more than just erotic thrills: his patient, skilled tuition at the life class, and generous championing of her work; the easy, joyous atmosphere of George and his community; their unique new Cornish home. Wasn't it self-destructive to renounce so alluring a future – and most unwise to do so when she was on an emotional high, still giddy with relief at the baby's safe delivery?

She looked down at it again and, all at once, it gave a gigantic yawn, puckering its mouth and stretching its whole face. 'You're tired,' she murmured, 'as weary as your mother.' She held the baby up a little, so it could see Amy, unimpeded. 'That's your Mama, right beside you. It's sad that she can't hold you now, but, once she's had a chance to recover, she'll love you as deeply as I do.'

But was that *true*, she wondered, with sudden new anxiety? Amy's lack of interest in the baby was hardly a promising start. Suppose she plunged into depression, as she herself had done; remained an ineffective mother for the child's first crucial years? And, if Hugo lost his job and reputation, things would be worse still: the upheaval of a house move, coupled with the problem of his finding future work. Her own mother and her mother's mother had both battled through adversity and, only with Amy, had come any hope of breaking the chain of suffering. If, God forbid, the suffering re-started, shouldn't she follow their example and keep that hope alive; help her daughter through the uncertainty and turmoil, and provide some sort of haven for her grandchild?

'Duty again, self-sacrifice … Isn't it time you broke your *own* chains?'

Felix's voice seemed to echo in her head, making it still more agonizing to reach any sort of conclusion. It was as if she were struggling through her own labour, as Amy had just done; exhausted, frantic, failing, yet facing a key moment of her life.

She focused on the baby again, which appeared to be drinking in her presence; imprinting her face and body on its mind, as if she were indeed its mother. Still irresolute, still torn, she registered its crumpled face and mottled, blotchy skin; its diminutive size and aching vulnerability. Whatever happened, she mustn't be swayed by sentiment, or by the inherent drama of childbirth – that wasn't fair to Felix, or even to herself.

Then, all at once, the infant hand reached out and grasped her finger, and the surprising strength of that grip cut through her vacillation; seeming to tell her at some deep, instinctive level, infinitely wiser and more discerning than any rational argument, that the two of them were inseparable. And she knew, suddenly, intuitively – and knew now beyond all doubt – that this child was her future. So long as it needed her and wanted her, she would and must be there, even if those needs continued until her death. It wasn't a question of 'sacrifice' or 'duty'; it was simply her new purpose and voca-tion, her way of redeeming the past. Her task in life was to help her grandchild to flourish; to repeat Hanna's role, not out of obligation, but because it was more essential than any other calling – more sacred, even, to use a Catholic word.

Felix wouldn't understand that. For all their sexual intimacy, there was a troubling gulf between them when it came to that whole other world of devotion, dedication, the sacredness of family ties. She loved him, yes; desired him, *yes*; craved everything he offered, yet her greater, deeper craving was to nurture a child who, had Fate been less benevolent, might never have survived. Despite all her doubts and fears today, the baby was actually *here* – living, perfect, all its systems functioning. And it promised a new relationship, one not dependent on staying young and sexually attrac-tive, but which would utilize the very strengths that age itself had brought: compassion, patience, wisdom. Even her long training in economy – deplored by Felix as self-denial – might come in handy if Hugo was out of work. And her training in art could also prove invaluable, because if she passed on all she'd learned about colour, light and composition, the *child* might be the artist, the one who'd leave behind a legacy of inspired, important work. She would encourage it in every way; maybe transform the Northumbrian cottage into a mini-Cornish idyll, to inspire and foster any talent it might have.

And, however great her anguish over Felix – and his own disappointment; maybe scorn and anger – she knew he would bounce back. He had his art; had George and the community, and his chapel-home, close by, and – perhaps most crucial – a buoyant, upbeat temperament that could cope with change and break-ups. And when he found a replacement mistress, she must strive with every fibre of her being to be glad for him and wish him well, rather than waste her precious energies on jealousy, regret.

'Do you have a name for your little girl?' Linda asked, still trying to rouse Amy from her state of shock and lethargy, and persuade her to take an interest in the baby.

Amy, however, appeared too shattered to make any response whatsoever, so Maria answered for her. 'Yes,' she said. 'She's called Hannah Maria – Maria after me.'

As if acknowledging its name, the baby opened its eyes again; its hand still clasping her finger, a symbol of their bond. 'I'm your grandmother,' she stated, slowly and distinctly, returning its attentive gaze, 'and you're perfectly safe with me. I shan't let any harm come near you.' Even newborns could respond to sound, according to the midwives, so, although her words were unintelligible, the baby might absorb their gist and spirit, and at least know it was protected and secure. 'Sadly, your grandfather isn't with us, but—'

She broke off, aware only at this moment that the poem she had recited for Silas, exactly twenty-four hours ago, applied equally to Amy and Hugo, and to Felix, and to *her*.

Begin again ...

She, too, was starting afresh, and in a far less intangible sphere than that of Silas. For him, the words might have been a trifle facile; a deceitful gloss on death. But for her, they related directly to this new stage of her life. Whatever might transpire, be it Hugo's disgrace, Amy's depression, or even her own loneliness – a loneliness honoured in the poem – she would somehow steer a path through all that lay ahead. *Every beginning is a promise ...*

'Hannah Maria,' she whispered, still feeling the pressure of the baby's trusting hand, 'things may not always be easy, but I give you my solemn word – so long as I live, I'll be here for you.'

And, looking up at the window where, behind the murky glass, a new, sunlit day was struggling to reveal itself, she pronounced a silent, fervent, exuberantly enormous *yes*.